REALITY

REALITY

[The Novel]

Jeff Havens

Academy Chicago Publishers

Published in 2006 by
Academy Chicago Publishers
363 West Erie Street
Chicago, Illinois 60610

Printed in the U.S.A.

Library of Congress Cataloging-in-Publication Data on file with the publisher

To McCall, an awfully nice woman
who was nice enough to marry me

And to reality television, without which
this book could not have been written

Part One: [JULY]

"Half the world is composed of idiots, the other half of people clever enough to take indecent advantage of them."
—Walter Kerr

[CHAPTER ONE]

It was during his fourth visit to the set of *Last Man Standing* that Trent Tucker realized how much he hated reality TV.

"I don't think I'm asking for too much here," Gary said. Everyone back at the Tank had dubbed him the Moron, mean and massive and as redneck as they come, a big hit with Southern males. He was standing now with both enormous arms crossed in front of a chest the size and shape of a refrigerator, looking at Trent with the same dull, slack-jawed expression he probably wore every waking minute of the day.

Trent finished his cigarette with a long drag, pulled at the hair on the back of his skull, and failed to repress a violent shudder. It wasn't that Rachel had bailed on two days' notice and the General had sent him in her place, or that Todd had done the same two weeks before, or that a visit to the camera-clogged beaches of Easter Island in the sweltering July heat was hardly his idea of a tropical getaway. Right now, Trent hated his job because never in his wildest dreams had he expected that anybody with a Masters from Stanford, or from anywhere for that matter, would ever have to explain to a grown man why he couldn't have a banana.

"For the last time," Trent said with his eyes closed, "you can't take anything from private property. The contract was very specific on that point."

"But they got thousands of 'em." He could *hear* Gary shrugging his gigantic, stupid, bionically-enhanced shoulders. "No one's gonna miss a couple."

Trent looked to the sky and exhaled a sharp breath through his nose. Why did he put up with this? Hemingway wouldn't have put up with this. Old Papa would have shot Gary as soon as he opened his gap-toothed mouth. Where was an elephant gun when you needed one?

"Listen," he said with an effort at conciliation, "the only reason we're allowed to be here is because we promised the Chilean government that we would not disrupt the lives of any indigenous people."

Gary stared at him.

"Natives," Trent said with a sigh. "The people who live here. Those little people with the little houses who don't speak English? If you steal anything, we could all be forced to leave, which is something we don't want. Do you understand me?"

"I just don't—"

Fuck conciliation. "Look," Trent hissed, "I'll make this simple. If I catch you within half a mile of a banana plantation I'll have you pulled midweek, no matter *what* the at-home viewers say! Under*stand*?" He was itching to take a swing at the man, a stiff uppercut right in the jaw, something that would shut him up for a while. But he didn't. Gary may have been congenitally defective, he might have been more inclined than most to marry within the family, but he was not the kind of man who lost a fight.

Instead, Trent stormed off down the line of other contestants, all of them waiting amid hundreds of supply crates and storage trailers while the cameramen got everything set up for the individual interviews. The scrawniest of them couldn't have weighed less than two-twenty. Bruisers, the lot of them, former Army Rangers and weightlifters, lumberjacks and strip club bouncers who could break up a brawl with a single punch. Guys who ate nails for breakfast and slept with their guns. Was it any wonder that these were America's newest television stars?

The concept was simple enough. Twenty men were airdropped onto a deserted island with no fresh water source and forced to survive by whatever means possible: eating scorpions, collecting rainwater, laying snares, building huts, and occasionally pillaging the stockpiles of their fellow contestants. They'd been given no tools, no maps, and had not been told which plants were poisonous. Those who succumbed to thirst, hunger, illness, injury, or the displeasure of the viewing public, were systematically eliminated, one each week. Never mind that Easter Island was neither deserted nor devoid of water; no one at home knew exactly where the show was being filmed, and they probably wouldn't have cared even if they did know. And never mind that all but one of the illnesses and brushes with starvation had been staged. After all, reality had never been a terribly important component of reality TV. The important thing, at least from the network's point of view, was that in its first week, *Last Man*

Standing had surpassed *Survivor: Bikini Atoll* as the most popular television program in the world.

"Trent!"

Trent groaned. All he wanted at the moment was five minutes alone with his cigarettes and the soothing sound of the ocean crashing endlessly along the beach. He turned in time to see Patrick barely avoid falling over a knot of electrical cords.

"What's the hurry?" Sort of a dumb question. Patrick was always in a hurry. It was impossible for the Director of On-site Operations not to be in a hurry. He'd probably been born premature.

"Hey," Patrick said. He looked like he'd run the length of the island; his short red hair was plastered to his forehead in uneven strands, and the clipboard at his chest rose and fell in great swells. He needed a few seconds to catch his breath. "We need . . . we need you over at Studio C. Alan just broke Jack's hand."

"*What*?" Not today. Please, not today. "You're kidding, right?"

"I wish I were."

"Tell me you're kidding."

"I wish I were."

Well, wasn't *this* a nice little kick in the nuts. "Where's Max?"

"I don't know. I think he's—"

"Find him. Tell him to meet me. I'll be right there."

Patrick stumbled off down the beach, and Trent headed for Studio C. It wasn't a studio, really, just a semicircular strand of eucalyptus trees that provided an excellent backdrop for filming. It was also about a quarter mile away, well beyond earshot of where the interviews were now getting underway. Trent pushed himself to jog and swore under his breath. *Why* had Rachel picked this weekend to come down with a suspiciously convenient case of diphtheria? He did not relish the idea of mediating a conflict between four hundred and fifty pounds of angry men. Of course, he might not have to. It was entirely possible that one of them would have killed the other by the time he arrived—if he was lucky.

Unfortunately, that wasn't the case. When he got there the two men were sitting on opposite sides of the depression. Alan looked all right, if a man who'd given himself the nickname of Barbarian could ever really look all right. He was sitting on a grassy bank, cleaning his fingernails with a sliver of wood. Jack, though—the Sensitive One, huge with female viewers—had taken a beating. His left eye was swelling shut, and his left wrist looked like a softball. There was no way around it, Jack would have to be sent home. The General was not going to be happy about this.

"What the *hell* are you two doing?" Trent shouted. It was best to shout at men like these. "You're supposed to be over at Anakena for the interviews. Is it broken?"

Jack nodded, teeth clenched.

Trent glared at Alan. "Care to explain?"

Alan looked entirely unconcerned. He'd been a Navy Seal for seventeen years, unit commander for twelve. At forty, the man was in better shape than most college gymnasts and could probably have dispatched an entire Olympic rifle team with a tuning fork. "I caught him stealing my food."

"I told you it wasn't *me*!"

"Calm down, Jack," Trent said. "When?"

"About 0300," Alan said. "I'd holed up for the night inside a tree and stashed my stores in a hanging bundle. Around 0300 I heard a noise and—"

"Wait, wait a second," Trent said. "A hanging bundle? What the hell for, to keep *bears* away? There aren't any bears on this island, Alan."

"You can never be too careful. Anyway, I came out to find my line cut and someone"—he jerked his head at Jack—"running east with my supplies."

"It wasn't me!" Jack jumped up, stifling a grimace. "I told you, I was asleep by the cove, five hundred yards *west* of you. You woke me up with all your crying."

"You weren't there at 0130."

"Yes I was."

"I didn't see you during my recon."

"You must have done a poor sweep, old-timer. I was there."

Alan stood up slowly. "You trying to suggest something?"

Trent had visions of his own imminent and very bloody death. "Guys, come on, calm down."

"Maybe I am," Jack said with a sneer.

"One broken wrist not enough for you?"

"Guys, I'm *really* not in the mood for this."

"What I'm *saying*, pal, is that you give me a fair chance instead of coming at me from behind, I'll kick your dick into your asshole!" So much for sensitive.

"I'm not doing anything right now," Alan said. "Tell you what. I won't even use my left hand. How's that sound?"

"Alan, sit down!"

But they weren't listening to Trent. Alan continued his slow advance, and Jack moved to meet him, his blue eyes consumed by malevolence. Trent rather doubted that he would be able to defuse two men who had both spent the greater portion of their adult lives learning how to kill people in a variety of ways. He was pretty certain that a battle between warriors had never been successfully halted by a 170 pound lawyer's son with a smoker's cough and a fifty dollar haircut.

But he tried anyway.

"Guys! Step back! Alan, Jack, get away from—do you have any idea what'll happen to both of you if I get—"

It was rather fortunate that at that moment Max came striding over the hill.

"Whoa whoa whoa, fellas, what's going on here? You know what, fuck it, I don't wanna know. Alan, over there. Jack, over there. What's the matter, you didn't hear me? No, I already told you, I don't want to hear it. Move your ass over . . . look, I don't care if he fucked your grandma, you got two seconds to do what I say or I'm gonna make sure you never make it into even so much as a deodorant commercial for the rest of your lives, understand? All right, that's more like it. How's it going, Trent?"

Trent smoothed his shirt and counted to make sure he still had all his fingers. "Better, thanks."

"Couldn't handle this by yourself?"

"It's been a long day." Trent lit a cigarette. "Fuck you, by the way."

Max laughed. "Sorry, pal. That was rude of me. All right, now who wants to fill me in?"

Alan obliged. Jack did not interrupt.

"Jesus Christ," Max said, shaking his head. "You fucked up, fellas, do you understand that? You've really fucked it up. All right, this is what we're gonna do. Jack, we're gonna have to send you home. Look, I don't wanna hear it, you can't compete with a broken wrist and you know it."

"It's not fair!" Jack bellowed, tears welling in his large, blue, sensitive eyes.

"Look, pal, life's not fair. I've been in love with Nicole Kidman for ten years, and do you think she knows who I am? No. That's not fair, right, but it's life, so live it or die. But we're not finished here, all right Jackie? This is just the beginning. Two weeks from now we'll have you on Regis *and* MTV. You don't know this, but *People* magazine's been dying for an interview. Play your cards right, you might have a shot at being the next Bachelor. That sound all right?"

Jack nodded silently, his moist eyes swimming with the golden prospects of fame.

Trent unbuttoned his collar. "We're going to have to send you home too, Alan."

For perhaps the first time in his life, Alan looked afraid. "Wait a second. You can't do that to me. I didn't—"

"Don't give us any shit," Max said. "You know you crossed the line. I'm pretty sure they teach you how *not* to break somebody's wrist in SEAL School. Trent, how's Alan been testing?"

Trent put his cigarette to his lips in order to suppress a smile. Max knew the answer to that; he was just making Alan sweat. He affected an indifferent shrug. "Not spectacular. Women want a survivalist they could bring home to Mom and Dad, and he hasn't made that happen." Trent enjoyed the flash of fear that crossed Alan's face. "He's made a modest spike with males eighteen to twenty-five, though. We might be able to get him a spot on Regis after Jack, kind of a tell-his-side thing."

Max nodded as though the idea were an original one. "All right. Let's see, what else can we do, what else can we . . . All right, Alan, I've got an idea. What would you say to some action movie walk-ons, maybe work as a stuntman?"

"All the greats got their start as stuntmen," Trent added. "Wayne, Willis, Stallone." Complete bullshit, of course, but Alan wouldn't know that. Unless he'd been a closet fan of the Italian Stallion's earlier work. Which was something Trent did *not* want to know.

"What do you say?" Max asked.

"Absolutely," Alan said, so quickly that it seemed as though he'd been hoping for this all along.

"Good," Max said with a self-satisfied smile. "I'm glad we got that taken care of. But there's one more thing we gotta do. We're gonna have to film the fight."

"Why?" Alan asked.

"We can't have you two leave the show without an explanation," Trent said.

"But it's already happened," Alan protested.

Trent pinched the bridge of his nose and shook his head. Was it a requirement that reality contestants were the stupidest people in America? Or was that simply a happy coincidence? "You're going to act it out, Alan. You and Jack."

"How are you going to get rid of this?" Jack said, pointing to his left eye, which by now was brilliantly purple and swollen completely shut.

"Trust me, it's not that hard," Max said. "If we wanted to make you look like Ethel Merman, we could."

"We'll film you from the right side," Trent said.

"Look, you two leave the camera work to us, all right? Both of you, go tell Patrick we need a full crew to Studio C. And listen. If I hear that either of you so much as touches the other between now and when you get back, then so help me God I'll see to it that the closest either of you gets to Hollywood is working toll booths on the San Joaquin. Now get outta here. Jack, tell Patrick we need to start rolling in half an hour, before your wrist gets any worse."

Jack and Alan left, silently and single file, careful to keep a discreet distance between them as they hurried down the path toward Anakena Beach.

"Well," Max said when they were gone, "*that* was fun. Looked like they were about to turn you into soup. You doing all right?"

"Yeah." Trent finished his cigarette and flicked the butt onto the ground. He started to light another one and stopped, suddenly too tired to make the effort. Instead he sat down on the smooth, white trunk of a eucalyptus tree that had been cut down specifically for that purpose. With the toe of his Aubercy shoes—not a bright idea to wear *them* onto the set—he ground the remains of his cigarette into the mud. When they had arrived, Studio C had seemed like an ideal place to build a small cottage with large windows to let in the soft sounds of the ocean at night, maybe get a massage from that girl working the dolly—what was her name, Jasmine? Now, though, thousands of footprints and tons of camera equipment had reduced the pristine valley to a swamp of mud and debris. Dozens of water bottles speckled the ground, half-submerged in the slime. Trent noticed one of them and stared at it.

"Hey pal, you awake?"

"I'm just tired," he said softly. Then, with more animation: "And fucking an*noyed*. I didn't get into television to break up fights between men twice my size. You may as well get that guy from Springer—what's his name, Stan?"

"Steve."

"Whatever. All I'm saying is, I didn't go to Stanford to explain to terminal halfwits like Gary why he couldn't have any goddamn bananas. Is this really all it is?"

"Trent." Max sat down beside him and rested his elbows on his knees. "What the hell are you talking about?"

"I'm just *tired* of it, you know."

"Look, you're just having a bad day. What else could you ask for here? We're in control of the whole world."

"I don't know." Max was right, though. And what a comforting thought *that* was. "Do you realize," Trent said, "that more people in America can sing the theme song to *Last Man Standing* than the national anthem? That more of them would recognize a picture of Jack or Alan than the president? And look at them! Do you want your sister's kids, *any*body's kids, growing up to be like them? Do you really think we should be turning these people into role models?"

Max rolled his eyes. "So what do you wanna do, make everybody watch TV versions of the classics? Do musical renditions of *Crime and Punishment* on TNT, that kind of thing?"

"I don't know," Trent said, wishing he didn't sound like a moping child. "Maybe. At least they had something to say."

"No they didn't. Where do you wanna start? Kafka? I read Kafka, and I don't think too many people wanna watch a show about a guy who turns into a bug and dies alone in his room because nobody understands him. What's the message there? You want to adapt *A Farewell to Arms*, show people that the best way to deal with an unplanned pregnancy is for the girl you knocked up to conveniently die? Or maybe *Oliver Twist*, teach kids in the slums that all they need to do is be good little boys and girls and sooner or later they'll come into their inheritance. Come off it, pal. The classics are as full of shit as everything else."

"Maybe." He'd heard all this before, although Max did have a maddening ability to choose different examples each time. "I'm just not sure we're doing a good thing here."

"You're missing the point. As usual." Max grinned and put an arm around Trent's shoulder. "We've struck gold here, pal. Gold! For the first time in the history of television, we're letting people make their own decisions about who they love and hate. No bullshit cello music to tell you who the bad guy is. Freedom of expression, that's what we're giving them. They get to choose who goes and who stays. It's *democracy*, the only true democracy left."

Trent barked a laugh. What a delightful world, where the most insipid, shallow, thoughtless, spiteful people had their fingers on the button. A warm and happy place, where the future of the world rested in the capable hands of the fat, flatulent couch-bound whale that was the average American. Armageddon couldn't be more than a week and a half away.

"Look," Max went on, "we don't have time to argue about this right now. I'm not saying things are perfect. There's a lot we could be doing that we're not doing, you know what I'm saying? So instead of bitching about it, why don't you figure out how to make it better?"

"You're right," Trent said. "I'm sorry, it's just . . . it's been a long day."

Alan and Jack soon returned, still maintaining a comfortable distance between them. Behind them was Patrick's assistant, Eric, fashionably bald and sweating a great deal. His shirt was open to the fourth button, and the walkie-talkie at his waist was alive with the sounds of people relaying instructions.

"Crew's on its way," Eric said from the top of the short rise. "Couple shoulders and a dolly track. Steven's coming to choreograph."

Trent perked up at the mention of the dolly track. What was that girl's name? Julie, Ginger? "Where's Patrick?"

"Jack, Alan, over here," Max said. "Let me tell you how this is going to work."

"Local disturbance," Eric said to Trent. He switched his walkie-talkie off. "Some Rapa Nui claiming a couple of his sheep were stolen the day before yesterday."

"Perfect," Trent said. "Does he have any proof?"

"Says so. Max, you need me to call a scriptwriter?"

"I can handle it. We'll overshoot and cut later." Max glanced at Trent. "Look, I can take care of things here. Why don't you go help Patrick deal with whatever it is."

Trent would have much rather attempted to deliver a pregnant hippo. "Where is he, Eric?"

And he was off, back the way Eric had come, past the camera crew making its cumbersome way toward Studio C, past the girl—Gina, that was her name, bouncing along with that perfect body he'd have to wait another two weeks to see—past the line of weathered survivalists eating boxed lunches and sipping Dr. Pepper while Gary told the viewers back home about his latest brush with dehydration, past the white sands of Anakena and the tranquility it promised and was never able to deliver. For a moment, the incessant cacophony of the set faded away, only to be replaced by a new sound, raucous and raw, the sound of an enraged farmer shrieking murder in rapid, incomprehensible Spanish.

Trent tensed his shoulders and reached for another cigarette. As soon as he got home, the first thing he was going to do was get himself laid. All he had to do was find someone willing to oblige.

[CHAPTER TWO]

For once, Trent managed to pull his Jaguar into his parking spot Monday morning without jumping the curb. He squealed to a halt, grabbed his briefcase, finished his cigarette, activated the alarm, and headed into work, if what he did could actually be called that.

The Tank, or Nova Creative Consulting as it was formally called, was a small, white, nondescript building on the 1100 block of Santa Monica's Colorado Avenue. It was called the Tank for two reasons. First off, that's what it looked like, a squat, bloated, almost windowless tank whose architects must have been going through the "airport terminal" phase of their artistic development. And secondly, that's what it was, a think tank for the networks, the source of some of the most innovative ideas in Reality Television, like last year's smash success, *Gangland Romance*. Too bad the two stars had gotten themselves imprisoned for stealing a car three hours after their wedding. They could have had a real future.

Trent pushed through the double doors and took the stairs to the second floor. Most days those thirteen steps constituted his entire cardiovascular workout. His doctor had told him to exercise more, but then his doctor's idea of physical activity was driving his golf cart between eighteen holes of water hazards and sand traps. Besides, Trent thought as he reached the top, there'd be plenty of time to get in shape when he was dead.

"Morning, Lynette," he said as he opened the door. The familiar sound of the office air conditioner reminded him how much nicer Easter Island would have been with central cooling.

"Good morning!" she chirped without stopping her typing. She was a very chirpy woman, the kind who might occasionally describe her children as "bushy-tailed." Her tightly curled hair had not yet begun the slow unraveling that would occupy Lynette for most of the afternoon. He'd seen it get away from her once; she'd looked like a startled porcupine. "You'll never guess who I saw this morning!"

Trent didn't care. Lynette was a nice enough woman, but her obsession with celebrities was something he couldn't even fake enthusiasm about. It was really too bad that the only actress she even vaguely resembled was the school secretary from *Ferris Bueller's Day Off*—what was her name, Edie something? Not to mention that when your only literary pursuits were *Vogue* and *Entertainment Weekly*, it was time to expand. "I don't know, Julia Roberts?"

"Brad Pitt!" she squealed with wide, loving eyes. "I'm sure it was him, I must have been beside him on Wilshire for like fifteen seconds!" She sat back and sighed as though she'd just climaxed.

"That's exciting," Trent said, attempting to sound interested. How come he couldn't inspire that kind of reaction in anyone? Brad Pitt could induce hysteria by going to the post office, and Trent couldn't land a third date if he bought the girl a car. Or maybe that wasn't true. Maybe he'd unwittingly caused a dozen amazing orgasms on his drive into work. He decided to go with that. No reason not to. Besides, who'd be able to prove him wrong? "Have they started already?"

"What? Oh, yes, five minutes ago. You're late again." She seemed to be restraining an impulse to wag her finger.

"Traffic," he lied. "Any messages?"

Lynette handed him a small stack of notes. Wallace from ABC, Ty from Fox—nothing that couldn't wait until afternoon. "Thanks," he said as he headed for the meeting room. "Let me know if anyone famous calls."

"I will!"

Trent shook his head. How exciting could it possible be? *Hi, this is Tom Cruise, can I speak with someone important, please?* Was that anything to swoon over? The next time he visited the *LMS* set he'd have to remember to get Lynette a scrap of Derek's clothing—he was her favorite. She'd probably put it behind more glass than the Shroud of Turin.

The conference room door seemed louder than usual when he opened it. "Sorry I'm late," he said, pretending to be out of breath.

For a split second, nobody said anything. They all just stared at him, the whole crew—Max, Taylor, Todd, Tad, Rachel, and the General—and Trent got the feeling, as he had numerous times before, that he had accidentally stumbled into a taping of *The Real World*.

"Nice of you to join us," Max said.

"You're always late," Taylor pouted. She was the company's Token Harlot, bleached blonde and as artificial as they came. Every part of her body was fake—fake nails, fake eyelashes, fake eyebrows, a fake tan, and fake breasts she made no attempt to hide. She'd probably had a fake liver inserted just to be trendy. Her office was a collection of emery boards and glossy pictures of herself and her obnoxiously beautiful friends. When she wasn't telling the country's women what they needed to watch, she divided her time between reapplying her lip gloss and twirling her hair. Needless to say, Trent couldn't stand her and desperately wanted to sleep with her.

"I'm sorry."

"How come *he* can be late all the time and nothing happens?" Todd said. "If that was me, I'd be cut loose and you *know* it!"

Trent sat down beside Rachel. Todd was the Angry Black Man—more Omar Epps than Samuel Jackson—forever fighting the oppression and injustice that plagued him every single day. Tall, bald, and blessed with the athletic physique that seemed to be the birthright of all African-American men, he rarely failed to point out a new way that the ubiquitous White Man was attempting to crush him and his brothers beneath the steel-heeled boot of bigotry. His office was decorated with pictures of Malcolm X and Louis Farrakhan. He had brilliant teeth, large well-manicured hands, and almost never spoke quietly when he could shout. Trent had a suspicion that Todd shouted in order to make up for the fact that he had never participated in a demonstration of any kind. Needless to say, Trent did *not* want to sleep with him.

"I'm sorry, Todd. Traffic was—"

Todd slammed his fist on the table. "For the last time, my *name* is Komunyaaka!"

Trent wasn't in the mood for this. Every couple of months it was something different, Baraka or Muhammed or Tanzulu, whatever the hell that was supposed to mean. But he wasn't about to call anybody Komunyaaka who'd never read a book of poetry in his life. "Look, is there any coffee left? I'm dying here."

"*Some*one's in a lovely mood," Rachel said—the Taskmistress, thin lips and thin heels and thin-rimmed glasses and a mass of dark hair held up with a pair of thin chopsticks. She looked the way Jennifer Aniston might have looked if someone had jammed a tree branch up her ass as a child and no one had ever bothered to remove it. It was no secret that she wanted to become the Tank's next VP, a position the General had only recently announced he was trying to fill. Trent thought there was also the remote possibility that she moonlighted as a dominatrix—he could picture her lashing network execs with tassled whips as a memorable way to close a deal—but he couldn't be sure. She handed him a cup.

He took a sip. Tepid, but it would have to do. "I see you've recovered from your diphtheria."

"It was touch and go for a while," she said without a trace of sarcasm.

"Oh, stop," Tad said. "Seriously, you two, it's always fight fight fight, like two little cats. Meow! Can't we all just get along?"

Obviously, Tad was the Flamboyant Homosexual, short and slender with frosted blond highlights and wrists that flipped so much they were bound to fall off someday. He ate strange foods, wore linen shirts, and debatably spent more time on his nails than Taylor did on hers. The story was that he'd walked into the Tank five years ago with no experience, no credentials, no references, and an idea for a show called *I Think My Brother's Gay*. He'd been hired on the spot, and four months later NBC's self-described "Queer TV" was the biggest thing on Thursday night.

So there they were: the Bombshell, the Militant, the Schoolteacher, the Fairy, Max the fast-talking Sicilian, and himself, the newest and—in his opinion—least insane among them. Trent looked at each of them with something akin to awe. Had the General planned it that way? Had he hand-picked his crack team to cover every possible viewing demographic? Probably not; Trent didn't think the General was creative enough for that kind of tactical strategy. But on the off chance that he had, then which one was Trent supposed to be? The Nice Guy? The Struggling Artist? Maybe he was the Office Heartthrob, the guy that made women everywhere wet with passion. That sounded nice. Every office needed one of those.

"No, Tad," Todd said, "we can't all just get along. Not while my black brothers and sisters are suffering the oppression of the white man!"

"Oh, *please*," Tad said, and there went the wrist, "don't even *start* with me about oppression."

"You know," Max said, "it'd be interesting to see which of you two would be on top."

"That's enough," the General said in his usual imperious way. "We've got more important matters to discuss. Trent, I understand there was some trouble on the set this weekend?"

P.T. Beauregard. The real reason that Nova Creative Consulting was more commonly known as the Tank. Sixty-two years of telling people what to do and how quickly to do it had hardened his face and eyes until they could have dented iron. He'd been brought up in Boston, raised by parents who must not have known they'd given their son the same name as a famous Confederate general. But from the moment of his birth, P.T. must have taken his unknown namesake to heart. It was impossible to imagine him as a child. He had always been an old, ruthless businessman, always plotting the subjugation of his next corporate victim. Nobody in the office knew what the General had done before founding the Tank, nor why he had suddenly decided seven years ago to move to the opposite end of the country. Some thought he might have run foul of the Mafia, others that he had once been a family don. It was Trent's feeling that, as with a woman's age, it was best not to ask. As it was, they were fortunate enough that the General tolerated their incessant bickering, which was rather inevitable, considering the crew he had assembled.

"An unexpected problem," Trent said, watching the ashes from his cigarette drift into his ashtray. Thank God P.T. didn't abide by California's regulations about workplace smoking. "We had to can Jack and Alan."

Apparently Max had not informed everybody, because Taylor's eyes grew suddenly large. "Really? That's too bad. Jack was so *cute*."

"You said it, sister," Tad added.

"Alan's not a loss," Trent said. "Any one of those guys'll hit the eighteen to twenty-fives. But we're going to need someone to pick up the women fourteen to twenty-eight."

P.T. took off his rimless glasses, which he did a lot; Trent didn't think he really needed them. "So we need a new nice guy. What about Clark? Michael? Anyone will do."

"My thought exactly, sir," Max said. "I had Patrick film Michael rescuing a sheep from somebody's snare. We could use that."

P.T. shook his head. "Sheep's no good. Too . . . I don't know. Doesn't sit right."

"Not cuddly enough," Taylor offered.

"What about a *llama?*" Tad said.

"No. Too big."

"Tiger cub?" Todd said in a normal voice. About the only time he ever used one was in these meetings, and only half the time at that.

"Thought about that," Max said. "Endangered. It'd take months on the paperwork. Real shame, too, that'd be a good one."

"Oh!" Taylor said, with a clap of her hands. "I know! What about a koala bear?"

"A koala bear," P.T. said, chewing on the frame of his glasses. "A koala bear . . . I like it."

"But there aren't any koalas on the island," Trent said.

"Then we'll fly one in. Do I have to do all the thinking for you?"

Trent didn't think that would ever be a problem.

"A koala's not bad," Rachel said, "but maybe we should—"

"We're going with a koala bear," P.T. said. "I've made up my mind. We need to keep our female audience, and Taylor thinks a koala will do the trick. That's why I hired her, you know, so we could keep our finger on the pulse of the American woman. That and her tits, of course."

Taylor sat up a little straighter. "Thank you, sir."

Trent could feel the waves of hatred coming from Rachel, whose pursed lips looked about ready to crack. He shifted in his seat and took another sip of his lukewarm coffee. Someday Rachel would go after Taylor so hard even Lennox Lewis wouldn't be able to break them apart. "Try not wearing a jacket all the time," he whispered.

The look she gave him would have made Alan cringe. "Try fucking yourself."

So much for trying to help. "Well," he said, turning his attention back to the rest of his colleagues, "if we're settled there, that should take care of *LMS* for another week. Everything else seems to be in order."

"Good." P.T. nodded. "I'll want a status report by the end of the day. Todd, how are things shaping up for *Gangland Romance 2?*"

Trent thought it deliciously ironic that Todd's biggest score so far was a show that portrayed black people as violent drug-using car thieves with facial scars and more illegitimate children than Strom Thurmond. Todd, however, didn't seem to be suffering from an ethical dilemma. The prelims were apparently fine; the Latin Kings were holding out for better weapons, but it was nothing the lawyers wouldn't be able to sort out.

"I think we've got a real star in Lil' Nig," Todd was saying. "Definite crossover appeal."

Max's face twisted into a smirk. "You did explain to the happy couple that we'll provide them a car for their honeymoon, right?"

"Look," Todd said, eyes wide, "that wasn't my fault, all right! Old habits die hard."

"Let them do what they want," P.T. said. Have them steal *two* cars, the last one was great for ratings." He straightened the stack of papers in front of him, papers which Trent knew from vast experience were predominantly blank. "So, I assume that takes care of the old business? On to new matters, then."

Speech time. Trent settled back in his chair and let his eyelids slide closer together. It was the same every Monday morning—he'd heard this speech so often he could have recited it himself, complete with all the hand gestures and dramatic removing of eyeglasses. But at least P.T. kept it short.

"We're doing all right here. *Gangland Romance*, *Files of the Unfaithful*—and let's not forget our golden boy, *Last Man Standing*. These are good things we've done. We've got our finger on the pulse of America. I can't tell you how many calls I have to return today from people desperate to secure our services."

Trent stifled a yawn. That took care of the ego-stroking. Now it was time to remove the glasses and get down to business.

"But frankly, it's not enough. I didn't found this company with the notion of being a competitor. It has always been my intention, and I've said this before, to be *the* source of creative concepts for the entire television industry." And there went the glasses. "I'll make this plain. Twelve months from now, I don't want anybody to remember that Dyson Associates ever existed."

As always when the subject of Stewart Dyson came up, Trent made a point to look at something other than his boss. Dyson was their biggest rival, founder of the agency that had given NBC two of the most profitable Reality shows ever, *Temple of Lust* and the surprise sensation, *What's My Gender?* It was this last one that had pushed the General over the edge. The day it aired, P.T. had locked himself in his office and gone on such a furious rampage Lynette had actually called the police. As far as Trent knew, there was only one person in the world that P.T. hated more than Stewart Dyson.

It seemed to take the General longer than usual to cool himself down, during which time everyone was careful to look thoughtfully at the table, except for Taylor, who looked thoughtfully at her nails. When he did speak again, it was with the tight restraint of a man who was evidently trying very hard not to throw something.

"Our *prob*lem, ladies and gentlemen, is that we've been too conservative. It's time to start pushing the envelope. Sooner or later people are going to tire of survival shows and arranged marriages. We're seeing it happen already. Last week *LMS* went from an eighteen to a sixteen share. If we want to be number one in this business—and we *do*—then we'll need to stay ahead of the curve, look at things from a new angle, think 'outside the box'." He actually used air quotes. "I don't want variations on existing shows, people. I want something new, something fresh, something . . . magnificent."

On that significant word, and with a significant narrowing of his eyes, the General stopped. There was a short silence while Trent and his coworkers pretended to process their boss's latest inspirational gem. As if he'd said anything new. Trent looked at the wall, lined with framed photographs of every cast member of Nova's Reality shows. The longer he looked, the more he hated them, clustered together with their borrowed clothes and airbrushed smiles as if they weren't all anxious to see their new friends bite it in the ass. He shook his head. What he needed more than anything was some fresh coffee. It was impossible to be nice or creative at 9:15 on a Monday morning without a few more cups of searing caffeine.

"What kind of show are you looking for?" Tad asked.

"I don't know," P.T. said. "Something new. It's your job to figure out what; that's what I'm paying you for."

"Well, what hasn't been done before?" Rachel asked.

"We've never had people kill each other," Max said.

"Oh!" Taylor's perfect forehead crinkled in disgust. "Who'd want to watch that?"

"Lots of people," Todd said.

Trent shook his head. Usually the conversation didn't get ridiculous until at least the second minute. "We can't kill people on national TV."

"What's with the can't, pal? Why do you have to be so negative?"

"Shut it, Max. Does anyone else want more coffee?" Trent got up to make another pot.

"We could fake the killing," Tad offered.

"It'd be complicated," Rachel said. "Maybe some maiming or eye gouging, but even that's dicey."

"Let the networks worry about how to do it," Max said. "All we have to do is give them the idea."

"I think Rachel's right," Todd said. "Besides, that kind of show would only reach a male audience, and you're already competing with sports and porn. And we're not going to make a dent in either of those markets no matter what we come up with. We need something with broader appeal."

"All right," Max said, "*you* come up with something, huh? What's *your* great idea?"

"I like puppies," Taylor suggested.

Rachel looked like she wanted to hit her.

"She sounds like she's genuinely trying to help," Trent whispered as he sat back down.

"Go fuck yourself," Rachel said—two for two.

"Animals are good," Tad said. "Women like animals."

"That's been done before," Max said. "*Crocodile Hunter*, *Animal Police*. The field is tapped out."

"We could *kill* the animals," Todd said.

Taylor slapped him repeatedly in the shoulder. "You—are—such—an—*ass*hole sometimes!"

"Come off it, girl. I was just playin'."

"I don't know, honey. It *would* be new."

That was it. "Oh, Jesus Christ, Tad, you can't be serious." If they wanted to dick around for the next half hour, he'd at least let them know what he thought of it. "I've got an idea. Taylor says women like animals. Todd says men like sports and porn. I think they're both right. Why don't we combine all three? How about *The Schnauzer Super Bowl*? Or, better yet, spice it up and throw some people in there. What about a new reality show called *Who Wants to Fuck My Donkey?* How's that sound?"

Everyone just stared at him. Every one of them—Taylor, Tad, Todd, Rachel, Max, even the General was staring at him, his imperious mouth wide open. Trent sat back down. Why couldn't he learn to keep his mouth shut? He wouldn't have said anything if he'd already had his second cup of coffee.

Todd was the first to speak. "That's not a bad idea."

"I think it's *brilliant*."

"You might be onto something there, pal."

Now it was Trent's turn to gape. "Guys, look, I was just k—"

"Yes, Trent," Tad said, "we know you were kidding about the title. We couldn't get away with that today, no way no sir. But the *idea* is so . . ." He sat back, apparently overwhelmed by his proximity to genius.

"What about *Who Wants to Marry My Donkey?*" Rachel suggested.

"Why limit it to donkeys?" Max said. "Why not call it *Very Special Pets*? Or *Animal Lovers*?"

"Donkeys are so *hairy*," Taylor said.

"And puppies aren't, honey?" Tad asked.

"*You* know what I mean."

"Better call it *Extreme Animal Lovers*," Todd said. "People like things that are extreme."

"The more extreme the better," Tad added.

"Guys," Trent said, "you can't be serious."

"Why not?" Max asked. "*Extreme Animal Lovers*, it'll put *Fear Factor* right out of business. Who's gonna watch people eat bugs when they could see 'em fuck cattle instead?"

"I agree," Rachel said. "But how are we going to show that on TV?"

"Let the networks figure that out," Taylor said. "They should have to do *some* of the work, don't you think?"

"We could just film them going into the stable or . . . wherever," Todd said, his face twisting at the thought. "The audience would get the idea."

"That might add a nice element of suspense," Rachel said. "Kind of a 'did-they-really-do-it?' thing."

"I'm thinking we might tap Hatch for this," Tad said.

"From *Survivor*?" Taylor said. "The fat naked guy? Ewww, why? He's got to be sixty by now."

"Tad's right," Max said. "I think this would be right up his alley."

"Let's worry about casting later," Rachel said. She cleared her throat and sat forward. "First things first. What kind of animals are we talking here?"

"Guys," Trent said with a certain amount of desperation, "this is insane."

"Of course it is!" Max said. "That's why it's going to be a hit."

And for the next ninety minutes Tad, Todd, Rachel, Taylor, and Max ironed out the logistics of the show that was already officially being called *Extreme Animal Lovers*. The entire time P.T. said nothing, and neither did Trent, too stunned for speech, listening for ninety minutes to a conversation that should have been possible only between Rod Serling and Richard Matheson. How had this happened? He'd been joking, for Christ's sake! The very thought of holding a casting call turned his stomach, and here Rachel was explaining how they could successfully incorporate female contestants into the show! He didn't even want to try picturing that one.

"I don't want to be remembered as the guy who introduced bestiality to primetime," he muttered, but no one was listening.

Well, he decided as he stared at the bottom of his coffee cup, one thing was certain. There was no way on Earth he'd do an onsite evaluation for *this* little wonder. Forget faking diphtheria; he'd go out and *find* someone with Ebola to sleep with before he helped anybody prep reluctant horses for the camera.

Eventually, P.T. reined it in. "I think that's enough for this morning. I have a good feeling about this one, ladies and gentlemen. Rachel, you and Todd put together a working script. Taylor, you're on liabilities. Max, give me your *LMS* status report by noon, then get on location search. Tad, you're wardrobe and set design. I'd like to start shopping this by the weekend. And Trent," he said as he stood up, "I'll need to see you in my office."

Great. Rarely was a visit to the boss's office a desirable thing. Trent obeyed, though, following P.T. past Tad's fastidious cubicle and Todd's more revolutionary one. Cubicles. Weren't they making enough money to afford doors?

"Listen," Trent said as soon as he'd closed the door to P.T.'s office. "I'm sorry I was late this morning. It won't—"

"Have a seat, Trent." P.T. eased into the chair behind his desk, a massive structure of glass and brushed steel that would have looked perfect in a Kubrick film. He pulled a cigar from his desktop humidor and struck a match. He did not offer one to Trent.

Trent sat down. All the chairs in the General's office were about six inches too short for ordinary people, which had to have been intentional. He extended his legs to keep from feeling like a giant fetus.

"Well," P.T. said, punctuating the word with a wreath of smoke, "let's get right to it, shall we?"

Right to what? Was he being fired? "Sure."

"You hit a grand slam in there today, Trent. It's fresh, risky, attention-grabbing—it's the first original idea this company's come up with in five years, that's what it is. Frankly, I didn't think you had it in you."

"Thank you." Sort of. "Just doing my job."

"And that title of yours." P.T. inhaled deeply. "Perfect. Sharp, shocking. Max is right, it'd knock *Fear Factor* right off the charts. That's a twenty-share title, maybe twenty-five. It's a real shame we can't use it. But unfortunately, not everybody shares our . . . vision."

P.T. stood up then, turning toward the windows behind him. One hand held the cigar to his mouth, and the other rested against the small of his back. For a while he said nothing, staring at the world beyond his office. It would have made a more impressive picture if the building had been twenty stories instead of two.

"Do you know whose picture that is?"

"What picture?"

"On the wall behind you."

Trent turned to look. He recognized the man instantly: Ronald Armsburger, chairman of the FCC—the only man in the world the General hated more than Stewart Dyson. Everyone in the entertainment industry knew who he was. But where in the world had the General found a poster-sized picture of Ronald Armsburger? You probably couldn't find one in the bin at Sam Goody's.

"*That*," P.T. began with a hiss, "is the man who is single-handedly killing television. Have you ever met him? Well I have, and if he had his way every station in the country would be airing *Leave it to Beaver* and *Gilligan's Island* twenty-four hours a day. As if that's what Americans want to see anymore. What does *he* know about America, anyway? We're the ones in the trenches, we're the ones who know what people want! I'm telling you, Trent, if somebody doesn't do something to stop him, Ronald Armsburger is going to destroy everything America stands for."

Trent thought that was perhaps a little excessive. Imposing a standard of decency on television programming was the only reason that *Sesame Street* wasn't followed by graphic footage of anal sex. Besides, considering that shows like *Joe Millionaire* and *The Swan* had been made, how strict could the FCC really be? But Trent knew better than to argue. There was a look in P.T.'s eyes that Trent had seen somewhere before. *Scarface*? *The Shining*? Either way, it wasn't a look that invited discussion.

P.T. drew again on his cigar, which seemed to calm him down. "Tad's right. That title is ahead of its time, and right now we have to make certain concessions until we can get somebody in there who understands what it is we're trying to do."

"*Extreme Animal Lovers* should sell," Trent said. Had he actually just said that? "It'll start slow, but once word gets around—"

"You're right. It's a solid title. Just not as strong as it could be."

Yeah, and that was too bad, wasn't it? Too bad they couldn't call it *Fuck the Fuckers* or *Ass Badger Pussy Pie*. "I think it'll work out all right."

P.T. nodded absently and returned to his seat. He ground the remains of his cigar into an ashtray and clasped his hands in front of him. "I didn't call you in here to talk about Armsburger. The man has a way of putting me out of sorts."

"Maybe you shouldn't have his picture in your office?"

"I need it to remind me what we're up against." P.T. leaned back. "You surprised me today, Trent. I must admit I underestimated you. I like a man who's not afraid to stick it right up the FCC's Puritanical ass. That's the kind of thing I'm looking for in a vice president."

Vice president? Was that an offer? Without thinking, Trent sat up straighter. "Thank you."

"Don't get too excited, I'm not promising anything yet. But I've got my eye on you now. Another couple ideas like this morning's, and I'd say your future here at Nova is a lock."

"Thank you."

"Now, I trust this conversation will remain between you and me."
"Absolutely."
"All right. Now, get back to work."
Trent leapt to his feet. "Yes, sir. I'll do my best."

[CHAPTER THREE]

I am such a whore.

That was the only complete thought Trent was able to formulate for the rest of the day. He called the people he needed to call and wrote the reports he needed to write, but all the while that single thought careened through his brain like a drunken ballerina. *I'm a big, fat, corporate whore.*

But at least he was honest with himself.

He cut out half an hour early, hopped onto Wilshire, and drove to Garibaldi's in the heart of Westwood to meet Adam, the only one of his graduate school friends he'd cared to keep in touch with. Adam had chosen to tackle the movies, or rather be tackled by them; so far none of his screenplays had made it past the treatment. Meeting at Garibaldi's had become a ritual for them, a comfortable place to drink sake bombs and steel themselves for the week to come. It also didn't hurt that all of the waitresses were unbelievably gorgeous, UCLA coeds and struggling actresses that Trent would have been able to find plenty of work for.

"You're early!" Candy said when he walked in.

Trent gave her a kiss on the cheek. Candy. What kind of parents named their daughter Candy? Probably ones who knew they'd created a knockout and didn't expect her to adhere to any strict code of morality.

"I'm making up for being late to work this morning. Is Adam here yet?"

"Not yet, sweetie. Grab a seat, okay?"

Trent slid into his favorite corner booth, plush blue leather and completely '50s. Lining the wall at his back were three rows of photographs, black-and-whites of some of the most famous names in Hollywood: Turner, Brando, Basinger. He could imagine Grant and Bogart sitting in this very booth, preparing for a film in a time when that word still meant something, before anyone in the entertainment industry could possibly have conceived of a show called *Extreme Animal Lovers.*

"Here you go, sweetie," Candy said, setting two tiny glasses of purple sake on the table.

"Thanks," he said, draining the first and moving the second in front of him. "You'd better bring some for Adam, too."

"I thought I had. Long day?"

"Something like that." It was always a long day for a big, fat whore like himself. "Bring a couple more for me, will you? Tell you what, bring six. I'm sure we'll drink them."

Candy left, walking heel to toe as if she thought a director might be watching her.

A moment later Adam arrived, looking characteristically hurried and walking with his shoulders slightly hunched as though he was bracing for an attack. He was wearing black, of course, black shoes with a black shirt and his black hair tucked into a black beret. He sat down with a sigh and, as usual, declined the cigarette Trent offered him.

"You're here early," Adam said. "Losing the war?"

"It's not looking good."

"Well, I've got you beat. Guess where I've been all day?"

"Adam!" Candy returned with a tray of drinks, set them down, and gave Adam a starlet's hug—all wrist, no palm. "New outfit?"

"Very funny. Maybe someday I'll be able to afford one."

Trent took the liberty of removing their drinks from the tray. "Candy," he said, draining his second sake, "have I ever told you that I love you?"

"Every Monday."

"So when are you going to let me take you home?"

"As soon as you get me a spot on one of those TV shows you're always making."

"Believe me, you don't want anything to do with our latest idea."

"Well, believe *me*, anything would be better than working here the rest of my life. Let me know if you need anything, okay?" And she swished away.

Trent was pretty sure that being mounted by an eager ram was, in fact, worse than slinging drinks. That'd be a tough one to explain to the parents. *Mom, Dad, I've hit it big! Watch ABC Wednesday night at 7, I'll be the one being fucked by a minotaur.* But then, who was he to judge? For a lot of people, that might constitute a step up.

"So," Trent said, "you want to hear about our newest stroke of genius?"

"Let me tell you about my day first," Adam said. He removed his glasses—black-rimmed, naturally—and started cleaning them. "So last night I got a call from Jake Dozander. You met him a couple weeks ago at Shelly's. Tall, blond ponytail, sounds a bit like Nicholas Cage? Anyway, I'd given him a copy of *The Long Road* to read, just for feedback."

"It's a great script."

"Thanks. Well, Jake calls me last night at one in the morning. Calls me on my home number, which I hadn't given him. At first I couldn't figure out who it was, right? But then he starts going on about how he'd just finished reading my screenplay. Said he thought it was the best thing he'd seen in a year. That's exactly what he said, 'Adam, this is best script I've read in a year.'"

"That's encouraging."

"I thought so too. He said he'd just got off the phone with his agent at Black Forest—he'd actually called the guy up in the middle of the night—and set up a meeting for ten o'clock this morning."

"Adam, that's *great*."

"Just wait, it gets better." Adam put his glasses back on and sipped his sake. "So this morning I get over there at ten on the nose, which is a miracle because I was stuck on the 405 for thirty-five minutes. So I get over there, right, and . . . have you ever been there?"

"No."

"Well let me tell you, it's like an institution. You'd think there'd be pictures of their clients on the wall, right? Not a single one. The walls are com*pletely* bare, and the secretary sits behind this huge desk—thing must have weighed half a ton. Anyway, there I am, ten o'clock sharp, and she tells me to wait. No big deal, right? Guess what time they called me?"

"I don't know. Noon?" A two-hour wait wasn't unusual in the film industry, especially for people who hadn't been "discovered" yet.

"Two-thirty," Adam said with a mirthless smile. "I lost count of how many people came in after me and were sent right in. And their chairs are all too short, I swear they must have been designed for children. It was impossible to get comfortable."

Trent had some experience with that. "It's probably a power thing."

"So anyway, there I am, sitting for four and a half hours. I think I read every magazine they have, including *Teen People*, that's how bored

I was. Seriously, what kind of talent agency has a subscription to *Teen People*?"

"One that represents twelve-year-olds."

"I guess so. I've got about fifteen ideas for my next hairstyle, if I can ever afford to get it cut. So I waited for over four hours, but whatever. I shouldn't be complaining, right? I mean, I'm fifty feet away from pitching my script to the best agency in Hollywood, what's the big deal about having to wait?"

"So what happened?"

"All right. Two-thirty rolls around, and finally the secretary tells me that Mr. Dietrich is ready to see me."

"Wait a second." Trent's hand stopped before it could bring his third glass of sake to his lips. "Karl Dietrich?"

"That's the one."

"Adam, that's *huge*."

"I know it. So I'm in there, right, I'm in Dietrich's office, and all around me are posters of films he's had his hand in. I'm telling you, Trent, the man's done *everything*. I swear, from his window you can see Universal's production lot. Anyway, he stands up, shakes my hand and says—get this—'I've been looking forward to meeting you. You're the first person Jake's ever called me about.'"

"You're killing me, Adam. What happened?"

"I'm getting to it. He sits me down and says, 'So, what have you got?' So I start in, right, all the basics—Poland, 1937, small town just outside Warsaw—you know what I'm saying. I tell him it's *The English Patient* meets *A River Runs Through It*."

"Yeah yeah yeah. What *happened*?"

"So," Adam said, leaning forward, "about forty-five seconds in he stops me. I haven't even made it to the second half yet, and he stops me and says—I swear to God, these were his exact words—he says, 'Sounds good. But where are the tits?'"

Trent, who had unwittingly been holding his breath, exhaled in the long, slow way that a dying man might breathe his final breath. "Tell me you're kidding. You've got to be kidding. You're kidding, right?"

"I wish I were."

That called for another sake bomb. "So what'd you do?"

"What *could* I do? I told him that there weren't any. So then he says—get this—'Does anyone die soon?'"

"Jesus Christ."

"At *this* point," Adam said, downing another drink, "I'm thinking he might be joking. But he's completely serious. So I told him, 'Nobody dies.' And he goes, 'How can you have a movie about the Holocaust where nobody dies?' Like it's a selling point or something. Like people go to movies about the Holocaust for the dead bodies."

"Or the naked prisoners."

"Ex*actly*. So I say, 'What about *Life is Beautiful*?'"

"Good example."

"And *he* says, 'I'm not sure America's ready for another Be-nigg-knee.' That's how he said it. Be-*nigg*-knee. I almost threw my chair at him."

It was impossible not to laugh. Trent drained his fourth sake bomb—or was it his fifth?—and spilled a little down the side of his chin. What a piece of work was man. How noble and infinite, pretty and paragonical. And yet, what was man but a quintessence of bullshit? "I'm sorry, Adam. I'm not laughing at you. It's just—"

"—the stupidest goddamn thing you've ever heard? Me too." Adam fell back against the booth and stared at the ceiling. "Oh, well. Back to the drawing-board, right?"

"Don't give up on it. It's a great script."

"Yeah, well . . ." He picked up an empty glass and ran his finger along the rim. "Thanks. So, what have you got for me?"

Trent launched in. He expected Adam to laugh a little, or at least chuckle a bit. But his friend apparently wasn't in a mood to appreciate the absurdity of a show that would require feed harnesses and dozens of foot-long prophylactics.

"Is that *all* anyone wants any more?" Adam asked. "What happened to art? Doesn't anyone have any integrity any more?"

"How do you think I feel? I came *up* with the idea."

"Yeah, but at least you're getting paid for it. I don't know how much longer I can afford to write scripts nobody wants to read."

"Listen," Trent said, starting to have trouble making his words end where they were supposed to, "don't let them beat you. Keep fighting."

"That's easy for you to say, Trent. You're making six figures a year to come up with shows about albino transsexuals." Adam threw his glass on the table, then covered his eyes with his left hand. "Look, I'm sorry. I shouldn't have said anything. It's . . ."

"No," Trent said, "you're absolutely right. I'm nothing but a big, fat, bloated, Armani-suit-wearing whore. You know how far I've gotten on my book? Nine pages. *Nine*. Know why? Because I spend seventy hours a week thinking up shows like *Paraplegic Beauty Queen*. We actually pitched that one, 'Because cripples need to feel pretty, too.'" Trent emptied another glass, hoping to rinse the taste of filth from his whorey mouth. "We'd have made it, too, if it hadn't been for Armsburger. At least *somebody* knows where to draw the line."

"You guys look so serious over here," Candy said. "You need more drinks?"

"I think we're fine," Adam said.

"Keep 'em coming," Trent demanded. He felt like drinking until he turned into a puddle. How had he let things get away from him like this? Why couldn't he just tell them all they were destroying the world? They may as well have been pouring oil on baby seals for all the good they were doing. He would have said so, too, if his Jaguar hadn't been so much fun to drive.

Trent buried his head in his arms. "Jesus, Adam, I'm such a whore."

"About to be a vice-presidential one, it sounds like."

"Maybe. Hey." Trent sat up, suddenly possessed with a genuinely good idea. At least it seemed like a good one. Drunk ideas often did. "If I make VP, I might be able to hire you on as a creative consultant."

"What, so we can *both* make shitty television?"

"It doesn't have to be bad. We could change it together. We could shop *The Long Road* as a miniseries, maybe run it by HBO. Tom Hanks did that with *Band of Brothers*."

"That's because he's Tom Hanks."

"Yeah, well, *fuck* Tom Hanks." Trent turned his cup to his mouth and was surprised to find it empty. Candy must have forgotten to fill it. "*Big* was a shitty movie. No tits in that one, by the way, Mr. Dietrich."

"There almost were."

Trent made a noise he had meant to be a laugh, but it didn't come out that way. "I've seen fewer clothes on seventh graders."

Just then a slim blonde girl—was *every* girl in Hollywood blonde?—stopped by the side of their booth. She had pale skin and looked as if she belonged in a library. Her eyes grew wide. "Are you Adam Caruthers? *The* Adam Caruthers? Oh my God, I've been *dying* to meet you, I'm like your biggest fan!"

Adam smiled. "You'll have to wait until Thursday to sleep with me. I've got a three-day backlog."

"Bullshit," she said, setting her cosmopolitan on the table. "I'm better than all of them, anyway."

"Why don't women come up to me like that?" Trent wanted to know. He gave her another look. She seemed to be going for the Gwyneth Paltrow thing, tall and willowy and probably planning to name her first-born child Bon-Bon or Carrot. Still, she'd have done in a pinch.

Adam moved over to let the girl sit down beside him. "Trent, this is Angela. We met a couple weeks ago."

"Pleasure," Trent said, extending a hand that felt only partially attached to his body.

"She's a theater student at UCLA," Adam said.

"I do a little extra work, too," she added. "Tomorrow I'm an audience member for a cooking infomercial."

"Sounds fascinating," Trent said. Gosh. A theater major in Hollywood. Who'd've thought?

Adam put an arm around Angela. "Just so you know, Trent's the most soulless, corrupt person I know."

"What do you do?" she asked. "Write sit-coms?"

"Worse. I come up with ideas for Reality TV shows."

Trent had described his job to hundreds of people, and their reactions always fell into one of two categories. There were the aspiring actors and avid reality show viewers who looked at him as if he were their new Messiah and would probably have followed him around wearing cellophane and jester hats if he'd asked them to. And there were the others, struggling artists and their friends, who looked at him as if he'd just eaten a baby and still had a tiny finger sticking out of his mouth. There wasn't any middle ground; people didn't have mixed feelings about it. And Trent could tell Angela fell into the latter classification.

She did a good job of trying to hide it, though. "Do you like it?"

He shrugged. "It pays the bills."

"Very well, I might add," Adam said.

"Why do they call it Reality TV?" Angela asked around her drink. "I mean, take *Joe Millionaire*. How real is that?"

"I've never had fifty women fighting over me at the same time," Adam said.

"You're not trying hard enough," Trent said.

"And you have?" Angela asked.

"All the time. It's happening right now. They're out in the alley fighting it out with broken bottles. If you listen real careful you can hear 'em."

"You're drunk," Adam said.

Trent smiled and raised another glass. Drunk, psssshhh. What did *they* know? There wasn't enough alcohol in the world to make him as drunk as he wanted to be.

"What are some of the shows you've done?"

"Has Adam told you about his meeting with Mr. Dietrich?" Trent asked, eager to talk about something other than himself. He didn't think she'd be terribly impressed to learn he was the architect behind *Child Custody Court TV*.

"No! Oh, baby, I'm sorry, I completely forgot! How'd it go?"

"Terrible," Adam said. He seemed to have gotten over some of his frustration. "I'll tell you about it later."

"Have you read his script?" Trent asked.

"Oh, my God, it's incredible," Angela said. Jesus Christ, she'd almost put a hand to her chest when she said it—one of *those* theater girls. "It's the best thing I've ever read."

"Stop it," Adam said.

"I'm serious, baby. Mamet's got nothing on you."

"I read it as kind of a cross between Cormac McCarthy and Thomas Pynchon," Trent said. He had no idea what he was talking about.

Angela nodded vigorously. "I can see that."

"Give me your keys," Adam said. "You're drunk."

Trent was fishing his keys out of his left pocket when the right one began to vibrate. "Hole on a second," he said to Adam, then opened his phone. "Trent Tucker . . . hey Max, how's . . . what? . . . he *did* . . . this weekend? . . . well, of course I want to go . . . yeah . . . all right, call me later . . . yeah." He closed his phone and sat there, swaying gently to the warm, happy music that had just begun playing in his head.

"What was that about?" Adam asked.

"P.T. wants me to do a casting call this weekend."

"I thought this was your weekend off."

"It is."

"You seem pretty upbeat. What's the show?"

Trent answered with a long, slow, ridiculous smile.

Adam leaned back. "Oh, you've *got* to be kidding."

"What?" Angela asked. "What are you guys talking about?"

"It is, isn't it?" Adam went on. "I can't believe you. You have got to be the luckiest fucker on the planet."

"I guess my job isn't *all* bad," Trent said.

"It's got its perks."

"Some."

Angela leaned forward. "Would *someone* tell me what the hell you two are talking about?"

[CHAPTER FOUR]

Following the overwhelming success of *American Idol*, television networks across America began a frantic scramble to find other ways to capitalize on *Idol*'s format. Nova conducted an intensive analysis of the show and soon uncovered the key components of its massive appeal. Unsurprisingly, the choice of music was the biggest factor. It translated easily to a visual medium; it raked in billions of dollars a year from people of every demographic; and, perhaps most importantly, there are millions of people who couldn't carry a tune if their lives depended on it, guaranteeing the show's producers an unlimited supply of horrendous outtakes to satisfy the public's need to mock their fellow Americans. What was needed, the crew at Nova determined, was a different form of entertainment that could meet all three criteria.

So they went to work, researching every conceivable type of artistic expression, proposing and discarding idea after idea until they finally hit upon the perfect combination of music and spectacle, a vocation that generated untold amounts of money in revenue each year. It was such an obvious choice, so simple and brilliant, that it seemed impossible no one had thought of it before. It was the answer to their search, an answer that would resonate with viewers from Atlantic City to Cheyenne.

An answer called stripping.

Thus the concept for *Take It Off!* was born. Designed as a complement to the *American Idol* model, *Take It Off!* would pit fifty girls against each other, professional and would-be strippers battling it out before a live audience, competing for a $250,000 modeling contract and a chance to make their heavily-pixellated breasts more popular than Jenna Jameson's. Preliminary reports suggested that *Take It Off!* would be an enormous hit with women under thirty and males from infancy to death.

When Trent, Max, Todd, and Taylor arrived at the United Center in Chicago, the line of girls waiting to audition was already seven blocks long. The ones at the front must have slept there, huddled on the cold, filthy sidewalk in clothes that would have blown off in a light breeze. Judging from the size of the bags each girl was carrying, there was enough makeup on Madison Street to bury Bangkok.

"Aren't a lot of black girls," Todd said as they got out of their cab.

"It's probably a conspiracy," Max said. "Seriously, who wants to see black women on TV?"

"You *tryin'* to start something?"

"Oh, Jesus," Trent said. "Give it a rest, Komunyaaka."

"Why do you guys have to fight all the time?" Taylor asked. "Can't we all just put aside our differences and watch all these women take their clothes off?"

On that remarkably profound note, the four of them went inside.

There seemed to be as many people inside the building as out, cameramen and ushers and the United Center's security staff, all of whom had probably requested the assignment and were waiting as impatiently as the girls outside for things to get underway. Dozens of voting booths had been converted to makeshift powder rooms, and the glare of harsh halogen lights made everyone—even Taylor—look sallow and washed-out. There were representatives from ABC, all wearing dark suits, all huddled together near the empty husk of a popcorn stand. And, most significantly, there were two lines of velvet ropes leading down to the stadium floor, where two stages had been erected—one for the actual contestants, and one for . . . the others.

"I'm on first selection," Todd said.

"We know," Taylor said. "You've said it a dozen times."

"Are you the guys from Nova?" A light-skinned black man with electronic equipment attached to every seam of his clothing came up and shook hands. "Great, glad you're here. Axle Jones, VP development, ABC. We're all very excited about this show. I trust the flight was okay? All right, we're about ready to get started, so if we can get one of you over at first selection, we'll start letting them in. Which of you are going to be helping us judge?"

"Max and I are. Trent Tucker, we spoke on the phone." He turned to Max. "We're on thirty-minute shifts, right?"

Max nodded. "Which do you want first? Tell you what, let's flip for it."

Trent called heads. It was tails.

"Naturally," he said. He hadn't thought about "the others" when he'd agreed to come. It was not an appealing thought. "I hope it doesn't spoil me for the rest of the day."

Axle clapped his hands together. "All right, let's get this rolling."

Todd went back to the main entrance and took his place at the point where the two lines of velvet ropes diverged. Taylor gave herself a quick review in a nearby mirror and headed for the knot of ABC reps, where she would laugh, wink, maybe flash something, and pitch as many new show ideas as she could. That left Max and Trent, who descended to the stages on the arena floor, identical in every respect—lights, poles, catwalks—except for the women who would be appearing on them.

It made sense to do things this way. Like with *American Idol*, there were only two kinds of contestants—those with talent, and those without. And, given the talent they were looking for, it didn't take a great deal of time to figure out which girls had it and which girls should have stayed home and done a few thousand sit-ups. It made sense to have a separate stage for each. And you couldn't very well have one filled with judges and the other completely empty. But that did not mean anyone should have to endure what Trent and Max would both witness at thirty-minute intervals for the next ten hours.

He looked at the stage on his left as though it might try to hurt him. How could he have forgotten about "the others"? But it was impossible to leave now. Already the girls would be coming in, and Todd would be directing each one to her appropriate line like a German soldier at Auschwitz. *You, to the right; you, to the left. Sieg Heil!*

Trent took his seat beside the other judges. Standard Reality fare—the stuffy British aristocrat and an out-of-work actress drowning in Maybelline. Where did ABC find these people? Was there a casting call for judges, too?

"How's it going?" Trent said, though he didn't particularly care.

"Smashing," the aristocrat said. "Evan Withers, pleasure. Brilliant idea, this, I can't believe you got it past the FCC."

"Hi," Maybelline said. "I'm Sunshine." She gave Trent a wide smile and a generous view of her cleavage.

"They're lovely," Trent said to Sunshine's breasts, paying her the compliment he knew she was waiting for. Sunshine. It's time to face the truth, lady, your light went out decades ago.

"Uh-oh," Evan said, nudging Trent in the side, "here they come."

Trent turned. Indeed they were, snaking down the aisles in two dynamically segregated groups, like stripteasing Elois and Morlocks. The line heading toward the other stage was filled with remarkable girls with washboard stomachs and impossibly perky breasts. They were wearing satin camisoles and lacy teddies, things a "good" girl would never dream of wearing in public. There wasn't a girl among them who didn't look capable of advancing to the next selection.

And in the other line, closing in on Trent like a bloated centipede, were the Morlocks—fat girls and short girls and worn-out grandmothers with drooping flesh and vermillion mascara tattooed above rheumatic eyes. There was a girl with burns on her arms, for Christ's sake. And the *clothes* they were wearing. Had they even bothered to look in a mirror? Or had their mirrors all shattered at the first viewing?

"Oh, I can't believe it," Evan said, masking his laughter by putting a hand over his face. "This is *too* perfect. Simply smashing."

"Is this really about to happen?" Trent asked.

"You should have been in New York," Sunshine said. "I can't even describe how horrible it was."

"We had a girl there with a prosthetic leg," Evan added.

Trent stared at the ceiling. "Just tell me when it's ten-thirty, all right?"

The show began at once. Fifteen girls were called at a time, one for each pole on the stage, and told to follow whatever impulse the music gave them. Six cameramen moved slowly back and forth at the base of the stage while the hopefuls puffed and strained in woefully unerotic attempts to remove shirts five sizes too small. Rarely were they given ninety seconds before Evan or Sunshine shut it off and explained why none of them would be asked to return.

"I don't know what you were trying to do up there, but it wasn't dancing."

"I don't want to be rude, ladies, but I've been more aroused by my own *dog* than by any of you."

"Look, I'm sure you'll all have better luck somewhere else. Like the rodeo."

Trent didn't say a word. He could barely bring himself to watch such a horrendous and humiliating display. If there hadn't been a thick curtain separating the two stages from each another, he'd probably have spent the entire time with his head turned in that direction. Max was probably throwing dollars on the stage by now.

"What time is it?"

"Ten after," Evan said. "Don't get squeamish on us now, the fun's only starting."

Occasionally there'd be a girl whose performance was so atrocious it would merit a repeat performance. Evan would stop the music and say, "All right, girls, that'll be all. You there, in the pink . . . whatever that is, I'd like you to stay." Then the woman in question would do another number alone, slithering and writhing like a landed fish until it was certain there'd be a stellar clip for the outtake reel. After perhaps a minute, Evan would cut her off and say, "Thank you. I think we've seen enough." And the girl would be led off the stage, still beaming, while the next fifteen were escorted up.

"It's *awful* how you lead them on like that," Sunshine said.

"They've brought them on themselves," Evan said simply. "Nobody forced them to come. Seriously, what can these girls *possibly* expect?"

Trent wondered the same thing. When was the last time anyone had seen a two-hundred pound stripper? Most people would have paid these girls to keep their clothes *on*. What did their families think? Had they told anyone? Or were they hoping to make it a surprise, sit down in front of the TV at Thanksgiving with all the cousins and watch themselves wriggle half-naked and grunting while Mom passed around the cranberry sauce?

"What time is it?" Trent asked.

"Quarter of eleven," Evan said. "I'm sorry, ladies, maybe the casting announcement wasn't clear. We're looking for talented women."

While the next round of hopeless hopefuls waddled their way onto the stage, Trent got up and stormed through the curtain to the other judges' table. "Max!" he said harshly. "You know what time it is?"

Max jerked his head toward Trent. His eyes were glazed. "What? Oh, shit, it hasn't been half an hour already, has it?"

"Forty-five minutes. Get up."

"Thank you, girls," one of the judges said, "that's enough. Numbers three, six, and seven, if you'd stay up there, please."

Max reluctantly got out of his seat. "Man, time flies, you know?"

"Not over there it doesn't."

"That bad?"

"Ever read *The Jungle*?"

"Oh, come on, pal, it can't be *that* bad."

"Sorry, man." Trent lit a cigarette. "How's it here?"

Max whistled. "See for yourself."

Trent looked up—and found himself in an earthly paradise. Three gorgeous women—blonde, brunette, and redhead; it was *too* perfect—were slowly removing clothes that hadn't covered anything in the first place. The blonde leapt upon her pole like an animal, climbing until she was seven feet off the ground and then suspended herself upside-down, held in place by the strength of her silky thighs. The redhead was crawling on the stage, inching her seductive way forward, breasts pressed together by the stage floor. And the brunette . . . he didn't think what she was doing was even *possible*.

"I'll be back at eleven-thirty," Max said.

"No hurry," Trent said, feeling for his seat with his hands. "Take your time."

Let Max suffer through forty-five minutes of shameless atrocity, Trent thought as he settled into his chair. He'd earned *this* moment. This was a reward long overdue.

The next flight began, and Trent spent most of the time attempting to keep his mouth closed. Every one of them was impossibly beautiful, former Victoria's Secret models and dorm room pin-ups, girls of such intimidating loveliness most guys wouldn't have the courage to approach them. And they *all* knew how to move, how to grind against their poles like lovers, how to slink and slide and slither in ways gravity should not have allowed. Where did girls like these hide? He'd been to Chicago a dozen times and never seen a single woman like the ones who were now dancing for him. Ahhh, for *him*. What else could a man ask for?

As soon as the judge at his side—Carter something or other—called an end to the audition, Trent realized he had no idea how to rate what he'd seen. "How am I supposed to judge that?" he whispered. "They're all amazing."

"You don't have to do anything," the man whispered back. "You're here as a courtesy, you know that. Just sit back and enjoy. Thank you, girls! That will be all."

Well, Trent thought, that suited him just fine.

Another group came up on stage, then another, and another, each more gorgeous and uninhibited than the last. Despite the other judges' repeated insistence that their decisions were made independently of how many clothes the contestants wore, none of the girls believed them. Every time Carter switched the music on, the women on stage began removing a wardrobe's worth of skirts and wet T-shirts, crimson sarongs and black thongs the size of quarters. When that was no longer enough, some of the girls started dancing with each other, pressing their chests together and giving each other long, slow, wet kisses. The first time it happened, Trent almost fell out of his chair.

After half an hour, twenty groups of hopefuls—three hundred semi- and completely naked women—had passed beneath Trent's expert and attentive eye. That was more than most men saw in their lives, at least without the aid of the Internet. Carter called for the twenty-first group.

And then, a terrible thing happened. Trent started to get bored.

At first he couldn't believe it. How could this happen? What kind of cruel, wicked, spiteful, vindictive God would allow such a thing? Frantically he lit a cigarette, hoping the sweet rush of nicotine would jumpstart his inexplicably stalled libido. But it was no use; they were all starting to look *the same*. Was this some kind of divine punishment? He'd been to church a few times; he'd paid his dues. He drank a glass of water and tried to concentrate harder—still nothing. Why? Why, God, why?

By the twenty-sixth flight, Trent was thoroughly bored. He should have known it was going to happen. He'd always been this way at strip clubs. All his friends could sit through a dozen lap dances without blinking, but after two he started to find the whole thing monotonous. Especially since he knew it'd never go anywhere. What was the point of paying a girl to arouse you and then not do anything about it? Most guys could find that kind of sexual frustration at the mall.

Exasperated, Trent tilted his head back and stared at the ceiling. Were there other guys like him, maybe some seasoned pornstars who groaned when it came time to go to work? *God, I am so tired of these tedious threesomes. Why didn't I finish accounting school like my mother wanted?*

"Sorry, pal," Max said over his shoulder, "time to trade."

Numb, and feeling royally cheated, Trent gave up his seat. However uninspiring these girls had become, it beat hell out of the alternative.

"I don't know what you're complaining about," Max said. "I had a great time. Those girls are hysterical. There was this one—total walrus, right, I'm talking huge, and she—"

"Tell me about it later," Trent said with a shudder. He'd probably see the girl's twin sister in five minutes.

And so it went. Every half hour Trent flipped between grossly unattractive women making asses of themselves and sultry vixens whose sexiness was so ubiquitous it had become commonplace—the worst of both worlds. The only thing missing was for one of them to accidentally fling her stiletto heel right through his eye. That would lend just the right amount of pique to lunch. Which they didn't get to take, he reminded himself. They were too busy deciding which girls American husbands would fantasize about while having sex with their wives.

About one o'clock, Evan and Sunshine started laughing. "Oh, *God*," Evan said, "she takes the cake."

Trent, who'd been staring at the table wishing it would come alive and go on a murderous rampage that would allow him the opportunity to escape, looked up. On stage was absolutely the most obese woman he had ever seen. She made the mother in *Gilbert Grape* look like an understudy for Kate Moss. She could have been standing there completely naked without revealing anything indecent. Trent closed his eyes, uncomfortable by just knowing a person of her size existed. How had she even made it into the building? They must have let her in through the cargo doors.

"All right, girls," Sunshine said once she gained control of herself. "Here you go."

Trent couldn't bear to watch, but he couldn't force himself not to. She was *horrendous*, her fat, sunken face red from the strain of more exercise than she'd probably had in years. Some of the other girls were forced to move out of her way in order to avoid being crushed beneath her titanic bulk. Evan and Sunshine snickered the entire time and made little effort to keep the girls on stage from hearing them.

Mercifully, Evan brought it to a speedy end. "That'll be all, ladies," he said, still laughing. "You. Yes, you, the one I'm pointing at. Stunning performance. We'd like you to do a solo for us."

"You've got to be kidding," Trent whispered harshly. "She's repugnant."

"I know. Isn't she priceless? We can make an entire *episode* out of this. That's right, move to the center of the stage, please."

Trent shoved himself away from the table and stood up. This was the most degrading travesty he'd ever seen in his life. He'd rather *participate* in *Extreme Animal Lovers* than sit through another minute of this. Without a word he stormed up the bleachers toward the main level. He should have walked off hours ago, and the fact that he hadn't made him even angrier.

Evan and Sunshine didn't bother to stop him, which was wise of them; if they'd said anything, he would have done something they'd probably regret. They didn't need him, anyway. Anyone could sit there and round out their number. Like Todd, or Taylor, or Kermit the Frog for all he cared. He was through.

Hundreds of girls were still waiting outside for their moment in the spotlight when Trent left the arena floor. He made it about fifteen feet before he realized Todd was nowhere to be seen. There was a different guy directing the hopefuls to their respective lines, a man with ears the size of coconuts.

"Where's Todd?" Trent asked him.

"Don't know. Said he needed about forty-five minutes to take care of something. Whoa, miss, you're in the wrong line. Move to the left, please."

He found Taylor, who was sitting in a green director's chair surrounded by half a dozen men in suits. For once her brazen beauty didn't affect him. "Taylor! Come here for a second."

"What do you want?" She sounded annoyed. "I'm just about to sell these guys on—"

"You know, they'll wait for you. Do you know where Todd is?"

"Haven't seen him. What's it matter?"

"If you see him, tell him to find me, all right?"

"All right."

"I mean it."

"All *right*," she said. "Jeez. Relax a little, try to have fun. Look at where we *are*."

They were in a meat house, that's where they were. But Taylor probably didn't even see them. Beautiful girls had an uncanny ability to ignore unpleasant sights whenever it suited them.

"C'mon, fella!" one of the suits shouted at Trent. "Stop hoggin' her. We're lonely over here!"

"Tell you what, buddy, why don't you—"

"*Trent*," Taylor whispered. "Stop it. I'll be right there, boys!" She gave him a cold stare. Her eyes were green today. "Honestly, Trent, sometimes I just don't understand you at all." She left him and returned to her seat, ass wriggling like an eager puppy.

He fished out a cigarette, lit it, and found a seat by himself.

About five minutes later Max came running out of the arena. "Where you been, pal? They told me you'd split. Man, you should've seen what I just saw. I'll point her out when she comes up. I mean, *this* girl, I'm telling you, they've got to be the size of my head. You feeling all right?"

Funny, Trent thought. The breasts on the girl *he'd* just seen were the size of his torso. Sometimes, bigger wasn't better. "I need a break."

"But it's your turn over on the good side." Max wasn't even attempting to keep his voice down, and the girls in line for the outtake stage were less than ten feet away.

"Take my turn. Go on, I'm all fleshed out right now."

"You sure? Suit yourself, pal, I'm not gonna fight you on that one."

Just then a raven-haired girl wearing nothing but a black thong and a sequined bra came up and thrust herself in front of Max. She had a tattoo above her ass that read LEGENDARY and was carrying the rest of her clothes in her left hand.

"You're one of the judges, right? I saw you down there. Listen, I will do *anything* to get on this show, do you understand me? *Anything*."

Trent perked up. "I'm one of the judges, too."

She turned to face him. Her breasts were large, fake, and heavily powdered. She smelled like honey and looked like a girl with more experience than he could ever hope to acquire.

"Are you? Well, then you'll do, too. I don't care who it is or what I have to do, but I *need* to get on this show. I'll do anything."

"Look, miss," Max said, "what's your name?"

"Sheila."

"Look, Sheila, that's not how we do things here. Can you imagine what kind of zoo we'd have on our hands if that's the way it worked? Girls would be running around all over the place trying to sleep with anyone wearing a name tag. There'd be riots, people'd go to the hospital. We'd be sued out our asses."

"He's right," Trent added, though he thought it might be acceptable to make an exception now and then, especially for someone with lips like hers.

"I've been to other auditions," Sheila said, looking defiantly at him and the people who were watching their exchange. "I know how it works."

"Maybe at other places," Max said, "but not here." He put an arm around her. "Come on, put your clothes on."

"You don't under*stand*," Sheila said, beginning to cry. "I *need* this. I *have* to get on this show. I don't know what I'll *do* if I don't—"

"Hey, now, stop crying," Max said. "I'll take care of this, Trent. Look, you wanna talk? Fine. Let's go talk about this someplace else so you don't have to let everyone watch you cry." He led her away, the word above her perfectly sculpted backside disappearing like a ship into the darkness.

Trent looked at the girls in the outtake line who had witnessed everything. "Don't get any ideas," he said. Dear God, there was a thought. If *that* group started trying to win spots on the show by forcing themselves on the staff, somebody was bound to die. The thought alone was almost enough to persuade a man to live a life of celibacy.

"I'd *never* do something like that," one of the girls said. She had crooked teeth and was maybe a hamburger shy of exploding out of her jeans. "That's so degrading."

Trent managed not to laugh. And standing in line for sixteen hours to expose herself in front of hundreds of people wasn't?

"Besides," she went on matter-of-factly, "that would never work for me, anyway. I don't have what it takes."

Trent blinked. "Then what are you doing here? Hoping to make it into the outtake reel?"

Suddenly her entire face lit up. "That'd be *won*derful. Do you think I have a shot?"

Oh, my, *God*. "What about you?" he asked the girl next to her. She'd have been quite pretty if it hadn't been for her face, hair, clothes, and body. "Is that what you're shooting for?

She shrugged. "Anything's better than nothing."

Trent looked at the ceiling and made a sound that might have been a laugh. "You know what, you're right. This really is the opportunity of a lifetime. I hope both of you have a chance to be ridiculed on national television."

"Thank you!" one of them shouted as he was leaving.

Trent pushed past the group of ABC men salivating over Taylor and up the ramp that led to the mezzanine, fishing for another cigarette. One wasn't going to be enough to calm him down, though. The whole pack probably couldn't do it. What he needed was the actual plant, an entire field of them that he could devour like candy. Or maybe a few pounds of uncut heroin; that ought to dull the pain. Better yet, a dozen hits of acid. That way he'd be able to pretend this was all some kind of wild hallucination.

There was nobody on the second level when he got there, which was a tremendous relief. He took a seat in the balcony and threw his feet on the chair in front of him, smoking in silence and watching the circus play out on the arena floor below.

It didn't seem real from up here. The girls looked like dolls, or marionettes, pulled and tugged by strings they'd attached to themselves. On the far stage were the outtake girls. They had to have seen the difference between the line they were in and the other one; they had to know they didn't have a prayer of making the second round. And still they waited, eager to sacrifice themselves on the altar of temporary fame.

And there were the others, ripe and tight and willing to do anything to make it to the main stage. They were the kind of girls who waited backstage after a KISS concert, soaking in lip gloss and wondering if they should fuck the band members individually or all at once. When it came down to it, was there really any difference between the two groups?

For a while he just sat there, listening to the heavy saxophone of the music clips and the occasional comments of the judges. The smoke from his cigarette drifted up in a thin cloud. Gradually, the distance made things tolerable. After about half an hour, he got up and went downstairs.

"Where did you go?" Taylor asked when he returned. She was alone for a change, primping before a compact mirror the size of a dime.

"Nowhere," he said. "How do you see anything in those things?"

"You get used to it," she said, still looking at herself. "I think I sold them on *Julie's Surprise*."

"Congratulations," Trent said, mostly to be polite. *Julie's Surprise* was Taylor's pet project, a Reality show exactly like *The Bachelorette* except that "Julie" wasn't a woman. Hence the surprise. "They weren't worried about liabilities? You know, like one of the contestants killing her . . . him . . . committing murder when they found out?"

"Not at all." She snapped her compact closed. "Something like that would be great for ratings. You could do a whole Court TV spin-off with a murder trial. Not that they *want* that to happen."

"Of course not."

"But if it *does*."

"There you guys are," Max said, looking as if he'd just done a few laps around the United Center. "Sorry I had to leave like that. Everything all right? Did I miss anything?"

"We're fine," Trent said. "You look like you've been through it, though. What happened to your shirt? Did Sheila get violent or something?"

"No," Max said with a quick smile. "Well, yes, but . . . whatever. Listen, we're going to need to add her name to the list of finalists."

"Ooh, I like her," Taylor said. "She's spunky."

"She certainly is," Max said.

"Why?" Trent asked. "Because she broke down? Max, if we took every girl that could cry at the drop of a hat we'd—"

"It's not because of that," Max said. "I just have a feeling about her. I think she'd really add something to the show. I saw her on stage, she's got this . . . I don't know what you call it, stage presence maybe . . . anyway, I think she's the real thing."

Suddenly, and with devastating clarity, Trent understood. His eyes narrowed. "You slept with her, didn't you?"

"That is *not* true. She slept with me." He took a deep breath. "Twice."

"Twice?" Taylor said. "In thirty minutes?"

"I didn't think I had it in me, either. That's what I'm saying, this girl will bring a lot to the show. I introduced her to Mel—he's the casting director, Taylor met him—and I think he'll agree with me."

This was *so* unfair. "I can't believe you slept with one of the contestants."

"I can't believe you haven't," Taylor said. "What are you waiting for? Isn't that why you got into this business in the first place?"

"She's got a point," Max said. "Don't worry, we'll find you somebody. Fair's fair."

Just then Todd appeared. "Hey, everybody. Sorry I bailed on you like that, I had something come up. Look, we're gonna need to make room on the list for this girl, Cindy. I met her in line. She's got two kids, but you'd never know it to look at her. I mean, *man*. Anyway, I think she'd really help take the show to the next level."

Trent looked at Todd, then at Max, then back at Todd, then back at Max.

"You all right, pal?" Max asked.

"Yeah, yeah, sure. Fine. Never better." Trent turned to Taylor. "So, you want to go have sex?"

Taylor stared at him for a moment, then burst into laughter. "Oh, *Trent*," she said, covering her mouth with her hand, "sometimes you say the funniest things."

[CHAPTER FIVE]

Back at the office on Monday, Trent took some satisfaction in the knowledge that other people had had an awful weekend, too.

"Frank's called three times this morning," Lynette said as soon as he walked in. Frank was Nova's CBS contact.

"It's not even nine yet." For once he was early, though not intentionally.

"He's in New York this week. You should call him now, he sounds worried."

That went without saying. Frank was always worried; the man's whole stomach was an ulcer. "I'll wait until after the meeting."

"Don't. P.T. told me to make sure you called Frank as soon as you got in."

That was something. Any excuse to get out of the Monday meeting was more than welcome. "Thanks. Which number's his cell?"

"The first one. Oh!" Lynette jumped in her seat and reached for her purse. "I almost forgot!" She handed him a folded piece of paper.

"What's this?"

"An invitation. Albert and I are throwing a *Last Man Standing* party this Sunday. Say you'll come! Oh, it's going to be *so* much fun."

Trent stared at the unopened invitation. He'd been to one of Lynette's Reality-themed parties before, complete with "authentic" Wal-Mart Tiki torches and Jell-O appetizers shaped like exotic insects. Lynette and her husband would be sporting twelve-dollar Hawaiian shirts made in Mexico, and khaki jungle shorts so they could show off their bone-white legs.

"You have to come," Lynette insisted. "Luke and Dara always ask about you."

Ah, yes, and who could forget the kids? Trent knew that a mother's love was blind, which explained how Lynette could allow her ten-year old son and eight-year old daughter to balloon to the size of redwood tree stumps. But it must also have been deaf and dumb, because Luke and Dara had to be the most obnoxious children in Marina del Rey. They were the poster children for Planned Parenthood. *Do yourself a favor*, it would say underneath their marinara-stained faces. *Abort.*

"I'll try to make it." That sounded too uninterested. He tried to cover. "Any sightings this weekend?"

Lynette sighed. "No. The new mailman looks a little like Leonard Nimoy, but I don't think it's him."

"Probably not."

He went to his desk and sat down. Tacked on his cubicle walls were pictures from famous films—Marlon Brando as General Kurtz, Orson Welles as Citizen Kane. He'd always thought it would be fun to hang a picture of Rasputin next to the one of Charlie Chaplin, just to make people look twice. But posters of wild-eyed maniacs were difficult to find, except for James Belushi.

Enough stalling. He called Frank. "Frank. Trent Tucker."

"Trent? Oh, thank *God* it's you, you know how many times I've tried to call? What time do you guys open out there, noon? Never mind. Oh, thank God it's you. Look, I'm in a terrible fix here."

"So what's new?"

"I'm serious, Trent, they've got my asshole tied in a knot. Have you seen the latest Nielsens? We're *fourth*, Trent. Fourth! Fox is beating us, NBC, ABC. We're going to be down with C-Span in a month at the rate things are going. Walter's furious, he's threatening to fire all of us—*all* of us, Trent—if we don't come up with something big. Please, for God's sake, tell me you've *got* something."

Trent tried to imagine Frank as a Little League coach and thought it would be best for America's youth if such a thing never happened. "I'm not sure. What are you looking for?"

"*Any*thing! Do you understand what's going to happen to me if we have to run another season of *Judging Amy*? We'll be ruined! You've got to help me, tell me you've *got* something."

"I'd love to help you, Frank, but NBC's outbid you on everything. Get Walter or Dan or whoever's in charge of your spec budget to loosen the reins a bit."

"That's not going to happen unless I give them something to *look* at. What have you got?"

At the moment, nothing. Everything they had was already optioned or in production. Except for *Extreme Animal Lovers*, he reminded himself with a shudder. But P.T. wanted Fox to have first refusal. It was a fitting program for their network, he'd said, and Trent couldn't disagree.

"I'm going to need a week."

Frank's reaction was predictable. "A *week*! I don't have a week, Trent! My ass is going to be out the window by *Wednesday* if I don't give the board something sensational. Sensational, Trent, I'm talking never-been-done-before stuff, you understand? I'm desperate here, I'm begging you, please—"

"Frank, shut up." Jesus *Christ*, the man was annoying. "You know me. You know our track record. How many of our shows have bombed?"

"Four." He said it like a chastened schoolchild.

"That's right. Four. Out of thirty-eight. And *Diaries of a Male Ballerina* would have been a huge hit if ABC had gone with an ex-con like we told them to." He could not believe it was possible for those words to be put into the same sentence. "So when I tell you I'll have something by next week, you can be certain it's going to be something good. If you can't wait seven days for a successful show, then call Dyson and take your chances." The General would have gutted him if he'd heard that.

"I already did."

"Oh. So now we're your last resort?"

"Look, Trent, I didn't mean—"

"I'll call you next Monday, Frank." He hung up. If Frank was as desperate as he sounded, he could at least have the decency to be grateful. Trent leaned back in his chair. Let the man sweat; it'd do him some good. Well, that probably wasn't true, but whatever.

He lit a cigarette, thinking. Actually, this might be just the opportunity he'd been waiting for. If CBS was eager enough for a new line-up, they might be willing to take some risks. He might be able to feed them an idea with teeth in it, something less vacuous than *The Hairstylists' Challenge*. Something meaningful. This might be his chance to put something worth watching in front of a national audience.

The only question was, what should it be?

"Too good for the meeting?"

He looked at Rachel. "Good morning to you, too. I had to make a call. Very important, could change everything. P.T. signed off on it." Let her chew on *that* for a while.

She smiled the way people do when they want to beat you over the head with something heavy. "Yeah, well. Taylor said you asked her to sleep with you."

"As a joke." Which it had been. Mostly. "Did she tell you why?"

"Something about Chicago. I don't know, I never listen to her for more than ten seconds."

"I know." They stared at each other. "So, did you stop by just to criticize me for being a bad employee, or was there something on your mind?"

Rachel stood up straighter. "Go fuck yourself," she said, and stormed off.

Trent looked at the place she had just been standing. That settled it; all women were officially insane.

Oh, well. He'd have plenty of time to figure out how to fuck himself tomorrow, or the next day; it sounded like an interesting challenge, and if he could figure out how to patent it he could make millions. Right now he needed to come up with an idea.

The trick was to find something meaningful without making people think they were watching anything important. A show that spoke to the human condition, something with a theme people could rally around.

All right. Now to pick a theme. Life? Death? Religion? Love? Not love. Too many shows dealt with love, or at least claimed they did, and too many people confused love with sex. People would expect hot tub orgies and elaborate scenes with pink roses. No, it would have to be something else.

Religion was a bad idea, too. Putting six or seven people of different faiths on the same show was just *asking* for trouble. The last thing he wanted to do was start a jihad; most studies agreed that jihads were bad for ratings.

So, it was life or death. That's what everything boiled down to, anyway. All the good books and movies, even some of the bad ones like *The Scarlet Letter* and *Benji*, were basically about one or both of those things. Maybe he could combine the two. But death was such a downer. Who wanted to tune in every week to watch someone die?

Actually, now that he thought about it, a lot of people did.

"A lot of people what?"

Trent whirled around and saw Tad standing in his doorway, or where the door would have been if his cubicle were an actual office. "Was I talking out loud?"

"You were buzzing like a little bee over here, buzz buzz buzz. Listen, do you have a minute? I'm *totally* stuck here. You know the show I'm working on?"

"The sequel?" NBC had demanded a follow-up to *I Think My Brother's Gay*. Naturally. "What on Earth makes you think I can help? *I* don't know anything about being gay."

"Oh, *non*sense," Tad said with a delicate flip of his wrist. "Inside every straight man is a little tiny gay man trying to come out. It's true, it's really true. Anyway." He knelt by Trent's chair in a position that, from the hallway, might look compromising. "I want it to be *bigger*, you know, something that will grab you by the collar and say, 'Hey, buster, you need to watch me.' You know what I'm saying?"

"Yeah," Trent said, thankful Tad hadn't taken hold of his shirt to illustrate the point. "What demographic are you targeting?"

"Well, I've got the queers locked up. They're easy. But you straight people . . ." He shook his head. "You're tough nuts to crack, you know that? I just don't know *what* to do with you."

"Have you ever thought that maybe—just an idea here—that maybe straight guys don't want to watch a show that makes them wonder if their brother's having sex with everyone in his drama club? Just a thought."

"Oh, *stop* it," Tad said with a *tee-hee* kind of laugh. "That's ridiculous. We watch shows about straight people all the time."

"Fair or not, there's a difference."

"Well then what do I need to do? Have him play basketball, be a mechanic, what?"

"Not basketball. All that butt slapping, you know. Mechanic's not a bad idea." Except of course that it was. The entire show was a bad idea. Unless . . . "Why don't you change the format, call it *I Think My Sister's A Lesbian*? That might work. Guys like lesbians."

Tad's eyes lit up. "Lesbians. Of *course*."

"Lesbians sell. Look at Britney Spears and Madonna. 'Course that had the whole mother-daughter element in it, but I don't think you should go there."

Tad smacked himself on the forehead. "I can't believe I didn't think of it myself. Oh, you're *so* smart. Thank you! I can see it now. A couple posters of Tori Amos on the wall, maybe some cargo pants."

"Don't forget the lipstick lesbians. They're already screen-tested."

"Lesbians. It's so simple. Everybody loves lesbians. How come *they* get to have all the fun?"

"I don't know. It's a crime."

"Who do you think I can ask about lesbians?"

Trent shrugged. "Try Taylor. Her nails are nice, she might be one." You never knew. She *was* always hugging her friends in the photos on her walls. "You got your hair done."

Tad's hand flew to his head. "Can you tell? Does it look all right? Be brutal, Trent, does it make me look *too* gay?"

Too gay? Was that possible? Did gay men rate each other like that? *I liked Steve and all, but he was just a little too homosexual for me*. "Looks good. It's just frosty enough." Better to pacify him than make Tad rush back to the hairdresser in flamboyant hysterics. "Anything else?"

"No, you've been a doll. I'd kiss you, but I don't think the little gay man inside of you is ready to come out yet. Someday, though. Ta." He strolled out, his highlighted hair bouncing like a ball of frosted flame above the cubicle wall.

Trent watched Tad leave, feeling as though some of his own integrity had left with him. Lesbians. Was that really the extent of his own creative abilities? Was he seriously unable to come up with a show with more substance than co-eds rubbing each other down with body wash?

Oh, well. No point in lamenting. What he needed was a show that would impact people, encourage them to do something positive. Something to make viewers *help* people instead of cut them down from the safety of their living rooms. Something uplifting and engaging at the same time. It would have to be a show that addressed an aspect of life everyone could relate to, even if it had never happened to them personally.

And then, like a bolt of lightning, it hit him.

With a sharp cry he leapt out of his chair. It was perfect. It would transcend demographics. Families would sit down together to watch and then be inspired to do something, to help combat a problem they'd never thought about before. He scrambled out of his cubicle and raced for the office of the only person who might be able to appreciate it.

"Max!" He burst into Max's cubicle and hung in the doorway, panting from the run. That was it, he had to stop smoking—or quit running through the office. Probably the latter. "Max, I've got it."

"Gimme a second, pal," Max said, holding his hand over the telephone receiver. "Look, Charlie, we go back a ways. I want to help you out. But if you can't come up to a million five, I'm gonna have to shop this somewhere else. I'm trying to do you a favor here, pal. I'm *handing* you a twenty-share show. . . . All right, you get back to me. Tell Sandra hi. Talk to you tomorrow." He hung up and swiveled in his chair. "You've got what?"

"The next breakthrough in television."

"Well, don't keep me waiting here. What is it?"

Trent let it out in a rush. "Organ transplants."

Max's forehead scrunched into a ball. "I don't follow you."

"Here's what we do. We find a family—a real one, no actors, I'm talking totally real here—with a kid that needs a new heart or kidney or something. I'm thinking seven, eight years old, young enough to really grab people, you know? Anyway, we follow them around, film everything, from the first moment they find out what's wrong, right up through the operation. We'll throw in random facts throughout each show, teach people a bit about the process. It's like *ER*, except completely real, and without the doctors all having sex with each other. It's perfect, Max! It's real, it's immediate, it's something everyone can relate to, it'll have a happy ending—we'll have to make sure of that, you know—and then when it's all over you can bet some people will be inspired to *do* something, volunteer at hospitals or donate money for research or something. We won't have to script anything, Max, the show will practically film itself. And think of the sequels! AIDS patients, cancer victims. And I'm not just talking medical shows, either. We can run this anyway we want, a day in the life of a firefighter or schoolteacher or whatever, take your pick. And for once we'll be making shows that *mean* something, you know? We can raise awareness, set up charity funds, *any*thing." He was out of breath, drunk on his own vision. "What do you think?"

Max turned off his computer monitor and ran his tongue over his teeth. "Well," he said after a moment, "to be honest, pal, I'm not crazy for it. I think you're forgetting what it is we actually do here."

As with anyone whose brilliance was not greeted with the adoration it deserved, Trent became immediately hostile. "What are you talking about?"

"It's our job to make shows people wanna watch, pal, and I don't think they'll—"

"Don't give me that. They'll watch whatever we give them."

"That is not true and you know it. What about *Celebrity Boxing*, huh? *The Tom Green Show*? You know how many shows get pulled midway through their first season?"

"Of course I do."

"And you know *why* they do? 'Course you do, but I'll tell you anyway. It's because they forget to give people what they want. And right now, pal, people want entertainment. They want shows that make them feel like anybody can be famous and live in a thirty-room mansion, even if it's only for a few weeks. You wanna know what I think?"

"Not really. But you're going to tell me anyway."

"Don't get mad just because I don't think this idea of yours is gonna fly. You didn't see me get all bent outta shape when you put the kibosh on *Amish Centerfolds*. And you were probably right, the country's not ready for that kind of show. Yet. Look, I'm just trying to help."

"All right, all right, I got it." It was like getting a lecture from his father, on those rare occasions when the man had been sober enough to talk. "Get to the point."

"You wanna know why *Lifestyles of the Rich and Famous* never went number one? I'll tell you, it's because people couldn't relate. Who wants to sit around and watch a show about people with more money than you'll ever have living in houses you'll never live in? That's *depressing*, man. Robin Leach is doing Campbell's *soup* commercials now, for Christ's sake, and the reason is that people don't wanna turn on the TV and be depressed. You wanna know why the porn industry rakes in billions of dollars a year?"

"Wow," Trent said. "From Robin Leach to porn in one sentence. Most people would have needed two or three."

"Just follow me, will you? You wanna know why porn's such a huge success? Two words: Ron Jeremy. That two-hundred-and-fifty-pound gorilla did more to revolutionize the film industry than the Warner Brothers. And you know why? Because *he* made the fantasy real. If he could get laid, then every man in America could. He's a saint, the man should have his own day of honor."

Trent couldn't quite picture that. Where would they put it, between Washington and Martin Luther King? Or maybe next to Arbor Day; that would be oddly appropriate. Lawmakers would have too much fun deciding on a name for the celebration. "That's a fascinating theory. What's it have to do with anything?"

"Because that's exactly what Reality TV tries to do," Max said. He drained the last of his coffee. "We make it possible for everybody to have a chance at stardom. You're a corporate accountant with an overbite and a beer gut? Not a problem. You're an Iranian midget with a cleft palate and three teeth? We can work with that. That's the beauty of it, Trent, you don't have to be beautiful or talented or eloquent or even nice anymore. With Reality TV there are no requirements, no standards. We've made fame attainable for anyone who wants it. And this show of yours," he went on, "will undo all of that. All of a sudden you've got to be this seven-year old kid with leukemia or kidney failure or whatever. That's not—"

"You're wrong," Trent said. "We're not creating some happy socialist model for bringing fame to the people. All we do is let people feel superior to the people they're watching. Why else would we spend so much time on the outtakes?"

"It's that too," Max conceded. "And your idea won't let people do that, either. Who wants to make fun of some little girl because she has an inoperable brain tumor? That's crossing the line, pal. Even Simon Cowell would balk at that one. I think. Whatever, you get my point."

Trent wasn't about to give up. "Look, this is the first honestly good idea I've had in the two years I've been working here, and I'm not going to throw it away just because—"

Max held his hands up. "Whoa, pal, no need to get angry. You do what you want. Run it by P.T., see what he says. Just don't be surprised when he tells you it's not gonna work. You gonna tell him now?"

"I haven't fleshed out all the details yet." He didn't want to talk about his idea anymore, at least not with someone who didn't understand what it could mean. "What are you working on?"

Max flicked his computer monitor back on. "I've got this idea for a new show. You remember *Cheaters*, the one where they'd hire a private detective to follow you around and see if you were cheating on your wife or whatever? Well, I thought, why not take it a step further. That's what we're about, isn't it, pushing the envelope? So I came up with—"

Just then there was a tremendous crash from P.T.'s office, followed by a roar that sounded like it had come from the belly of a rampaging lion. Trent spun around.

"What the hell was *that*?"

Another crash followed the first, and this time Trent could tell, from the dull slap that echoed throughout the office, that it had been caused by a chair being hurled violently against a wall.

[CHAPTER SIX]

"I'm not going in there."

All seven of them, Lynette included, were gathered around Max's cubicle, staring at the door to the General's office. There were no sounds of breaking windows or picture frames being splintered, just an eerie silence that grew more ominous the longer it lasted.

"I'm not going in there," Todd said again. "White man gets angry like that, you just know he's waiting to take it out on a brother."

"Well, *some*body has to go in," Rachel said.

"Why don't you go, Taylor," Max suggested. "You have tits, that ought to pacify him."

"They *are* superb," Todd added.

"If you're into that sort of thing," Tad said.

"Rachel has tits, too," Trent offered.

"Go fuck yourself."

"Fair enough. I deserved that one."

"What could have upset him like that?" Tad asked. "Trouble at home? Does anyone know if he's even married?"

"Did somebody put Equal in the coffee?" Taylor asked.

"Ooh, that'd do it," Tad said. "I just get furious when somebody messes with my—"

"We don't care, Tad," Todd said. "So, who's going in?"

"Not me."

"Me either."

"Well, one of you white people has to," Todd said. "No telling what he might do next."

"Do you think he's okay?" Lynette asked.

"All right," Max said, "enough talking. We'll draw for it." He tore seven strips of paper. "Short one goes."

"Oh!" Taylor squealed. "I have a better idea! Let's just make Trent go."

"Fine with me."

"Yeah."

"Good thinking, Taylor."

Somehow, Trent knew that was coming. "Every one of you owes me a drink later." If he lived long enough to collect. "Max, give me a cigarette. I'm not going in there unarmed."

The door to P.T.'s office swung in silently. The first thing Trent saw was the hole in the wall, about the size of somebody's head, punched in and grinning like Edward Norton in *Fight Club*. He was right; it had been a chair. In fact, it was the one he had sat in last week when the General had called him in. Hopefully that was just a happy coincidence; otherwise Trent may as well hurl himself through the window before P.T. had a chance to.

"Morning, sir," he said. The word sounded odd; he didn't usually call his boss sir. But since graduate school hadn't prepared him to deal with violently unhinged employers, he thought it was best to err on the side of formality.

"Come in," P.T. ordered. "Shut the door."

Vaguely certain he was walking into a trap, Trent did so. "Is everything all right?"

For a moment, P.T. said nothing. He didn't *look* upset. He was standing by his desk with both hands on its burnished steel surface. It was true that everything on the desk had been swept to the floor—except for the humidor; apparently P.T. had maintained enough presence of mind not to smash that—but he looked more like a man stretching before a jog than anything else.

"Oh," he said. "You guys heard me?"

"I think the Dodgers heard you, sir."

"Well," P.T. said, straightening, "I'm going to have to call that soundproofing guy. He obviously did a chop job." His fingers curled into fists. "I'm going to *kill* that motherfucker."

Trent felt sorry for the soundproofer. "I could come back if you'd rather be alone."

"*Nobody* fucks with P.T. Beauregard and gets away with it. By the time I'm through with him he'll wish he was never born."

"I'll just come back later."

"No." With a visible effort P.T. mastered himself. "Trent. Sit down."

"I think I'll stand, if that's all right with you. It's easier to dodge things that way."

"Sit down, Trent. I'm not going to hurt you." P.T. sighed. "It's Armsburger. He's forced ABC to cancel *Take It Off!* before the pilot aired. He threatened sanctions if they went ahead with it. I just got a call from Jerry, they're pulling the plug as of this morning."

"Oh." Trent wished he'd said something more profound. But the only thing he could think was the girl—what was her name, Shelly? Shirley?—whatever, the girl Max slept with. Boy, was she going to be *pissed*.

"He cut our legs out from under us, *that's* what he did." The fire was returning to P.T.'s militant eyes. "He thinks he can tell everybody what they can and can't watch. He wants to take us back to the fifties? Well, let me tell you something, the past is over, and it's *never* coming back."

"Is there anyth—"

"Do you *hear* me?" P.T. shouted. He was looking at the poster of Armsburger now, which had miraculously remained unharmed. "*I'm* the one who knows what America wants, *I'm* the one who's willing to give it to them! You're *nothing*! Do you hear me! *Nothing*!!"

Trent wondered how hard it was to get a bottle of Xanax without a prescription.

"You want a war, you've got one. You want to go fifteen rounds with me, just name the *time* and the *place*. I'm the one America needs, not you. Not you, not your family, not the FCC, not the government, none of you. *I'm* what this country wants, and I'm going to win."

"I don't understand, sir," Trent said. "We got paid for the idea. ABC can't take their money back."

"It's not the money." He grabbed a cigar but did not light it. "It's the principle. ABC didn't make any secret about the show. He waited until they'd already started auditions, already put millions into pre-production. Think of all those girls whose hopes he crushed. But this wasn't about them, or about ABC or any of the other networks. It's about us, about you and me and everyone else trying to provide this country with some decent entertainment. He waited until we'd all invested our time and money because he wanted to show us that he's in charge."

P.T. came out from around his desk, making no effort to avoid the debris scattered on the floor. "Back in Boston, in my old line of work, if you had a problem with somebody, you took it right to them. If you did me wrong, I'd come to you. Not your family, not your friends—you. Armsburger has a problem with me, he should come see me, not this cowardly stab-you-in-the-back bullshit. Make no mistake, Trent, this was directed at *us*, nobody else. I know what he's doing."

Once again Trent wondered what P.T. had done for a living back in Boston, and once again he was glad he didn't know. "So what are we going to do?"

With the unlit cigar in his mouth, P.T. smoothed his hair. "First things first. Jerry needs a new show by Monday. We have to show the FCC that for every idea of ours they knock down, we've got ten more waiting. I want all of you on it, top priority. I do *not* want Dyson getting this one. As far as Armsburger goes? Don't you worry about that. I'll take care of him."

][

Trent was out of the office before noon. It was best, he decided, if he wanted to keep himself from going crazy. Some days simply weren't cubicle days, especially ones where your boss breaks his own furniture and all but says he's going to strap some guy's legs to a pair of cinder blocks and dump him somewhere off the Malibu coast. And it wasn't like he was skipping work, at least not according to P.T., because Trent had managed to give himself the assignment of market research.

He hopped in his Jaguar and headed for the nearest mall. Ah, the sweet freedom of market research. All you had to do was sit around eating gyros all day long, staring at teenagers and recording what stores they went into and what they bought. It was like being a wildlife naturalist, except that he wasn't allowed to tag their ears.

When he arrived at the mall, Trent double-parked and went in through the food court. At noon on a Monday in July, the place was crawling with its usual clientele: groups of the elderly who came for their morning walks and stayed because they had nothing better to do, stay-at-home moms constantly on the prowl for another skirt or throw rug or vase they didn't need, and gaggles of fourteen-year-olds with multi-colored hair and more disposable money than any other demographic in America. They were the real targets, these kids, the ones to whom every entertainment industry geared its products, the ones trend analysts wished they could implant with tracking devices. These kids, with their braces and lip rings and minimum-wage jobs, were the true leaders of America's cultural evolution.

He approached one of them, a pale girl with blue-black hair and a quarter-inch of mascara surrounding each eye. She was working the gyro counter. "Two pepperoni gyros and an orange-mango juice, please." At least part of his meal should be healthy.

She went to work on his order with the lack of enthusiasm that was the trademark of high school employees. "Eight fifty."

"Just out of curiosity," he said as he was paying her, "what's your favorite TV show?"

"None of them. I don't watch TV."

"Really?" Good, affected interest. "Why not?"

"Cuz it all sucks. There's nothing on but all those fake reality shows that are totally not real."

By 'real' he assumed she meant 'depressed and morose'. A lot of girls her age did. "Have you ever seen *Last Man Standing*?"

"I can't stand that stuff. How come they don't have any women on that show? Do they think women can't survive as well as men?"

"I'm sure they'll do a sequel with only women." Which was true; NBC had already contracted for one. "I hear they're also thinking about a reality show with gothic people."

The girl's eyes lit up a little. "That'd be cool. It'd be *real*."

Of course it would. Because wearing black clothes and torn fishnets meant you were deep. "Thanks. Keep the change."

Trent found a table and sat down. Too bad for Morticia that the gothic demographic wasn't large enough to merit a show. It would have been fun, too, filmed on location at coffeeshops and public parks and the occasional Denny's. They could run a soundtrack with bands named *Dysfunction* or *Ennui*.

He ate his gyro, which was somehow too greasy, and watched a group of four teenage girls go into a five-dollar jewelry store. One of them, falsely tanned and with a stomach that decent people would have kept covered, was wearing a pink T-shirt that said "Your Boyfriend Likes Me" in bright, glittery letters. Trent suspected false advertising. With a shirt and jeans at least two sizes too small for her, the poor girl looked like a busted can of biscuits. She was a *Swan* girl, or a *Bachelorette*, something where an ordinary girl like herself could wake up beautiful and desired by millions. Nothing new to learn there.

Then there were the guys in the music store, aspiring thugs with blue bandanas and pants twenty-seven sizes too large—a somewhat paradoxical fashion concept, since it made running from the scene of a crime almost impossible. They were *Gangland Romance* material for certain. Probably they'd like a spin-off starring white gangsters, *Honkeez for Life* or *Cracker Posse*. They might also watch a Reality competition for freestyle rappers. Trent pulled out a pad of paper and made a note. P.T. would like that idea.

He finished eating and headed to the bookstore, which admittedly was hardly the place to spot trendsetters. After all, books with multi-syllabic words and no pictures were so not in anymore, except for magazines. He went straight to the magazine rack and took note. Not like he needed to; it wasn't as though anything had changed in the last ten years. Women's magazines were still plastered with seventy-five pages of makeup ads and 532 tips to dress like a model. The cover for this month's *Seventeen* magazine promised over seven hundred ways to look naturally beautiful, an irony too obvious for even high schoolers to miss. Men's magazines were really no different, each of them bursting with airbrushed photos of girls who would never sleep with you but who were paid to look like they would. Every magazine in America was the same, with the same headline every issue: *YOU ARE BROKEN, AND WE CAN FIX YOU.*

As he picked up *Cosmopolitan* to learn how he could make his hair more luxuriant, Trent realized he was being watched. A blonde girl in dark capris was staring right at him and making no attempt to hide it. From the looks of her, she was definitely a *Joe Millionaire* girl, stopping her life once a week so she and her sorority sisters could tell each other how much better the show would have been if they'd been chosen instead of the flighty bimbos Fox had selected.

"Excuse me," she said. She had a high, soft voice. "Aren't you that guy from *Survivor*?"

Trent's answer was only a split second in coming. "Yeah, I am." If he couldn't get them with the truth, he'd have to settle for lying.

"Oh, I *knew* it!" She looked as if she was about to melt. "I knew it was you, I could just tell. You were in the Marquesas, right?"

"That's right." It wasn't exactly a lie. He hadn't been to the Marquesas, but he *had* been to the Canaries. They were both islands.

"Wow. My name's Jill. Oh, I'm so embarrassed, I watched every episode and I can't remember your name."

"Trent," he said. There hadn't been a Trent on the show.

"*Now* I remember! Oh, wow, that must have been incredible! I'm sorry you didn't win."

"It's all right."

"I voted for you, though. You didn't seem to be in it just for yourself, you know?"

Trent smiled and pretended to look modest. "That's nice of you. I appreciate it. I'm not upset, though. It was great just being there. The Marquesas are incredible, if you have a chance you should go sometime."

"Oh, I'd *love* to."

Trent managed to put his *Cosmo* back on the shelf without her noticing. "I'm not doing anything right now. If you want I'd be happy to tell you about it."

"Oh, my God, are you serious?"

"Sure. Do you like coffee? I know a great place near here."

][

When Trent arrived at Garibaldi's a few hours later, Adam was waiting for him. "Dude, where've you been?"

Trent slid into the booth across from Adam, who was already on his third sake bomb. "Sorry. I lost track of time." That tended to happen during sex. Well, during *good* sex.

"I tried calling," Adam said. "Is your phone broken?"

"Had it turned off." It would have been rude to keep it on. "I've got a question for you. You've seen *Survivor: Marquesas*, right? Is there anybody on that show who even remotely looks like me?"

"Shit, I don't know. Gabriel, maybe, *maybe*, except for the hair. Why? Somebody think they recognized you?"

"More or less. Is Angela coming?"

"She's at an audition. A real one, not some *Law and Order* walk-on. What do you think of her?"

"I've only met her once," Trent said, which was a more polite response than calling her an overdramatic theater wonk. She probably didn't think much of him, either. "She seems nice. Are you two . . . ?"

"I don't know. Maybe. We'll just see where it goes."

"You sound like a woman."

"I should be so lucky. They're the ones in control of every relationship." Adam finished his drink and waved for Candy. "How was the casting call?"

"Not everything I'd dreamed of."

"How's that possible?"

He told Adam about the outtake stage. "I swear, man, some of them looked like they were dying. I've never seen people humiliate themselves that badly before. And for nothing—we found out this morning that ABC's pulling the show."

"What for? Was it testing bad?"

"No. It would have buried everything. The FCC threw its weight around, and ABC caved."

"I'll bet P.T. wasn't happy about that."

"You could say that. Thanks, Candy." He watched her set them up with a new round of drinks. "Any luck with the script?"

Adam shook his head. "Couple people who'll get back to me, you know how that goes. I might start shopping it to independents, but there's no money in that. Not enough to pay the rent, at least."

"It's a great script, Adam. Don't give up on it."

He shrugged. "Yeah, well. I've started another one."

"Really? What about?"

"It's kind of tough to explain. I'll let you read it when I'm finished. It's coming real fast, I should be done by the end of the month." Then Adam sighed, the big depressive sigh of a guy watching the girl of his dreams dancing with somebody else. The kind of sigh the girl at the gyro counter might have sighed. "I've got a favor to ask."

"Sure, man. What is it?"

Adam stared at the glass he had just drained. "I need to . . . I was . . ." He closed his eyes. "There's really no good way to ask, so . . . I was wondering if I might be able to borrow some money. I'm not going to make the rent this month if I—"

"You don't have to explain anything, man. How much do you need?"

"About a thousand."

"Sure, man. Sure."

"I'm not asking for a handout here. I'll pay you back."

"I know you will."

"I mean it, Trent."

"I know." Trent took a drink, primarily so he would have something else to do besides stare at his miserable friend. "I'll be right back, okay? I've got my checkbook in the car."

When Trent came back, Adam still looked as though he'd confessed to a major crime. Trent wrote the check. Was there a non-awkward way to give someone money? Of course, looking uncomfortable was part of the game; benefactors didn't want their recipients to be too excited. Still, this wasn't how it was supposed to be between friends.

"Here," Trent said as he ripped the check out of his book. "There's fifteen hundred. Don't worry about the other five hundred, it's a birthday present. I'm sure I missed a few in there."

"Thanks," Adam said. Things *must* have been bad; he didn't even pretend to put up a fight about the extra five hundred. "You know, the whole 'starving artist' thing isn't as glamorous as people think. I'll bet Van Gogh'd be happy to trade his current fame for enough money to buy bread while he was alive." Adam had another drink. "I can tell you one thing. Whatever smug bastard came up with *carpe diem* never had to worry about rent."

"So," Trent said, anxious to talk about anything other than money, "my secretary's hosting a *Last Man Standing* party on Sunday. You want to come?"

"God, no."

"Come on. You can't let me go alone." He'd have invited Jill, except he didn't have her number. It was best that way. Sooner or later she'd figure out that he wasn't that guy from *Survivor*, and then she'd feel cheated. This way she'd have something to brag about to her friends. Really, he was looking out for her best interests.

"Look, man, I know I owe you, but one of those was enough. Why are you going?"

"I promised I would." Adam was right; he'd probably hate it. But there was no denying that Lynette was a phenomenal cook. And that went a long way with a guy whose refrigerator was filled primarily with liquids.

"Well," Adam said, removing his glasses to clean the lenses, "if it's all the same, I'll pass. I'm anxious to get this next script finished so I can start shopping it. I think it's got a decent chance."

"You think it's better than *The Long Road*?"

"It's hard to compare them. They're very different. You'll have to wait until I'm finished."

Candy came up behind Trent and slid into the booth beside him. "You two doing all right over here?"

"Couldn't be better," Trent said. "Especially with you sitting next to me. How's tricks?"

"Wrong girl," she said. "If it's tricks you want, talk to Suzanne."

"That's awful," Adam said.

"Sometimes the truth hurts." She nudged Trent. "So when are you gonna make me famous?"

"Soon. I'm putting together a show for you right now."

"Yeah, yeah." She stood up. "You need anything else?"

"Just the check."

"You leaving already?" Adam asked.

"I've got some errands to run," Trent said. Specifically, he had to swing by Target or K-Mart and pick up some khaki cargo shorts and a Hawaiian shirt for the weekend. Who knew, maybe he'd splurge and get himself a straw hat and a leather fanny pack. Jesus. It was like he could *hear* Jimmy Buffett's stock rising.

[CHAPTER SEVEN]

Trent pulled up to Lynette's house in the stupidest outfit he had ever worn in his life. It wasn't the blue and white Hawaiian shirt or the round-rimmed safari helmet or the dark brown sport shorts suitable for hiking and/or kayaking. It was the combination of all three at the same time, especially on a man who had not been camping since he was twelve. He looked like one of those New Yorkers who went to Nashville and bought cowboy hats and chaps. Everyone else better damn well have dressed up too, or he was gone.

Lynette's house was cute and yellow, which made perfect sense. There were little flower gardens along the edges and around the cement birdbath in the side yard. Inside were Norman Rockwell dishes hanging in the dining room and lots of lacy doilies. It was obvious that Lynette's husband, Albert, had not been consulted about the décor. From what Trent had gathered, Albert was a quiet man who spent most of his time in the basement watching golf and, probably, certain movies Lynette didn't know they owned.

He went around back. The gate to their privacy fence was open, and inside about twenty people were standing around the swimming pool and drinking pina coladas out of hollowed coconuts. A host of citronella candles dangled from bamboo poles, sending puffs of watery black smoke into the air.

Lynette had really outdone herself this time. She was wearing a painfully bright pink sarong and a floppy hat the size of a tractor tire. Luke and Dara, bigger than ever and wearing swimsuits that exposed the top inch of *both* of their asses, took turns doing cannonballs into the pool in an attempt to sink the inflatable palm trees that were floating in it. Everyone else from work seemed to be there, except P.T. and Rachel, who never did anything outside of work anyway.

"Hey, pal!" Max looked just as out of place in his equatorial gear as Trent. "Late as usual. Nice hat."

"Thanks. Maybe before I leave I'll beat you to death with it. Hey, Taylor."

"Hi." She was wearing a grass skirt and a seashell bra that had somehow pushed her breasts up against each other. Her eyes were blue today, probably to match her nails. She took a sip from her coconut. "Have you tried these? They're fantastic."

"Jesus Christ," Max said, staring at her chest, "are those things weightless? Seriously, Taylor, you could put someone's eye out. How is that possible?"

She shrugged. "One of the perks. Everyone should do it."

"Where's Trixie?" Trent asked. Trixie was Lynette's Pomeranian, who at the last party had spent five solid hours barking at a plastic bag.

"Locked up somewhere, thank God," Max said. "I've never understood the point of little dogs. Any dog you can fit into a purse is not a real dog."

"Oh, that's not true," Taylor said. "Trixie is *so* cute."

Max shook his head. "Dog like that, I'd just shoot it and put it out of my misery. Please, Taylor, save me the indignant gasp. You can't even keep plants alive."

"*Trent*!" Lynette waved and bustled over. "You made it. I was starting to worry. Here." She handed him a coconut. "Try it, I made them myself. You wouldn't be*lieve* how much coconut I've got now. It looks like we'll be eating German chocolate cake for the next three years!"

"That's a lot," Trent said. Luke and Dara would be awfully pleased about that.

They must have heard him thinking about them.

"Uncle Trent, Uncle Trent!" Both kids popped out of the pool and ran toward him, their fat faces red and greedy. "Whadja bring us, huh? Whadja bring us?"

Trent looked at them. The first time he'd been to Lynette's house he'd bought presents for the little porkers. It had been a mistake. Now Luke and Dara expected them, and the one time he hadn't brought anything they'd raised such an atrocious noise it had been an effort not to kill them.

Lynette was beaming. "Aren't they precious? Now now, children, don't get Uncle Trent wet."

Too late. "Here you go." He brushed standing drops of water from his shorts and pulled their gifts from his back pocket.

Luke turned his over. "What's this?"

"It's a book."

"I know it's a *book*. What's it *for*?"

For giving yourself paper cuts, dumb ass. For eating. For beating your sister over the head whenever she steals the remote. "You read it. This is what people did before they had television."

Luke stuck a finger in his nose. "What's a hobbit?"

"You'll have to find out. I think you'll really like it, that was my favorite book when I was your age."

"Did they make it into a movie?" Dara asked. He'd given her the same thing.

"Yeah, but the book's way better."

"How can a book be better than a movie?" Luke said. "That's impossible."

"All right, kids," Lynette said, "tell Uncle Trent thank you."

"Thank you, Uncle Trent," they said in sullen unison.

"You're welcome," you ungrateful, ignorant blobs. "Are you guys ready for school to start?"

"No *way*!" Luke said. "School sucks."

"Yeah," Dara echoed.

Ah, the future.

"That was sweet of you," Lynette said when her kids had scampered off. "It's so hard to know what to buy for tweenagers."

Trent shuddered. Tweenagers. He *hated* that word. It was nothing but an excuse for parents to blame their children's behavior on some fictitious developmental stage rather than on their own parenting. "Yeah, well."

"I'm sure they'll both love it," Lynette continued. "Oh! You know what you need to try. I made some mini quiches, they're so good. I'll go get some."

"Is it just me," Trent said when Lynette had gone, "or are Luke and Dara the most—"

"Don't say it," Max said. "She'll hear you. Mothers can hear people talking about their kids from a mile away."

"Besides," Taylor said, "they're cute."

"Sure they are," Trent said. "A quarter ton of fun."

"You're just pissed because they didn't like your present, pal."

Max had a remarkably annoying way of understanding him. "It wouldn't kill them to read a book once in their lives."

"Whatever. I don't have anything against reading, but seriously, what's the point anymore? You can get your news by watching TV just as easily as reading the newspaper, and if a book's any good they just turn it into a movie anyway. Face it, pal, reading's a dying art. Bookstore revenues have been falling for the past decade, you know that. It's just not necessary like it used to be."

Trent scratched his forehead where the helmet was beginning to make him sweat. "It is necessary."

"How? Why? Besides, who has *time* for reading? We work eighty hours a week, pal. What was the last book you read?"

"Don't argue, guys," Taylor said. "Have some of your coconut, it's really good."

Trent managed a partial smile. Taylor probably wouldn't have made a very effective conflict resolution therapist. *Now, Sally, I know your husband cheated on you with your sister, but if you just have some tea I'm sure this will all work itself out.* But it didn't matter. Todd was walking over and, as usual, he looked extremely oppressed.

"Does anyone else realize that I'm the *only* black person here?"

"It's probably a conspiracy," Max said. "Seriously, who wants to have black people at a party?"

"What'd you say?"

"I said they're probably all in the kitchen washing dishes."

"Why you snide mother—"

"Guys!" Trent said. "This really isn't the place. Max, stop being such an ass. Todd, try to relax. Nobody's here to oppress you."

"I think black guys are sexy," Taylor said. "I wish there were more of them here."

"Oh my *God*." Tad came up in a flutter. "Have you guys tried the cheese dip? It is *ab*solutely incredible, you *have* to try some, it's better than sex. Well, all right, it's not better than *good* sex, but we can't always have good sex now, can we? I've had some ogres in my day, let me tell you."

"Please," Max said with a wrinkled nose, "don't."

Tad raised his eyebrows and sniffed. "Well, *some*one's in a crappy mood. What's the matter, Mr. Pouty Pants?"

Trent blinked. Mr. *Pouty Pants*? "Hey Tad, do you ever stop to think that maybe you're just reinforcing the stereotype?"

"What are you talking about?"

"Nothing, Tad. Never mind."

Lynette came back with a tray piled with quiches in all manner of interesting shapes, cockroaches and scorpions and even a couple tarantulas with legs made of pretzels. She must have spent a week preparing for this party.

"Wow," Trent said, "these are great. Do you think Albert would mind if I borrowed you for a week? I'll pay you."

She laughed. "I'll have to ask him."

Max spoke around his food. "Where is old Al, anyway?"

"Oh, he's inside, getting everything ready for the big show." Lynette's hat seemed to quiver with excitement. "So, which one's your favorite?"

"Favorite what?" Todd asked.

"*Last Man Standing*. Who do you want to win?"

And they'd been having such a nice time not talking about work. "I don't care," Trent said, "as long as it's not Gary."

"Really?" Lynette said. "Why not? Max and Dara just *love* him."

Somehow, Trent wasn't surprised. "I've had to deal with him a couple times. He's not the shiniest penny in the barrel."

"That's diplomatic," Max said. "You seen Jessica Simpson?"

"Of course I have," Lynette said. "On TV, not in real life. I haven't been *that* lucky yet."

"Yeah, well, Gary's dumber."

"Is that even possible?" Tad asked. He'd never been to the *Last Man Standing* set. P.T. had decided, wisely in Trent's opinion, that some of the contestants might not approve of Tad's alternative lifestyle.

"You'd have to meet him," Max said. "I'm going for Gilbert."

"Gilbert," Taylor said with a giggle that made her chest quiver. "That's such a funny name."

"I wouldn't say anything about it to him," Trent advised. "He's a bit sensitive."

"And heavily armed," Max added. "Even without weapons. I'm pretty sure he kills animals with his bare hands."

"Just the kind of role model America needs," Trent said.

Max shrugged. "Better than Gary."

"I'm rooting for Leroy," Todd said.

"We all kind of guessed that," Max said. Leroy was the only remaining black contestant on the show. Originally there had been three, a percentage even Todd had found satisfactory. Of course, he'd gone on a rampage when Campbell had been the first one voted off. If Leroy didn't win, there was a decent chance Todd would show up to work the next day with a machete.

"*I* want Barry to win," Taylor said. "He's *so* sexy. Mmmmm." She actually made that noise. Mmmmm. Like she was digesting a meal.

"You wanna cover for me next time I have to go?" Max asked. "I'm sure the two of you could work something out. Guy like that, alone on an island with a bunch of other guys? You'd be a welcome sight."

"Oh, we've already slept together," Taylor said.

Trent choked on his drink. "*What*? How? When?"

"Last time I went. And let me tell you, there's *nothing* small on that man."

"Good for you," Max said.

"I can't believe this," Trent said.

"You slept with *Barry*?" Lynette asked. Her eyes were glowing. "You *have* to tell me all about it sometime—when the kids aren't around."

"Sure."

"Come on, Lynette," Max said. "I'm sure Max and Dara'd love to hear about it. They gotta learn sometime, right? And who better to teach them than an easy girl like Taylor?"

"I'm not easy," she said indignantly. "I'm liberated. Honestly, you men all think you're so high and mighty. You should be grateful. Without girls like me, you'd all have to sleep with each other."

"See?" Max said to Lynette. "Whaddya say, should we call the little ones over?"

"Oh," Lynette blushed, "they're still too young."

Trent was pretty sure Max and Dara knew the game; anybody who watched shows like *Confessions of a Bigamist* were bound to pick up a few things. But right now, he was devoting far more attention to Taylor. Was she really that beautiful *and* generous? How had he failed to capitalize for so long?

He was pulled from his fantasies by Lynette's husband Albert, whose pasty white legs glistened like the white, flaccid bodies of cave fish. "It's about to start, everybody!" he shouted from the porch. "Come on in and get a good seat!"

Max and Dara squealed and rushed inside, flinging water on everybody they passed. The rest of the gathering started piling inside like cattle going to the slaughter—or, perhaps more appropriately, acolytes convening at the altar of their harsh, demanding god.

"You coming, pal?" Max asked.

"I'll be there in a minute," Trent said. "I need a cigarette."

He managed to find one poolside chair that Max and Dara hadn't drenched, sat down, and pulled out his pack. Yet another reason to smoke—it gave him a legitimate way to excuse himself from situations he didn't like or people he couldn't stand. *No, really, I'd love to hear more about your appendectomy, it's just that I . . .* In most cases, the slow process of acquiring lung cancer was infinitely preferable to the alternative, and this was no exception. God had invented tobacco for the same reason He'd come up with alcohol and Angelina Jolie: to make the world an easier place to endure.

It wasn't until his second cigarette that he noticed one copy of *The Hobbit* floating in the pool, its pages swollen and distorted with water. It had to have been Max; Dara wouldn't throw hers away until later. Trent fished the book out and set it on the concrete. Had Max even opened it? Maybe next time he'd bring them each a .357 and let evolution take its course.

"Not interested in the show?"

Trent looked up. An older man, probably mid-forties, was standing at his side. He was dressed as if he'd just come from work, and in any case didn't look capable of pulling off a tropical outfit.

"I didn't know anyone else was out here," Trent said. He stood up. "You smoke?"

"No thanks. You're Trent, right?"

Trent suddenly remembered he was wearing a safari helmet and took it off. "Yeah. I don't think we've met."

"I'm an old friend of Albert's." Which didn't explain how he knew Trent's name, since Trent had only met Albert a couple of times. "You work at Nova, right?"

Trent's eyes narrowed. "Yeah. How'd you know?"

"I'm in the industry. You like working there?"

"Sometimes. I'm a little tired of Reality TV, if you want to know the truth. What's your name?"

"I am, too. Tired of Reality TV, I mean. It seems like we're doing the same thing over and over again. It's not creative anymore."

"I won't argue that. What's your name?"

The man reached into his pocket and pulled out a card. "My employer's been looking to take things in a different direction for some time now. He feels we're taking the country down the wrong road. I think he'd be interested in talking with you." He handed Trent the card.

With the vague feeling that he was accepting something illegal, Trent looked at it.

SIMON PETERSEN
VICE PRESIDENT, ACQUISITIONS
DYSON ASSOCIATES
(931) 227-1019

Trent looked up. "How did—?"

There was no point in asking the question. Mr. Petersen was already walking away, heading not toward the house but rather the open fence gate. Ten seconds later he was gone.

][

"Morning, Lynette. Any messages?"

Trent didn't really want to know. He half expected to have a message from Petersen, or from Dyson himself, a possibility that had kept him up most of the night. What could Dyson want with him? The two of them had never met and never spoken; all Trent knew about the man had been learned secondhand at industry events or from the General's frequent diatribes. Why had Petersen approached him instead of Todd or Taylor or anyone else? Trent wasn't sure he wanted to know. But on the other hand, he hadn't thrown the card away, either.

"Frank called," Lynette said. "Twice. He wants you to call him right away."

"Anyone else?"

"That's it."

"All right. Thanks." He started to walk away, then stopped. "Does your husband know anyone in the television industry?"

"*Al*bert?" As though he might have meant her other husband. "Good lord, no! Not that I know of. Why?"

"No reason," Trent said absently. How had Petersen known where to find him? And what the hell did he want? "Just curious."

"Did you have a good time last night?"

That wasn't a real question. Lynette only wanted to hear that everyone had had a wonderful time, and he didn't feel like saying otherwise. "Great. Yeah. It was a lot of fun."

"Oh, *good*. I'm so glad you came. And Max and Dara just *love* your present."

Trent raised his eyebrows. "Is that right?"

"Oh, yes. I went to tuck them in last night, and they were *both* reading. I could hardly get them to go to sleep."

"Is that right?" Trent said again. "That's great. It'll be fun to talk to them about it next time I'm over."

There was a subtle shift in Lynette's smile. "I'm sure they'll look forward to it."

Trent nodded and walked away, smiling. He knew *some*one who'd be stopping by the video store on her way home from work.

He joined everyone in the conference room and made it through the Monday meeting without saying anything. The General seemed to be in a tolerable mood today. At least he didn't launch any furniture through the wall.

"Well," P.T. said in his wrapping-up tone, "that's just about all. One last thing. NBC's finally ready to start filming *Last Woman Standing*. The lawyers should have all the papers by next week, but in any case I need a few of you to volunteer for location search this weekend. Any takers?"

Nobody raised a hand. Rachel looked at her pencil; Tad tried to sink into his chair. This act of defiance was only effective for about two seconds.

"All right," P.T. said. "Tad, Todd, Taylor, I want you on this. I'll arrange a flight Friday night. That will be all."

Trent slipped away before anyone could yell at him for not being chosen. Location searches were absolutely the least exciting part of the job. The idea sounded great on paper, until you did it a few times. But after a while, every uninhabited island started to look the same, and walking up and down empty beaches quickly got extremely boring. Not to mention the stinging insects, aggressive scorpions, and other lovely amenities standard for each of these unlivable hellholes. And what was the point? They could have filmed everything on a studio set and nobody would have known the difference.

He did not, however, go to his office. The only thing waiting for him there was on the other end of his phone—Frank, frantic and blustery and probably convinced that nothing would be good enough. It was a proven fact with television people that the more desperate they got, the more they expected from others. Well, he had a show for Frank that would make CBS a competitive network again. But he couldn't make the offer until it was approved by P.T.

"Sir," he said when his boss came out of the conference room, "do you have a minute?"

"Is it a pitch?"

Trent nodded. "For Frank at CBS."

"Why didn't you run it by all of us at the meeting?" He raised a hand to prevent any attempted answer. "Doesn't matter. Come on in."

Trent followed. He caught Max looking at him, shaking his head vigorously. "Don't do it," Max mouthed, but Trent ignored him. It would be nice to show Max that you could have a successful television show without bloodshed or incest.

The door to P.T.'s office closed. Everything looked the way it had a week before; the hole in the wall had been repaired, the broken chair replaced. Still, there was something different about the room, some subtle yet major change. Something . . .

It took Trent a moment to figure out what. The picture of Armsburger had been altered. A target had been painted around his head, bright red with three circles of decreasing size zeroing in on the FCC chairman's hawklike nose. Trent tried not to stare at it.

"Well," P.T. said, "what's the pitch?"

Trent sat down in one of the room's undersized chairs, then decided he'd do a better job standing. Then, he began.

". . . possibilities are endless here. We can run cancer patients, meningitis scares, hemophiliacs, whatever you like. We can get the camera crews from *ER* to choreograph the hospital scenes. The networks can set up charity fundraisers, it'll make them look like philanthropists. It's real, it's different, and it'll give people something to *think* about. What do you think?"

"Is that it?"

"That's it." He realized he was leaning against his boss's desk and stepped back. "What do you think?"

P.T. took off his rimless glasses and held them in his right hand. "Frankly," he said, "I think it's the worst idea you've had since you've been here."

"Thank you, sir," Trent heard himself say, which made absolutely no sense. All the blood began to pool in his feet; he began to feel like one of those inflatable clowns whose only purpose was to be beaten.

Which is pretty much what happened. "I'm serious, Trent. In my seven years in this business that's the worst idea I think I've heard. *Cancer* patients? You ever heard of a show starring a terminally ill person?"

"There've been a few. *Mask*, *My Life*, *Life Goes On*."

"Don't give me that *Life Goes On* bullshit. You know Down's Syndrome is different. They look funny, and that sells. Now I know I said I want something new, but this . . . Jesus Christ, this would bury us."

"With all due respect, I disagree. I think it would get people thinking about—"

"Exactly!" P.T. struck his desk with an open palm. "That's exactly what it would do, it would get people thinking. And that is not what we're here for. *Thinking*? You think people want to come home after a long day at work and *think* about anything? That's not what television is designed to do. Our job is to *keep* them from thinking. You know that, I shouldn't have to tell you. Bottom line, nobody wants to think about the kind of world you want to show them. That's why people move to the suburbs and put up privacy fences and buy cars with tinted windows, to keep the real world *out*. That's why more people are watching our shows than the evening news, because we know how to give them what they *want*."

Trent wasn't ready to give up yet. "There's more to—"

"Look." P.T. made a rapid motion with his hands. "It's no big deal. You had an idea, and it sucked. Happens all the time, don't get bent out of shape about it. I know you're under pressure from Frank to give him something immediately, but we've got standards to maintain. I'm trying to run a successful business, not some two-bit flea market hawking shit and calling it china."

Oh, right. How could I have forgotten. Because *Donkey Fuckers Unlimited* would be *such* a quality show. "I don't—"

"Look," P.T. said again. He stood up and pinched the bridge of his nose. "You've been working hard, you're tired, you don't know what you're saying. The Trent *I* hired knows when to abandon a sinking ship and move on to something else. You know what you need? You need a vacation."

Trent blinked. A vacation? Why was it that every time he sat down in his boss's office he expected to be fired or hit with something?

"That's what you need," P.T. continued. "Get out of town, relax for a few days, get your head straight. Because Jesus, *cancer* patients? That's horrible. It's fucking awful, that's what it is. You should know that. Anyway, I want you to join the others on location search this weekend. I think it'll do you some good."

He stared at his boss, trying to fathom the twisted synapses that operated his dysfunctional brain. The word *vacation* implied comfort and ease, not being crammed into a helicopter to survey some godforsaken piece of barren land. What, did P.T. unwind with leisure hikes through Death Valley? What the hell kind of fucked up—

"I'd say that settles it," P.T. said. "Call Frank and tell him you'll get back to him next week. Let him bitch all he wants, but he'll wait for you. Then call Eddie and tell him to make arrangements for four. I'm sure by next Monday you'll have your head together. Oh, and one other thing." P.T. opened his humidor and pulled out a cigar. "It's going to be hot there, so when you're on the island, see if you can get some pictures of Taylor for me. Topless if possible. Thanks."

Trent left without a word, feeling vaguely as though he were part of somebody else's sadistic little dream. He drifted back to his cubicle, turned off his computer monitor, and unplugged his phone. For the rest of the day he did nothing that could be called work. A few times, in an almost unconscious way, he opened his wallet and pulled out the card Petersen had given him the night before. But always he put it back again, and did not call.

[CHAPTER EIGHT]

They'd been flying for so long that Trent didn't even hear the sound of the helicopter engine anymore. Beneath him stretched the ocean, blue and endlessly blue, broken everywhere by thousands of tiny whitecaps that, from their height, looked like clouds bursting into existence only to immediately disappear. It was a sight that should have inspired awe, the sapphire vastness of the sea with its rhythmic, hypnotic motion that had beckoned to mankind for thousands of years. It had, too, for the first couple hours. But now it was only monotonous.

"Are we there yet?" he asked no one in particular.

The answer came through the speaker embedded in his helmet. "Less than an hour now," the pilot said. "Try to get some sleep."

Trent sat back. Fat chance of that, wedged as he was between Todd and Tad. The two of them were staring out opposite sides of the helicopter. Somehow Taylor had fallen asleep, leaning up against the helicopter's interior wall in what could not possibly have been a comfortable position. She didn't seem to mind, though. She also managed to look pretty doing it, which shouldn't have been a surprise; beautiful girls probably didn't drool on their pillows.

"Isn't it just *magical*?" Tad said at one point. He'd said it seven times now.

"It'll be magical when I can get off this thing," Todd said. "I feel like a sardine."

"Oh, come on now," Tad said. "You're not scared, are you?"

"Hell no, I ain't scared."

"You *are*!" Tad clapped his hands. "Oh, that is just *precious*. Don't worry, Todd, I'll make sure nothing happens to you."

"Fuck you, Tad."

Trent sighed. "Are we there yet?

]I[

Three hours after leaving Kiribati, and more than twenty hours after flying out of Los Angeles, the Nova crew touched down on a small rock platform overlooking a desolate stretch of beach. The whirling helicopter blades sent sand and driftwood scattering in all directions; strange-looking crabs scuttled out of the way and frantically rushed into the surf or buried themselves in the sand. The pilot waited for the propellers to stop spinning before opening the doors.

"Wake up, Taylor," Trent said. He didn't see how the landing hadn't jarred her awake. "We're here."

She opened her eyes—green today, with a bit of yellow near the pupils. She'd worn the same ones to the set of *Take It Off!* Those must have been her traveling eyes. "That wasn't so bad."

"Speak for yourself. I'm taking your seat on the ride back."

"Fine. See if I mind being sandwiched between two men."

That was *not* a fair thing to say. Now he was going to have to walk around all day with his hands in front of him.

"We should only be a couple hours," Trent said to the pilot as Taylor got out. The pilot nodded and picked up his clipboard. Trent removed his helmet, then jumped out of the helicopter and onto the ground.

There was literally nothing to see. A long stretch of sandy beach lay before them and curved gently around to the left, where it was obscured by low dunes and the beginning of the island's dense forest. The only sounds were the wind, the ocean, and the constant murmur of ten billion insects. The air reeked of salt.

"Would someone explain to me why we're looking at an *actual* deserted island?" Tad asked. He'd exchanged his safety helmet for a wide-brimmed straw hat and looked exceptionally out of place.

"NBC wants it that way," Trent said. "They've had some trouble dealing with the Easter Islanders, local autonomy and so on. Apparently this'll be easier."

"It seems so barbaric, don't you think? Who'd want to put themselves *through* this?"

"Two words," Trent said. "*Extreme Makeover.*"

"You've got a point."

"Ow!" Taylor screamed. "Something just *bit* me!" Suddenly she was engulfed by a pungent cloud of bug repellant. "Whose idea was it to make bugs in the first place?"

Trent didn't think this was the time to tell her about the insects' role in the delicate balance of nature. "This won't take long. Let's get started. Todd, did you get an aerial?"

"I thought Tad was supposed to."

"Oh, no! No, no, no, that was *your* job, mister."

"Great," Trent said. "How are we supposed to know which way to go?"

"Don't you start bossing me around," Todd said.

"I say we go this way," Taylor said. She'd already removed her shoes and was walking in the sand.

"Can't hurt," Tad agreed. "We'll get aerial shots on the way back. Don't be such a stick-in-the-mud, Trent. Pretend we're on an ad*ven*ture."

There really wasn't much of a choice. They started walking, following Taylor as she stopped to pick up seashells or watch sandpipers run alongside the surf. The sky was clear, the sun was hot, and the air was wet with enough humidity that Trent's shirt was clinging to his skin after five minutes. Perfect. Just what he wanted. All they needed was to find a den of poisonous snakes to fall into.

Speaking of which. "Anyone know if there's anything poisonous on this island?"

"Poison?" Taylor whirled around. "Who said anything about poison?"

"Ooh!" Tad said. "This would be a good spot for filming."

"The whole beach would be good," Todd said. "Does this place even have a name?"

"Not that I know of," Trent said. "What do you want to call it?"

"Zulu," Todd said immediately. "Zulu Island."

"I think the word 'fabulous' should be in there somewhere," Tad added.

"I like puppies," Taylor offered.

Hmmm. The Fabulous Zulu Puppy Island. *You've seen grown men struggle to survive the harsh environment of Easter Island, but that's nothing compared to what you're about to see when ordinary women are forced to endure the brutal climate and dangerous animals of . . . Fabulous Zulu Puppy Island!!* "Great," Trent said. "I think you've picked a winner."

"This would be a good spot to film," Todd said, "with the dunes behind us."

"Agreed," Trent said. "All right, let's check out the interior." He looked at the tangled wall of undergrowth just past the sand dunes. "Anyone see a way in?"

"Nothing good," Todd said. "Do you think there's any poison ivy in there?"

"Why?"

"I'm allergic."

"I'm pretty sure there's no poison ivy in the tropics," Trent said, though in truth he had no idea. And of course he was wearing shorts.

"I can't see a *thing* through all that mess," Tad said. "Boy, wouldn't it be wonderful if we had some aerials?"

"Don't start with me," Todd warned.

"Hey, guys!" Taylor called. "There's a stream up here. You can follow it in."

"What do you mean 'you'?" Trent asked when he'd reached her. The stream she'd found was about five feet wide and fairly fast-moving—enough fresh water for everybody.

"Well, I'm not going in there. You've got to be crazy, all those *bugs*? No way. I'll stay here and guard the beach."

Guard it? "From what?"

"Stuff. Things. Whatever. Just get in there, you're wasting time."

"So," Tad said, looking at the stream and the thick foliage on either side of it, "who's going in first?"

"Not me," Todd said.

"Oh, *come* on." Trent realized that both Todd and Tad were standing behind him, like he was some kind of shield. "Didn't you guys ever go camping?"

Tad made a noise. "You've got to be kidding. *Camp*ing? Seriously, Trent."

"Just start walking," Todd said. "We'll be right behind you."

"Ow!" Taylor shrieked, and again she disappeared behind a fog of repellant. "Would you hurry *up*? I don't know how much more of this I can take."

Trent reached the stream. What had P.T. been thinking when he assigned these three to this job? He would have done better to hire a group of quadriplegics. "Let's go, guys. Taylor, don't go anywhere." Then, feeling like a Scout leader with a bunch of ten-year-olds, Trent started into the forest.

The temperature fell fifteen degrees as soon as he entered the forest shade. For a while he was able to walk alongside the stream. But the trees, large-trunked things with spindly limbs and exposed roots, gradually narrowed the gap until the rude path he was following disappeared.

He cursed. "Into the water, guys."

"Are you crazy?" Tad said. "You want us to jump *in* there? Do you have *any* idea how much these shoes cost?"

"What did you expect?" Trent asked. "We're on a deserted island. Did you think there'd be roads to walk on?"

"Don't take that tone with me, mister. It's not just the shoes. There might be *leeches* in there."

Todd's eyes got big. "Leeches? Aw, no. No, no, no, no, *no*. Nobody told me nothing about any fucking *leeches*."

"There's nowhere else to go," Trent snapped. "You think this is my idea of a good time?" It was true he'd been camping before, but he'd never liked it. And then it had been easy, with wide paths and a car waiting at the end. It certainly hadn't involved wading through an ankle-deep stream just begging to be attacked by God only knew what.

In they went. "It's *cold*!" Tad squealed.

Trent clenched his teeth. "Just pretend you're at the day spa."

The stream soon narrowed so that they had to walk single file. Overhead, birds and frogs made a symphony of noises, punctuated at times by the shrill drum roll of something that sounded like a giant cicada. They were in *Indiana Jones* country, wading their way toward an ancient temple that no one had ever returned from alive. Or maybe it was *Friday the 13th*, and Jason was waiting for them just around the turn. The only thing missing was the sound of a discordant violin and the gratuitous sex that always came right before the murder.

It couldn't have been five minutes before Trent decided they were wasting their time. "I can't see anything that we can use, guys. Let's go back to the helicopter and do the aerials. Then we'll know where to look."

Tad and Todd were quick to agree. They turned around and fairly sprinted their way out of the jungle. Taylor was waiting for them on the beach, jumping around and flailing wildly at the air.

"Get them *off* of me!" she shrieked. "I'm too *pretty* to get bitten!"

"Come on," Trent said, grabbing her by the arm, "we're going back to the helicopter."

For once, all three of them followed without complaint. Occasionally Taylor would swat at the air or the person nearest to her, swearing she'd seen another bug. Todd was checking his legs for leeches, and Tad spent the walk back lamenting the destruction of his patent leather shoes. Trent picked up the pace, dreaming of the cigarettes he'd left on the helicopter the way newly married men thought about their wives.

Ten minutes later they rounded a gentle curve and saw the helicopter. The pilot was sitting in the front seat, apparently taking a nap. Trent wondered why he hadn't bothered to remove his seatbelt, unless maybe it gave him support. At the moment, though, he hardly cared. The sooner they were in the air, the better.

"All right," Trent said, climbing into the back of the helicopter, "we can't do anything until we get some aerials."

The pilot didn't acknowledge him.

"Hey, wake up." Trent moved closer. "Charlie? His name's Charlie, right?"

"Yeah," Taylor said. "I think so."

"Hey, Charlie." Trent shook the man's shoulder. "Charlie, wake up."

Charlie still did not move.

Suddenly Trent began to get a *very* bad feeling.

"Charlie!" He squeezed his way into the co-pilot's seat and grabbed Charlie's arm. "Charlie, come on, come on Charlie, wake up, wake up. Jesus, wake up, will you!" He found the seatbelt release.

Charlie's body fell forward into the instrument panel and did not move. His head was turned toward Trent by the impact.

Trent stared at him. "Oh, my God." The man's chest wasn't moving. "Oh, my God." His eyes were partially open. "Oh, my God." He was not breathing.

This was not good.

"What's going on?" Todd called from outside.

Trent opened the door at his side and scrambled out. "Um." This couldn't be happening. "Um, I think um, I think the pilot's dead."

Instantly the color left everyone's face.

"What?"

"*Dead*?"

"You're kidding, right?"

Trent ran both shaking hands through his hair. "No, I um, I think he had a heart attack or something. He's not breathing, he's . . . I think he's *dead*, guys."

Tad's hand flew to his mouth. "Oh, my God."

"Hurry!" Todd said. "Someone's got to do CPR or something."

"CPR?" Taylor said with a frightened gasp. "*I'm* not touching a dead person."

"It wouldn't do any good," Trent said. "The man's dead. Look at his face."

Taylor started pacing. "Oh, this can't be happening. This can't be *happening*! I can't be stuck here on a deserted island! I have a *party* to go to tomorrow night!"

"I think we've got more important things to worry about than your social life!" Todd screamed. "What the hell are we going to *do*?"

"Oh, my God," Tad said. He sat down on the rock. "Oh, my God, I feel faint. I feel faint. I think I'm starving to death."

"You're not starving to death," Trent said. "Let's just calm down and think this through, okay?"

"Wait!" Taylor shouted. "I've got it!" She ran to the helicopter and jumped in. For a moment all Trent could hear were the sounds of things being thrown in several directions. Finally she emerged, holding her purse triumphantly. "I've got it!"

"Got what?" Todd asked.

"My cell phone." She dug through her purse, then breathed a sigh of relief. "Oh thank *God* it's still got a full battery." She started dialing.

Trent didn't know how to tell her. "You're not going to get a signal, Taylor. We're two thousand miles from—"

"Shut up!" She held the phone to her ear.

Everyone waited.

Suddenly she screamed and threw her phone as hard as she could against the ground. It shattered, and she started to cry. "We're going to die here, aren't we? We're never going to get off this island alive!"

"We're not going to die," Trent said as calmly as he could. "They'll know something's wrong when we don't get back to Kiribati tonight, okay? By tomorrow morning they'll put out a search party, and the first place they'll look is right here. Nobody's going to die here, all right?"

They seemed to be listening. Taylor had stopped crying, and Tad didn't appear to be starving anymore.

"Todd," Trent said. It was nice to notice that in times of crisis, Todd didn't insist upon his African name-of-the-month. "Help me get Charlie out of the cockpit."

Todd blanched. "Why?"

"So we can see if we can get the radio working."

"If Taylor's cell phone won't work, what makes you think the radio will?"

"I don't know. Maybe they're different."

Together, Trent and Todd pulled Charlie's corpse out of the cockpit. It was quite a job; dead bodies were extremely heavy, and neither of them wanted to be holding Charlie in the first place. For the next twenty minutes Todd and Trent attempted to figure out how to turn on the radio. They managed to start the engine but got no farther, and when Todd accidentally started the propellers, they decided they should probably stop before they found themselves in the air with no idea how to land. There was a manual, but it was written in such incomprehensible English that Trent couldn't make any sense of it.

"The radio's out," Trent said when he and Todd re-emerged from the cockpit. Tad and Taylor were about thirty feet away, equidistant from the pilot's corpse and the forest at their backs. "We're just going to have to wait for someone to come get us."

"You really think they'll be here by tomorrow?" Taylor asked.

"Almost positive. It can't be longer than two days."

"Two *days*?" Tad gasped. "How are we supposed to survive out here for two whole *days*?"

Trent looked at his companions—Taylor, with her long fingernails and bug repellant; Tad, with his frosted hair and bleached teeth; and Todd, who was currently looking at Charlie's body as though it might rise up and attack him—and began to despair. The crew from *Gilligan's Island* had been better equipped to handle this kind of situation.

"Oh, God," Tad said. "I'm starving. I can *feel* my stomach shrinking."

"Shut *up*!" Todd said. "You're only making it worse by talking about it."

Trent massaged his forehead. "All right." Someone had to take charge, and it was obvious that none of them were up to the task. "Here's what we're going to do. We're going to need food, fresh water, and a place to sleep since we can't all comfortably fit in the helicopter. We also need—"

Todd interrupted. "Wait a second. What are you, some kind of Boy Scout?"

"As a matter of fact, I was." It was a damn good thing his father had insisted on dragging his horribly disinterested son through Cub Scouts. *"You'll never know when you'll be stuck on a desert island somewhere and need to tie a clovehitch."* The man had said those exact words every Sunday night for five years. God, the irony was oppressive. His father was certainly laughing in his grave right now.

Too bad Trent had quit when he was fifteen.

But at least he knew what to do, if not how to do it. "We're going to need some wood for a fire. It'll keep us warm tonight in case it gets cold, and it'll give search parties something to see in case they start looking tonight. Todd, you remember where that stream was? Why don't you see if there are any canteens or plastic bags in the helicopter and fill those up. Taylor and Tad, you two can gather firewood. I'll see if—"

"Whoa whoa *whoa* there, buster," Tad said. "What makes you think you can tell us what to do? I don't remember anyone electing you leader."

Trent stared at him. "I'm not trying to boss you around."

"Oh, yes, you are," Taylor chimed in. "Todd do this, Taylor do that. What if I want Todd to get firewood?"

"It doesn't matter who does what, as long as—"

"To tell you the truth," Todd said, "I don't really feel like walking all that way to get water. Did you assign that to me because I'm *black*?"

"What the hell are you guys talking about? We need to—"

"Don't take that tone with us," Taylor said with a warning finger. "I'll vote you off this island so fast your head will spin."

Trent's mouth fell open. "*What* did you say?" She hadn't really said that, had she? "You can't vote me off, Taylor! We're not on television here. This isn't *Survivor*!"

Tad's hand flew to his mouth again. "Heresy!"

"For the love of Christ, people, this isn't a reality show! We have to work together!"

"Right," Todd said with a maddening chuckle. "Like people who get stranded on a desert island all of a sudden put aside their differences and start working *together*, is that what you're saying? Seriously, man, what planet are you from?"

"Well, then, what do *you* want to do!" Trent shouted.

Todd shrugged. "I guess I can go get water. But I'll be damned if I do it because you *told* me to."

"Come on, Taylor," Tad said, "let's go get some wood."

"Don't expect me to pick any of it up," she said. "I'm not about to break a nail. Do you have any idea how much they cost?"

"Honey," Tad said, pointing to his shoes, "don't even *start* with me about that, okay? You can get leaves for the roof. Big ones. Oh, it'll be just like a sleepover!"

The three of them went in their respective directions. Trent watched, speechless. What had he done to make God so angry with him? This had to be a cruel punishment, some kind of divine retribution for decades of sinfulness. Maybe he'd murdered children in a previous life. Nothing else could possibly explain why this was happening to him.

"I swear," he said to the sky, "if you get me out of here I promise I'll go to church. I mean it this time."

There was no answer, of course. God was probably thinking it over.

[CHAPTER NINE]

Trent threw another stick onto the fire. "I can't believe the human race ever managed to survive."

It was night. The sun had set two hours ago, sinking into the ocean in a spectacle of flashing reds and oranges that would have been dazzling if they weren't stranded. The four of them were sitting in front of a small fire; behind them, the helicopter stood guard, silent and slightly ominous in the flickering light. It was a miracle they'd been able to start a fire at all, even with Trent's lighter. Lighters—yet another reason to support smoking, even if being stuck on a deserted island wasn't quite as common as emphysema. Still, Philip Morris might look into a new ad campaign.

"I don't know," Tad said, leaning against a small hump in the sand, "I'd say we're doing pretty well."

"Compared to whom?" Trent asked. The process of gathering the basic essentials had illustrated their overwhelming inability to survive on their own. Two trips to the stream and Todd was whining about blisters; Tad and Taylor had spent fifteen minutes gathering firewood before declaring their exhaustion and refusing to work any more; and the only food Trent had managed to find was a strange-looking green fruit nobody wanted to try for fear it might be poisonous. It was sitting in the middle of their circle, one side blackened from its constant exposure to the heat. And thank God the sky was clear, because their attempt to erect a shelter had been a complete disaster. The wreckage was beside them, a jumble of branches, leaves, and vines that Todd had tried to use as rope. It was probably for the best; anything they'd built would more than likely have collapsed halfway through the night and crushed them in their sleep.

"How do you think they did it?" Taylor asked.

"Who?" Todd asked.

"Old people." She nibbled on the end of a granola bar, one of six that Trent had found in the helicopter. It wasn't much, but for a girl like Taylor it might constitute an entire meal.

"What do you mean," Tad asked, "like forty-year-olds?"

"No, silly. *Old* people, from hundreds of years ago. How did they get anything done?"

"They worked," Trent said. "The women worked too. Their nails must have looked horrible."

Tad shuddered. "Oh, it's too awful to imagine."

"I'm glad I didn't live back then," Todd added.

Trent felt the same way, but he didn't say so. He liked being able to drive his Jaguar to the supermarket and buy food that had been shipped in from halfway around the world. Technology made everything easy—so easy, in fact, that people didn't need to know how to do anything anymore. He couldn't milk a cow, or gut a fish, or catch one for that matter, or make plastic, or build a house, or find his own food, or make his own clothing, or figure out what half the buttons on his washing machine did. And yet the rest of them had wanted to vote him off the island because he tried to make them work together.

"Do you guys think we're doing the right thing?" he asked.

"What are you talking about?" Todd asked.

"The whole Reality TV thing." His voice sounded empty against the crackling wood and the endless surge of ocean on sand. "I mean we're making shows that basically encourage people to work against each other, every man for himself, and—"

"Or woman," Taylor said.

"You get my point. Anyway, all our shows make it look like the best way to win is to treat everyone else like an enemy, and in reality what we need to be doing is working together. I mean we're sending people the wrong message, don't you think?"

Todd shrugged. "We're just giving them what they want to see."

"Bullshit." Trent flung his granola wrapper into the fire. "People will watch *anything*."

"Oh, honey, that's not true," Tad said.

"Oh yeah? Then how do you explain TNT?"

"Well—"

"Lifetime? QVC? *Full House?*"

There was a brief silence.

"You have a point," Tad conceded. "But we're different. We give everyone a chance to be famous."

Trent had heard that argument before. "That doesn't bother me." It *did*, but that wasn't the point right now. "It's what we *do* with them that I'm not sure is right. Couldn't we have a show where people don't stab each other in the back all the time and work together instead? Would that really be so horribly unpopular?"

"How should we know?" Taylor asked. "It's never been done before."

"Oh yes it has," Tad said. "Look at *Queer Eye*. Those men are just *fabulous* together. Plus you get to make fun of some poor straight guy with the fashion sense of a billy goat." Tad laughed, his frosted hair dancing like a show pony in the slight breeze. "Some of the men they find for that show, I tell you, I just wonder how in the world they found *anyone* to sleep with them."

That's the problem, Trent wanted to say. We're turning the world into a bunch of mindless, drooling, sniping idiots. We're turning people against each other. We're glorifying spitefulness and stupidity, avarice and selfishness. We're hastening the decline of civilization as we know it, and we've got to stop. But they wouldn't understand. Nobody did.

"What's the matter, Trent?" Taylor asked. "Still looking for your show?"

"What?"

"Your show. The one you want people to really remember. You know, like, 'Oh, Trent Tucker, he's the one that did . . .' Like *Hamlet* for Shakespeare or *The Odyssey* for that guy who wrote it."

Trent rolled his eyes. "Homer."

"Yeah. Him." Taylor stretched her legs. "You know what *my* favorite show is? *The Swan*. Because it's so *real*, you know? And it's doing such a good thing. Nobody should have to be unattractive."

"You don't think people should learn to love themselves the way they are?" Trent asked.

Taylor gave him a look. "That's what people *always* say to ugly girls. You think beauty just happens? No sir, it takes a lot of work. You've got to want it. And those girls do, and they get it. That's what's so great about that show."

She sat up and leaned in closer to the fire. "But what I want to do is go beyond the surgery table. See, it's not just about changing your appearance, it's about getting a whole new *life*. So I want to take some really unattractive woman—I mean, *really* unattractive—from like Iowa or something, give her the makeover, and then, totally change her identity. Give her a new name, move to a new, hip city—Seattle or Austin or San Francisco or something—and follow her around, watch the guys hit on her, let her see what she's been missing. *Then*, after six weeks or something, we'll take her back to her family in Iowa and let her choose which life she wants! Does she want to stay with her ordinary family and her unattractive husband, or does she want to live the glamorous life of a hot city girl?" Taylor clapped her hands excitedly. "Isn't that just *perfect*?"

"So," Trent said after a moment, "you want to make a show that basically says that beauty is the most important thing a woman can have?"

"Oh *please*," Tad said, "don't pretend it's not. Look at magazine covers, actresses, talk show hosts. It's the only thing that matters."

"That's the problem. You're basically encouraging people to get divorced." As if anyone needed additional help from television on *that* front.

"Pssh," Tad said with a dismissive flip of his wrist. "You're such a downer sometimes. I think it's a marvelous idea, Taylor. I think P.T. will just eat it up."

She brightened. "You really think so? That's *such* a relief. I've been sitting on it for a *month* now, and I just haven't got up the courage to tell P.T. because I don't think I could take it if he didn't like it. I'm still not sure what to call it, though. *The Choice*, maybe?"

"No good," Todd said. "It'll sound like a show about abortion."

"Oooh. Good point."

"What about *Total Switch*?" Tad offered. "Or *Life 360*? You know, like 360 degrees?"

"You mean one-eighty," Trent said with a small laugh. "Three-sixty would take you right back where you started."

"Whatever, Mr. Math Wizard. Look, just because we're stuck out here in the middle of nowhere doesn't mean you have to be so crabby."

"I'll think of a title for it," Taylor said with dreamy eyes. "And when I do, it's going to be the biggest show in the history of television."

"Second biggest," Todd said. "After mine."

She arched an eyebrow at him. "Oh, yeah. What's *your* great idea?"

Todd dug into the sand as though he'd been waiting to explain. "You know *Gangland Romance*, right? Well, I'm proud of that. I feel like I've really done something there, you know, shown people what it's really like in the ghetto. Tupac and all them, they talked about it, they told the world about Compton and all that, but I've been able to put a face on the plight of the modern black man."

"And woman," Taylor added.

"Please, honey," Tad said. "And just when did you become a feminist?"

"Anyway," Todd said, "that show has opened eyes, but it doesn't offer a solution. What I want to do is bring *hope* to my brothers and sisters, show them that they don't have to be the white man's servant. I want the world to know what we're capable of."

"That sounds great," Trent said. Had he misjudged Todd for the last two years?

"So what I want to do is make a show that will let *everybody* know that if you fuck with us, you're gonna get what you deserve."

No, Trent thought, looking to the sky as though expecting a meteor to fall on him any second. He hadn't misjudged Todd at all.

"See," Todd went on, "*Gangland Romance* is a good show, but it doesn't fix anything. It's still blacks killing blacks. We're waging a war against our*selves*, and that's not the way it should be. The black man is not my enemy. You white people, you're the enemy."

"You're right," Trent said, pinching the bridge of his nose. "In fact, just last weekend I lynched a black kid for walking on my sidewalk."

"You *know* what I'm talking about. We're still second-class citizens. We still have to endure the chains of discrimination every single day."

"Don't even *start* with me about discrimination," Tad said. "At least *you* can get married. Not that I understand why anyone would want to do that."

Todd turned to Trent. "You can't deny there's still discrimination."

"I'm not arguing that. But—"

"And there are too many of my brothers and sisters who think there's nothing they can do about it. They think that's the way things are, and that's the way they'll always be. It's been almost fifty years since the marches, and are we really any better off than we were? I don't think so."

"I think things are better than they were in the fifties, yeah."

"Maybe," Todd said, "but it's not enough. We need to stop fighting ourselves and focus our energy on the source of the problem. So what I wanna do is take the struggle out of the ghetto and into the white man's world. I've even got the title worked out: *Suburban Warfare*." Todd's eyes were wide with excitement. "What do you think?"

"Sounds fun," Taylor said.

"It does have potential," Tad admitted. "That's what *Queer Eye* did by putting five gay men in a straight man's home."

"What about you, Trent?" Todd said in a challenging tone. "You got a problem with it?"

Trent felt as though he was being hit over and over with a rusty hammer. He was in hell. He had died and gone straight to hell, nothing else could explain it. Any minute now little demons would start poking him with kabob skewers.

"I said, you got a problem with it?"

Trent stared at him. "I think it's the worst idea you've ever had. I think it's the worst idea in the history of television. You'd do better to have a show about incest."

"Incest," Tad said thoughtfully. "Now *that's* something we haven't tried yet."

In the face of Todd's outraged silence, Trent continued. "You want to enfranchise black people by telling them to start a *war*? What about working together, for Christ's sake? Why not give people a show where a whole bunch of blacks and whites and Asians and Mexicans live together in a big house and get the fuck *along*! Is that too boring for you?"

"Wake up, Trent," Todd said. "You can't just expect people to get along with each other. That doesn't work. It's *never* worked, and you know it. You can't get people to listen to you without violence."

"Is that right?" Trent laughed because it was better than screaming. "What about Martin Luther King?"

"Malcolm X," Todd countered.

"Fine, then. Gandhi. Mother Theresa. Jesus Christ, for Christ's sake."

"Yasser Arafat. William Wallace. Joan of Arc. George Washington. Abraham Lincoln. They all fought for what they wanted, and they're *heroes*."

"Ooh," Taylor said. "Good one, Todd. What do you say to that, Trent?"

"Shut up," Trent said. God, he *really* wanted a drink. "Those people turned to violence as a last resort, not some kind of publicity stunt. Todd just wants to skip the negotiation table and head right for the armory."

"Shit," Todd said. "Talking never accomplished nothing."

"Of course not! Because people like *you* were more interested in blowing shit up instead!"

There was a silence after that. Tad lay back and stared at the sky, and Taylor busied herself by making little pyramids in the sand. Todd was looking into the fire as though debating whether or not he should fling a burning brand at Trent's head. And as for Trent, he gazed out on the blackness of the midnight ocean and wished he could disappear into it.

"I don't know about you guys," Tad said, "but I should sure go for a pizza right now."

"Don't start talking about food," Todd said. "I'm starving."

"Is there any more water?" Taylor asked.

Tad passed her the canteen. "Do you really think they'll come tomorrow?"

"They have to," Trent said, more hopeful than certain. "By now they have to realize we should have been back. They've probably tried calling us on the radio. I'm sure they'll send somebody out first thing in the morning."

Taylor sighed. "I'm supposed to be at a party right now."

"I'm sure it's a snoozer," Tad said.

"Thanks," Taylor said. "I hope so." She lay back and stretched out. Her shirt, too short to begin with, stopped just short of exposing her chest, and it drew Trent's gaze like a magnet. Her deliciously fake breasts pointed like missiles toward the sky, defying every rule of gravity known to man. Newton may have been smart, but he had never factored silicone into his equations.

Taylor sighed again. "What do you think everyone back home is doing?" She looked up and caught Trent's eyes.

He found something else to look at. "I don't know. Rachel's probably telling somebody to go fuck themselves."

"No," Tad said, "that's just you."

"Lucky me."

"Max is probably halfway to some girl's apartment," Todd said. "You ever go out with him, I mean outside of work? That boy is *always* trying to score. He'll say the craziest stuff, too, shit nobody'd believe, but he makes 'em believe it. I don't know how he does it. He could talk your grandmother into his bed if he wanted to."

"You can't have too much trouble yourself," Tad said. "Seriously, Todd, I'd be all over you like—"

"Don't say another word, man. That's disgusting."

"Don't knock it 'til you try it."

"I hear he's not that good," Taylor said. "Max, I mean."

"You *hear*," Todd asked, "or you *know*?"

"None of your business."

"*Please* don't tell me you've slept with Max," Trent said. There were certain things in this world he simply could not deal with right now.

Taylor shrugged. "All right, I won't."

There was another break in the conversation. The island's insects continued to chirp and whirr and creak, and the fire still crackled its quiet, unabated song. But now they all sounded different. It was as if they were whispering: *Max slept with Taylor, Max slept with Taylor, Max slept with* . . . Trent groaned. Now he'd never be able to get to sleep.

Tad yawned. "I'm bored."

"Me too," Taylor said. "No wonder nobody lives here, there's *nothing* to do here. What do you think old people did for fun?"

"Who knows?" Tad said. "Counted rocks, maybe."

"Invented things," Trent offered. "Wheels and plumbing and stuff. Probably slept a lot, too, after working all day."

Taylor wrinkled her nose. "I'm so glad I didn't have to live through all that. Working all day? That's no fun."

"What are you talking about?" Trent asked. "We work like seventy hours a week."

"Yeah, but it's not like *work* work. You know, gardening and stuff?" Taylor held out her hands and looked at her nails. "I just couldn't do that."

It's a good thing you didn't have to, Trent kept himself from saying. The human race would never have made it.

"Well," Todd said, "I know one thing they did. No electricity, no TV, there's only one thing you can do. I could sure go for some right now."

"Who couldn't?" Tad asked. "Oh, God, it's been *weeks*."

There was a momentary pause. Todd looked at Taylor.

"So," he said, "you wanna have sex?"

Trent blinked. "What?"

"I wasn't *talking* to you. Taylor, you wanna have sex?"

"Right here?" she asked.

Todd shook his head. "I was thinking in the helicopter—little more private."

She seemed to be thinking it over.

"We don't have anything better to do," Todd said.

And that apparently did it.

"Why not?" Taylor said.

"*Whoa*!" Trent said. "*What* the hell just happened?"

"Stay out of our business," Todd said, getting to his feet. "This doesn't—"

"Wait," Trent said to Taylor, who was already standing and brushing sand from her clothes. "You mean that's *all* you have to do? Just tell a girl she's got nothing *better* to do? You're telling me I've been wasting all this time going on *dates* and getting to *know* a girl before sleeping with her?"

"We're on a deserted island, Trent," Taylor said. "It's different."

"Yeah," Tad added. "Ordinarily Todd would have to buy her a drink first."

"Shut up," Todd said. He put his hand on Taylor's back. "You ready?"

"I'm always ready," she said. They started to walk away.

"Wait!" Trent scrambled to his feet. "Wait wait *wait*! I asked first, remember? I asked in Chicago, I get first dibs!"

"That was different," Taylor said.

"Well then can I at least join in?"

Taylor looked at him for a moment. Was she considering?

No. An instant later she started laughing. "Oh, Trent, you are so *funny* sometimes."

"Someone needs to keep Tad company," Todd said. "We don't want him getting lonely. Come on, Taylor." He led her toward the helicopter. "We'll be back in an hour or two."

Trent watched them open and shut the helicopter door with an utterly blank look on his face, his mouth open. He had no idea how long he stood there, staring at the door until he couldn't see it anymore. It wasn't possible. It simply wasn't possible.

"Get over it, Trent," Tad said. "You snooze, you lose."

Somehow he made himself sit down by the fire next to Tad. The silence between them was noticeably louder than it had been before.

"You know," Tad said eventually, "you don't have to sleep alone tonight."

Trent glared at him.

"Just a suggestion. You don't have to look at me like that."

And then, because things weren't bad enough, it began. The helicopter started to shake, a tremendous, rhythmic quiver of steel and aluminum; and above it, piercing the air with maddening regularity, was the sound of Taylor's voice: "Yes! Yes! Harder! Harder! Yes! Yes! *Yes!*" Over and over, thrust after thrust after thrust like a devil pounding on an enormous drum.

"Wow," Tad said. "They didn't waste any time, did they?"

"Can you see anything on my forehead?" Trent asked suddenly. He leaned into Tad and pushed his hair back. "Anything? Like a number or something, maybe three sixes?"

"Yes! Yes! Yes! Oh, *God*, yes!"

"No," Tad said. He didn't get it.

"Just checking." Trent sat back. God must have put it somewhere else. Because there was no doubt about it—he was cursed, doomed to endure horrors no man should have to endure.

"Harder! *Harder!* Is that—the *best*—you can *do*—oh!"

"Come on," Tad said. "Let's try to get some sleep."

"Oooooooohhhhhhhhhh!!!!"

Trent didn't think that was likely to happen.

[CHAPTER TEN]

When Trent woke up the next morning, the sun was above the trees, beating down on him with an uncomfortable intensity. Embers from last night's fire still smoldered in the pit, and a thin trail of smoke trickled into the sky. He stood and stretched, his legs and back as stiff as boards. As soon as he got back to civilization, the first thing he was going to do was make an appointment with his masseuse—Skyler, or maybe Julie, or maybe both of them. He'd earned it.

It took him a moment to accept the fact that last night had not just been some horrific dream. There was the helicopter, sitting in what seemed like an unnatural silence after last night. So, it had happened. Taylor had slept with Todd—if you could call it that. Now he understood why some kids thought their daddy was hurting their mommy whenever they accidentally walked in on their parents.

It took him another moment to realize he was alone. He looked up and down the beach—nothing. Where could they be? Taylor and Todd might have stayed in the helicopter, but what about Tad? Certainly Tad hadn't decided to head into the forest on his own. Then again, the canteens were gone, so maybe he'd gone to the stream to refill them.

He started walking. In a way it was nice, being alone on an empty beach with no screaming children or ringing cell phones to distract him. It was almost possible to forget the fact that he was stranded on a deserted island with people he could hardly stand. All he needed was something to eat and he could almost have been on vacation.

It was not a feeling that would last long.

Soon he became aware of a figure coming toward him—Tad, he assumed, coming back from the stream. But unless Tad had grown a few inches and changed the color of his skin, that wasn't him.

"Todd?"

"Morning!"

"What are you doing here?"

"Getting water. What's it look like?"

"I thought you were—" He couldn't finish. No, that wasn't true; he just didn't want to.

"No. I slept on the beach last night. Man, that girl wore me *out*."

"Yeah, that's great. Please, tell me all about it. Because I couldn't hear everything that was going on." He grabbed a canteen. "Where's Tad?"

"Don't know. He was laying next to you when I came out. Wasn't there this morning, though. Man, that girl wore me *out*."

Trent wondered what Todd would look like with a canteen lid jammed into his eyeball. "So you haven't seen him?"

Todd shook his head. "Haven't seen Taylor either. She's probably asleep in the helicopter. Man, I'm telling you, that girl—"

"I know," Trent snapped. "I know."

They walked back to their camp. Still no sign of Tad. He couldn't have gone into the forest; there wasn't anything resembling a path to follow. And he couldn't have gone down the beach the other way because there weren't any footprints in that direction. In fact, there were only two sets of tracks he could see—a jumbled trail leading to the stream they'd just come from, and another one going from the fire to the helicopter. Which meant Tad had to be . . .

Oh, my, *God*.

Without a word Trent flung his canteen on the ground and sprinted for the helicopter. With a grunt he threw the door open.

And came face to face with Taylor and Tad, sleeping side by side, both of them naked to the waist.

No. It couldn't be.

Tad opened a sleepy eye. "Oh, hi Trent. Is the rescue plane here already?"

It just couldn't be.

"Well, don't stand there all day, mister. Are we rescued or what?"

"What's going on here?" Trent croaked. His voice was hoarse, as though someone had scraped it raw with a grill brush.

"What, this?" Tad stretched and propped himself up on his shoulders. "Oh, nothing. Well, not *nothing*. Taylor just—"

Trent put a hand in the air to silence him. "Tell me you didn't sleep with her," he said, eyes closed in an effort to appear calm. "Just tell me nothing happened, and I won't have to kill you."

"I'll tell you that if it'll make you feel better," Tad said. "But I'd be lying."

"What's going on here?" Todd came up and peered into the helicopter. "Whoa." He looked at Tad with a curious smile. "Did you . . . ?"

"Mmm hmm. After you came out and fell asleep—and let me say, you looked like you'd come out of a hurricane, which I com*pletely* understand now—anyway, after you fell asleep, Taylor came out to see if there was any food, which of course there wasn't. But she wasn't tired yet, and I wasn't tired, so . . ." Tad shrugged. "What's a guy to do?"

"But you're *gay*!!" Trent screamed.

"Of course I am. But you know, honey? Sometimes you want the cream, and sometimes you want the sugar."

"Way to go, man," Todd said, grinning like a fool. "How was it?"

"Are you kidding? Oh my *God*, I haven't done some of those things for *years*. I told you, Trent, you snooze, you lose. Maybe if you hadn't been asleep—"

"Shut up, Tad." Suddenly Trent was possessed by a single, violent shudder. This went beyond bad luck. This was a conspiracy. They'd planned it from the beginning, hadn't they. They'd probably gone out for drinks the night before they left L.A. and worked it all out, right down to Charlie's heart attack. They'd probably laughed about it, too: *Oh, I can't wait to see the look on his face when he finds out.*

"You don't have to get all snippy, mister."

"I think I'm entitled to be a little *put out*."

"Could you guys keep it down," Taylor mumbled. "Some of us have only been asleep for an hour."

Trent looked at the sky and started to laugh—not a fun laugh or a happy laugh or the kind of laugh little kids have when their parents give them piggy-back rides, but the kind of laugh you might hear from a stranger just before he pulls an AK-47 from his trench coat and riddles you with bullets.

"You okay?" Todd asked.

Trent turned to him. "Me? Oh, I'm fine. Never better! This has been the best weekend of my entire *life*. Hasn't it been fun? I can't wait to do this again!"

"I think the heat's getting to him," Tad said.

"Shut the door," Taylor groaned. "It's too bright outside."

"Hey," Tad said before Trent had a chance to slam the door closed. "You guys haven't found any food yet, have you?"

"No," Todd said, "and I'm starving."

"Well, if you find any, could you bring us some? That'd be great."

"Why don't you help us *look* for it?" Trent said through gritted teeth.

Tad laughed a delicate laugh. "After what Taylor put me through? Honey, I don't have the energy to traipse through the forest right now. But if you could just—"

Trent didn't hear the rest. He slid the helicopter door closed with such force that the propellers quivered.

"Man," Todd said, still smiling, "who'd have thought, huh? I mean *Tad*, of all people. Tell you the truth, I'm impressed. Aren't you?"

"Thrilled."

"Aw, don't be so mad. You'll get your chance. Shit, everyone else has."

Trent did not need to be reminded. "Come on, let's find something to eat."

"Actually," Todd said, "I'm still pretty tired myself. I mean man, that girl wore me *out*. You mind if I—"

"Yeah, I mind," Trent said. "I'm not doing everything by myself."

"Don't be such a dick. I got the water."

"I don't—"

"Look, just find something and bring it back, okay? It's not that hard." Todd sat down next to the ashes from last night's fire and made a pillow out of sand. "You know, if this *were* a reality show, you'd have been voted off in the first week. I don't know why you have to be so difficult all the time. It's not like *you've* been oppressed your whole life." And with that, he took off his shirt, put it over his eyes, and went to sleep.

There was nothing else he could do. Trent stormed off toward the stream, looking to the sky every few seconds. That rescue chopper had damn well better come soon. Otherwise there were going to be three more dead people for the coroner to examine.

]I[

"Wow," Max said. "Sounds like you guys had a great time."

"Oh yeah," Trent said. "It was special."

It was Tuesday. They were all safe now and back at the office, sitting in Nova's conference room two days after Trent had opened the door on Tad and Taylor's unholy union. Their rescuers had come that evening, conveniently before Trent had a chance to capitalize on Taylor's hospitality.

"You guys must have been starving," Rachel said, looking vaguely irritated as usual.

"Oh my *God*," Tad said, "you wouldn't believe it. I've never been so excited to see a McDonald's in my life, I swear. Oh, I just *pigged* out when we got back. There was nothing to eat on that entire island."

Trent winced. That wasn't entirely true. By mid-afternoon of their last day—and while everyone else was still sleeping off their midnight exertions—Trent had become so hungry he'd decided to try some of those green fruits he'd found. They tasted all right; but there had been some rather unpleasant side effects he did not like to remember.

"That's it." P.T. had been listening to their story with a scowl on his face. "This weekend you're all signing up for pilot lessons. There's no excuse for anyone being stranded on an island with a perfectly good helicopter. Hell, I was flying Cobra attack copters by the time I was nineteen years old."

"Don't you think that's a little excessive, sir?" Trent asked.

"Excessive, hell. Be prepared for everything. That's the only way to stay alive in this business."

So, Trent thought, because their pilot died on them, they were going to have to learn how to fly? Why not make them take a jet engine repair course, just to be safe? Or better yet, why not learn how to mine their own iron and build a ship fueled by coconut oil? May as well learn how to grow their own food, just in case all the farmers in the world suddenly died. Or how about—

"Um," Taylor said, "do you think that could wait until next weekend? I could really use some down time."

"I think we've earned a break," Todd said.

P.T. considered. "I suppose so. Max, Rachel, you two can start this weekend. And Rachel, if you come down with typhus or polio or any other disease before Friday, you're fired, understand?"

"Yes, sir," she said.

"All right then, people, if that's all? Then let's get down to it. NBC's been waiting for your status report for the past three days. What did you guys find out?"

There was an awkward silence while everybody stared at the table.

"Spit it out, people. We don't have all day."

For some unknown reason, Tad decided to speak up. "Well, actually sir, we didn't really get a, um, a very good look at the island."

"Excuse me?" P.T. removed his glasses and put them in his pocket, which was never a good sign. "What do you mean you didn't get a good look? You were there for two days. What the hell else did you have to do?"

"Quite a bit, if you want to hear about it," Trent said. That earned him a cold look from Taylor and a jab in the ribs from Todd. As though he cared.

"The beach is nice," Todd said. "Long, sandy, relatively unbroken. Ideal for filming."

"What about the rest of the island?" P.T. asked.

"We didn't get a good look," Tad admitted. "The forest was *really* thick."

"And there were a lot of bugs," Taylor added. "Like, a *lot*."

"There is fresh water," Todd said.

"And a helicopter," Trent added.

"What about aerials?" P.T. asked. "Tell me you got some aerials."

Trent felt it was safest not to say anything. P.T. already knew the answer to his question, and nothing good could come from provoking him.

"So." P.T. put his glasses back on, which somehow made him look even angrier. "The four of you were supposed to spend two hours scouting the island, and you're telling me that after two *days* of sitting on your asses the only thing you can report is that the island has *beaches* and *water*!"

He stood up suddenly. "This isn't a game, people! Do I need to remind you that I'm paying you to do a *job*? In case you've forgotten, Stewart Dyson is right down the street with his own team, trying to put us out of business. And he *will*, too, if you can't do better than this!"

Nobody dared to speak. The General towered over them. The blood vessels were standing out on his forehead, large enough that Trent could see the man's pulse. Chairs and staplers might start flying across the room at any second.

"Now." P.T. inhaled through his nose and sat down. The arteries in his skull began to sink. "Some of you are going to be returning to that island to get some decent information. But we'll deal with that later. Right now, I want to hear some new ideas for television shows, and they'd better knock me out of my chair. I'm not talking about an *LMS* sequel or another *Bachelor* ripoff. I want something extreme, something the world has never seen before. Because make no mistake, ladies and gentlemen, we are at war. And there is no room for second place."

Taylor didn't waste any time. "I've got one."

"It better be good. Your tits aren't going to save you today."

"Yes, sir." She coughed once and looked as if she wished she hadn't said anything. "Well, I don't have a title for it yet, but—"

"Get on with it."

"Yes, sir." And she did, highlighting every facet of her horrendous idea—the Iowa farmwife, the plastic surgery, the transplantation, the unadulterated sex, and the return to her drab home for the ultimate decision. Nobody else said a word while she talked; indeed, it was doubtful whether anyone else was breathing. The air in the room seemed to turn cold and gather over Taylor's head in a cloud that could burst at the slightest disruption.

". . . go beyond shows like *The Swan*, you see? I think it would really add to our portfolio." She drummed her nails on the table. "What do you think?"

P.T. was massaging his chin. "It's not enough."

Taylor's face turned desperate. "But—"

"It's not *enough*! The problem, which none of you seems to understand, is that these ideas of yours aren't going *far* enough. What's the climax here? Some homely cowgirl makes a choice? That's not drama! I want action, I want a show that rips people's hearts out. I can turn off a show about a woman making a choice. I want shows that people *can't* turn off! I want them *glued* to their televisions sets. I want children going hungry because Mom and Dad are too busy watching our shows to make dinner. Don't just take it to the next step, people. I want you bringing television to an entirely new *plane*. Have I made myself clear?"

Amid the stunned and somewhat wounded silence of his coworkers, Trent found a reason to smile. He'd heard enough. It was time to do something he should have done a long time ago. If he didn't, he'd never be able to salvage any of his dignity.

"I have an idea," he said, and he looked his boss right in the eyes. "I have a great idea. Fuck . . . this . . . *job*."

There was a sound like a jet taking air into its engines. Tad gasped, his hand flying to his mouth. Rachel looked at Trent and blinked. Max shook his head over and over again. Taylor and Todd seemed to shrink into their chairs. And P.T., the almighty General, narrowed his eyes and cleared his throat.

"Excuse me?"

"You heard me. Fuck this job. It's not worth it. Every Monday we sit here and listen to you complain that we're not doing well enough. We're the top creative consulting firm in the *country*. How much better can you get? But it's never good enough for you, is it?"

"Be careful what you say," the General warned.

"I'm picking my words very carefully," Trent said. *God* this felt good. "You know something? I've been working here for almost two years, and I've never heard *you* offer a decent show suggestion. What's the matter? Your little brain can't come up with anything good? Is *thinking* just too much work for you?"

"Oh, you are so fucked," Todd said.

"*Shut* up," Trent barked. He turned again to P.T. "You want something extreme? You want a show nobody's thought of before? Here's an idea for you. It came to me when I was stuck on that island this weekend—I don't know, sort of an inspiration, I guess, being stranded with these three. Here it is. You take four people, right, three guys and a girl. You don't tell them they're going to a deserted island, you don't let them audition for the job, you just take them, kidnap them from their homes and throw them in the back of a cargo plane, then dump them on some godforsaken waste of land and leave. No supplies, no tools, no nothing—none of that *Last Man Standing* bullshit—just four people alone on an island with no hope of being rescued. No film crews either, just hide some cameras in trees and rocks. Totally candid, none of that three-quarters interview shit. Then, let *them* figure out how to survive on their own. It'll be hysterical, right, because seriously, what paralegal or accountant or creative consultant is going to know how to find their own food? If that's not enough, make sure the island has some predators on it, tigers or cannibals or something. And bugs. Lots of big, fucking, *bugs*, and *no* bug repellant. That oughtta be a hoot."

Suddenly he thrust his chair away from the table. "What's the point of this show? Why would anybody watch it? Because it's *real*. Because everybody *loves* seeing others suffer, right? I mean, that's what we're doing, isn't it? Except we're doing it all fake. The people on our shows *want* to be on them. Think about what you'd get if the contestants *didn't* want to be there. Wouldn't that be special? I think it'd be a big hit, getting to watch these poor sons of bitches cry and argue with each other while they slowly starve and die from exposure. And if they *do* die, so what? That'd be great for ratings, wouldn't it? Everybody *loves* dead people, especially when it's *real*. And then, maybe after thirty days or something, go pick them up, tell them it was all a big joke, ha ha ha, lots of fun, everybody back home just loved it. Can you imagine the looks on their faces when they find out they've been forced to endure that kind of torment just for other people's entertainment? It'd be priceless, don't you think?"

The smile on Trent's face simply wouldn't go away. He'd done it. He was free. He hadn't felt so liberated in two years. So what if P.T. threw him down the stairs on his way out the door—it couldn't be any worse than what he'd already gone through. "Well? What do you think? Is that the kind of shit you're looking for? Huh? Is it? What's the matter, don't know what to say? At a loss? Come on, P.T., spit it out. What do you think?"

The General didn't say anything. He stared at Trent through his rimless glasses with an unreadable look. Everyone else at the table had moved back, pushing themselves against their chairs in a tiny effort to get away from the impending carnage. But P.T. didn't raise a finger. He just kept staring, his eyes sparkling with a glint that could mean anything.

"I'm getting bored here," Trent said finally. "Come on, *sir*. What do you think?"

"Stand up, Trent."

Trent was happy to do so.

The General removed his glasses and, for a moment, remained silent. He looked as if he was trying to figure out exactly what to say. Then he stood up too.

"Taylor," he said softly. "Tad. Todd. Rachel. Max. *That*"—he pointed a finger at Trent—"is ex*actly* the kind of thing I'm looking for."

Suddenly, Trent's delirious glee lost some of its luster.

"That's what this company *needs*, ladies and gentlemen. People with vision, people who aren't afraid to take chances, people who can tell America, 'You're going to listen whether you want to or not.' I could have done without the personal attack, Trent, but I understand what you were doing."

What was happening? "No, I don't think you do."

"Of course I do!" P.T. said. He was smiling. He wasn't *supposed* to be smiling. "You wanted me to get into the heads of these people you're talking about, the unwitting stars of your new show. And it *worked*. Harsh, gripping, riveting—I half-believed you were seriously angry at me for a minute. Powerful stuff. And that's exactly what'll make America watch this show."

In the face of Trent's stunned silence, P.T. came around the table and put his arm around Trent's shoulder. "Ladies and gentlemen," he said, "I'd like to introduce you to your new vice president. Congratulations, Trent. You've done a fantastic job."

Part Two: [AUGUST]

"Only two things are infinite, the universe and human stupidity, and I'm not sure about the former."
—Albert Einstein

[CHAPTER ELEVEN]

"Vice president, huh?"

Trent nodded over his glass. He and Adam were at Garibaldi's, exactly six days after his attempt at quitting had been turned into a promotion. The bar was crowded today, more crowded than normal at least, filled with young executives and aspiring actresses waiting to be seen. Angela was there as well, sitting against the booth and looking as theatrically languid as possible.

"Congratulations," Adam said. "So what does that mean?"

"No more location scouting, for one thing." He'd already told them about his escapade on the island. Angela had listened raptly, especially when he got to Taylor. Which was hardly surprising; bisexuality was a must for any serious theater girl. It was probably written into UCLA's bylaws.

"That's too bad," Adam said. "I know how much you enjoyed them."

"Or talent hunts, or status reports," Trent added. "No more flying to Easter Island once a month to talk with people like Gary about bananas."

"You lost me there," Angela said.

"I'll tell you later," Adam said, caressing her hand. "So, what *do* you have to do?"

"Don't know yet. So far all I've done is moved into my new office." And he was in no hurry to find out. A job with no responsibilities—could it get any better? "I've got a door now."

Actually, moving offices had occupied most of the last week. The one thing he *had* done, which he didn't care to tell them about, was call Frank at CBS, who at this point was almost rabid with desperation, and pitch his latest ideas. He'd given him both, the kidnapping survival one and the awareness-raising medical reality show. Frank had responded predictably. *'Cancer patients? Are you out of your fucking mind?!'* Of course he'd leapt at the other. It had not been Trent's proudest moment.

"A door," Adam said. He took another sip of sake. "Fancy. Does it pay more?"

Trent nodded. "A little." Actually, a lot, enough that he didn't think he'd live very long if his coworkers found out.

"That's great," Adam said.

He felt awkward talking about money with Adam, considering their exchange last week. "You know, I could—" He cut himself off. Angela was right there, and he didn't know how much Adam wanted her to know. "Things are going pretty well."

Adam seemed to understand. "Thanks."

Angela yawned and leaned into Adam. "How come you didn't quit?"

Trent looked at her. Leave it to the theater girl to get all judgmental. He tried to understand where she was coming from. She was young, still in college, unused to the harsh realities of the working world. Someday she'd understand that you couldn't always have things exactly your way. Sometimes you had to make compromises in order to get where you wanted to be.

Besides, it really was a lot more money.

"I thought about it," he said, quickly so he wouldn't start calling himself a whore. "This isn't exactly how I envisioned making my mark. But now I feel like I might be in a position to make a real difference now. My boss respects my opinion, so I'm hoping I can steer him in the right direction."

"It just seems like you should have quit on principle," Angela sniffed.

"Maybe I should have." Did she really just *sniff* at him? Who the hell sniffed anymore? "But you can't change anything if you take yourself out of the game."

"Hurray for cheap rationalizations," Adam said with a smile. "The *true* opiate of the masses."

Trent scowled into his sake. "Shut up."

"Don't get mad. You've got it made. You're an executive now, man. Women will be lining up to sleep with you." Adam finished his drink and gestured with his head. "Here comes the first one now."

Trent turned. Candy was making her rounds, replacing drinks and taking orders in a loose shirt and pleated skirt that left little to the imagination. She strutted over to their table and held her empty tray in front of her chest.

"You guys doing okay over here?"

"Set us up," Adam said. "Hey, Candy, did you know Trent just made vice president?"

Candy's eyes widened. "Is that right?"

"That's right. He's going to start making a lot of decisions about who gets to be on TV."

"Is that right?" she said again. Suddenly her breasts seemed to swell. "Well you *know*, Trent, if you're ever looking for somebody . . ."

"I haven't forgotten," Trent said. "How could I forget about a girl like you?"

She leaned in. "I can make sure you never remember another girl in your life." She winked. "I'll be right back with your drinks." And she drifted away, heel to toe, heel to toe, ass shaking like a pendulum.

"Dude, you're drooling."

Trent forced himself to look away. "Thanks a lot."

"What are you com*plain*ing about? Dude, she's practically *begging* for you."

"I know. But there's a problem."

"*I'll* say," Angela chimed in. "She's too eager. She's basically throwing herself at your feet. She should have more respect for herself."

No, that wasn't the problem. Eager was never a problem. Eager girls made it easy; they took all the pressure off. And he didn't have a problem with promising a television role to a girl with no previous screen time—after all, it wasn't like Reality TV required its stars to have any talent. The problem, Trent thought as he lit a cigarette, was Angela, all pouty and full of indignant morality. A man couldn't do anything with one of *them* sitting across the table. Now he'd have to wait until the next Monday—unless she came then, too.

He decided to change the subject from his frustrated libido. "How's the new script coming?"

Adam and Angela exchanged a glance. "Actually," Adam said, "it's done."

"Really? When did you get it finished?"

"Last Sunday. I know, it only took three weeks. I've never written anything that fast, it practically wrote itself. Anyway, I was going to bring you a copy last week, but you were busy being stranded on a deserted island, so . . ."

"What's it called?"

Adam looked at the table. "*Deadly Justice*. I know, it sounds like a Steven Segal movie, but it's more than that. The title's a toss to the industry."

"Fair enough." As if a guy who came up with shows like *Take it Off!* could really criticize someone else's title. "When can I read it?"

Adam reached under the table, pulled out a small white box, and slid it over.

Trent took it anxiously, then looked at it. "What's with the tape? You don't want me to open it?"

"Not here. And I don't want you asking questions about it, either, because then I'll start answering them and giving you a biased view of the script. That's why I haven't told you what it's about. I just want you to read it cold and give me your honest opinion."

"I can't wait."

"You're going to love it," Angela said. "It's absolutely amazing."

"Better than *The Long Road*?"

Her eyebrows contracted. "It's hard to compare. They're completely different. This one's more—"

"Stop," Adam said. "Don't tell him anything. Just let him read it and decide for himself."

Trent set the box on the seat beside him. "Any luck with *The Long Road*?"

Adam shook his head. "Nothing. After Dietrich I managed to get fifteen minutes with Blaine Pascow—don't ask how, it's a long story—but he didn't . . ." Adam's shoulders fell. "I've given it to some indie directors. They'll all get back to me, you know how it is."

"Don't give up on it. It's a great script."

"Yeah, well. I think this one's got more commercial appeal. It's a little—never mind, I don't want to start talking about it until you've had a chance to read it. It's just the first draft, so keep that in mind."

"Sure," Trent said. "I can't wait to get to it."

][

The next day Trent was only three minutes late to work, which was quite impressive considering he'd almost been run off the road twice by the same 900-year-old lady. He wanted to be angry with her, but really he should have known better. Anyone who ever tried to pass a cream-colored Cadillac was asking for trouble.

"Morning, Lynette," he said when he opened the door. "Any messages?"

"None this morning," she said brightly, then leaned in as though about to impart a secret and added: "Mr. Vice President." She giggled when she said it, just as she had every day for the past week.

"Okay. I'll be in my office."

"Your *new* office, Mr. Vice President."

"Yes, Lynette, that one."

Lynette giggled. "Well, enjoy your day, Mr. Vice President. Oh! I almost forgot. You won't be*lieve* who I saw this morning."

"I give up. Mel Gibson?"

Her eyes grew wide. "At 14th and Pico. How did you know?"

"I paid him to drive around that intersection this morning so you'd see him. Vice presidents do things like that. If you like I can have him stand in your shower tomorrow morning."

"Oh, *stop*."

Trent slinked past everyone else's cubicle on the way to his office. He still wasn't sure how well his promotion had gone over. The past week had been a quiet one, and he thought his new title might have had something to do with that. Still, they hadn't taken his door off the hinges or burned him in effigy, so maybe they weren't that upset. After all, except for the addition of a door and ceiling, some windows, more wall space, a bigger desk, nicer chairs, and his own coffee maker, his new office wasn't much different from his cubicle.

OK, so maybe they *were* upset.

He closed the door behind him, sat down, and stared at the wall. He was going to have to get some more pictures; Marlon Brando and Orson Welles looked lonely against all that off-white space. He could use a couple lamps for the corners, too, especially when the blinds were drawn.

And now that he thought about it, a coffee table would look nice on the other side of his desk—a glass one perhaps, something tasteful. Maybe he should take the rest of the day off and go shopping for works of art and other aesthetic necessities.

All right, so they were probably extremely upset.

"Trent."

That was P.T.'s voice. Trent looked down. There was a silver intercom next to his phone. It hadn't been there yesterday.

He pressed the button. "Sir?"

"I need to see you in my office." The man's voice sounded grainy but no less authoritative.

Trent groaned and got up. P.T. probably wanted to tell him what his new duties as vice president were. Alas. All good things had to come to an end eventually.

But when he got to his boss's office, Tad was there, too, sitting in one of P.T.'s too-short chairs and looking as though he'd swallowed something sour. That was no surprise; personal meetings with the General had a tendency to lower your morale. P.T. was standing behind his own massive desk, hands clasped behind his back, eyeing Tad with an inscrutable expression that nevertheless didn't look good.

"What's going on?" Trent asked.

P.T. answered slowly and deliberately. "Tad has an idea for a show. I want him to tell you about it, and then I want to hear your opinion before I give him mine."

Well, Trent thought cheerfully, this had disaster written all over it. *Hey, everybody, let's play Read the Boss's Mind.* "All right." As though he had the option of refusing.

"Go on, Tad," P.T. said. "Tell him your idea."

Tad bit his lip. "Okay. Well, um, let's see. Okay, so, well—"

"Spit it out, Tad."

Tad looked as if he'd been struck. He closed his eyes and held his palms away from him. "So you know how we have shows for people on both sides of the fence—straights and gays, steers and queers, bucks and—"

"I got it," Trent said. Such a barrage of imagery.

"Yeah, well, I was thinking. What we *don't* have is a show for bisexuals—or bi-curious, if you'd rather, some people are a bit sensitive about their labels. Anyway, so what *I* was thinking is that we could have a show where we get the contestants to go on two dates at the same time. Kind of like *Elimi-date* except with men and women at the same time."

Tad was beginning to warm to his subject. "I think it'd be fun. You could have all three of them in the hot tub and have Barry—that's such a *manly* name, I just *love* it—turn to Susan or whatever and *then* turn the other direction to Steve. I think the audience would just eat it up. I've got the title and everything. Now, granted, this is just a working title, so if you don't think it'll fly we can work with it, but I was thinking, *The Curious Polygamist*. I know I know, it's not *really* polygamy, but I just thought that would rope 'em in, you know." Tad smiled awkwardly and tilted his head down. "What do you think?"

Trent did not want to answer. He looked at P.T., whose face betrayed nothing that might give away his opinion. Great. Then again, what was the worst thing that could happen? He'd guess wrong, P.T. would go off on him, and maybe he'd be removed as vice president before he actually ever did anything. That wasn't so bad. Plenty of vice presidents made their livings doing nothing; the only difference was that their careers usually lasted longer and involved a better retirement package.

P.T. was waiting. May as well get this over with.

"So," he said with a sigh, "you want to run a show where guys make out with women, then make out with men, and put it all on camera?"

"Pretty much. I'm talking about a huge market we've been neglecting so far."

Trent nodded; then, because he felt like it, nodded some more. "And you want my opinion."

"Not really," Tad said. "But I don't have a choice here, do I?"

At least that was honest. And, since they were all being honest . . . "I think it's a terrible idea."

Tad's face fell. "But why?"

For a million reasons. Because it was empty, meaningless, vacuous television. Because it was the same tired, worthless piece of shit they'd been making for years, an old whore with a fresh coat of makeup in a pathetic effort to look desirable again. Because no straight man or woman in the world wanted to watch two men go at it. Now bisexual *women*, that was a different story. Everyone liked them, college girls in oversized shirts with their sorority sleepovers and homoerotic pillow fights. It wasn't fair, but it was the truth.

Tad was waiting for an explanation. "Look, Tad, I wish I liked it, but I—"

"Don't apologize," P.T. interrupted. He placed both hands on his massive steel desk. "Tad, I agree with Trent one hundred percent. This show of yours has no future. We're trying to attract viewers, not repulse them. How many times do I have to tell you people, I want shows that are *extreme*. I want shows that will make *that* man"—he pointed to the picture of Armsburger on his wall—"shit himself in fear. Am I making myself clear?"

Tad looked miserable. "Yes, sir."

P.T. stood up. "Now so far, Trent here is the only one who's managed to come up with an idea like that. By the way," he turned to Trent, "CBS called this morning. Frank made his pitch yesterday and they loved it. They're calling it *Tropical Abduction*. Thought you'd like to know."

Trent tried to sound excited. "Thank you."

"You see, Tad," P.T. went on, "I want to do more than make television here. I want to change America. People like Armsburger, they want to hold America back. If they had their way, we'd all be living like the Puritans. And the only way to stop them is to keep pushing. You understand that?"

Tad leapt to his own defense. "But I thought I—"

"Yes, Tad, I know what you thought. And you were wrong." P.T. pulled a cigar from his humidor. "New policy. From now on, all show ideas need to be approved by Trent before coming to me."

"Whoa, sir." The words were out of Trent's mouth before he had a chance to stop them.

P.T. lit his cigar and exhaled a blue cloud of smoke. "Is there a problem?"

"No," Trent lied quickly. "No, not at all. It's just, are you sure that's a good idea?"

"You're the only person here who seems to understand what I'm looking for. And I've got more important things to deal with than listening to dozens of *Temptation Island* makeovers every week. Besides, it'll give you something to do. You didn't think I promoted you to vice president for nothing, did you?"

Trent said nothing. He glanced at Tad, who was looking back at him with hot, resentful anger in his eyes.

"Are we clear?" P.T. said. "Excellent. Now get back to work. Tad, try to come up with something decent for a change. Make me remember why I hired you. And Trent." He took the cigar from his mouth. "Keep up the good work."

Trent hurried back to his office before Tad had a chance to tell everyone what had happened. Perfect. Just perfect. *None* of them was going to like this. Monday meetings should be a whole lot more enjoyable now. Maybe he'd start bringing his own fireplace poker so they could take turns beating him with it. Why couldn't he be like other vice presidents and just go golfing every day? Was that really too much to ask?

[CHAPTER TWELVE]

"What do you mean you don't fucking *like* it?"

Yeah. They definitely didn't like the new policy.

Trent looked at Todd, who had just leapt out of his chair and looked ready to charge, his nostrils the size of tuna cans. Angry tuna cans. The kind of tuna cans that might fling themselves at you when you passed them in the grocery store.

And it was only nine-thirty—on the first day.

"Listen," Trent said. "All I'm saying . . . look, can you sit down, please?"

"It's because I'm black, *isn't* it."

"No. I'd ask white people to sit down, too."

"You *know* what I'm *talk*ing about! You're turning this idea down because I'm black. If one of the other crackers that work here had come up with it, you'd be sending it right on, wouldn't you? But you're gonna make the *black* man beg, aren't you, jump through your little hoops like I'm some kind of show pony. Well *fuck* that. I'm *nobody's* bitch."

Wow. Was this Todd's idea of winning someone over? "Could you sit down, please?"

"Hell no! You can't tell me what to do, just because I'm—"

"Oh, shut up, would you?" Obviously tact and reason was the wrong approach. "Now sit your ass down or get out. Pick one."

Still incensed, and with his nostrils still flaring, Todd took a seat.

"Look, Todd—"

"Call me Azi*ki*we, cracker!"

Trent stared at him. "Todd. It's not because you're black. The problem's not your skin color, it's the idea."

"What's wrong with it?"

"Well if you'd shut up for a second, I'd be able to *tell* you." Trent pinched the bridge of his nose. That was it—after work he was going to buy some of those nicotine patches. Two or three of them at a time should keep him calm all day. "The problem is that we can't do it."

"Why not?"

"You can't have kids running drugs on national television," Trent said, a statement he thought should have been fairly self-evident. "It's illegal."

"I'm telling you, *Urban Entrepreneur* will be huge with—"

"It won't be huge with anybody, we're not going to do it. It's illegal. The government will arrest people. That's not good for TV."

"The hell you talking about?" Todd asked. "Of course that's good for TV. Look at *Law and Order.* They've got like nineteen versions of that show."

"They're *fake*, Todd. That's why they can make that show, because it's not real. Fake. You do know the difference, right?"

"Don't *pat*ronize me, you—"

Trent cut him off. "Do you really think it's a good idea to have a show encouraging kids to sell drugs? Is that the message you want to send to people?"

"I don't see any problem with it."

He didn't see any problem with it. Of course he didn't, he was a moron. Why should that be a surprise? "Look, we're not going to do it."

"What do you—"

"We're not doing it, Todd. No. N. O. Understand?"

Once again, Todd burst out of his chair. "This is because I'm *black*, isn't it?"

"Yes," Trent said. Being hit by a bus was looking awfully good right now. "Yes, Todd, it's because you're black. I don't like black people, or their black ideas."

Todd's eyes were as wide as Trent had ever seen them. "You better watch yourself, cracker." He stormed through the door and slammed it closed behind him.

Trent listened to the angry echo of Todd's exit. Well, he was just making friends all over the place, wasn't he?

He wondered if P.T. had promoted him specifically for that reason. Maybe this was all part of some twisted experiment, the General's own personal *Big Brother.* Maybe he'd installed cameras in the walls so he could watch the entire drama. He could be watching right now, sitting in his office eating popcorn and laughing his dour ass off. Well, not laughing; the man didn't look capable of laughing. But snickering, at least.

Trent was actually about to start checking his walls for microscopic holes when there was a knock at his door. A delicate knock. "Come in."

"Are you busy?" It was Taylor, decked out in a yellow top and a blue skirt the size of a lipstick case. "Do you have a minute?"

"Sure," he said, a bit confused. She couldn't have a new idea already, only a week after her last one; none of them worked that fast, despite P.T.'s continual harangues. "What's on your mind?"

She shut the door behind her with a gentle *click*. "Oh, nothing."

He watched her walk across the room slowly, languorously, the way a beautiful girl did when she had nothing better to do than walk and be watched. She went right up to him, still slowly, and leaned forward, putting her elbows on his desk. Her shirt fell open enough for him to notice that her bra opened from the front.

"I just wanted to talk to you about my show," she said in her breathiest whisper.

Trent smiled. So, that was what she wanted. And this was how she planned to get it. Ordinarily he would have leapt at the chance—literally leapt, across his desk and into her like a tidal wave, or at least a modest swell. But he didn't. For some reason, he suddenly felt as if he had a better idea.

"What do you want to talk about?" he asked in his most casual tone. God, this was going to be fun.

"Well." She stretched forward until her fingers were almost touching his chest, which raised her ass into plain sight. "It's just that, I *really* want to make this show, but P.T. said it's not good enough, and I . . ." She put a finger to her bottom lip and pulled on it gently. Ooh, that wasn't fair at all. "I'd *really* appreciate it if you could talk to him and try to change his mind."

"You'd really appreciate it, huh?" Trent pushed his chair away from the desk before his libido took complete control. "Well, I don't know. He seemed pretty upset by it, you know. How much would you appreciate it?"

She leaned forward even further. This time her feet left the ground. "Oh, I'd *really* appreciate it. I'd do just about *any*thing."

"Just about?" It was an incredible effort to keep a straight face. "I don't know. 'Just about' doesn't sound too good. There's a big difference between 'anything' and 'just about anything,' you know. What exactly are you talking about?"

Taylor smiled. With a single, sinuous motion she pulled herself off the desk and stood up. Then, slowly, and with her eyes on Trent the entire time, she walked around the side of his desk and up to his chair. The sound of each heel on the carpet was distinctly audible. She curled her fingers around the armrest of his chair and turned him so that he was facing her.

"Well," she said. Slowly her legs opened, moving apart until her skirt was stretched to its utmost limit. "What exactly did you have in mind?"

Trent sighed. What he was about to do was perhaps the single most painful and yet satisfying thing he had ever done in his life. "I'm sorry, Taylor. I'm not going to pitch your show to P.T."

Without missing a beat, Taylor sank to her knees and placed her hands on Trent's thighs. "I'm not sure I heard you right. What did you say?"

"I said I'm not going to pitch your idea to P.T."

She leaned closer. "Are you sure?"

"Positive."

Even closer. Her head was now between his knees. "I think you should reconsider."

"I'm not going to reconsider, Taylor. It's a terrible idea."

And with that, her act was over. She shot to her feet, eyes blazing. "*What's* your problem, Trent? I thought you wanted me!"

"I do. Everyone does."

"Of *course* they do!"

"But if I slept with you, then how would I be able to respect myself? Or you?"

That wasn't why he was turning her down. His reason was far less noble—he wanted to spite her, to get revenge on her for being so disinterested in him until now, and for thinking that he'd be so easy to manipulate. Would he regret it tomorrow? Probably; after all, how often would a chance like this come along? But at the moment, the look of disbelief on her face was well worth it.

"Look," Trent said in the face of Taylor's violent breathing, "I'm not going to take P.T. an idea he already doesn't like, especially when I don't like it either. These are people we're talking about, Taylor. We're—"

"They're not *people*!" she shouted. "They're actors!"

Trent decided to ignore that. "Listen, I'm not pitching a show that's going to promote divorce. Do you realize what kind of message that show would send to the country?"

"Yes! If you're ugly and you hate your life, *do* something about it!" She stormed toward the door. "You are such an asshole, you know that?"

"Bring me a show P.T. will like. Then we can sleep together."

"*Fuck you!*" she shrieked, opened the door and slammed it behind her.

Well, Trent thought as he watched his pictures vibrate on the walls, that was two of them. Probably three, if he included Tad. Not bad for his first week as vice president. Forget the effigy; pretty soon they were going to start burning him for real. He wouldn't put it past them to throw gasoline on his head while he was smoking a cigarette. Which reminded him that he desperately needed one.

He pulled one out and lit it. Why couldn't he play the game like everyone else? Why couldn't he be an ordinary vice president and do nothing except golf and sleep with the occasional willing coworker? That's why they were mad at him—because he wasn't acting the part.

So why didn't he?

He knew the answer. It was because now he had a real chance to make a difference. Thanks to P.T.'s horribly misplaced trust, Nova wasn't going to produce a single show without Trent's approval. And just what did that mean?

Trent smiled. It meant an end to Reality TV as the world knew it. No more empty-headed exploitations of attention-hungry clowns; no more derisive, incendiary attacks from people supposedly on the same team. It meant no more *Extreme Makeover* or *Niggas with Guns* or anything like it—that's what it meant. For the first time in its brief and embarrassing history, Reality TV might finally redeem itself, and all because of him. And if it meant pissing off his coworkers in order to save the American public from its own depraved appetites, well, he could live with that.

At least, so long as they didn't gang up and kill him. Maybe he should enroll in a self-defense course.

Just then there was a knock at the door.

Trent jumped a little. Hopefully this wasn't a preemptive strike; he wasn't even a white belt yet. "Who is it?"

Max stuck his head through the door. "It's me. Gotta minute?"

Great. Couldn't they space their visits out a little? "Yeah, sure. I suppose you want to tell me I'm full of shit, too, huh?"

Max shut the door. "No, pal. Though I did see Taylor run out of here a minute ago. Jesus, pal, what'd you tell her? You know what, never mind, it's none of my business. Besides, women get worked up about everything. I'm sure she'll be over it by tomorrow."

"I doubt it. What did you want?"

"Nothing, really." Max sat down. "You know this office is bigger than it looks from the doorway. I've never actually been in here. I like what you've done with it."

"Thanks."

"Look, I'm not being jealous here. The boss needed a V.P. and he picked you. That's all it is. I wish it had been me, I won't lie about that, but I'm glad he picked you instead of some suit from Beverly Hills. Or Todd, because I hate that guy, but that's no surprise, right?"

"Not really," Trent said, relaxing a little. Maybe Max wasn't planning to beat him over the head with a crowbar.

"Hey, P.T. knows what's best for the company, right? I don't think that man's made a mistake in his life, if you want to know the truth, and if he thinks you're the guy, well, then, you're the guy."

"Thanks for the flattery. So what's your pitch?"

"I don't have a pitch, pal. I just heard Taylor tell you to fuck off—actually we all heard it, except Rachel, which is too bad because she would have loved it, I mean *loved* it—anyway, I just thought you might like to know that I'm on your side. It's gotta be hard, right? I mean one day you're the same as the rest of us, and the next you're supposed to tell us what to do. And some people don't like being told what to do, you know, especially from a guy who used to have a cubicle just like theirs."

"It's been a rough start."

"Let me guess. Taylor tried to seduce you?"

"Yeah. How'd you know?"

"What do you mean how'd I know? That's what she does, it's all she knows how to do. Now I don't know why you turned her down, personally I'd have fucked her for all I'm worth. I've been trying to get in there for *months*, man. But if you don't have anything to offer her, you don't have a prayer."

Well, that was something. It was nice to know he wasn't the only one who hadn't slept with her. Although Rachel probably hadn't, either. That'd be something to watch, though.

"But whatever," Max continued, "I'm sure you had your reasons. Anyway, I just thought you might like to know that some of us appreciate that you've got a job to do same as the rest of us."

"Thanks, Max."

"And next time I bring you an idea and you tell me it's not good enough, I'm not gonna take it personal. Not that I want you shooting down my ideas, don't get me wrong. But a business is a business, right?"

"Is this how you manage to sleep with so many women? You just keep talking until they fuck you to shut you up?"

Max grinned. "Not at all, pal. Women, I just tell them what they want to hear. I'm being sincere here. Seriously. You have a job to do. I mean shit, if Taylor couldn't persuade you, what chance do I have?" He grinned. "Hey, you ever been to the Slow Bar?"

"It's been a couple years."

"I know, I know, it's not what it used to be. Still, it's worth going just for the waitresses. You wanna catch a drink after work?"

"Yeah," Trent said. It suddenly occurred to him that he had never gone out for a drink with anyone from work since he'd started. "There's a couple things I have to do first, but I could meet you about, I don't know, seven?"

"Perfect," Max said. "That'll give me a chance to get a head start."

Just then the door opened and Rachel walked in. Not surprisingly, she hadn't bothered to knock. "Oh," she said when she saw Max. "What are you doing here?"

"Good to see you too," Max said. He smirked. "I was just talking to our new vice president. Too bad you didn't get the job. Better luck next time, right?"

"Go fuck yourself," Rachel said. And Trent had thought he was the only one she felt that way about.

"Sounds like a fantastic idea," Max said. "If anyone needs me, I'll be in the bathroom. Trent, see you at seven, right? All right." On his way out he brushed Rachel, who reached for her hairsticks as though to yank them from her hair and plunge them into his back.

"So," Trent said after Max closed the door. At least this would take care of all of them. "What's going on?"

She didn't waste any time. "*First* of all, I want you to know that I can't *stand* the fact that you're vice president. You know how much I wanted this job."

"I didn't ask for it." Not like that would make a difference.

"*Secondly*," she said, ignoring him, "don't think that just because you're P.T.'s golden boy means you're entitled to any special treatment from the rest of us."

That was so absurd Trent almost laughed. "Have you ever given me special treatment?"

"*Third*—"

"Look, I'd love to sit here and find out everything that's wrong with me, but is there a point to this?"

"I heard what happened with Taylor," she said. "And let me make myself perfectly clear. If you try to make me do *anything*, I'll—"

"Wait, wait. You've got it all wrong."

"Got *what* wrong?"

Trent put his cigarette out. "I didn't say anything to Taylor. She tried to seduce me so I'd take her show to P.T."

Rachel laughed—a sarcastic, derisive laugh, but still. He'd never heard her laugh before. "Right. She tried to seduce you. And you turned her down. I don't think so."

"You don't have to believe me. But that's what happened."

"*Bull*shit." She took her glasses off and pointed them at him like a gun. "You'd have taken her in a heartbeat."

"What can I say? I didn't."

"You wouldn't have turned her down. Everyone wants to sleep with her."

"Well, that's what happened." Something interesting was happening. He felt that he was close to figuring something out, something supremely important.

"I don't believe you," Rachel said, but she was beginning to falter; some of the steel had left her eyes.

"Believe what you want. But do you think she would have been so offended by that suggestion that she would have run out of here? Her?"

There was a change in Rachel's expression, as though she were suddenly regretting everything she'd said so far—a sentiment that Trent hadn't thought was possible in her. She cleared her throat, put her glasses back on, and touched her hairsticks. "So, why'd you turn her down?"

"I don't know. Because I wanted to, I guess."

"Why?"

"Because I did."

"But why?"

This was going to get awfully repetitive. "Because I didn't feel like sleeping with her."

Rachel swallowed. "But I always thought you wanted to."

And at that moment, Trent understood. How he understood it, he couldn't say. But finally, and for perhaps the first time in his life, Trent knew what a woman was thinking.

"Do you want to have dinner with me tonight?" he asked.

Rachel blinked. "What?"

"Do you want to have dinner with me tonight? Dinner. You know, food?"

She was now completely confused; the muscles in her throat were moving constantly, and she couldn't seem to stop blinking. "Wh—why?"

"Because I'm going to be hungry later, and I thought you might be too. You can tell me to fuck myself if you want, I just thought I'd ask."

"Why are you asking?"

Trent leaned forward. "Because I want to."

Clearly she hadn't expected that. "Well, why didn't you ask Taylor? Not like she ever eats anything, but still I don't . . . I don't . . ."

For once, Trent knew exactly what to say. "Why would I ask Taylor when I can ask you instead?"

][

As it happened, they decided to skip dinner.

"Oh, my God, oh, my God, *oh—my—God*!"

They were at Rachel's apartment. There were a pair of Japanese screens in one corner and bamboo placemats on the dining room table. Trent had seen them when he walked in. He couldn't see anything now, though, because he was wearing a blindfold.

"Oh, my God, oh, my *God*."

"How does *that* feel?" Rachel said.

"Oh, my God, *oh*, my God."

"Not yet."

They were in her bedroom. The sheets were satin, or silk, something smooth that slid and bunched with every movement.

"Oh, dear Lord. *Jesus* Christ."

"Don't you dare. Not yet."

"Jesus."

"Not yet."

Too late. With a shudder strong enough to register on a seismograph, Trent exploded.

"I told you not to."

"I couldn't *help* it," he managed. He took in air with large, ragged gulps. "You're unbelievable."

"I know."

"What did you *do* to me?"

"Things."

Trent rolled over, or tried to, sweating and utterly exhausted. He shook his head and managed to wriggle the blindfold up over one eye. "I can't . . . I can't . . ."

"That's the idea."

Gradually, he got his breathing under control. "I haven't had that kind of a workout since high school."

"Oh, we're not finished yet."

"You've got to be kidding." He put his head back and stared at the ceiling fan, which was rotating slowly. "What time is it?"

"Eight-thirty."

"Shit. I was supposed to meet Max at seven."

Rachel rested her head on his chest. "I guess you're not going to make it."

"You think he'll understand when I tell him why I didn't make it?"

She raised her head. "Now listen to me. If you tell anyone about this, I mean *anyone*, I'll kill you."

"OK."

"I mean it, Trent. I'll kill you."

"Got it."

"Good. Now." She climbed on top of him. "It's *my* turn."

"Wait," he panted. "I'm not ready."

"You'd better be."

"I'll do what I can. Do you think you can untie me?"

"I guess so," she said.

A few moments passed.

"Oh," he said.

"There," she said. "That's more like it."

"Oh, my God," he said.

[CHAPTER THIRTEEN]

"What happened to you last night, pal? I waited until ten."

Trent didn't know how to answer. He still wasn't sure himself what had happened to him. He'd finally passed out sometime after midnight, and when he woke up to the jarring sound of his alarm clock—which he didn't remember setting, and which was in his apartment, which he didn't remember driving to—Rachel wasn't there. He was half inclined to think he'd dreamed the whole thing, except for one thing: every muscle in his body was sore. It had taken him five minutes just to get out of bed and reach the shower. For the love of God, what had she *done* to him?

"I'm sorry, Max. I . . . something came up."

Max waved it off. "Don't worry about it, I kept myself entertained. What about tomorrow night, you up for it then? We could invite Rachel, I'm sure you'd love that."

Trent's head jerked up so fast it hurt. "What?"

"Do you wanna ask her, or should I?"

Then he saw. Rachel had just come around the corner and was walking toward them with the same peremptory stare she gave to everyone. There was no indication at all that she'd done anything unusual the night before, and she certainly didn't look as though every movement made her wince.

"Max," she said. Then, more coldly: "Trent."

"Hi, Rachel," Trent managed. What was he supposed to say? *Morning, Rachel, I think you broke me in half last night*. Why did the morning after always have to be awkward?

Rachel played her part perfectly. She was as icy as always, even when the two of them were alone. And when there were others around she outdid herself; at one point Trent actually thought she was going to beat him to death with her clipboard.

But that Friday night, and again the following Tuesday, the two of them ended up back at Rachel's place. There was no foreplay, no candlelit dinner or trip to the theater or pretense of having coffee; as soon as the door to her apartment was locked she leapt on him like a cyclone. Each time he was left in serious need of a licensed chiropractor. And each morning after, she glared at him through her thin-rimmed glasses and told him to fuck himself.

Well. If that was the way she wanted it, that was the way it would be. He wouldn't say anything, and he definitely wasn't going to tell anyone about it. If that's how she acted when she was aroused, he'd hate to see her when she was really angry.

][

The second week of Trent's vice presidency went more smoothly than the first, primarily because nobody tried to pitch him anything. And since he didn't have anything to pitch to anyone else, he spent most of his working days playing poker on the Internet, which he was very bad at.

Then, on Friday, P.T. called an unexpected meeting.

"I want you all to see something."

Trent shifted uncomfortably in his chair. P.T. never called an afternoon meeting, and certainly not on a Friday, unless something bad had happened.

"What is it?" Taylor asked.

"Just watch."

P.T. flipped a switch on the wall, and a projection screen descended from the ceiling. He turned off the lights, then moved to his chair at the head of the table and stood behind it. He did all of this without talking, which did nothing to ease the suspense. By the time he turned on the projector, Trent was expecting something hideously grotesque, like news footage of burning children or emergency room video footage from *Celebrity Heart Transplants.*

So when the ashen, hawk-nosed image of Ronald Armsburger appeared on the screen, somber and standing behind a podium in some D.C. press room, Trent relaxed. This should be nothing new, another Q and A with bored, uninspired journalists. Nothing to get overly worked up about—except, of course, that P.T. already was.

"This interview took place last night," he said, then pushed play.

". . . ceived a report from ABC," one of the reporters was saying, "alleging that they had been forced by the FCC to drop two of their prospective reality shows after they had started production. Now NBC is considering canceling its sequel to *Confessions of a Bigamist* to avoid similar sanctions. Is this accurate?"

"It is indeed," Armsburger answered in a voice that sounded eerily like an angry Richard Dreyfuss.

"Would you care to comment on why the FCC is suddenly taking such an active role in the censorship of these shows?"

"I take issue with the word 'censorship,'" Armsburger said. "There is nothing illegal or immoral about our actions. We are a regulatory agency whose function is to maintain a minimum—and I stress the word 'minimum'—amount of integrity in the communications industries. Our actions were in accordance with federal guidelines, and considering the tenor of the shows we're talking about, I have no regrets. Next question."

A different reporter spoke. "How do you respond to critics who claim that recent FCC actions are a direct violation of the First Amendment?"

"Son," Armsburger said, gripping both sides of the podium, "the constitutional right to free speech is not absolute. If it were, children would be able to watch pornographic videos at all hours of the day, and I think you're going to have a hard time convincing anyone that the First Amendment should guarantee them that right. The shows we're talking about, the kind of *tele*vision we're talking about, falls into the same category."

"How do you—"

"I'm not finished yet," Armsburger said severely. "Companies like Dyson Associates and Nova Consulting are providing our television networks with shows of absolutely no redeemable value. It is their unstated mission to remove whatever vestiges of morality are left to our airwaves, and it is my job as chairman of the FCC to ensure that they do not succeed. The shows in question were removed because they violated certain indisputable standards of decency. They are a new kind of pornography and must be treated as such. Next question."

The image died. The projector was pulled into the ceiling, and P.T. turned on the lights.

"That . . . *man*," he said with a slight shudder, "is becoming a serious problem."

Trent wondered if his boss were angrier at Armsburger's actions or the fact that he'd named Dyson first.

"He's turning this into a crusade, people." The cigar was there, unlit and clenched in his fist like a dagger. "And now he's made it personal. I had hoped *Take It Off!* was an isolated case, I had *hoped* the man would know when to stop. But apparently, he does not."

"How many people heard that speech?" Tad asked.

"Nobody, it aired on C-SPAN. But that's not the point. The *point* is that those words were spoken at all."

"What do you want us to do?" Max asked.

P.T. put his cigar between his teeth and held it there. "Here's what I want, Max. You issue a press release explaining our position. Let me see it before you send it out. Taylor, Tad, you two come up with a"—again with the shuddering—"*nice* show."

Tad's hand flew to his mouth; Taylor gasped. "But *sir*," she said, "that's—"

"I *know* what it is!" P.T. roared. He managed to refrain from striking the table. "I know. I'm not pleased with this, either. But trust me, this is only a temporary solution until I can work out something more . . . permanent."

Trent bit his tongue. Permanent? What, like Jimmy Hoffa permanent? What exactly *had* P.T. done before he'd moved to L.A.?

"Todd," P.T. went on, "call NBC. Rachel, call ABC. Pitch them whatever you've got, don't worry about running anything by Trent this time."

"Yes sir," they said in unison. Todd seemed particularly pleased about that.

"And as for you, Trent," P.T. said, "you're going on *The Ann Vapid Show*."

Trent felt as though he'd just swallowed something sharp. "Me?"

"It's time for the world to get a glimpse of the people behind their favorite TV shows. You're going on Monday at four. There should be a few million people watching. And so will I, so"—he grinned around his cigar—"make me proud."

][

In the opinion of most of those in the industry, Ann Vapid hosted the most banal, inane, superficial show in the history of television—and for a medium that had given airtime to Anna Nicole Smith on more than one occasion, that was saying a lot. It was generally assumed that an hour's exposure to *The Ann Vapid Show* would lower your IQ by at least three points. Naturally, it was America's number one daytime talk show and had been since its first season.

Trent pulled into the studio's rear parking lot with a sullen screech of his tires. No part of him wanted to be there. Well, that wasn't entirely true. He was looking forward to meeting Jennifer Gerrigan, Ann's celebrity guest *du jour* and star of the summer blockbuster *Friends for Life*, for which she had reportedly received over ten million dollars and additional benefits that probably included her own island and a team of Sherpas. She'd been featured on at least one tabloid cover every week for the past two months, alternatively cast as a bulimic, psychic, transsexual, Fidel Castro's secret lover, the expectant mother of Elvis Presley's twin children, and a space alien. Personally, Trent was pulling for the Castro angle—the others were just so overdone.

He was met at the door by Ann Vapid's personal assistant, Tracy, a harried woman with a pursed mouth who looked as though she'd never had fun in her life. "You're late."

"Sorry. Traffic, you know."

"Yeah, well. You're not planning to wear *that*, are you?"

Trent looked at his clothes. "What's wrong with them?"

Tracy sighed. "Don't worry about it, I'm sure we have something that will do. Come on, they're waiting for you in the dressing room."

He followed her into the building, a rat's maze of dark hallways and cinder block walls. Stagehands and caterers were hurrying everywhere, opening and closing doors incessantly.

"We've pushed you back to seven minutes," Tracy said as they wove their way through the corridor. He'd originally been scheduled for ten. "You understand, of course."

"Of course," Trent said. What he understood was that his interview, which had the potential for turning into something vaguely intellectual, was nowhere near as important to the audience at home as finding out about Jennifer Gerrigan's secret fears. Not that Trent cared; he didn't want to be there in the first place, and he certainly didn't want to say what he was going to have to say. But P.T. was sure to be watching.

"What's the lineup?" he asked, already feeling the urge to wash his whorey mouth with soap.

"The mimes are up first, then you, then—"

"Wait. The . . . the *mimes*?"

"Yes. The mimes. They're fantastic. It's all the rage now, didn't you know? I'd stay away from them if I were you, though. They'd been slated for twenty minutes before you were added in, and they're *not* happy about that."

Indeed they weren't. For at that moment, as Tracy led Trent into the men's dressing room, he saw a gang of seven small men in whiteface, all dressed in black, every one of them sitting on an invisible chair and smoking an invisible cigarette. And as soon as they saw him, each one shot to his feet and glared at him, unblinking and utterly silent. It was eerie, the way they all scowled at him with the same expression, like Stephen King's *Children of the Corn*. Except, of course, that the only weapons these men carried were imaginary. Still, it didn't feel nice.

"Sorry, guys," Trent said awkwardly. "This wasn't my idea."

They said nothing, naturally. Slowly, each man returned to his invisible seat. One of them opened an invisible newspaper and began reading it. Another pulled out an imaginary fingernail clipper and pretended to trim his nails. All of them pointedly ignored him.

It was impossible to be sympathetic. There was a reason their art had died out decades ago. "Where's my chair?" he asked Tracy. "Preferably a real one."

He was taken to a dressing booth on the other side of the room, where a pair of women in black clothes and white aprons applied his makeup. It wasn't the first time Trent had been prepped for the camera, but he wasn't a seasoned professional either, and he had trouble keeping his forehead smooth and his eyes from blinking while they lathered him in enough cosmetics to satisfy Elizabeth Taylor. When they were finished he looked like he was made of plastic.

As soon as the makeup girls removed his bib, Tracy led him to the wings just out of sight of the studio audience. Ann Vapid was there, her long blonde hair twirled into the characteristic bun that guests occasionally tried to get her to let down. She was talking to Jennifer Gerrigan, every bit as beautiful in person as she was on screen. Numerous critics had compared her to Audrey Hepburn, though most conceded that the star of *My Fair Lady* would probably never have agreed to the kind of lesbian shower scene that *Friends for Life* had required. But maybe that was because no one had ever asked her.

"Ann," Tracy said as she led Trent to the two women, "this is Trent."

"Trent!" Ann held her arms out as if she was planning to hug him. "Trent, *dar*ling, so good to see you."

"The pleasure's mine," he said. And, as long as they were lying . . . "I'm really a big fan of the show."

"Oh, you're *too* sweet to say so. How's P.T. doing? I haven't seen him in *ages*."

That was news. "I didn't realize you two knew each other."

"Are you kidding? He and I go *way* back, I can't *tell* you how many times he's helped me out."

Which explained why she'd been so accommodating about this interview. "He's doing well. Except for Armsburger, of course."

"Of course." Ann nodded sympathetically. "That man, *honestly*. Did you know he came after *my* show once? It's true, he did, and accused me of indecency. Me, of all people!"

"The nerve of some people," Trent said with a somber shake of his head. It was almost fun, making up this much bullshit.

Jennifer Gerrigan coughed. It sounded like a legitimate cough, not the can't-you-see-I'm-standing-right-here kind, but it had the same effect.

"Oh, I'm *so* rude. Jennifer, this is Trent Tucker. Trent, Jennifer Gerrigan."

"Hi," she said in that breathy voice of hers. She extended her hand.

"It's a pleasure," he said, much more sincerely this time. "I'm a big fan."

"Thank you."

"Jennifer," Ann said, "Trent's the vice president of Nova Consulting. They—"

"I know what they do."

"Ms. Vapid." A tall black man wearing a headset came up. "We're on in five."

"Of course," she said. He left, and she turned to her two guests. "No rest for the weary, is there?" An indulgent laugh. "If either of you need *any*thing, Tracy will take care of you. Bronson, where are my mimes?" She hurried away, calling to a dozen different people for a dozen different things.

Which left Trent to stand alone next to the biggest movie star in America.

"So," he began lamely, "how do you know what I do?"

"Doesn't everybody?" She laughed. "Seriously, though, I'm a *big* fan of your work. A big fan. Nova's the company that came up with *Last Man Standing*, right? Was that your idea?"

"It was a team effort. I did help, though."

"*God*, I can't *tell* you how much I love that show. Do you know when Alan was voted off I actually cried?"

Cried? Over a guy nicknamed the Barbarian? "You watch the show?"

"I don't know what I'd do with*out* it. I know I'm a . . . 'big movie star' and all, but really I'm no different from other people."

Too bad. He was hoping she was.

"Say." She started nibbling on the corner of her bottom lip. It was an odd gesture, more embarrassed than erotic. She looked like a teenage girl waiting backstage at a Britney Spears concert. "Do you think there's any way you could get me in touch with him?"

"Who, Alan?"

Jennifer nodded. "I'd . . . really like to meet him. He's *so* . . . mmm."

Well, Trent thought, that did it. If being on a reality show meant having beautiful, bi-curious actresses dying to meet you, then he was going to cast himself on the next one they ran. "I'll see what I can do."

][

"Hello everyone!" Ann said above the thundering roar of studio applause. "And welcome back to *The Ann Vapid Show*! I'm Ann Vapid, and let me just say—*wow*. Wasn't *that* something? I don't know about you, but I think that's the most fun I've ever had. Well, *al*most." She put a scandalous hand to her mouth; the audience hooted.

Trent sat in the couch across from hers and tried to seem appropriately interested. He looked at the studio audience—two hundred starstruck people probably wondering who the hell he was—and couldn't decide if he'd look better with his mouth closed or slightly open. Not like it mattered. It wasn't as though he was going to leave the show with his dignity intact anyway.

"*Now*," Ann said, and the audience quieted down, "our next guest, as you may have guessed, is not our normal visitor. But he is an old and dear friend, and I think you'll be interested in what he has to say. Please welcome the vice president of Nova Consulting, Trent Tucker."

The audience reacted as expected, with polite but unenthusiastic applause. He knew what they were thinking. *You mean he's not a moo-vie star? Why waste my time for this shee-it?* He understood. He was thinking the same thing.

"So," Ann said, leaning toward her guest, "*Trent*, what exactly do you do?"

"Well, Ann, we work with the country's major television networks to come up with successful shows."

"What kind of shows?"

"Reality TV, mostly."

Ann turned to her audience. "Did you hear that? And you thought I was giving you a *dud*." She smiled at their laughter. "Let's see if I can remember some of the shows you're responsible for. *Gangland Romance*, *Julie's Surprise*, *I Think My Brother's Gay*, and of course, who could forget, *Last Man Standing*!" There was a collective gasp from the audience at that one, an electric, almost fanatical sound. "Isn't that right?"

Trent smiled in order to keep himself from wincing. "That's right, Ann."

"I just can't *tell* you how much I love *Last Man Standing*, oh my *God* it's so good. Don't you all agree?"

The audience cheered.

Trent gave his new fans a small wave. "We've . . . we've been very pleased with its success."

"Have you met any of the contestants?"

"All of them, actually."

"Well, I'm sure we're all *dying* to hear what you have to tell us, aren't we? *But*," she added with a wagging finger to her audience, "we're going to have to wait for *just* a little bit. First, I have a couple questions."

"Shoot."

"Now I know everybody *here* likes Reality Television, don't we? But it does have its critics. Some people think it's immoral, others think it's setting a bad example for our children, and so on and so on. *My* question is, what would you say to someone who thinks you're helping to create a harmful product?"

"You make it sound like we're making assault rifles," Trent said with a smile. He could feel the makeup on his face like a weight, eager to crack under too much stress. "We're talking about television here, not toxic waste."

Ann slapped playfully at his wrist. "I know *that*."

"But seriously, Ann,"—and here it came, the intellectual equivalent of selling his body to pay for heroin—"this is something that all entertainment industries have had to deal with. Movies, music, television, you name it. We have to come to terms with the fact that times change. Fifty years ago people thought rock music would bring about the downfall of America, which didn't happen. It did change the way we dress, but it didn't turn us into Communists. This is something that always happens whenever a new art form enters the mainstream."

"Uh-huh," Ann said. She said it slowly, like she was still trying to figure out what he'd said.

Too many big words, Trent told himself. Remember who you're talking to.

"So," Ann said, "you don't think you're corrupting the youth of America?"

"Of course not." There, he'd said it. That wasn't so bad. Certainly no worse than a new mother having her baby come out sideways. "It's important for people to realize that we don't determine what shows make it on the air. The people at home determine that. If they don't like a show, they have the option of not watching it. It's as simple as that. The reason Reality TV is so successful is that people want to watch it."

"Do we *ever*!" Ann said. "Oh, I just can't get *enough* of it. Still, I can see how some people think that some of those shows are a little over the top."

"Maybe so. But there are more than five hundred channels to choose from."

"Very true. Very true. So, what's next for Reality TV? We've seen survival shows, dating shows, cosmetic shows, home improvement shows, I can't even re*member* all of them. So tell us, Trent, what do you have in store for us next? Or is that a *big* secret?"

"I'll tell you," Trent said, "if you'll let your hair down."

"Oh, you are *bad*," Ann said. Then she gave him a curious look, turned toward the audience, and reached for the hairsticks holding her hair in place.

The crowd's reaction was immediate. A chorus of hooting and howling rose to an almost deafening pitch, like monkeys at the zoo simultaneously screeching at the wind. The women especially were in an absolute frenzy, and when Ann's hair fell in a golden cascade to her waist, Trent actually thought some of them might rip their chairs out of the floor in their fervor.

For a full two minutes the entire audience was transformed into something incomprehensible. Trent watched, fascinated. This was the true secret of the media, the ability to show people things they thought they weren't supposed to see. Everyone was a peeping Tom, glancing surreptitiously through the neighbor's windows when nobody else was around, peeking into the shopping carts of the others in line at the grocery store, devouring tabloids to learn a shred of private information about celebrities they'd never meet. And Reality TV, with its host of invasive cameras and 'candid' interviews and endless stream of sordid details, fed that desire like gasoline on a flame.

Slowly, and with practiced dexterity, Ann returned her hair to its original position. She was smiling slyly, not at Trent but at herself, and he knew why. Because now she *had* them. These people were hers now; they'd go to work tomorrow and tell everyone how they'd *been there* for the great unveiling. These people would always watch her show now, until the Botox injections stopped working and the network forced her desiccated husk into retirement.

"*So*," she said, and her face adopted a serene expression, "tell us what we have to look forward to."

"I think it's going to be a bit anticlimactic now," Trent said, and the audience laughed, perhaps embarrassed by their overzealousness. And perhaps not.

"Well," he said, "let's see. We've got a sequel lined up for *Last Man Standing*, this time with women." He paused while the crowd applauded. "In fact, next season you should see a host of sequels for all your favorite shows."

There. That should satisfy P.T. But Trent couldn't stop there. Ann had given him an unexpected opportunity, and if he didn't take it he'd never forgive himself.

"And we're also looking in a new direction. As it stands right now, Reality TV provides plenty of entertainment, but not a great deal of information. What we'd like to do is come up with some reality shows that raise public awareness about important issues. Like cancer research. Now that's just an example, but it is my hope that by next season, we have some shows on the market that provide the same caliber of entertainment while teaching viewers a little more about this amazing world we all live in."

When he was done he allowed himself a brief moment of congratulations. He'd said what he needed to without saying anything that P.T. could criticize.

"Well," Ann said, "*I* think that sounds marvelous. *Now*,"—she leaned forward—"tell us what all those *Last Man Standing* men are *really* like."

After his interview, Trent was taken back to the dressing room. The mimes were already gone, which was nice. Although they could have been in the parking lot, waiting for him to come out so they could give him the imaginary beating of his life.

He changed into his own clothes and was heading out the door when his cell phone rang—a number he didn't recognize. "Hello?"

"Trent. It's P.T."

Here was the moment of truth. He'd kind of been hoping for that moment to happen later, when he'd had time to make out a will. "I assume you were watching the show. What did—"

"I need you back at the office. *Now*."

"What's going—" But there was no point. P.T. had already hung up.

Trent got in his car and started the engine. Well, that answered that. Trent had stuck his neck out, and P.T. was ready to chop it off. Or sever it slowly with a rusty butter knife. Either way, it wasn't going to be pretty.

He lit a cigarette. Maybe he should just drive his Jaguar off a bridge and save P.T. the trouble. It would mean less for his boss to clean up. Really, he thought as he pulled into traffic, it was the only considerate thing to do.

[CHAPTER FOURTEEN]

An empty office building can be a rather menacing place. Cubicle walls and copy machines assume an almost sinister appearance, dormant demons ready to pounce at any moment. The sound of your feet on the carpet is suddenly too coarse and loud, the whisper of your breathing becomes a harsh tattoo. Overhead, the all-night security lights seem to create more darkness than light, and who knows what unspeakable thing might be waiting in the shadows. Yes, an empty office building can be an intimidating place.

Of course, most places are intimidating when you think someone is about to tear you a new asshole.

Trent opened the door to P.T.'s office and stepped inside. "I'm here, sir." He decided against closing the door behind him. If things did go badly, he wanted as few obstacles as possible between himself and the exit.

P.T. was sitting at his desk, one hand on his chin, the other holding an unlit cigar. The only light in the room came from the two metal lamps on either end of P.T.'s massive steel desk. He looked up when Trent spoke, looked directly at him, but said nothing.

"Look, if this is about the interview, I—"

"It's not about the interview," P.T. said. "Have a seat."

Now Trent was thoroughly confused. He sat down, for once not thinking to complain about the size of the chair, and waited.

He didn't have to wait long. "I want you to see this."

"What is it?"

"Just read it," P.T. said. He slid two sheets of paper across his desk.

Trent was forced to stand up in order to reach them, and once he did he decided to stay standing. He hated reading in front of people; he always felt he was taking too long. But it didn't take him long to figure out what it was.

"*Lives in the Balance*. This is a show proposal."

P.T. nodded.

"From Dyson Associates," Trent added.

P.T. nodded again.

"How'd you get this?"

"Never mind *that*. Just read it."

Trent obeyed, curious enough that he would have done so anyway. He had no idea why P.T. was so worked up over a show proposal, or why this couldn't have waited until tomorrow.

By the time he had read the first page, though, it was completely clear.

"This is . . ."

". . . the same show you pitched to me three weeks ago. Medical reality show, cancer patients, endless possibilities, the whole thing." P.T. lit his cigar and took a long, slow inhale. "Anything you care to tell me?"

Suddenly Trent wanted to be very, very far away. It was not uncommon for companies to develop similar ideas for television shows, especially reality dating, but this was different. The resemblance here was uncanny. It was as though Dyson had read Trent's mind.

"Did you go to Dyson with this?"

All the blood in Trent's body froze. "No! No, sir, I—"

P.T. slammed his hand on his desk and shot to his feet. "Then *how* do you explain that!"

"I can't, sir. It's . . . listen, I know this is similar to—"

"It's not *similar*, Trent, it's the same goddamn *show*!"

Trent took an involuntary step backwards. "Look, I've never talked to Dyson in my life, I swear. Check my phone records if you want."

"I already have," P.T. said. "But you also have a cell phone."

He'd already checked his *phone* calls? "Listen, sir, why would I give anything to Dyson? What good would that do me?"

"That," P.T. said more calmly, "is the one thing I couldn't figure out." He sat down and stared blankly at the papers he'd handed Trent. "Has your apartment been broken into recently?"

"No."

"What about your car?"

"No. Besides, it wouldn't matter. I didn't write anything down."

That stopped P.T. for a moment. He put the cigar between his teeth and chewed on the tip. "Did you tell anyone else about this idea of yours?"

Trent paused. He had told Max. But there was no way Max had leaked anything to Dyson. "No, sir. Nobody but you."

P.T. nodded, but didn't say anything. He looked more like a general now than he ever had, the way MacArthur might have looked just before the landing at the Port of Inchon. It did nothing to lighten Trent's mood.

"I'm not sure what the real problem is, sir. You said my idea wouldn't fly anyway, I don't see why it would be different for Dyson."

"That's not the issue," P.T. said. "Have a seat."

As soon as Trent sat down, P.T. stood up. With unnerving deliberation, he walked around the side of his desk. In a few moments he was behind Trent, pacing back and forth, his footsteps slow and steady on the thin carpet. There was no comfortable way for Trent to face his boss, so he stared at the man's dim reflection in the window.

"I want to talk to you about loyalty," P.T. said. "You know what loyalty is, don't you?"

Trent knew better than to answer that.

"*Loy*alty is the most important element of any business. Without loyalty, there can be no trust. Without loyalty, there can be no . . . progress. Without loyalty, Trent, there can be no business."

"Sir, I—"

"How*ever*, loyalty is not something that is freely given. Loyalty must be earned. If I want my employees to be loyal, I need to give them a reason to be. That's the way it works. That's the way it *should* work. So the first thing we should be asking ourselves is, have I earned it? So let me ask you, have I?"

Trent swallowed. "Y-yes, sir."

"Do I pay you well enough?"

"Yes, sir."

"Do I let you leave early when you need to take care of personal matters?"

"Yes, sir."

"Haven't I rewarded you for your ideas?"

"Yes, sir."

"Have I asked you to do anything you haven't wanted to do?"

Now was not the time to get into a philosophical debate. "No, sir."

"All right. Then I believe I have *earned* your loyalty. So now the question is, have you given it to me?"

Suddenly P.T.'s hands were on Trent's shoulders. Against his will, Trent flinched. In the window's reflection he could see his boss's face above his own, cigar wedged into the right corner of his mouth, smoke curling out of the left. If this was his boss's idea of creating a happy workplace environment, it was not working.

"So, Trent, have you?"

"Yes, sir."

"Did you take this idea of yours to Dyson?"

"No, sir. Why would I do that? What would it accomplish?"

"I don't know," P.T. said. "Maybe this one is particularly important to you. Maybe you wanted to see it on the air no matter what it took."

Trent shook his head, which felt awkward with P.T.'s hands on his neck. "I've had a dozen of my shows get a pilot. Besides, this isn't anything personal, right? Just business."

"Business is never personal," P.T. said. "But when someone is disloyal, it's important to address that problem immediately."

"I've already *told* you," Trent said, with far more force than he thought he could muster. "I didn't go to Dyson!" He stood up and turned around, glad to have his boss's hands off his neck. "Don't you trust me? Isn't that an important part of business too, trust? And if you can't trust your vice president, then who *can* you trust?"

There was steel in P.T.'s eyes; he obviously did not like being talked to defiantly like that. But almost immediately it disappeared, replaced by a look that might almost have been respectful.

"You didn't go to Dyson?"

"No," Trent said firmly.

"And you have no idea how he came up with this idea?"

"Not at all."

It was the same thing Trent had been saying for the past ten minutes, but for some reason, this time it seemed to work. P.T. gave him a curt nod, then returned to his chair. He sat down, leaving Trent standing, and set his cigar in the ashtray.

"I don't know how many ways I can say it, Trent, but this business of ours, television? It's not a business, it's a war. And in a war, you have to choose sides. And if you're not with me, you're against me."

The war metaphor was getting awfully old. "Look, if you find out I went to Dyson with this idea, you can shoot me yourself."

"I'll remember you said that," P.T. said. Then he smiled. "You're free to go. I hope this conversation hasn't spoiled your evening. I'll see you tomorrow."

][

The entire way back to his apartment, Trent was thinking about his cell phone. It was sitting in his pocket, tugging at him with the gravity of a neutron star. He thought about reaching for it a dozen times, and each time he restrained himself—and checked the rearview mirror to see who might be following.

How had Dyson come up with that idea? There was no way he could have known, unless he'd managed to put listening devices in Nova's offices. He wondered if P.T. had tried to do the same at Dyson's office. Certainly the idea had crossed the General's mind.

Of course, there was one other way Dyson might have learned of Trent's idea.

At the next stoplight Trent took out his phone and dialed. On the second ring, the call connected.

"Hello?"

"Max. It's Trent."

"What's up, pal? Saw your interview with—"

"We can talk about that later. Did you tell anyone else about my idea?"

"What are you talking about?"

"My show idea, the medical reality show."

"The one with the cancer patients?" Max laughed. "Hell, pal, why would I tell anyone about that?"

"I don't know. Did you?"

"No. I told you, that idea's a complete piece of shit."

Trent decided not to remind Max that he had once tried to sell P.T. on a show called *Amateur Tattoo Artist*. "You're sure you didn't tell anyone?"

"No, I didn't. What's going on?"

He could tell Max was telling the truth. "Nothing. I'll talk to you tomorrow."

"Look, pal, if—"

Trent hung up. Again he looked in the rearview mirror, but nobody seemed to be following him. Not that he'd have been able to tell.

Well, back to square one. How had Dyson come up with that idea? It was possible that the whole thing was a coincidence, although that seemed unlikely. How had he done it? And what was his motivation for doing so?

There was only one way to find out.

At the next light, Trent pulled out the card he'd kept in his wallet for the past month. The paper had grown warm and soft, its edges bent and frayed, but the writing was still quite legible:

SIMON PETERSEN
VICE PRESIDENT, ACQUISITIONS
DYSON ASSOCIATES
(931) 227-1019

It was the only way. Slowly, and with covert glances out each of his windows, Trent dialed. The ringing seemed abnormally loud.

Suddenly there was a connection. "This is Simon."

"Mr. Petersen. Trent Tucker."

"Trent!" The pleasure in the man's voice was evident. "Excellent. We'd just about given up on you."

"I need to meet with Dyson."

"Well, I can assure you, Mr. Dyson is quite anxious to meet with you."

"I'm sure he is," Trent said, not knowing exactly what he meant by that. "When's good?"

"How about right now?"

"Now?"

"Sure. Mr. Dyson is in his office now. I'll tell him you're coming. You *do* know how to get here, don't you?"

Trent looked in his rearview mirror. There wasn't a car behind him. "I'll be there in fifteen minutes," he said, then hung up.

As soon as the light turned green he took a hard right across two empty lanes onto Palisades Beach Road. The sound of his tires screeching on the pavement was sufficiently portentous. As he drove, he thought perhaps he should have waited until tomorrow. That way he could have swung by his insurance company and added a death and dismemberment clause to his life insurance policy, just in case P.T. ever found out.

He looked again in the rearview mirror. Jesus Christ. What was he getting himself into now?

[CHAPTER FIFTEEN]

"It's good to see you again. Please, come in."

Trent followed Petersen inside. He'd parked in the rear lot, which could only be accessed by a small alleyway. Except for the driver of the street sweeper, nobody would know he was there. Unless, of course, he really had been followed.

"I was afraid I'd frightened you off after our first meeting," Petersen said. "I hope you've been well in the meantime."

"Fine, thanks." He was looking at the offices. They had walls, *real* walls that went all the way up to the ceiling. They'd been painted, too, each office a different color. Burnished gold, vermilion, cinnamon, Georgia peach, Tuscan red—warm colors. Inviting colors, the kind that could make you actually want to go to work.

"Looks nice."

"We try. This way."

Petersen led Trent around a corner, past a row of plants—which weren't made of plastic—and a stone cherub that served as a drinking fountain.

"I hope the water comes out of his mouth."

"Everybody asks that. It does. You can try it if you like."

"That's all right." Tad would have loved it, though. Or been disappointed, he couldn't tell.

At the end of the hall, Petersen opened a door and gestured Trent inside. It was a waiting room, small but tastefully furnished, with appropriately boring magazines for people to read while they sat and waited. Nova didn't have a waiting room. In fact, he couldn't remember the last time a client had come to their office.

"Do people actually come here?"

"All the time. Mr. Dyson prefers doing things face to face. It's a bit antiquated, perhaps, but Mr. Dyson feels it's best for everyone. His office is on the other side." He paused, and added: "I hope I was right in approaching you." Then he closed the door slowly behind him, leaving Trent alone in Dyson's waiting room.

For an instant, Trent had an urge to run. He could have done it; Petersen wouldn't have stopped him. But he decided to stay. He'd already come this far, and he was more than a little curious about his boss's biggest competitor—and the generator of an idea so uncannily similar to his own. So, with a deep breath, Trent opened the far door and stepped inside.

The room he entered was the same size as P.T's, but there the resemblance ceased. The walls were paneled mahogany, dark and rich in the dim lamplight. An overstuffed leather couch and two matching chairs were set around a low glass table, a scene that would have fit just as well in an art-house coffeeshop as a presidential suite. Framed pictures hung on the wall, including a large reproduction of *Starry Night*, which somehow didn't seem out of place. Along the back wall, near windows that did not face a brick wall, sat Dyson's desk, large and wooden and more inviting than P.T.'s, if only because you didn't run the risk of impaling yourself on its edges. And standing next to that desk was Stewart Dyson himself.

"Trent," he said warmly, as though they'd known each other a long time. "I'm glad to finally meet you."

He crossed the room and took Trent's hand. Dyson was smaller than Trent had expected, thinner and a little older than P.T. He looked a bit like Ben Kingsley in *Schindler's List*, kind and somehow sad.

"You don't look like you slaughter children for fun," Trent said.

"Is that what P.T.'s told you?" Dyson smiled. "Well, that doesn't surprise me. He's been like that since Vietnam."

"You knew him in Vietnam?"

"The two of us were in the same battalion. We weren't together very often, but I learned enough about him to know what he's like. I think he wishes the war had never ended." He moved to a wet bar recessed into the wall near the door. "So now he's chosen a different war to fight. Please, have a seat."

Trent sat down in one of the chairs, which of course was the perfect height. It was nice not to have his knees pressed against his lungs.

Dyson poured himself a glass of scotch and set it on a glass tray. "Would you like anything? Wine, bourbon?"

"I'm fine, thanks." Now that was really almost too much. Normal chairs, a boss who offered people drinks from his own collection—what was going on here? Was he being filmed?

"You know," Dyson said as he sat down on the couch opposite Trent, "if your boss finds out you're here, there's going to be some trouble."

"Don't remind me."

"And yet you came anyway." There was a pause. "I have to confess, when Simon told me he'd talked with you, I thought he'd lost his mind. In fact I almost fired him for it. I thought he'd moved too soon. But here you are. Congratulations on your promotion, by the way."

"Thanks." This was all *way* too cordial. He may as well have been drinking tea with Margaret Thatcher. "Look, I came because there are a few things I need to know. Like what Petersen was doing at Lynette's house in the first place."

"Ordinary surveillance. Checking up on the competition. P.T. does the same with our people, I imagine. I'm surprised you aren't a part of it, to be honest."

"Don't you think it's a bit risky to show up uninvited to someone's party?"

"Would you have noticed him if he hadn't come up to you?"

Good point. "I guess not."

"The best kind of reconnaissance is done in the open," Dyson said. "Something I learned a lifetime ago."

"All right, next one. Your latest show idea. How did you get it?"

"Petersen gave it to me."

"Then how did *he* get it?"

Dyson sipped his scotch. "I assume he thought of it."

"So it's just a coincidence?"

"Maybe I don't understand what you're asking."

"That idea," Trent said. "*Lives in a Palace* or whatever it's called. The medical reality show, raising awareness and all. That's my idea. I pitched it to P.T. a few weeks ago."

"Is that right?" Dyson's face broke into a slow, radiant smile. It was eerie, in a way. The only time he'd seen his own boss look that excited was when Ronald Armsburger had been admitted to the hospital for chest pains.

"Where'd he get it?" Trent pressed.

"I can assure you," Dyson said, still smiling, "we didn't steal it. I'd tell you if we did, I have no reason to lie to you. But I must say, this is exceedingly good news."

"*What* is? Why did your vice president tell me to give you a call? And why did I *do* it?"

"I think you know the answer to that."

Trent leaned forward. "What do you want with me?"

"Ah." Dyson finished his drink and stood up. "The answer to *that* is going to take some time." He returned to his liquor cabinet. "Are you sure you don't want something to drink?"

"No, thanks."

"Suit yourself." Dyson poured himself another scotch but did not return to his seat. Instead he stood there, statuesque, looking at the floor in an effective pose of thoughtful meditation.

Trent dug in and waited.

"Let me tell you a little about myself," Dyson said eventually. "I've been in this business a long time. Longer than you've been alive, I imagine. After Vietnam, the country was begging to move into a new era. The lifestyle of my parents' generation, their quaint morality, their inability to tolerate other forms of government or ways of life, had failed them. It failed *us*, Trent, it gave us a world where nothing made sense, where people died for no reason. We were sent to the slaughter because our parents couldn't *talk* with the Vietnamese, because they feared what was different. And I saw television as the best way to counteract the damage they'd done."

This was a bit more in-depth than Trent had expected. Still, he didn't think about interrupting.

"I wanted to push every envelope," Dyson said. "All the things you're not supposed to talk about, all the things you're not supposed to do in polite society, I worked to put on the air. I wanted to push every moral conservative in America back into their caves, I wanted all the Jimmy Swaggerts and Pat Robertsons of the world to feel the persecution they'd doled out on my generation. I was going to change the world, Trent. *I* was going to make everything right."

He returned to his chair then, sitting down with a quiet rush that betrayed his intensity. "For twenty years I gave myself to this business, and for twenty years I felt as though I was beating against a brick wall. Nothing I did seemed to work, nothing was good enough. I can't remember how many times I thought about giving up. You have no idea what it's like to feel as though you've wasted your life on an unreachable dream. Or maybe you do."

Trent leaned back and didn't reply

"By the time the nineties came around," Dyson continued, "I had all but given up. I thought America was lost. We were never going to get past our Puritan heritage. People weren't ready to break down their barriers and actually *talk* with each other. I thought I'd wasted my life. And then, in '92, MTV came up with *The Real World.*"

Dyson set his drink down. "You have no idea what a revelation that was. Seven people, all of different backgrounds, all with different ideas, together in the same apartment? Forced to deal with each other's problems, forced to *talk* about life and love and politics? For the *first* time, Trent, for the first time, television had gotten inside our heads. All the things you're not supposed to talk about, all the sordid details and ugly squabbles of our everyday lives were suddenly out there for millions of people to see. It was revolutionary, absolutely revolutionary—and wildly popular. I thought that if only we'd had something like this when I was your age, maybe we'd never have gone to Vietnam in the first place."

"Don't you think you're exaggerating just a little?"

"You have to appreciate how I felt then. Back then I thought reality television was the answer to all our problems. Now," he sighed, "now I feel differently."

"Meaning?"

"First things first. After *The Real World* aired, I threw myself completely into the Reality market. Finally, I thought, here is a way to shake America out of its cocoon. We came up with thirteen show ideas in that first year, each one more groundbreaking than the last. Then other companies picked up on the model, and the competition forced us to even greater heights. When *Temple of Lust* came out I thought it would ultimately lead to the end of sexual discrimination."

Trent had to laugh at that one. "I think you missed the mark on that one. The end of marriage, maybe."

"Yes, well, you're never too old to be naïve," Dyson said. "You'd do well to remember that."

"I'm still not sure what any of this has to do with me."

"I'm getting to that. You sure you don't need anything to drink?"

Trent shook his head, and Dyson rose to pour himself another glass. Outside, a soft rain began to fall against the windows. In the momentary silence, Trent could hear the drops hit the roof.

"For the past decade," Dyson said, "I've helped build Reality Television into a global industry. I've watched it dominate every major demographic in this country, and for the past decade I've been waiting for the revolution to come. A freer America, a more united America. And do you know what I've finally come to realize?"

Dyson sat back down again, his eyes more soulful and sad than before. His bald head reflected dimly the light from above, and it gave him the aspect of a cleric. Or a martyr.

"The revolution I've been waiting for is never going to happen."

Trent had trouble meeting Dyson's gaze. He felt as if he were observing someone's Catholic confession, pretending to be a priest while some poor sinner related the details of his workplace affair. "Maybe it's too early to—"

"Don't play devil's advocate. The fact that you're here means you know better than that. It's never going to come, at least not this way. Look at what we've done! These shows aren't dealing with reality. They're caricatures. We're a tabloid, Trent. We're a weekend gossip column. We take real people and make them into something to deride, something for people at home to make fun of and feel superior to. That doesn't breed unity."

"So what exactly are you saying?"

"I'm saying, Trent, that when I look back at what I've helped to create, I realize that I've wasted my life."

Ouch. That had to suck. At least Trent could take comfort in the fact that he'd only wasted his twenties. "I'm sure—"

"Don't," Dyson said. "I know what I know. I've created a nation of voyeurs, a nation of people who know more about characters on television than the world they live in."

"You can't take *all* the credit for that. What about sports shows? Or soap operas, for Christ's sake."

"I'm not responsible for them. And what they do, or have done, doesn't excuse my part in it. Reality Television takes the worst elements of human behavior—selfishness, greed, betrayal, lust—and turns them into models to follow. We're teaching our children to regard one another as enemies, we're . . ." He cut himself off and looked out the window.

Trent didn't say anything. So, Stewart Dyson was having a crisis of conscience. That wasn't a shock; it was fairly common in every facet of the entertainment industry, except hip hop. Most people dealt with it by taking a couple of mistresses or becoming alcoholics; Dyson obviously preferred the latter. Still, that didn't explain why Dyson had wanted to talk to him, or where all this was going to lead.

"I have a grandchild," Dyson said. "Did you know that?"

"No, I didn't."

"She was born a week ago. Her name's Isabella." For a moment, as he said her name, Dyson's eyes sparkled. But it disappeared quickly. "I don't want her to have to live in the world we've created."

"I can understand that. That's why I always wear a condom."

Dyson smiled. "It's time for us to fix the mess we've made of things. It's gone too far. We forgot that everything should be in moderation, and now our world, without any restrictions at all, is no better than the repressive world we were fighting against."

"So what are you saying? You want to get rid of Reality TV?"

"Ultimately, yes."

Trent shook his head. "Can't happen. Don't get me wrong, I'd love to see it all burn. But it's too ingrained now, it's too much a part of things. The Home and Garden channel has reality shows, for God's sake. You can't get rid of it any more than we can get rid of NASCAR, much as I'd like to."

"If there is a God," Dyson said, "there will come a day when our children look back on Reality Television and wonder what on Earth we were thinking. Like my daughter's 1987 haircut. I could show you some pictures if you'd like."

Trent declined. He remembered the bangs, those tidal waves of hair frozen in place with enough CFC's to choke a rain forest. "So what exactly is it that you want to do?"

"I want to fix things. We may have to live with our mistake, but that doesn't mean we can't elevate it to something a little more worthy of attention. That's why I'm pushing *Lives in the Balance*, because I think it could matter. But I can't do this alone. Which brings us to the reason that you're here."

"Wait." Trent cleared his throat. "You're not going to ask me to come work for you, are you?"

"The thought had crossed my mind."

Trent started shaking his head and found that he couldn't stop. "I, I can't do that, I . . . look, it's a great thought but I, no, I can't."

"I understand."

"No, I don't think you do. If P.T. found out—which he would, he'd have to—I don't think I'd make it out the front door."

"Trust me," Dyson said. "I understand that perfectly well. It must be a lovely place to work. Has he given you an ulcer yet?"

"I don't know. A few, probably."

"Well, I'm not going to ask you to leave Nova. But I am hoping that we can still work together."

"What do you mean? You want me to spy on my boss?" *That* wasn't going to work. Everything he knew about surveillance he'd learned from the movies, and most of the time those scenes ended in a gunfight between two cops and an entire gang of Yakuza. Not exactly what Trent had in mind.

"No spying," Dyson promised. "He's not a complicated man to read. His goals are a bit more . . . imperialistic than mine, so I already know what kind of shows P.T. is going to promote. No, what we need is to fight this war on two fronts. That's the only way to win."

"There's nothing I can do," Trent said. "I've already thrown this idea at P.T., he said it was the worst thing he ever heard. If it doesn't have midgets beating each other over the head with dead fish, he's not going to let me pitch it."

"Then start smaller. I'm not asking for a miracle. I realize that what I'm talking about is going to take some time. All I want is for you to try. The worst he can do is fire you, and if that happens, you can come work for me."

"That's not the worst he can do."

Dyson ignored him. "But if you're able to make even a small impression, that's a start. As long as we keep pushing, we'll eventually be able to make the kinds of shows we should have been making all along."

Despite his rather considerable fear of what would happen if P.T. ever found out what he was doing, Trent couldn't help being a little excited. Who'd have thought a CEO could be an idealist? Especially one whose company had once pushed a show called *Payback, Bitch!*

"So," Trent said, "all you want me to do is *try*?"

"All I want you to do is try. Which you're going to do anyway, that's why you pitched your idea—*our* idea—to P.T. But now you know you have an ally. And so do I."

"I can't promise anything."

"I'm not asking you to. But you're in a good position to make things happen. And if you think of something that P.T. shoots down, send it to me. Perhaps we'll be able to use it."

"If he finds out I'm talking to you . . ."

"He's not going to find out," Dyson assured him. He reached into his suit pocket and pulled out a card. "Here. If you need to get in touch with me, use this number. It's a Chinese diner I use as a cover. If anyone's tracing your calls, which wouldn't surprise me, they'll think you're ordering dinner."

Dyson stood; it was clear their interview was at an end. He led Trent to the door and opened it for him. Petersen, who had been sitting in the waiting room, got to his feet.

"I'm glad we had this chance to talk," Dyson said. He shook Trent's hand. "I feel like there may be some hope for us."

"If you call me, use my cell number, not the office line."

"I know. We'll be in touch. Petersen will show you out."

Trent followed Petersen through the office to the rear door, where his car was waiting. The alley was empty and completely silent except for the soft patter of falling rain. So he hadn't been followed. That was a relief. There'd be no horse's head in his bed tomorrow morning.

"Drive safely," Petersen said. "I trust we'll meet again." He closed the door on that note, and Trent was left alone in the parking lot.

Nice, Trent thought as he walked to his car. Apparently it was the fashion at Dyson Associates to end conversations on a cryptic note. Oh, well. Better that than some other things. Trent started his car and put it in reverse.

The whole evening had taken on a rather surreal quality. Had he really just met with his boss's archenemy? Had he really agreed to *help* the man? Did either of them actually think they could fix anything?

Just then his phone rang. The sound made his heart skip. What did it mean? Had someone been watching? But when he saw the number, he relaxed. "Hi, Rachel. I'm glad it's you." Instead of some guy named Vinnie.

"Where have you been?"

"Sorry, I had my phone off."

"What have you been up to?"

She sounded accusatory. Best to lie. "Nothing. I just had some things I needed to take care of."

"If those things include another woman, I'm going to hurt you."

At least some things hadn't changed. "You've got nothing to worry about. What are you doing right now?"

"Watching television."

"Anything good?"

"Not yet."

"Mind if I come over?"

There was a pause. "Sure. But you'd better hurry. *The Tonight Show*'s on in twenty-five minutes, and I don't want to miss it."

"Well, I'd hate to interrupt your television schedule."

"I'd hate that, too. They're interviewing Mitch Tanner, you know."

"I'll be there in five minutes."

"Hurry," she said, "or I'll start without you."

He hung up and pulled out of the alley. By the time he got there he'd only have twenty minutes. Not a problem. He'd worked with less plenty of times.

[CHAPTER SIXTEEN]

Trent drove to work the next day with more than a little hesitation. It was quite possible he was speeding toward his own doom, like some suicidal gazelle leaping into the jaws of a nearby tiger. By the time he arrived at the office, he'd already smoked half a pack of cigarettes. If this was to be his day of reckoning, then at least he'd enjoy himself while he could.

"*There* you are!" Lynette said as soon as he walked in. "Everyone's waiting for you."

"Waiting for me?" That couldn't be good. Waiting to do what? "What are you talking about?"

"In the conference room, silly." She looked as if she wanted to wag a disapproving finger at him.

"But it's Tuesday." Maybe he shouldn't have dismissed that impulse to buy himself some body armor.

"Don't ask me, Mr. Vice President. You're supposed to be the one who knows everything."

Then Trent remembered. Tad and Taylor were supposed to have come up with a nice show. Something family-friendly, something that might air on Nickelodeon or even Lifetime. They should have been ready yesterday, but both of them had begged for an extension.

Suddenly Trent stopped worrying that someone was going to throw a shuriken into his spine. What kind of show had they come up with? *Mr. Fuzzy's Petting Zoo*? *The Happy Fun Train*? Such endless possibilities. "Thanks, Lynette," he said, and went to the conference room.

And just in time. P.T. was mid-harangue, standing imperiously above the rest of them, his ubiquitous cigar in hand. Tad and Taylor looked as though someone had poured bleach into their laundry. Or as though they were about to get fired.

"I'd hate for you to be on time," P.T. said, scowling as Trent walked in. But he turned to Taylor and Tad. "Well, what do you have for me?"

"Um," Taylor said.

"Quit stalling."

"Now keep in mind," Tad said, "this is a very rough draft."

"What's the title?"

Tad cleared his throat. "Well, we were thinking, *The First Year.*"

"Or *Ultimate Responsibility*," Taylor added.

"The second one," P.T. said. "What's the pitch?"

Taylor turned to Tad. Her breasts didn't seem as perky this morning, Trent noticed. Maybe she'd forgotten to inflate them.

"Well," Tad said, his eyelashes fluttering and his fingers fully extended, "here goes. Now keep in mind you wanted a nice show, not a good one. We wouldn't have come up with this if you wanted a good one."

"Get on with it," P.T. said.

"So." Tad stared at the conference table. "We get this couple—young, married, not too much money—and have them adopt a kid. The kid will be five, six years old, big enough to yell and scream and so on. And the idea is to watch them deal with the"—Tad paused for a long sigh—"pressures of raising a child."

There was a short but profound silence. Trent chewed on the tips of his fingers. It was obvious that nobody liked the concept. The problem was, it wasn't terrible—not great, but certainly a hell of a lot better than some of the other horrors they'd come up with. *If this were Dyson's meeting room*, he thought, then stopped himself. There was no telling what he might inadvertently betray if he started thinking like that.

He settled on something safe. "We might be able to work with that."

"Are you kidding?" Max rocked back in his chair. "We may as well film some little girl playing with her dolls. 'Would you like some more tea, Mr. Wiggles?' Jesus Christ, are you kidding me?"

Taylor whirled on him. "*You* try coming up with a nice show! Do you know how *hard* that is?"

"Thankfully, I don't."

"This isn't getting us anywhere," Trent said. "We need a nice show, and this is a nice show. I say we give it a shot."

"Well spoken," P.T. said. "Except that this idea is an absolute piece of shit."

"What do you want from us?" Tad asked. "We can't—"

"It's not your fault," P.T. said, cutting Tad off before he could work himself into full hysterics. "It's Armsburger's fault. Every goddamn problem in this world is Armsburger's fault. That man is a cancer. And the only way to kill cancer is by killing a part of yourself along with it."

"So what are we going to do?" Todd asked.

"We're going to run with this," P.T. said. "We're going to take this to production, and we're going to take a loss on it. That's what we're going to do. And let me tell you one other thing. Every one of you is going to come up with a show like this."

"But sir—"

"Don't worry, Max, we're not going to pitch them. If we did that we'd be out of business, which of course is exactly what Armsburger wants. No, all I want is to have some more ideas like this on file so we can at least look like we're making an effort. It's all about appearances."

"But what about this one?" Tad asked.

"This one we're going to pitch," P.T. said. "This one will be our sacrificial lamb. But not like this. There has to be some bite to it."

Now was Trent's chance to start pushing. "I think we should run it like it is. It'll be great P.R., especially with the adoption angle. We'll be able to point to this show as evidence of our concern for—"

"That is *exactly* what I want to avoid," P.T. said. "Concern? This is television, Trent, not charity. I want to give Armsburger just enough to pacify him, nothing more."

"What if we stage an abduction?" Todd said. "Get a couple guys in ski masks to break in and steal the kid around week six?"

"You can't be serious," Trent said.

"It would give us a ratings spike," Rachel offered.

"Sure," Trent said. "In fact, let's just skip the kidnapping and have them kill the little shit. I say we have them throw him out a window. That'll *really* get people watching."

"Trent's right," P.T. said, "we can't do that for this show. But I like the idea, Todd, abductions are always a good sell. Like *Tropical Abduction*, right, Trent? Maybe we can work an abduction into another one. Work on it."

"How about there's a bully at school or something?" Taylor suggested.

"A *bully*?" Max leaned forward enough to look at her around Tad. "Jesus, what is this, an after-school special? *Full House*?"

"That show was huge," Rachel said.

"Ooh!" Tad raised his hand, then started talking anyway. "I know. We could find the kid's real mom and have her try to take him back!"

"A custody battle," P.T. said. He seemed to be chewing on the idea.

"It's already proven. *Child Custody Court TV* was an enormous success, especially with young mothers."

"Too derivative," Max said. "It'll look like we're running out of ideas."

"Not if we stay out of the courtroom," Tad countered. "If we film it from inside the house—both houses, once we get the real mother on the show—I think it'll work."

Trent looked at Tad as though he were some kind of monstrous, bloated ogre. "You're kidding, right? What about the *kid*, for Christ's sake? You're just going to—"

"Oh, *please*!" Tad said. "Don't pretend that you care about some random child's welfare."

"You were the one who came up with *Child Custody Court TV* in the first place," Todd reminded him.

It was a mistake, he wanted to say. Every idea I've ever turned into a television show has been a mistake. *Pregnant Hookers* was a mistake. *Who Wants to Marry My Rich, Dying Grandmother*? was a mistake. They all were. But nobody there would understand.

"A custody battle," P.T. said again. There was a pause. Then, the inevitable. "I like it. Good work, Tad. Taylor, you too, I'm sure you did something. The rest of you, come up with some nice shows we can put on the shelf. And Todd, let's see if we can work that child abduction into a *real* show."

Trent went back to his office with the heavy trudge of a prisoner returning to his cellblock after being gang-raped in the shower. Well, all right, so maybe things weren't *that* bad, but they seemed like it.

He hadn't been sitting there for ten minutes when the intercom on his desk buzzed to life. "Trent. Something's come up. I need to see you in my office."

Trent's blood froze. Was this about his meeting with Dyson last night? Had P.T. simply been waiting for a private moment to rip his vice president's heart out with a pair of ice-cube tongs? "I'll be right there, sir."

P.T.'s office looked less inviting than usual, especially compared to the relative warmth and comfort of Dyson's. As usual, Trent glanced at the chairs across from the massive desk and opted to stand. "Yes, sir?"

"I just want to clarify a few things." P.T. leaned back in his chair with a slow squeak. "If Nova's going to succeed, you and I need to be on the same page."

Same page? Had P.T. been reading self-help guides for bosses? Trent relaxed. Nobody who used the phrase "on the same page" was about to club anybody over the head with a nine iron. "All right, sir."

"Now I know what you were trying to do in there," P.T. said. "I said I was looking for a nice show, and you were just trying to help. But I need you to understand, the only thing I meant by that was a show that would pacify Armsburger and the FCC enough for us to make the kind of shows we *should* be making. Is that clear?"

"Perfectly, sir."

"All right." P.T. seemed to relax. "For a while in there, I thought you were actually *objecting* to the idea of a custody battle."

You're right, sir. I thought for a moment that you had developed some kind of conscience. I see now that I was wrong. Don't worry, sir, it won't happen again. Prick.

"Is that all, sir?"

"One more thing." P.T. stood up and opened the blinds behind his desk, which made Trent squint. "It seems Dyson has managed to drum up some interest for that show of his."

There was a surge of excitement that Trent found very difficult to quell. "Which one? *Lives in the Balance*?"

P.T. nodded. "I don't know how he did it, but apparently Foster at ABC thinks it might actually"—he closed his eyes and drew his lips close together—"be a hit."

Trent clenched his hands into congratulatory fists. Ah, the sweet taste of vindication. "You know, I *did* come up with that idea first."

"I remember." P.T.'s eyes grew hard. "I shot it down then, and I'd do the same now. I don't know what Foster's thinking. Only thing I can figure is that ABC's so desperate for success that they're willing to take this kind of risk."

"I don't think they're desperate," Trent decided to say. "They've had plenty of success in the last two years. You never know, Foster might be right."

"Are you defending Dyson's show?"

"No, sir. I'm defending my own."

P.T. gave Trent a long, humorless look, then turned his attention toward some papers on his desk. "Dyson's pitching another show as well. Different idea, same concept. Public awareness, family programming, all that shit."

"What's the show?"

"Doesn't matter." P.T. rubbed his chin. "He's up to something, Trent. He's trying to change the game on us." He kept talking, but his voice dropped, as though he'd forgotten Trent was in the room. "He doesn't know who he's dealing with. This is *my* world. *Mine*."

Trent started to feel uncomfortable, which made sense. Usually you felt a bit out of place whenever somebody was beginning to have a mental breakdown "What do you want to do?"

P.T. seemed to come back to himself. "Nothing. I'll take care of everything. You just keep coming up with ideas. And remember," he added, emphasizing the words with a pointed finger, "this is a war. There's no room for second place."

Well, well, well, Trent thought as he left his boss's office. Maybe there was a reason to hope. Already Dyson had two good shows on the market, and undoubtedly there were more on the shelves, waiting to be pitched. If he found a way to change the focus of reality TV, Nova would have no choice but to adapt along with him. And if *that* happened, it was just possible that Trent would be able to celebrate his thirtieth birthday without the help of Alcoholics Anonymous.

When he got to his own office, there were two messages waiting for him. One was from Frank, thanking Trent yet again for his help with *Tropical Abduction*. The CBS execs were already planning an entire series of abduction shows. Trent looked at the note and shook his head.

Tropical Abduction, *Arctic Abduction*, *Ghetto Abduction*, and so on. He slid the note into the desk's top drawer and tried to convince himself it didn't really exist.

The second message was from Adam, which was odd. Adam always used Trent's cell phone number, not the office line. But a quick glance at his cell phone told Trent that Adam had tried that, too. Something must have happened, something important.

He was about to call Adam when Max walked in. "Hey, pal, you gotta second?"

"Actually, no. Can you come back in five minutes?"

"Sure. It's just that I've got this show idea, it's been burning me up all day. It's a killer, pal, gonna knock everything else off the charts. You wanna hear it?"

I doubt it. You're a great guy, Max, but I'm sure this idea's a piece of shit. "Give me five minutes, will you?"

"Sure." But instead of leaving, Max came in and sat down. "All right, here's the thing. We get nine people—a Palestinian, an Israeli, a Klan member, a black guy, two lesbians, an Indian girl, a Pakistani man, and a Muslim—and make them all live together. I know, I know, it's sounds like *The Real World* all over again, right, *but*, with *this* show, there's a goal. A new goal every week. Maybe the first week it's to open a restaurant or clean up their neighborhood, work for Habitat for Humanity—there are tons of options here."

This wasn't at all what Trent had expected. "Not bad, Max. It sounds a little like *The Apprentice*, though."

"Exactly. Except with *The Apprentice*, it's all 'I'm gonna fuck you over as soon as I can.' But here, everyone has to work together, and if they don't, see, then *all* of them get kicked off, and we start fresh with a new team. Because that's what this world's about, isn't it? Getting along, working together despite our differences?" Max's eyes were feverish. "What do you say? We'll call it *Coalition of Love* or something and bill it as the first wave of the new Reality format—smart, sensitive, the kind of show that makes you want to hug people instead of kill them. What do you think?"

Trent was overwhelmed. It was happening. The transformation he had hoped for, the evolution Dyson was attempting to engineer, was beginning to take hold. And it wasn't as difficult as they all imagined. Decent shows *could* be created, and people *would* watch them. "I think it's . . . I think it's fantastic, Max. I think it's the best—"

Max cut him off. "Wait, wait. Trent. Pal. You didn't think I was serious, did you?"

Trent's face collapsed. "You weren't?"

"*Shit*, man!" Max started laughing, the sound pouring from him like air he'd been trying to hold in. "I was just . . . Oh my God. Trent, *Trent. Coalition of Love*, are you fucking serious? What, you turn into a John Denver fan all of a sudden? That's the worst idea I've ever *heard*."

Trent forced himself not to throw his coffee cup at Max's head. "It doesn't sound bad to me."

"Trent." Max stopped laughing. "Seriously, pal. An Indian and a Pakistani living in the same house? Do you want to start World War III? I mean I know you're an idealist, but come *on*, even *I* have my limits. No, pal, that's one for the shelves, something for P.T. to pull out if the FCC starts in about decency again."

"Was that the only reason you came in here?"

"Look, don't get all upset. I was just kidding. *Jesus*. As a matter of fact, I have a real idea I wanted to run by you."

Trent sighed. If there was a God, He was definitely an angry, spiteful, vindictive God, not that other kind some people liked to talk about. "What is it?"

"All right. You know that old show *Cheaters*, right, about catching people cheating on their girlfriends or whatever? Well, I was thinking, why not take it one step further? Why not do a show called *Stalkers*? It's one thing to follow people around when they're doing something wrong, but following them around when they're *not* doing anything wrong. Think about it."

"*Stalkers*." He said the word, and for some reason felt that he was watching the first amphibian give up on progress and slither back into the river. "You mean like digging through people's trash."

"That, and sneaking into their homes, hiding in their cars—you know, all the shit stalkers do. I was thinking we'd start with celebrities, of course—*Fan-atic* basically laid the groundwork there—but eventually I'd like it to move to ordinary people. By the time you're done watching the first season, I want you to think there might be somebody staring at you through your own window."

Trent started to twitch. "And exactly why would we want to do that?"

"Because we *can*, that's why. Why do people spend ten bucks to see a horror movie just so they can leave the theater and wonder if some undead axe murderer's hiding underneath their car waiting to chop them to pieces? Fuck if I know, pal, but those horror movies make billions. Billions, pal. Think about that. Think of the market I'm talking about."

"You've got to be kidding. *Stalkers*? What's the tag line going to be? 'Just when you thought it was safe to leave your home'?"

"Hadn't got that far yet. That's a good one, though, we might run with that. What do you think, pal, is it a go?"

What was there to say? He was in Hell. There could be no other explanation. Somewhere along the line he had died, probably run over by some senile grandfather who had mistaken his Jaguar for a German Panzer tank, and now he was sitting in Hell.

"Get out of here, Max."

"Come on, what's the problem?"

"Get out of here, Max."

"Look, you still upset about that *Coalition of Love* bullshit?"

"Get out of here, Max."

Max stood up. "All right, all right. I'm sorry. Jesus, I didn't think you'd take it so personally. I'll leave you alone. But I want you to think about that *Stalkers* show, seriously. There's a whole market we're ignoring right now, pal, a big one."

"Get out of here, Max."

"I'm going, I'm going." Max opened the door to the hallway. "You know, instead of *Coalition of Love*, we could call it *A Small, Happy World*. Or how about *We're All the Same Color on the Inside*?"

"Get the fuck out of here, Max."

Laughing, Max departed.

Trent put the heels of both hands over his eyes and pressed hard against them. Okay, so maybe his and Dyson's vision of a more palatable world was still some way off. At least the thought was there. People had probably laughed about the possibility of ending slavery when it first came up, too. Maybe all he needed was a little more determination.

And an army on his side. That couldn't hurt.

He decided to call Adam before thoughts of military conquest became too enticing.

"Hey," Adam said. "Got my messages?"

"Yeah, both of them. You all right?"

"Yeah, fine. Just calling to see if you're up for Garibaldi's this afternoon."

"Sure. Sorry about yesterday. Business, you know."

"Yeah. I hope you'll forgive me if I didn't watch." There was a pause. "So . . . have you read it yet?"

"Read what?" The words were out of his mouth before he could stop them.

"*Deadly Justice*." There was no mistaking Adam's disappointment. "You haven't read it."

Shit. He had completely forgotten about that. The box was still in the back seat of his car, where it had remained since the day Adam had given it to him. It was a good thing no one had ever asked him to babysit; otherwise he'd probably be in prison right now for negligent homicide. "Listen, I'm an asshole."

"Don't worry about it. I'm sure you've been busy."

"No, that's no excuse." Trent opened the door to his office. "I'll have it finished by this afternoon."

"You don't have to hurry," Adam said. Then, with hardly a pause: "Do you think you can get it done by then?"

"Absolutely."

Again, there was a pause. "I'd appreciate it. Don't go out of your way, though."

"Trust me, there's nothing I'd rather do. See you at four."

"Thanks, man."

Five minutes later Trent was back in his office with Adam's manuscript. He ripped through the tape—Jesus, there was a lot of it—and set the entire stack of papers on his desk. It couldn't have been more than a hundred and twenty pages; he'd have it finished by lunch. He started reading:

DEADLY JUSTICE
By: Adam Caruthers

Scene One:
OVERHEAD EXT.
Night. A back alleyway (dogs barking, empty bottles, etc.). One broken-down car is parked against a wall, its wheels missing. A PROSTITUTE in a red dress walks by.

ZOOM INTO:
Two cars pull into the alley from opposite directions. One is blue, the other green. Both are fully loaded (running lights, spinners, etc.). Sound of tires on gravel. They come to a stop and people pour out, four from each car. Everyone is heavily armed with guns, knives, and chains. Both cars leave their engines running. One man from the blue car, TITO, a black man in his 20s, approaches the center of the alley. The leader of the green car, DAMAGE, larger and more heavily-muscled than TITO, does the same.

DAMAGE: You got the shit?

TITO: I got the shit.

DAMAGE: Well, lemme see the shit.

TITO: It's in the trunk.

DAMAGE: Tell your dogz to put their weapons down.
(To his men): Any of those motherfuckaz makes a move, gun his ass down.

TITO: Come on, take a look.

DAMAGE *(leaning into TITO)*: If you fuckin' with me, I'ma pound your ass into dog food, you got that?

TITO: I ain't fuckin' wit ya, DAMAGE. I value my life.

DAMAGE *(laughing)*: Shit. Life ain't shit but bitches and blow.

(General laughter.)

Trent put the first page of Adam's manuscript back on his desk and stared at the remaining pile. All of a sudden, Garibaldi's was the last place on Earth he wanted to be.

[CHAPTER SEVENTEEN]

"So," Adam said as soon as Trent sat down, "what'd you think?"

Trent bought himself some time by lighting a cigarette. For the last four hours he'd been sitting in his office, staring at the wall, dreading this moment and knowing he could do nothing to avoid it. Every cell in his body was screaming at him to leave, to fake a heart attack and stagger out of Garibaldi's before it was too late. But even that would only postpone the inevitable. Eventually, he was going to have to tell Adam that *Deadly Justice* was, without a doubt, the worst piece of shit he'd ever read.

"Come on, man, you're killing me here. What'd you think?"

Trent set his glass down. At least Angela wasn't there. "It's . . . different."

"Very. I told you it wasn't like *The Long Road*."

"No, that's for certain. It's . . . yeah . . . it's very different. You know it took me a little while to get used to it. The language and everything."

"I can understand that. It was a little awkward for me at first too, but after about twenty pages it all started to flow. I told you I finished it in three weeks, right? I don't know, it just . . . exploded, kind of. But what'd you think? Did it sound fresh?"

Oh, it was fresh all right. As fresh as a giant, steaming turd. "Yeah. Definitely. I don't think I've ever read anything quite like it. I particularly liked when the cop—what was his name?"

"Sedgewick."

"That's right. When Sedgewick said, 'I'm gonna fuck you so hard your eyes are gonna bleed.' That was . . . that was something."

"I was pretty proud of that. It sounded original, right?"

"Oh, oh yeah. Completely." Especially since the man had said it *to his wife*. "Yeah, I didn't see that line coming." Was that urban romance? What did they do on their anniversary, shoot each other in the legs?

"Good. Great, excellent." Adam took a drink. "So, what about the story?"

"The story?"

"What'd you think of it?"

"Well." Trent stalled by lighting another cigarette, even though his first was only half finished. The story. It would have helped if there had *been* a story, or at least something interesting enough to merit the torturous process of reading the horrible thing. "The story. Let's see."

"Don't hold back, man. Be honest with me."

Trent swallowed. Honesty was definitely not the best policy right now. "Well, I guess there were a couple, you know, one or two things that seemed . . . I don't know, kind of . . . improbable."

"Good." Adam looked as if he'd been waiting for this part of the conversation. "Like what?"

"Well, like the bedroom scene, for example."

"What about it?"

"Well." Trent desperately wanted Candy to come over and refill his drink. "All right, Damage has just been shot, right? Two or three times, I think."

"Five, but whatever."

"All right, so he's been shot five times. He's bleeding all over the place, and one of his hookers lays him down on the bed and has sex with him."

"Right." Adam paused. "So what's the problem?"

Trent bit his lower lip. Was this the Adam he had known at Stanford? "It just seems like if he's been shot five times, maybe they should take him to the hospital."

"But he can't go to the hospital. He's got to lay low. If the police find him, he's a dead man."

"Well, don't you think Bambi or whatever her name is—"

"Chocolate."

"—should maybe bandage him up instead of sleeping with him? Who'd want to sleep with a bleeding guy, anyway?"

Adam waved his hands. "You're thinking too literally. This is movie logic we're talking about, this kind of thing happens all the time. *Raiders of the Lost Ark*, *Desperado*, there's tons of examples. Damage probably *should* get medical attention, but that's not going to keep viewers in their seats."

"So then it's not a problem that in the next scene he's up and walking even though he was just shot in both legs?"

"I put in there that he's limping. Didn't you see that?"

That did it. Adam had officially lost his mind. "I guess I overlooked that."

"Well, it was in the director's notes. It's easy to miss it, especially if you're not used to reading movie scripts. Anything else?"

Yes, Adam. In fact, everything else. The whole goddamn idea was terrible. The script would have been better if a monkey had written it. "Let's see . . . um, I think there was just one other thing."

"Let me guess. The nightclub, right?" Adam nodded as if he'd seen it coming. "I was worried about that, I wasn't sure if it would seem too over-the-top. I mean, it *is* a little unlikely that anyone would start having sex right there on the dance floor. But I kept thinking that part of the script needed something . . . punchy, you know? It was just dragging a little for me."

"Punchy's the right word," Trent said, "considering that he somehow manages to get in a fight with three other guys and have sex with the girl at the same time."

"So it worked for you?"

"That part, yeah." Only because the sheer impossibility had made him laugh so hard he thought he was going to die. "There are a lot of movies I've seen that would have benefited from that kind of . . . initiative."

"Great." Adam took another drink. "That was really the only part I was personally worried about. Anything else?"

"Nothing comes to mind," Trent said. This had to stop. He was already feeling sick to his stomach. "Let me ask you, what . . . what were you *going* for here?"

"Good question." Adam took a breath. "I guess I wanted to write a script that was a little more accessible. More mainstream, I guess. *The Long Road*—"

"Is a great script."

"Thanks. But it doesn't *grab* people. At least it hasn't so far, and even if it does it'll drown in the indie market."

"So you wanted to write a script that would sell."

"Well, yeah. I need to eat, you know. And if I can't write movies people want to produce, then what good am I doing? You have to understand that."

"I do," Trent said quickly. "I do. It's just . . ."

"Just what?"

Oh, man, this was going to suck. "It's just, it seems like you're . . . settling here."

There was a change in Adam's voice. "What are you talking about?"

Trent sighed. "I just feel like this is an LCD movie."

Adam squinted. "LCD. What, like a computer screen? What the hell does *that* mean?"

"Lowest common denominator. It's the way we decide what kinds of shows to make. We pilot all our shows before they air, and if anything about them—title, plot, whatever—confuses anyone in our test audience, we change it. Everything we do is geared toward the least critical, least discerning, least analytical people we can find."

They were interrupted—blissfully—by Candy. "You guys doing okay?"

"I think we're each going to need another," Trent said.

"Make it two," Adam added, which pretty much told Trent everything he needed to know.

As soon as Candy left, Adam launched in. "So you're saying this script is worthless?"

"Not *worth*less. I'm just saying it's an LCD movie. That doesn't mean it's bad. There are probably a lot of people who'd like it. Look at *Scary Movie*. That was a com*plete* piece of shit, and they made what, seven of them?"

"So now you're saying my script is a piece of shit?"

"No, Adam, you're not listening. I think this script can sell. It's the kind of thing a lot of people are looking for right now. It's just not . . . I just think you can do better."

"Better." Adam repeated the word like he didn't know what it meant. "Better? How?"

Trent leaned forward. "Look. *The Long Road* is a great script. Someday people are going to look back at that and—"

With an abrupt, angry laugh, Adam shoved himself against the back of his booth. "Someday? *Someday*? I need to eat *now*, man. And even if you're right, what the hell good will it do me if I'm not around to appreciate it?"

"I just don't think you should give up on it."

"I'm not giving up on it. I'm still shopping it, it's still *out* there. But I can't afford to wait forever. And this one, this is the kind of stuff people want."

"I know," Trent said. "I agree. That's why I think it has a good chance of selling. It's just not my kind of movie."

"What the hell's *wrong* with it?"

Just then, Candy returned with a tray of drinks. She'd obviously heard their argument, because she looked carefully at the glasses as she set them on the table and walked away without saying anything. Trent watched her leave and wished he could go with her.

"There's nothing wrong with it," Trent lied. "It's just not my kind of movie."

"Why not? Too LCD for you?"

"I'm trying to be nice about this, Adam."

"Then tell me what's wrong with it."

"*Fine.*" Trent drained his drink and set the glass down hard enough to make the salt shaker quiver. "Do you really want me to tell you everything I don't like about it?"

"Do you think I can't take it?"

This would have been a good time for an out-of-control ice cream truck driven by an inebriated clown to come crashing through the front door. That would have helped a lot. But, since that didn't happen: "All right. For starters, you're a Jewish guy from suburban Connecticut trying to write a script about black gangbangers."

"So?"

"So, you have no idea how they talk. Nobody actually says, 'Fo shizzle,' Adam. The only place you'd ever hear that is on MTV."

"Oh, like *you'd* know."

"I know that no hungry gangster is ever going to say, 'I'ma bust a cap in that casserole.'" It was hard for Trent to say that sentence without shuddering. The very thought of the word 'casserole' being used in a gangster movie was almost too much. "But whatever. I could be wrong."

Adam seemed happy to accept that concession. "All right. What else?"

The whole damn *thing*. "I don't know. There's a bit more violence than I prefer."

"What are you talking about? What about *Fight Club*? That's your favorite movie, isn't it?"

Trent shook his head. "That's different. The violence in *Fight Club* is for a purpose. It's illustrative. A lot of this seems . . . gratuitous."

"For example?"

"Like lots of examples. When they shoot up the orphanage."

Adam shrugged. "One of the orphans stole the suitcase full of money. It's retribution."

"All right, then. What about the nun? Do they *really* have to decapitate her? It's a fucking nun, for Christ's sake."

"I needed something powerful. Guns are so overplayed, I felt like I needed an edge. What else?"

At this point Trent was completely exasperated. He felt that he was talking to a brick wall. "Do we have to do this? I didn't want to get into an argument."

"I just want to know why you don't like the script."

"Because I don't!" He finished his second drink and continued more quietly. "I just think you can do better than this."

"Who are you to talk to *me* about 'doing better'?" Adam asked. "Look at you! Look at what you do with *your* life."

"I know I'm not the best example."

"Then get off my back! Ever since we left Stanford you've been telling me to follow my dreams, stay true to myself, all that bullshit. And look at you! You make *shitty* television shows every day of your life. And you know what? You're making six figures a year and driving a two-year-old Jaguar be*cause* of it. I don't see a whole lot of integrity in that."

It didn't help Trent's argument that Adam was entirely correct. "I'm trying to change that."

"Is that right?" Adam smiled mirthlessly. "You know what I saw on TV last night? Tell me if this rings a bell. It's a new Reality show coming out next month called *Mega-Monopoly*. That sound familiar?"

Trent buried his head in his hands. *Mega-Monopoly*. NBC had been running prelims for so long he'd completely forgotten about that one.

"I take it that's a yes," Adam said. "So let's see if I got this right. You take ten people, give each of them $100,000 to start a restaurant, and each person's job is to drive the other nine out of business by the end of a year. Isn't that right? Drive them out of business *by any means necessary*? Isn't that it?"

"That's about right."

"So let me ask you. How do *you* sleep at night?" Adam didn't wait for an answer. "I'll tell you how you sleep. Pretty damn well, in your three-bedroom apartment on your king-size bed. You've got enough room for a family of five, and meanwhile I'm living in a basement with bad light and a leaking ceiling. But that's no big deal, right, because *I'm* keeping it *real*."

"I'm trying to change it," Trent said. "I'm trying to fix things."

"You've been saying that for the past six months, man. Longer, actually. It's never going to happen. And you know what? I don't care if it ever does. That's not my problem. I'm just tired of fighting."

"It's not hopeless."

"You don't *get* it!" Adam pulled at his hair. "I've got a family back home. I've got a little sister who's going to college next year. I want to be able to help out. And that'll never happen unless I start playing the game."

"It doesn't have to be like that. We can still win."

There was a considerable pause. Adam stared at Trent for a long time with a look Trent didn't particularly enjoy. Then, as though he'd come to some final conclusion, Adam stood up.

"Fuck it, man." He didn't sound angry anymore, but somehow that was worse. "Look, you made you choice, and you're where you are, and that's the way it is. But you can't have it both ways. You can't criticize me for doing the same thing you're doing. And you sure as hell can't use me to live your vicarious little life. You want to be true to yourself and follow your dreams and to hell with anyone who tries to stop you? Fine, go ahead. But let me tell you, it's not all it's cracked up to be." He picked up his last drink, finished it off, and set the glass down. "I've got to go, man. I'll talk to you later."

There was nothing for Trent to say. He watched Adam make his way through the crowd and disappear out the front door. When he was certain Adam wasn't coming back, Trent looked down at the few drops of sake left in his glass.

Some time later, Candy came up. "You guys okay?"

"I don't know," Trent said. He looked at the door again. "I don't know. Let me get the check."

[CHAPTER EIGHTEEN]

Trent and Adam didn't talk for the next three weeks. Trent tried calling a few times to see if Adam wanted to meet at Garibaldi's, or anywhere for that matter, but Adam never answered and didn't call back. After a while, Trent stopped making the effort. Adam would come around, eventually, when he felt like it. Until then . . . well, until then Trent would be drinking alone in his apartment.

On a more positive note, his relationship with Rachel—if the word "relationship" could legitimately be applied to two people who spent most of their time together naked—was going strong. At work she was still as icy and standoffish as ever, but outside of the office, she was beginning to warm up. A couple of times she even let him be on top.

"What is it exactly that you want?" he asked once. They were lying in bed together after an unusually sedate bout of lovemaking. Or maybe it was just that he had become acclimated to her style.

"What do you mean? With this?"

"Yeah." He propped himself up on his shoulder. "I mean, we never go out. I've never bought you dinner, or flowers, or anything really, and you don't seem to care at all."

"Do you want me to?"

"No. It's fine. Most guys dream of a girl like you."

"Then what's the problem?"

"There isn't one. I was just curious, what is it you're looking for?"

She thought about it for a moment. "Sex," she finally said.

"Just sex? How did we not do this earlier?"

"Just sex," she repeated. There was a brief pause. "No, that's not true. If all I wanted was sex I could take care of it myself. Really I guess what I'm after is power."

Trent blinked. "Power?"

"Power, control, whatever you want to call it. I like feeling like I'm in charge of things. And with you, I do." She reached over to the nightstand

and pulled out a cigarette. "I also wanted to one-up Taylor. It's nice to have something she can't."

"Wow. That's probably the least romantic thing I've ever heard."

"There's no such thing as romance. All that buying cards and flowers, it's just another way for women to feel superior. You don't see us buying anything for you guys, do you?"

"Now that you mention it, no."

"My point exactly. That's why I got into television, too, for the power. Of course, that's why *everyone* gets into television."

Trent wanted to contest that, but he couldn't. Even his own goal was essentially a way of exerting his will over everyone else's. The only difference was, *he* knew what needed to be done. *His* vision was right. "So what is it you want to do?"

"With television?" She exhaled a cloud of smoke. "I'm not sure yet. I don't feel like I've found my calling. When I do, though, you'll be the first to know."

"And you think I'll just let you run with it no matter what? What if I don't like it?"

"I know how to persuade you," she said. "You ready for more?"

Part of Trent's body went into revolt. *Please, for the love of God, a man can only do so much!* But he didn't listen. No self-respecting man in his situation would ever listen to the voice of reason. "You're going to kill me if you keep this up, you know."

She put out her cigarette. "Women have been doing that for centuries. How else are we supposed to get to the top?"

He had no idea if she was joking or not. But a minute later, he absolutely didn't care.

][

Back at the office, things had taken an unusual turn. P.T.'s insistence that Nova develop a stockpile of "nice" shows to pacify the FCC and other critics of Reality Television, which at first had been received with little enthusiasm, had suddenly become the latest fad. Soon it was the office joke, their substitute for compromising pictures of drunk coworkers from last year's Christmas party. Every two or three days someone came up with another absurdly nice show concept, which meant that every two or three days Trent had to listen to them.

"What about a show called *Fun with Cripples?*" Todd said one day. "We could have them play basketball, go to the mall, cook dinner and shit—just like normal people."

Taylor's suggestions were even more heartless. "I was thinking we could do something about body image? You know, get some fat girls—I'm talking *real* fat, like a hundred thirty or so—and let them compete to be runway models! Because it's what's on the *inside* that counts, right?" She couldn't help laughing at that. "Wouldn't that make you feel all fuzzy inside?"

But Tad won the prize for the most painful idea. "Okay!" he said one morning, bursting into Trent's office in a flurry of hand-waving excitement. "Okay, so here it is. Are you sitting down?"

Trent looked at himself sitting in his chair. "Yeah, Tad."

"Well, hold on to your armrests! Here goes." He took a deep breath. "So, what we do is, we get this guy, right? Total hunk, you know, like Andy Roddick, but without all the sweat. Then, we have him move into a nice suburban neighborhood and pretend he's gay. You with me so far?"

"Man pretending to be gay. It's not that hard to follow. And?"

"*And*, then we film his neighbors. Do interviews, see what they think about having a 'homo' living right next door. We make sure *tons* of guys are coming over all the time—and a couple girls, just to throw everyone off."

"What's the point?"

"Patience!" Tad hissed. "You straights are always in such a hurry. Bang, zoom, goodbye. Honestly, I don't know why women put up with you."

"Tad, I'm kind of busy."

"Oh, all *right*." Tad sat down, then jumped up again immediately. "The point, Mr. Impatient, is that we film the silent racism that the modern homosexual faces in daily life. The cold shoulders, the gossip, so on, so on. *Then*, at the *end*, we gather everyone together and reveal the truth—that their new neighbor is really straight. It'll be like holding up a mirror to everyone's *soul*, because if that changes their mind about him, then it'll reveal the hypocrisy and intolerance a lot of people have toward homosexuals. It'll be a *revelation*, Trent, a way to open the eyes of the average American and make them say, 'You know, I'm not being very nice. It shouldn't matter what people do.' What do you think?"

For a moment, there was a surge of hope that made Trent's skin tingle. Tad hadn't *said* this was a fake show. Maybe he was being sincere. "It . . . sounds great, Tad. How'd you think of it?"

"Do you think P.T. will like it?"

"I don't know. It's a bit cerebral for him, but I might be able to—"

"Wait," Tad said. "You don't think I'm talking about a *real* show, do you?"

Trent's excitement evaporated. Once again, the cruel hand of Life had bitch-slapped him in the face. "You're not?"

"*God* no!" Tad tittered. "Are you serious, a show about neighbor gossips? Can you say *boring*? Oh, I'd rather watch golf."

"A lot of people watch golf."

"Trent. Listen, I know you're trying to . . . do something different, but it's not funny anymore. Just put it on the shelf, will you? Or run it by P.T. if you think he'll get a giggle out of it. You're an angel. Ta."

There was one good thing that happened in those three weeks. Dyson's company was beginning to roll out a small battery of new reality shows, all geared around a thought-provoking concept of social betterment that P.T. found completely incomprehensible.

"What the hell is he *doing*?" P.T. roared at one of the Monday meetings. "No one's going to watch this shit. Has he lost his *mind*?"

Trent kept his mouth shut. He knew better than to say anything, and besides he was afraid he might betray a little of his enthusiasm. Finally, somebody was proposing ideas that didn't turn his stomach. Maybe Dyson's ideas *were* a little off—a show called *Helping the Elderly* was a bit too touchy-feely even for him—but at least he was trying.

"People will watch anything," Tad said. "At least for the first four weeks. We all know that. I think Dyson's counting on that."

P.T.'s back became ramrod straight. "Are you siding with him?"

"No, sir. Not one bit. I just think it's something we can't afford to ignore."

"*Trust* me," P.T. said, "I'm *not* letting this go. I'll take care of Dyson, one way or another. Don't you have anything to add, Trent?"

"He's a bastard, sir," Trent said automatically. The word "bastard" was always a good one to use in relation to P.T.'s enemies; it never failed to soothe him.

"It's obvious that he's desperate," Todd said. "We've outproduced him for the past five months, and he's—"

"We haven't done enough," P.T. said. "He's still there, threatening. I don't want to beat him, people, I want to de*stroy* him. There's not enough room for two of us. And if this new direction of his takes off . . ."

"That's not going to happen, sir," Rachel said.

P.T. turned his diamond-eyed stare on her. "Are you certain of that? Are you absolutely, one hundred percent certain?"

Rachel wasn't one to back down, but even she couldn't meet that gaze for very long. She lowered her head and drew her lips together. "No, sir."

"Then don't *tell* me it's not going to happen!" He slammed his open palm down on the table, and Taylor's coffee spilled over the edges of her cup.

In the extremely uncomfortable silence that followed, Trent re-appraised his boss. Something was wrong. He wasn't just angry at Dyson; he was worried. Something big had happened, something serious enough to threaten the General's sense of security, and Trent thought he knew what it was.

He waited to ask, though, until the others weren't around.

"Sir," he said when he walked into P.T.'s office, "what's going on?"

P.T. motioned Trent to close the door, then sat down behind his massive steel desk. The anger was still there, but it was tempered by a whisper of restraint. "It's Dyson's show. ABC's running with it. They're going to start filming next month."

"*Lives in the Balance*? You're kidding."

"Be careful, Trent. You almost sound excited."

"Sorry, sir. But it was my idea first."

"That still doesn't make it a *good* idea." P.T. turned in his chair until he was facing the windows—a useless gesture, since all he could see was the brick wall of the neighboring building.

Now was Trent's chance to press. "Shouldn't we retaliate? We've got a dozen 'nice' ideas on the shelf, and some of them aren't half bad. Maybe—"

"I'm not playing his game. I'm not going to let him dictate what we do."

"Businesses have to evolve, sir. Otherwise they—"

"*Weak* businesses have to evolve, Trent. Strong ones *make* the market. Strong ones makes others follow *them*. And that's what I intend this company to do."

Trent left without pressing further. Trying to reason with his boss was a lot like smashing his head against a brick wall, with the notable exception that the wall would be nice enough to eventually knock him unconscious. He sat down at his desk with every intention of wasting the next thirty-five minutes until he could justifiably excuse himself for lunch.

Two minutes later, though, Lynette walked in, cheery as ever. "Hell-oooo!"

Trent smiled. "Still thinking about Matt Damon?" Last night she'd seen him coming out of the restroom at the mall.

Lynette giggled. "It's just so *odd*! You don't think of celebrities doing the same things that ordinary people do."

He had to concede. In all his fantasies about Monica Bellucci, she had never been on the toilet. "What's going on?"

"Oh, nothing. Just delivering a message. I didn't know you had out-of-town company this week."

Trent took the slip of paper from her. Steve Cardigan. He'd never heard of anyone by that name. Out-of-town guests? What the hell? "Yeah, it was sort of a last-minute thing."

"Well, toodle-oo!" Lynette chirped happily out of his office.

Trent looked again at the note. The number was an unfamiliar one. He got up, checked his door to make sure Lynette had shut it tightly, sat back down, and looked at his phone. Then he remembered his evening conversation with P.T.

Maybe it'd be better if he used the cell.

"Hello?" A vaguely recognizable voice.

"Who is this?"

"Trent?"

"Yeah. Who is this?"

"Are you on your cell phone?"

What kind of question was that? "Yeah. Who *is* this?"

"Simon Petersen."

Trent's voice immediately fell to a whisper. Well, at least that explained the deception. "Why the hell are you calling me here?"

"You had your cell phone turned off. I didn't have a choice."

"Couldn't it wait?"

"Unfortunately, no. Can you meet for lunch in about an hour? It's kind of important."

][

Forty-five minutes later, Trent arrived at Firefly. It was appropriately inconspicuous—no sign on the door, no overt markings, and far enough away from work that no one he knew would be likely to spot him. He walked quickly through the bar to the patio at the far end. Dyson was there, sitting with Petersen at an outdoor table. If it weren't for the dull Los Angeles smog, it would have looked a lot like a Mediterranean villa.

"Trent," Dyson said warmly, rising and shaking his hand. "So glad you could make it."

"Do me a favor. Next time, don't call the office."

"We were as discreet as possible," Petersen said. "I'm sure your secretary's not suspicious."

"Even so." Best not to take chances, especially not with a boss who, by Dyson's own admission, actually *enjoyed* the Vietnam War. "So, what's going on?"

Dyson lifted a briefcase onto the table and clicked it open. He pulled out a manila folder and passed it to Trent.

"What's this?"

"A proposal."

"For a show? You called me all the way out here to give me a show proposal?"

"It's more important than you think. I'm sure you've heard that *Lives in the Balance* is about to go into production?"

Trent nodded. "P.T.'s not happy about that."

"I'm sure he isn't. We're changing the game on him. And high time we did, too, but I don't want to go into that again. You know where I stand."

Dyson smiled. "That proposal you're holding. I want you to pitch it to your boss."

"To P.T.?"

"Unless you have another I don't know about."

Trent looked at the manila folder. There were no markings on it, no indication of what lay inside. "If this is anything like what I think it is, he's not going to accept it."

"I don't expect him to," Dyson said. "You don't win a war with a single battle. But you can't *fight* a war on two fronts, not forever. If both of us are pushing, he won't be able to hold out forever."

"We've got half a dozen more like this," Petersen said, "and another four outlined. We can keep this going as long as it takes."

Ten shows? "How do you guys come up with so many ideas?"

Petersen shrugged. "It's not that hard. And it would explain, in case any of you had started to wonder, why you've outsold us for the last five months."

"That's not his concern," Dyson said gently to his vice president. Then, to Trent, and with even more warmth than before: "Take it home. Look it over, make sure you're satisfied with the concept. I'm sure you will be, but I don't want you running anything you don't believe in."

Trent cast a glance over his shoulder. The other diners were talking quietly, and none of them seemed to be looking his way. "When do you want me to run this by him?"

"Tomorrow, if possible," Petersen said. "The sooner the better. And if and when he turns it down, give us a call and we'll get you another one."

"And another," Dyson added, "and another, and another. Make no mistake, Trent. We are at war here, a war for the very soul of our nation. And it is one that we are going to win."

Trent left soon after that, Dyson's manila folder tucked tightly beneath his arm, and hopped into his Jaguar. Things were beginning to happen. For better or worse, the ball was in motion now—there would be no turning back. And although he did not relish the idea of confronting P.T. with an idea he knew the man would despise, at least he was starting to feel as though he was doing something worthwhile.

Besides, in all honesty, what was the worst that could happen?

[CHAPTER NINETEEN]

That night, in the dim silence of his apartment, Trent read through Dyson's proposal. It was short, only six pages, and the market analysis was condensed into a single paragraph. It was dense, too, written more like an academic abstract than a reality show idea.

And it was brilliant.

Speculatively titled *The Samaritan*, the concept was simple. Six contestants, each accompanied by two cameramen, would start in New York City and take separate, pre-arranged routes across the country to Seattle. Their assignment was to help as many people as they could in whatever capacity they were able—changing tires, fixing houses, feeding the homeless, rescuing puppies—all the while recording their exploits. They would be prohibited from accepting payment of any kind and would be disqualified if they did. There would be no audience voting, no capricious eliminations or sinister alliances. Instead, each contestant would continue to the end, where the audience would cast a single vote and determine the winner.

But that wasn't the end of the show. The winner would be awarded a substantial prize—speculatively a million—but was not allowed to keep it. The *real* twist, and what made *The Samaritan* so revolutionary, was that the winner was required to spend the prize money on someone else. It didn't matter if it was a needy neighbor or Habitat for Humanity; but once that decision was made, then all six contestants would join together for one last, collaborative round of philanthropy. The net result: the contestants didn't leave with *anything* except the knowledge that they'd spent twelve weeks working to make the world a better place. Whatever deals and endorsements resulted from their newfound celebrity were theirs to take or reject, but the show itself would have no part in making that happen.

Trent actually had to read the whole thing twice to make sure he hadn't missed something. No cutthroat competition? No backstabbing interviews? This wasn't Reality TV anymore; it was something *real*, something so good it didn't even seem possible. This show would resonate with everyone who had written off Reality Television as the province of the petty and overambitious. There were *millions* of those people, untold millions who would see this as a show worth watching, who might sit down with their children and watch together in a spirit that had not appeared in prime time for decades.

And Dyson had given it to him with the expectation that it would never be produced.

Trent poured himself a glass of whisky. That's what was truly unfathomable, that Dyson would throw such a wonderful idea into the fire. What did that mean? Did Dyson think it was a bad concept? Unlikely, especially since the man seemed to be as genuine as someone who worked in the entertainment industry could be.

So what, then? If he was willing to let this one fall through the cracks, what were the ideas he was still holding onto? Petersen had said they had half a dozen others in the wings, waiting for a more opportune moment. Was it possible they were even better? Was Dyson saving his best ones for last?

And if so, how much better could they get?

There was no way to answer that, no way for Trent to even begin to imagine what kinds of shows Dyson had on his shelves. But he knew one thing. *The Samaritan* was the first show proposal he'd read in two years that had excited him like this. He wanted to be jealous that someone else had come up with it, that Dyson or Petersen or one of their underlings had done what he himself had never managed to do. But his enthusiasm wouldn't allow him to sink to that.

He drained his whisky and poured himself another. This was a good thing, perhaps the first really good thing in the history of Reality Television, and he'd be damned if he'd allow P.T. to dismiss it with a cursory glance.

With a quick, hot burst, Trent finished his second drink. That was it. Tomorrow he'd march into P.T.'s office and present *The Samaritan* as the beginning of a new era in Reality TV. It was time to expand, time to reach out to the tens of millions of disenchanted Americans who needed something fresh. And when P.T. refused and said it would never work, he'd keep at him. He'd back P.T. into a corner if he had to. He had no choice. He *had* to do something. This one was too important to give up without a fight.

Just then his cell phone rang.

Trent walked over to the couch where he'd left it and looked at the number. An unfamiliar one, and unlisted as well. Odd. Still, he answered.

"Hello?"

"Oh, Jesus Christ, thank God you're there."

The voice on the other end was breathless, ragged and heaving with great, rasping gulps of air. "Who is this?" Trent asked.

"It's Dyson. Listen—"

"Dyson? Is everything all right?"

"*Listen*!" There was a faint, rhythmic sound underneath his voice, almost as though he were running. "He's sent someone after me."

"Sent someone? Who's sent someone?"

"P.T. It's P.T., I know it's him. He's trying to kill me."

Trent's blood suddenly turned to ice. "*Kill* you? What are you—"

"There's no time!" he shouted. "I'm in trouble, someone's . . . listen, they're right behind me, I wanted to warn you. You're in danger."

"Dyson, where are you?"

"I'm at the corner of—Oh, Jesus!"

"Dyson?"

No answer.

"Dyson."

Again, no answer.

"Dyson!"

A loud noise, like the phone had been dropped.

"Dyson!"

A different sound, slow and wet—a bad sound.

"Dyson?"

Abruptly the sounds stopped. It didn't take Trent long to realize what had happened. Dyson's phone had been turned off.

[CHAPTER TWENTY]

By the time Trent arrived at his office the next morning, he'd already downed four cups of coffee. He'd slept like hell, probably no more than two hours and neither of them very well. The silence at the end of Dyson's phone call still pounded against his skull like a throbbing headache. He'd woken up every hour, certain that he'd heard the phone ringing, but it never did.

He'd tried calling the number once, but there had been no answer. Maybe Dyson was just sleeping.

And maybe he wasn't.

In his tense, sleep-deprived stupor, Trent had almost forgotten to bring the proposal for *The Samaritan* to work with him. But there it was, sitting on the passenger seat beside him, small and unmarked and full of genius. He wasn't sure if he was going to pitch it today or tomorrow; it might be better to wait until he was able to stand up without his knees wobbling.

As it happened, the day seemed to have started without him.

"*There* you are!" Lynette chirped when he walked in. "We've been waiting for you, Mr.—" She cut herself off. "Trent, are you all right?"

"Fine," he mumbled. "Just tired."

"Oh, dear. You look *awful*."

Trent gave her a tight smile. Why did people invariably feel compelled to make that comment? Did they think he was unaware of his condition? You may as well remind Steven Hawking that his legs didn't work. "Thanks. What's going on?"

"I don't know. Nobody does. We're all waiting for you."

"Why is everyone always waiting—"

He didn't get a chance to finish. At that moment, every one of his coworkers came out of their cubicles and began the onslaught.

"Jesus, pal, where've you been?"

"*God*, Trent, we've been waiting for*ever*."

"The fuck took you so long?"

Trent put a hand to his eyes. "Whoa, guys. What's the deal?"

"That's the thing," Max said. "Nobody knows. P.T. walked in this morning like he just won the lottery or something, but he won't tell us what's up. Said he wanted to talk to you first."

"Personally," Tad said, "I don't think that's . . . hey, you all right? You look *terrible*."

"Shut up, Tad."

Tad held his hands in front of him. "Okay, okay, calm down, tiger."

Rachel arched an eyebrow at Trent. "Rough night?"

"Not like that. Where's P.T.?"

"In his office," Max said. "Waiting for you. Get in there, will you? We're dying out here."

Trent looked at his boss's door. "Is there any coffee left?"

Two minutes later, armed with *The Samaritan* in one hand and a lukewarm but caffeinated cup of coffee in the other, Trent opened the door to P.T.'s office. He expected his boss to be sitting at his desk, smoking a cigar or masturbating to stock figures or whatever else he usually did in the mornings.

But that wasn't what he saw.

P.T. was golfing. He was standing beside his desk with a seven iron, systematically whacking a row of golf balls out the open window. With each swing there was a loud grunt, something between a laugh and a shout, and then he would put his hand above his eyes like he was blocking out the sun and watch his ball sail over the brick building in front of him to land out of sight, possibly on the heads of unsuspecting pedestrians 175 yards away.

Too bewildered to process what he was seeing, Trent let his hand slip from the door, and it closed behind him with an audible click.

"Trent!" P.T. turned. The man had never sounded so happy. "Glad you're here! Sit down a moment, let me knock off a couple more."

For once, Trent didn't mind sitting in the short chair—didn't even notice it, really. He just watched as his boss, who might have been going crazy, started talking to each ball as he swung.

"That'll *teach* you." Whack. "You dirty son of a *bitch*." Whack.

"Um, sir?"

Whack. "Hope you like the *view*." Whack.

"Sir?"

"I *told* you." Whack. "This is *my* world." Whack.

"Could you please tell me what the fuck is going on here?"

Finally, after the last ball had soared over the next building's roof and into some unseen car's windshield, P.T. set his golf club on his desk. He was sweating, and his face was red, flush with some unknown triumph. "Trent, have a seat."

"I'm already sitting, sir."

"Oh." The General took his own chair. "So you are. Very good."

"Should I call your therapist?" He wasn't entirely certain the man had one, but it was a fairly safe guess.

Then P.T. did a thing Trent had never heard him do before. He laughed. The sound was ripped from him, jagged and hot, a *Clockwork Orange* sort of laugh.

"Therapist? Hell, son, I've never felt better in my *life*. And do you know why?"

"Nobody does. Everyone's waiting to find out."

"Of course. But I had to tell you first. You and I have a *lot* to talk about."

Trent took a long swallow of coffee, almost afraid to hear any more. "Like what?"

P.T. lifted a newspaper from his desk and tossed it to Trent. "Page 14, second column."

Trent turned to the right page. It was the obituaries.

All of a sudden, he started to get a very, very bad feeling.

"Go on, second column. You'll know it when you see it."

That was absolutely true. And when Trent found what he was looking for, what had catapulted his boss into such high spirits, he felt as though he'd been shot in the stomach.

Stewart Dyson, founder and executive director of Dyson Associates, was dead. He'd died late last night, apparently the victim of a massive and unexpected heart attack. He was survived by his wife, two children, and his infant granddaughter Isabella.

Another section landed in Trent's lap. Numbly, he picked it up.

"Page three," P.T. said. "At the bottom."

Trent read. Simon Petersen, vice president of Dyson Associates and heir apparent to the media mogul's now-empty throne, had announced his intention to resign. Citing "personal reasons" that were sure to cause no end of speculation, Mr. Petersen was stepping down immediately. There was no mention of the fate of the second-largest media consulting firm in Los Angeles, and there was some talk that without the guiding light of its visionary founder, Dyson Associates would sink quickly into oblivion. The paper would follow up on developments as they occurred.

"I *told* you this was a war," P.T. said. "And every war has its casualties."

Trent couldn't say anything. He was in shock, stupefied, unable to move or think or do anything but listen.

"This could not have come at a better time, Trent. That man was trying to change *everything*. You don't know this, but I've seen some of the shows he was trying to push through. Monstrous, Trent, things that should never have seen the light of day. *Lives in the Balance*, that was just the beginning. And *some*how—God help me if I understand how—he was starting to gain support. Foster told me, he actually told me once, that he wanted to see some things 'along the Dyson model.' That's what he called it, the Dyson model." The tendons on P.T.'s neck became momentarily visible. "I'm telling you, Trent, this could not have come at a better time."

P.T. leaned back and closed the window behind him. "I've known Dyson for a long time. We fought together in Vietnam, did you know that? In the same battalion, as a matter of fact. The man had no heart for it. He was soft, he was *always* soft, and if he'd had the chance he would have done the same thing to television. If he'd had his way there'd be no room for the kinds of shows we need to be making. Would you like a cigar?"

The man had never offered before. But Trent declined with a shaky wave of his hand. Right now, the thought of smoking made him nauseous.

The General lit one for himself. "The world is not a forgiving place. I think you'd agree with me there. I think you'd agree with me on most things, that's why I made you vice president. This world doesn't tolerate losers. There's no room for second place, never has been. The history of all life supports that idea. We didn't get where we are as a species by working *with* other animals, and we didn't get where we are as a nation by worrying about everybody else. This is the greatest country in the world, and it's that way because we *fought* to make it that way.

"And our television programs need to reflect that mindset. Survival of the fittest, Trent. We need to show people that the only way you can succeed in this world is by taking care of yourself. Sure, we need others—that's why all these shows start out with teams and groups and so on—but as soon as people outlive their usefulness, then it's our job to let them fall behind. Otherwise, we can't get anywhere ourselves. The human race didn't rise this far by always turning around and going back for the sick and elderly, that's for *cer*tain."

P.T. shook his head. "The America I grew up in, the America I fought for? She's dying, Trent. When I went to Vietnam, America was a strong country. She wasn't afraid of *anything*. Whenever someone punched us, then by God we punched them back. We didn't worry about how everyone felt; we did what was necessary.

"But *now*," he continued, getting out of his chair, "now, look at us. Look at what's happened to this country. We've become a nation of *pussies*. Look at Iraq. Couple thousand soldiers die and suddenly everyone wants to bring 'em all home. That's not how you fight a war! You don't stop fighting until you've won, that's the only way to do it. You have to win, no matter *what* the cost. Not to mention everybody's talking about how we have to be *equal* and *fair* to everyone, not because they deserve it, but because it's 'the right thing to do.' All this equal rights bullshit that's going on in the world—in *our* world, Trent. There are parents in this country who pull their kids out of school if someone's mean to them. In this country! How are those kids supposed to learn about the real world? How are they supposed to grow up and learn that the world doesn't have *time* for losers?"

P.T. started pacing. "And you know, if things keep up like this, we're all going to lose. The fucking Chinese are going to take over everything—and don't think they aren't ready for it, don't think they haven't been training for the past fifty years waiting for the right time to do it—and we're just going to let them walk all over us because it wouldn't be *nice* to fight back. Well, let me tell you something. That's not the world I want. That's not the world I fought for in Vietnam. I won't allow it, Trent. I won't *allow* that to happen."

Trent watched him, bewildered, frozen in place by a man he felt he was seeing truly for the first time.

"You know," P.T. said with a nostalgic smile, "there was a time when I thought about getting into politics. I did, I shit you not. That's not so hard to believe, is it, knowing me? But the one thing about politics is, you can't ever get away from your past. And there are certain things I've done, people I've associated with . . . well, you understand."

He sat down beside Trent, stuffing himself into one of his own undersized chairs. Trent felt a desperate urge to recoil.

"You know why I came out here seven years ago? I was doing fine in Boston, you know. I was respected, I had people who were loyal to me. I had a good business going. But it wasn't enough. And I finally realized, like a bolt of lightning from God Almighty, that the *real* power wasn't in politics or business. The *real* power in America is on the TV screen. Look at our country. Do you realize that the average American spends more time watching television than working? That the average kid spends more time watching TV than doing his homework? Of course you know that. The average family will spend more time in front of the TV each week than they'll spend at church in a *month*. Television is the new religion of this country—and *we*, Trent, you and me, are America's most powerful priests. We're the ones who tell them what to think, how to live, how to act, who to admire and who to despise. Their futures are in *our* hands."

He put a hand on Trent's leg. "You know, in a way I envy you. It took me sixty-two years to realize all this. But you and Max and everyone else, you guys are thirty years ahead of me. If I'd known then what I know now, America would be a very different place, I guarantee you that. A stronger place, a country that wouldn't have backed out of Vietnam and Grenada and Iraq just because some people at home didn't have the heart for it. I'm going to take this country back to where it belongs. *We* are, Trent. That's our mission. That's what we've been called to do."

Trent looked at the hand on his leg as though he didn't know what it was. This wasn't real. He was Keanu Reeves in *The Devil's Advocate*, waiting for Satan to pop out of Al Pacino's grinning mouth. He took another sip of his coffee, which by this time had grown rather cold. He hardly noticed.

P.T. stood up. "This is an unprecedented opportunity for us. With Dyson out of the way we don't have to compete with his softer vision.

We don't have to compete with *anyone*. We finally have the ability to do what I've wanted to do since I left Boston. This thing we've started, it's only beginning. We've haven't even scratched the surface yet, and now it's time to start the real push. And we're going to keep pushing and pushing until all the Puritans in this country, all the Ronald Armsburgers and poster-carrying PETA members and self-righteous moral police can't fight back anymore. We're going to make America strong again if we have to drag it by its fucking *teeth*. This is just the beginning, Trent. This is only the beginning."

"What about him?" Trent croaked. "What about Armsburger?"

"Don't you worry about him. His term is up in eight months. But even that's too long. Never mind, though, don't you worry about it. I have a feeling he's not going to be a problem for us much longer. And when he's out of the way, then there won't be anybody to stop us."

P.T. kept going, spewing his apocalyptic philosophy like a zealot in the desert, but Trent was no longer listening. He suddenly became aware of the manila folder underneath his arm, cowering like a gypsy standing before the Gestapo. There was no room for shows like *The Samaritan* in P.T.'s world. There was no room for anything in P.T.'s world except for more of the same, backstabbing and greed and unadulterated lust, each one more rapacious than the last until nothing meant anything and no one could trust anybody.

It was at that moment that Trent realized what he needed to do. Something clicked inside his brain, something molten was twisting in his heart. It wasn't a thought so much as an instinct, a primal urge that consumed him until he could concentrate on nothing else. And the more P.T. continued to talk, the more absolute the impulse became.

He had to kill his boss.

Part Three: [SEPTEMBER]

"Insanity—a perfectly rational adjustment to an insane world."
—R.D. Lang

[CHAPTER TWENTY-ONE]

"Have you lost your *mind*?"

Trent didn't exactly know how to answer that question. It was the first time he and Adam had met for a drink since their argument. He hadn't even been sure Adam would show up. But it had all worked out, and a good thing too, because Trent had no idea who else he could have called.

All day he'd been thinking about it, the thought growing on him like a fever. For the past five hours he'd been sitting at his desk, staring at the wall and replaying P.T.'s conversation over and over and over again. He could hear the man still, spouting his vision of the future. And the more Trent thought about it the more convinced he became. He had to do it. It was crazy—it was *more* than crazy—but it had to be done. P.T. Beauregard had to die.

"You can't be serious," Adam finally said. He sounded desperate, which Trent supposed was understandable. Most people probably would sound that way if one of their friends was planning to kill someone. "Trent, tell me you're joking. You just made this up so I'd come meet you, right? Right?"

"Keep your voice down."

"Look, I know we haven't been on the best terms lately, but this is—"

"I'm not kidding." Trent looked around at the other customers. There weren't many, even for two in the afternoon. Still, he lowered his voice. "I'm going to kill him."

"Jesus, man, you can't—"

"He killed Dyson. I know he did. That call, remember, the call I got the night before Dyson died? Dyson told me, he said someone was following him."

"That doesn't mean—"

"I *know* it was him. He paid someone to kill him, I know it. Why else do you think Petersen would be retiring? They threatened to do the same to him, I'd bet on it. *And*, Dyson said I was in danger. That's what he said, Adam. I *have* to do this. If I don't, think about what might happen to me."

"Even if you're right, that doesn't mean you can just . . . you can't just . . . you can't *do* this."

"Yes, I can." It was strange; the more he talked about it, the less nervous he was. "I have to, Adam. You didn't hear him this morning. If he gets his way, there won't be any way to stop him."

"Stop him? Christ, Trent, we're talking about *television* here."

"It's more than television." He lit another cigarette, the last of the two packs he'd smoked that morning. "It's more than television."

"Look, man, you can't just kill somebody because they disagree with you."

"People do it all the time. The Inquisition, the Salem witch trials, religion, politics, war. Look at the Bible, for—"

"Are you really comparing yourself to the Inquisition? You've lost your *mind*, man!"

Trent wasn't about to be deterred. "There are times when it's justified. The world would be a better place if some people weren't in it." Privately he estimated that number at around a billion, but he didn't think now was the time to bring that up. "Have you ever read *Crime and Punishment*?"

"What? Yeah, so?"

"There you go."

"What do you mean there I go? Are you insane? Have you forgotten about the '*and Punishment*' part? Most of that *book* was punishment!"

"I won't feel guilty."

"Jesus, man—"

"Look." Trent pointed his cigarette at Adam. "I've already made up my mind. This is something I have to do. I've been selling my soul for my entire adult life, which you were happy to point out to me a few weeks ago, by the way. Now finally, *finally*, I have a chance to do something that really matters."

"That's what Hitler thought."

Trent pulled on his cigarette as if it were oxygen. "I've made up my mind. It's the only way to save America, and it's the only way to save myself. Are you going to help me or not?"

"*Help* you?" Now Adam was truly baffled. "Who said anything about *helping* you? Why the hell would I want to get involved in this?"

"Because," Trent said in a low voice, "I don't know how to kill anybody."

"And I do?"

"Listen, I can't just walk into his office tomorrow morning and beat him over the head with a baseball bat." All right, so maybe Adam was right; maybe he was a little unbalanced. Either way, that was definitely the most fucked-up sentence he'd ever uttered in his life. "I need to cover myself."

"Trent." Adam looked at the ceiling, then back down at the table, then at the rest of the bar. "I don't know how to say this. If you go through with this, you're going to end up on death row being buttfucked every day by some guy named Chester."

"Nobody's going to find out."

"How do you *know* that?"

"I don't know. I haven't gotten that far yet."

There was a lull at that point, which both of them filled by finishing their drinks. This wasn't exactly how Trent had imagined it would go. How did Mob bosses do it? There had to be some in L.A., or at least some hit men—why didn't they advertise?

Instead he looked for Candy, who was nowhere to be found and who desperately needed to bring him more to drink.

"Trent." Adam sounded tired. "Trent, you can't do this."

"Yes, I can."

"What *good* is it going to do? There's just going to be another guy like him. You plan to kill all of them?"

"There *won't* be. That's where you're wrong. If Dyson's company goes out of business—which it will—then Nova's all that's left. And if P.T.'s not around to manage it, I'm next in line. Don't you see? *I'll* be the one making the decisions."

"It can't be that easy."

"It *is*. I'll be calling all the shots. I can hire you on if you want, we can change things together. That's what we always wanted to do, isn't it? Isn't it?"

"Not like this," Adam said. "Not like—look, man, you can't just *kill* somebody just because you don't like what they're doing!"

"I don't see why not. Happens all the time."

"You can't *do* this!"

"Look, I don't have time to run around in circles with you. Are you going to help me or not?"

Adam said nothing.

But Trent already knew his answer. Adam wasn't going to help. He shouldn't have been surprised, and he really wasn't; asking had been a long shot. But he was still disappointed. It would have been nice to have an accomplice.

For a while they just sat there, tilting their glasses back to catch the few drops that remained. Around them, the low hum of other conversations bubbled in the air. It was plain that no one had heard them.

"So," Trent said eventually, "any luck with the movie?"

It was an absurd change of topic, but it worked. Adam seemed to relax, and there was something like a smile on his face.

"Actually, yeah." He looked at his empty glass for a moment. "You remember me telling you about Karl Dietrich?"

"At Black Forest? The one who said *The Long Road* needed more tits?"

"That's the one. About a week ago I went back over there and met with him. Don't ask why he bothered to see me, but anyway, I pitched *Deadly Justice* to him, and . . ."

"And?"

Adam looked up. "And he liked it."

In the wake of Trent's stunned silence, Adam continued. "He said it was just the kind of script they were looking for—fresh, funny, violent, and plenty of tits. That's what he said, 'And plenty of tits.' So he ran it by someone at Universal—"

"You're not serious."

"—and Miramax, and Dreamworks. Trent, they're bidding on it. All three of them."

"You're kidding, right? All *three* of them?"

"I'm not kidding, man. It's going to happen. They're going to make my movie. Or at least option it."

"I don't believe it," Trent said. "When did all this happen?"

"Three days ago."

"And you're just *now* telling me?"

"You said you didn't like the script."

"Yeah?" That was true, it was debatably the worst script he'd ever read. "Maybe. But that doesn't mean I can't be happy for you. Adam, that's fan*tas*tic!"

"Thanks."

"So," Trent said with an attempted grin, "I guess you're not going to help me kill my boss, are you?"

"You can't go through with this, man. It's *crazy*."

Trent ignored him, as he usually did when people said he was crazy. If he'd paid attention every time he'd heard that . . . "What did Angela say when you told her?"

"Angela? Oh, her."

"Something wrong?"

"Not as far as I'm concerned. We broke up a few days ago."

"Oh. Sorry to hear that."

"I'm not. She was too theatrical, you know?"

Actually, Trent did know. But he didn't say anything. He'd learned from experience that as soon as you criticized a friend's ex-girlfriend, the two of them were bound to get back together.

"Besides," Adam went on, "I've found someone else."

"Really? Who?"

And at that moment, Candy walked up. "Hey, sweetie," she said to Trent. Then, as she turned to Adam, her voice dropped half an octave. "Hi, sugar."

Right away, Trent knew.

"I came in three days ago," Adam said, "after Dietrich told me that the bidding had started."

"You told Candy before you told me?"

"You said you didn't like the script."

"Isn't it *wonderful*?" Candy said. Her arm was around Adam's shoulder, her chest close enough to his face that he could have eaten off of it. "Isn't *he* wonderful?"

"She was very happy for me," Adam said with a grin. "Very, *very* happy."

"I'm sure she was."

"He's already promised me a part," Candy added.

"I'm sure he has." Trent got up. He wasn't in the mood to be the third wheel. "Look, congratulations, both of you. I've got to go."

"Where you headed, sweetie?"

"Trent's going to go kill his boss," Adam said.

"Oh. Well, good luck with that."

"Thanks. How much do I owe you, Candy?"

"Let me take care of it," Adam said. "I think for once I'll be able to afford it."

Trent didn't object.

][

He pulled out of Garibaldi's parking lot in silence. No music on the radio, no open windows—just the quiet rise and fall of his engine and the smooth, steady hum of his tires on the asphalt. The sound of his turn signal, the rustling of his shirt as he turned the steering wheel—every little noise seemed unnaturally loud. He drove that way for a long time, uncertain where he was going or what he would do when he got there.

So, Adam was on his way. After years of paying his dues, watching less-talented people eclipse him over and over again, Adam was finally going to get the fame and fortune he'd always wanted. And so what if his movie was an utter horror? The ends justified the means, right—and besides, considering how he'd spent the last two years, Trent wasn't really in a position to criticize. But that didn't mean he had to be happy about it.

Whatever. The real problem was that now Trent had no idea who he could turn to. He needed help—there was no doubt about that—but who would agree to it? More importantly, who could he even risk asking?

He ran down the list of people he might consider. He could always ask his hairstylist. Or his masseuse, come to think of it. But he doubted either of them would be up for it. *Yes, I will help you kill your boss, and then I will massage the knots from your back*. Doubtful.

So, the only people left were the people at work. Not the best of circumstances, but there wasn't much of a choice. So, who to ask?

Tad was out, for obvious reasons. He might have been a good decorator and a sharp dresser, but those weren't exactly the kinds of skills Trent was looking for. Just the thought of Tad holding a gun was enough to disqualify him. He'd probably faint at the first sight of blood.

Todd was out, too. He could talk a good game, but that was about it. And Taylor—Jesus, that was just an invitation to disaster. Tad might drop the gun in his anxiety, but Taylor was just as likely to shoot the wrong person.

That left Rachel and Max. Rachel was a definite possibility; Trent didn't think she'd have a problem killing anybody, including himself at times. And Max . . . well, it was a poorly kept secret that Max wanted to run the company.

Trent reached for a cigarette, then realized he was out. What did he know? He'd never done this before. It wasn't like asking a girl to the prom, and even that hadn't been easy. Oh, for the love of God, what was he *doing*?

But he couldn't give up. For *once*, once in his miserable, whorey life, he was determined to do something good. And if that meant putting himself into a few awkward moments, then so be it.

Only then did he realize he was on the southern edge of town. At the next light he turned left. There was somebody he had to see.

][

"So wait, wait wait wait wait. Lemme get this straight, pal. You wanna do *what*?"

Patiently, Trent explained again. They were at Max's apartment, which looked like a cross between a college pad and a love den. Framed movie posters hung on the walls, and there were candles everywhere, and lotions, and incense, and small colored glass bottles full of God knew what. A rope chair hung in the corner, and a highly polished wet bar stood fully stocked, waiting to be exploited. The door to the bedroom was closed, but Trent would have bet money that the bed rotated.

As soon as Trent finished, Max leaned back and shook his head as though he were trying to wake up. "You wanna kill P.T."

"That's right."

"And then take over the company."

"Pretty much."

"And if I help, you'll make me co-president."

He'd been thinking vice president, but now wasn't the time to split hairs. "That's the idea."

"Wow. That's fucked up, pal. When are you planning on doing it?"

"Don't know."

"How you gonna kill him?"

"Don't know."

"How are we supposed to get away with it?"

"Don't know."

"This isn't much of a plan, pal."

"First things first," Trent said. "Are you with me or not?"

Max paused. "Does anyone else know about this?"

"No. Yes, one person. But he won't tell anyone."

"How do you know?"

"I just know. And by the way, if you tell anyone about this conversation—"

"Hey, give me some credit, will you? I'm not a rat. Besides, you'd just deny it ever happened, and what'd that get me? Nowhere, except maybe fired for spreading lies about Nova's vice president." Max inhaled sharply through his nose. "So, you have no idea how we're supposed to do this, or how we're supposed to get away with it."

"More or less. Are you in?"

Max considered. A second turned into ten, which turned into thirty. Outside, a car alarm went off.

Finally, Max raised his eyebrows and shrugged. "Sure, pal. I'm in."

Trent blinked. "Really? You're serious?"

"Yeah, why not? It'll be fun. Is that all right?"

"No, that's great, it's just . . . that was easier than I thought it'd be."

"Eh, fuck the man. The way I figure, I don't owe him anything. Sonofabitch promoted you instead of me, remember? So, what now?"

"I don't know," Trent said. "To be honest, I didn't really think I'd ever get to this part of it."

"Fair enough. Well, how do you want to do it? Knives, guns, mustard gas, what?"

"Not knives." Way too messy, plus he'd have to stare right into P.T.'s eyes. "You don't think we could get our hands on any poison, do you?"

"Well, yeah, sure, I could pour some Drano in his coffee, but I don't think he'd drink it. Poison's like the Dark Ages, pal. Car crash?"

"No way. Too much paperwork." And, as if that wasn't an absurd enough thing to say: "We could sabotage his car, though."

"That's movie bullshit. You always see some clueless fuck driving along on the highway when he suddenly realizes his brakes don't work. I mean seriously, is that the first time he'd be trying his goddamn brakes? He'd know as soon as he left the parking lot. Let's do guns, how's that sound?"

"Sure."

"Guns are good. Nice, friendly, kill you quick. We don't want to torture the poor bastard, right? All right, you ever shoot one?"

"Fifteen years ago." In his more sober moments, Trent's father had loved nothing more than going out into the woods and shooting things. Mostly he'd shot trees, not so much because he hated them as because he couldn't aim for shit. "Does a BB gun count?"

"Not really, but it's something. You don't own a gun, I take it."

"No, do you?"

"Nah, but it's not hard to get one. Won't do any good if you can't shoot it, but we can take care of that easy." Max scratched his head. "Tell you what, give me a couple days to figure something out. I know some people who know some people, you know? We'll make this happen. Until then, just don't tell anybody. The fewer people who know, right?"

"Right. Good. OK." Trent stood up, eerily calm for someone who'd just finished making preliminary plans to kill his boss. He'd actually been more nervous about his audit last year. "So, I guess that's that, huh?"

"For now," Max said. "I tell you what, Trent, you are one crazy motherfucker. You know that, right? But I like it. This'll be fun, I haven't killed someone in years. Relax, I'm just screwing with you, pal, I've never killed anybody. But seriously, I think you're right. I think it's time to take this company to the next level, you know? Hey, you wanna go get a drink? I'm dying here."

[CHAPTER TWENTY-TWO]

It was strange for Trent to go back to work the next day. He felt as though everyone would know, as though there would be some bright symbol on his forehead for everyone to see. Worse, he kept worrying that he might accidentally give something away, that some psychotic impulse might encourage him to shout "I can't wait until I kill my boss!" at the top of his lungs while pouring himself another cup of coffee. Killers did that all the time on *Law and Order*, except without the coffee.

He arrived just in time to be late to a meeting he hadn't known about. Apparently no one else had, either, because all of them were sitting there looking completely confused. Max shot Trent a conspiratorial look as soon as he sat down, and for a moment Trent was certain everyone would see it. But nobody seemed to pay any attention.

"Trent," P.T. barked, "start getting here on time."

"Sorry, sir." God, it was going to be nice not to have to say *that* all the time anymore. "What's going on?"

"That's what we're all waiting to find out, honey," Tad said.

"I'll bet it's about Fox," Max said.

"All right, all right, enough talking." P.T. held up a copy of the *L.A. Times*. "Anyone read this yet?"

"Read the paper?" Taylor asked.

"Seriously, who has time?" Todd added.

"I didn't think so," P.T. said.

"I did, sir," Max said.

"Good. It's nice to know that at least *one* of my employees is literate. As for the rest of you, let me fill you in. The . . . FCC"—P.T. said the word like a curse—"has issued a two-million-dollar fine to the Fox network for last week's episode of *Extreme Dating*."

"But that's one of *our* shows," Todd said.

Tad gasped. "Two million dollars? Whatever *for*?"

"Indecency," P.T. said. "Anyone see last week's show?"

"I did, sir," Max said. "Never miss it."

"Good. Remember the lap dance? Well, Armsburger and the rest of his terrorist group have decided that it 'breached the boundaries of common decency'."

"What are they talking about?" Rachel said. "I saw it too, her ass was completely pixilated."

"She's right," Max agreed, "it looked like a blob. Two blobs, really. A bit disappointing, if you ask me, she looked like she might have a nice one."

"They didn't ask you," P.T. said. "Armsburger is calling it a flagrant violation of the FCC's new decency standards. He said, 'Any child watching that show would know there was sexual activity taking place.'"

Taylor sniffed. "I don't think sex is indecent. I think it's fun."

"Sexual activity?" Max was sincerely aghast. "*That's* indecent, because there's a suggestion of sexual activity? Well, hell, let's close everyone down, then. No more shampoo commercials, and what about Animal Planet? I've seen lions going at it for ten minutes at a time."

P.T. nodded. "Armsburger's threatening to triple the fine—not double, *triple*—for the next network offense. Not just Fox, but any network that airs a similar broadcast."

"That's extortion!" Todd roared.

Trent looked at his boss. The man was strangely quiet, almost calm. He might have been talking about his stock portfolio for all the anger in his voice, and that was not like him. Something else was going on, and that something was probably not a good thing.

"So what do you want us to do?" Trent asked.

"Nothing."

That couldn't be right. "Nothing?"

"Nothing. There's nothing for us *to* do. I only wanted you to be informed, that's all. Now get back to work."

Nobody knew quite how to respond to such an abrupt end to their meeting. The process of filing out of the conference room was silent and awkward. Trent got himself a cup of coffee and was about to leave when P.T. stopped him.

"Trent." He shut the door to the conference room. "You and I need to talk."

Immediately, Trent froze. He knew. He knew! Max must have told him; why else would he have been acting the way he did, sucking up like a goddamn leech. All right all right all right. All he had to do was call Max a liar. Nobody'd be able to prove anything.

"What is it, sir?" he asked. It was a miracle his voice didn't give out.

"We have a real problem on our hands."

"Oh?" Maybe it would be best to just start running. "What's that?"

P.T. put an arm on Trent's shoulder. Against his strongest effort, Trent flinched.

"It's Armsburger."

Trent's bones began to melt with relief.

"Ronald Armsburger," P.T. went on in a quiet, icy voice. "That spineless, soulless, conniving piece of shit. He's trying to ruin us, you know. He'd like nothing more than to see all of us dead and buried. I've just about lost my patience with him."

"I wouldn't worry about him," Trent said, suddenly happy and ready to talk about anything. "If you ask me, Fox has been asking for it for months. They are the ones who aired *Burlesque Mothers* between two cartoons. Some family channel."

P.T. smiled thinly but didn't say anything.

"So, what do you want me to do? Issue a statement, do an interview, what?"

"Nothing. There's nothing you can do. There's nothing any of us can do as long as that man is running the FCC."

"So what do—"

"Don't worry about it. I've got things under control. This time next month, I guarantee you, Armsburger isn't going to be a problem for us anymore."

Suddenly the room grew very, very cold. "What are you talking about?"

"Trust me, I'm going to take care of everything. And just so you know, this conversation? Never happened."

"What conversation?"

P.T. smiled again, this time more broadly. "That's what I like in a vice president. Now, get back to it."

Great, Trent thought as he headed for his office. Just great. Now P.T. was planning to kill Armsburger, too, unless by "take care of everything" he meant "have a reasonable discussion over a nice dinner," which Trent highly doubted. Now it was even more important that he stop P.T. before things got too out of hand. But how?

][

"I've got it."

Trent looked up from his desk. All afternoon he'd been fielding calls from frantic television executives trying to figure out if their networks would be the next to suffer the wrath of Armsburger's FCC. As if he knew. He was tempted to tell them all that if their shows involved honey, polygamy, whip cream, pixels, syrup, hot tubs, bedrooms, breast implants, string bikinis, hot waxes, camping, or dating multiple women at the same time, then it was a safe bet they would someday be targeted. But since that would eliminate every reality show ever made, he opted for the safer and less informative, "Use your best judgment." When in doubt, offer a platitude—that was Trent's motto, at least for today.

"Got what, Max?"

"I've figured out what we need to do. You know, about . . . *him*."

"Jesus Christ, would you shut the fucking *door* first?"

"Sorry." Max shut it behind him and sat down. "All right. First thing, we need to get guns, which I'll take care of."

"Shouldn't we talk about this somewhere else?"

"Jesus, Trent, what are you worried about? You think he bugged your room?"

"Actually, yeah."

"You're overreacting. Look, I know a couple guys can get us guns. Nobody'll be able to trace them back to us."

"How do you know a couple guys?"

"What do you mean how do I know them? I'm Sicilian, it comes with the job. Don't worry about that, just let me take care of it, all right? All right. *Now*, the next thing is, we gotta follow him."

Trent would have been much more satisfied if they'd been having this conversation at a coffee shop on the other end of town. "Follow him where?"

"Around. You know, see what he does after work. I think it'd look kind of suspicious if we killed him here."

"Could you keep your voice down? You don't know how thin the walls are."

"You're worrying too much, pal, he doesn't suspect a thing. Why would he? If someone were planning to kill you right now, would you suspect it?"

That was an awfully unpleasant comparison to make. "Just get on with it."

"All right. What we do is, we tail him after work. You know, see where he goes, what he does, all that. That's the only way to figure out where to get him. I don't even know where the man lives, and I'm guessing you don't either.

"Not a clue."

"So, we need to figure all this stuff out. After we know where he goes and what he does, we'll be able to decide the best time to take him out."

"You've been thinking a lot about this, haven't you?"

"Course I have. Haven't you?"

Trent didn't really want to answer that. The truth was, he'd been hoping it would just take care of itself.

"Meet me at my car after work," Max said. "We'll wait until he leaves, then follow him. Sound good?"

No, it didn't sound good. None of this sounded good. But it had to be done. "Yeah, I'll be there."

][

Waiting in a car for someone to come out of a building was, in Trent's opinion, the most tedious experience of his life. Time absolutely stopped, and there were two occasions when he would have sworn the digital clock on Max's dashboard had actually moved backwards. After the first hour, Nova's back door started to look blurry and hazy; by the time the second hour was almost up, Trent was starting to believe that the door hated him. It had to, otherwise it would have opened by now.

"Why does it hate me?" he finally said to Max, who was changing the radio station for the seventy-fifth time.

"Relax, pal. We're on a stakeout here, this is exciting shit. Haven't you ever seen a movie?"

Yes, he had, and in the movies the cops never waited for more than thirty seconds before something happened. Damn the movies with their time distortions! "I have to go to the bathroom."

"Hold it."

"I have been."

"Then use a cup." Max finally settled on classic rock. "You like Free-bird, right?"

Not particularly. "You sure we're not being too conspicuous here? I mean we're parked right across from him."

Max shook his head. "I told him my car wouldn't start. Said I'd call for a tow when I got home. He'll just think it hasn't showed up yet."

Just then, the back door opened.

"There he is," Trent hissed.

They watched P.T. walk around the side of his car, an imperial-looking Mercedes sedan so highly polished that the black looked almost silver. He opened the trunk, set his briefcase inside, then walked around to the driver's door. He got in, started the car, and began to back out. Not once had he looked in their direction.

"What'd I tell you," Max said. "Hold on, here we go."

They waited for P.T. to pull out of the parking lot and into traffic before starting after him. By now it was almost seven-thirty, and the traffic was thin enough that he was easy to follow. He took Lincoln to Pico and turned east, then north on Westwood. At one point he made it through a stoplight before they did, but luckily they were able to catch up at the next one.

"Get closer," Trent said.

"What, you want me to rear-end him? Would that be close enough?"

"I don't want to lose him again."

"Trust me, I know what I'm doing."

"Oh, right, because you follow people home all the time."

"Maybe I do. How would *you* know?"

In this way, the two of them proceeded. It wasn't exactly the playful banter between an experienced cop and his rookie sidekick, but it managed to pass the time.

As it was, Trent had nothing to worry about; P.T. drove like a grandmother. He never ran through a yellow light, and he accelerated to the speed limit about as quickly as an overweight jogger. Trent could conceivably have kept up with him on a skateboard.

"You'd think he'd drive a little faster."

"Hey, I'm not complaining," Max said. "Change the station, will you pal, I hate this song."

For the next twenty minutes, Trent saw nothing but the taillights of his boss's gleaming Mercedes. Whenever they flared to life as the car slowed down, Trent reflexively inhaled on his cigarette, and the tiny ember glowed bright in sympathy. There were more than a few times that other cars worked their way between pursued and pursuing, but every time Max managed to stay on the right track.

"Any idea where he's going?" Max said at one point.

"Not a clue. You?"

"I'm starting to think so. We'll see if I'm right."

"Where?"

"Let's just see if I'm right first."

Their question was answered soon enough. After taking a series of poorly-traveled side streets that Trent felt sure would give them away, P.T.'s Mercedes pulled into a circular driveway manned by a pair of liveried valets. Another pair of men, each about the size of an Abrams tank, stood on either side of a single, heavily-tinted door. There was no façade on the building, no indication at all what it might be, but Trent knew it anyway.

"That's LaRue's."

Max pulled slowly past the driveway and parked on the street about half a block up. "Yep. I knew it."

"I didn't know he was a member."

"Neither did I. Had a hunch, though. Shit."

Trent twisted himself around in the seat. From where he sat, he could just barely catch a glimpse of P.T. handing his keys to a valet and walking inside. "He's going inside."

"Of course he's going inside, where else would he be going? Jesus, you know how much it costs to belong there?"

About a year's salary, Trent thought. And that probably didn't include parking. He watched one of the bodyguards close the door behind P.T. and assume his previous Buckingham Palace stance. "So what should we do?"

"Wait for him, I guess. I'll pull the car around."

Max went up to the next intersection, made a screeching U-turn—"Did you *really* have to do that?"—and parked on the opposite side of the street. They now had a perfect view of LaRue's front entrance, although there wasn't much to look at. Aside from the occasional car driving past, nothing changed.

"How long do you think he'll be in there?" Trent asked.

"Don't know." Max paused. "What do you think he's doing?"

Trent had some idea. He'd heard of LaRue's, of course—everyone in L.A. had *heard* of it, although nobody he knew could afford to belong—but he rarely heard the same thing twice. Some thought it was just a gentlemen's club, a dark oak-paneled place with expensive cigars and colorless conversation about stock options and hip replacement surgery. Others thought LaRue's was a *true* gentlemen's club in the vein of *Eyes Wide Shut*, with perfect women writhing naked on brass poles until someone chose to take them to one of the club's spacious back rooms. Trent was certainly more intrigued by the latter possibility. "I have a couple ideas."

"So do I."

They waited. Trent leaned his head against the headrest and stared at LaRue's door with dull, half-opened eyes. Ten minutes turned into twenty, then thirty. Nothing happened. Thirty-one, thirty-two, thirty-two and a half. Oh, God, how did detectives put *up* with this?

"I'm bored," Max said.

"So am I."

Another minute passed.

"Are we gonna do this all night?"

"Looks like it. It was your idea, remember?"

"You're the one who wants to kill him."

Another ten minutes passed.

"Fuck it, pal." Max opened his door. "I'm going in."

Suddenly Trent was *wide* awake. "You're *what?*"

"I'm going in there."

"You can't just walk *in*, Max! What about *those* guys?" He gestured at the mounds of unsmiling muscle guarding the door.

"Them?" Max shrugged. "Not a problem, I can talk my way past them. I can talk my way into anything. You'd know that if you came out with me more often."

"What about P.T.? What if he sees you?"

"Don't worry, pal, I'll think of something. He's not gonna suspect anything, why would he?"

Trent grabbed Max's arm. "Don't."

"Watch me."

And before Trent could stop him, Max pulled himself free and was out of the car. Trent watched in horror as Max crossed the street, whistling—the bastard was actually *whistling*—as he approached the doors.

It was over in ten seconds. Max presented himself to the guard on the door's left side. Trent could see him talking, moving his hands in small circles. Then, just at the moment Trent expected Max to be thrown into the street, the door was opened for him, and he stepped inside.

He stared for a moment longer, then lowered his head onto the dashboard and hit it repeatedly with his forehead. It would have been better if Max *had* been flung into the gutter. Now Trent had to wait and see what happened.

The next forty-five minutes were intolerable. The door opened three times in that period, but the people who emerged were neither Max nor P.T. By the third one, Trent was certain something had gone wrong. Max had been spotted, or caught, or locked up by the club owners until the police could come and take him to jail. Or he'd run into P.T. and told him everything, spilled his guts right there at P.T.'s table. The two of them were plotting together, leading Trent into a trap that would cost him more than his job. Or maybe—

Then, when Trent's hope had all but disappeared, Max returned, leaving with the same nonchalance he'd had when he entered. He patted one of the bodyguards on the shoulder and hurried across the street. He was still whistling.

Trent assaulted him as soon as he got in the car. "What the *fuck* were you thinking? Do you realize you could've—"

"Relax," Max said easily. "There's nothing to worry about, pal. He didn't see me. Didn't see him, either, he must have gone to one of the back rooms."

"So what the hell were you *doing*?"

Max cleared his throat. "Well, I sat down in a booth—that place is unreal, pal, you wouldn't be*lieve* some of the art they've got on the walls—and this waitress came up. She asks what I want, right? So I say—"

"You were in there *drinking*?"

"Not exactly. So I said to her, 'What do you have?' And *she* said, 'Anything you want.' I was like, '*Anything*?' Then she leaned over—and she was something else, you should have *seen* what she was wearing—and said, 'Anything you can think of.'" Max shrugged. "So I thought of something."

"Wait." Trent closed his eyes. "Wait, wait a second. You're not telling me that you . . ."

"Oh, yeah. Yes, I did."

"You slept with her?"

"Trust me, pal, there wasn't any sleeping going on."

Trent stared at the roof of the car. "I don't believe it."

"Believe it. I have *got* to get myself a membership there."

"We're on a stakeout, Max! Do you understand what that means?"

"Hey, why do you think I went in there? I was doing *surveillance*. I just happened to do that waitress along the way."

"Sur*veill*ance, Max. That means you're supposed to pay attention to the guy you're following."

"Hey, I paid attention. He was definitely not in the room she took me to."

Trent was debating whether to strangle Max with his own hands or beat him to death with a croquet mallet when P.T. walked out of LaRue's. Instantly their argument ceased. They waited while P.T.'s Mercedes was pulled around, then allowed him to drive half a block. Then Max started the car, and they were off.

As before, P.T. drove like a student driver. He made his way to the 405 and headed north. At no time did he give any indication that he knew he was being followed.

"You ever been up this far?" Max asked at one point.

"Never."

"This is a long way to drive every morning. Why not just get a house in Bel Air?"

"Who knows?" Trent said. "Maybe they're not big enough."

As it turned out, that was exactly the reason. After getting off the 405 and making a series of turns past increasingly wealthy neighborhoods, P.T.'s Mercedes pulled into one of the biggest houses Trent had ever seen. It looked more like a compound than a single man's home, protected by a nine-foot adobe fence on all sides and a keycard reader by the iron gate. The driveway itself was over half a mile long, snaking down a gentle hill to disappear around the back of the house. P.T.'s Mercedes paused long enough for the gate to open, then proceeded inside. The gate closed quickly behind it. Max drove past and parked his car near the corner of P.T.'s property.

"Jesus," Max said, "it looks like a drug lord's home."

"Wouldn't surprise me. Let's get a better look."

The two of them got out of the car and walked up to the fence. Thick, leafy trees provided both a screen from passing cars and a hindrance to their own efforts. Eventually, Trent got on Max's shoulders and hoisted himself up to the top of the fence. His knees scraped against the rough plaster as he pulled himself up—so much for *that* suit—then he reached down to help Max. Fortunately, the fence was thick enough for them to sit on without too much danger of falling.

The view from their new perch was even more impressive. P.T.'s house was a monster, two sprawling stories of brick and stucco situated on a low hill and surrounded by acres of sculpted gardens. Beyond the far fence was a dark expanse of forest; P.T. had probably purchased the lot just to keep anyone else from developing on it. The Mercedes was still visible, winding its way down the long driveway toward the garage at the back of the house. There was a large patio on the home's east side, and, from where he sat, Trent could just make out the blue glimmer of a lit pool. A small, square guard house sat inside the gate, and another building, possibly a servant's home, adjoined the house on the west.

"Fuck me," Max said. "What do you think, thirty rooms?"

"At least. He could hide in there for hours and we'd never find him."

"That's not the only thing. He's got guards."

Sure enough, a pair of flashlight beams were cutting an orderly path around the perimeter of the home. The men were too far away to be seen clearly, but that didn't matter. Trent and Max watched for ten or fifteen minutes—long enough for one man to make his way from one end of the house to the other—and at no time were there fewer than two flashlight beams in sight.

"He's got a *lot* of guards," Max said. "Probably cameras, too, somewhere. I'll bet that guardhouse is full of TV screens."

"Do you see any way inside?"

"Not from here. Maybe there's a way in on the other side, but I doubt it. Doesn't look like the old boy is taking many chances."

"A guy like this doesn't have that many guards unless he's made some serious enemies," Trent said. "Do you have any idea what he used to do before he came to L.A.?"

"Not a clue. Come on, let's go."

Gingerly the two of them hopped off the fence and got back in Max's car. The engine sounded unforgivably loud in the cool night air, but nobody came running. Soon Max was pulling back onto the road and past the iron gate again. Trent tried to catch a glimpse of a guard in the guardhouse, but he didn't see anyone.

So, breaking into P.T.'s house was out of the question. And they couldn't very well shoot him down at LaRue's and expect to get away with it. There had to be a way, though. There just had to be.

"It's just going to take some time," Max said as they turned back onto the highway. "You can't decide to kill someone on Monday and take care of it Tuesday, that's just not how it works. Don't worry, though. It'll all work out. I'll think of something."

[CHAPTER TWENTY-THREE]

Trent and Max repeated their pursuit of P.T. for each of the next four nights. The General's routine was invariably the same: leave work at seven-thirty, drive to LaRue's, stay for ninety minutes, then drive home. There was no deviation from his routine, no opening that Trent and Max could hope to exploit. The man was a robot, an evil corporate cyborg whose monotonous regularity protected him from any possible attack. By the end of the week, Trent was beginning to lose hope.

"Cheer up," Max said as they were driving away from P.T.'s house on the fifth night. "How easy'd you think it would be? Come on, pal, try to have some *fun* with this. We're out tailing cars, stalking our boss, plotting to kill him—what else could you ask for?"

Trent didn't answer. It was good that Max was enjoying himself so much. It was also extremely weird and disturbing. But Trent couldn't manufacture that kind of enthusiasm. He wasn't some bored teenager looking for a thrill; this was serious. The future of America was at stake, and if he lost heart—or worse, if he failed—the entire country would be forever doomed to an endless barrage of soul-killing TV shows like *My Daddy the Pimp*.

"I think we should make it look like a robbery," Max said when they turned back onto the interstate. "Or a carjacking."

"How? I don't think we should do it at work, and the only other place he goes is LaRue's. And we can't do it *there* because the bouncers would recognize you." Trent had made Max swear he would not go back into LaRue's until after they took care of business, to which Max had reluctantly consented.

"We could run him off the road somewhere," Max said. "I've never seen anyone else driving up here."

"Can't. If we hit him, some of the paint from our car will get onto his. The police'd be able to trace it."

"You watched *CSI* last night, didn't you."

"Yeah."

They were silent for a while. The outskirts of Santa Monica appeared, and soon Max was turning onto Wilshire Boulevard, where Trent had left his Jaguar.

"I guess we'll have to break into his house, then."

"I guess so," Trent agreed. "Any idea how we're going to do that?"

"Not a clue, pal. Doesn't look like the old boy leaves a lot to chance, you know what I'm saying? But first things first. Open the glove compartment."

Trent reached forward and pulled the latch—and before he knew what had happened, there was a gun sitting on his lap.

"Jesus fucking Christ is that thing loaded?"

"Relax, pal. You act like you've never seen a gun before."

"Of course not, Max, I have guns fall in my lap all the *time*. Is it loaded?"

"No, it's not loaded, all right? *Jesus*."

Marginally appeased, Trent picked it up. It was a six-shooter, lighter than he expected and, judging by its appearance, well used. He popped the cylinder just to make sure it wasn't loaded, then clicked it back into place.

"Where'd you get this?"

"Don't worry about where I got it. I know people who know people, remember?"

"Was this the best they had?"

"What do you want, a fucking bazooka? Beggars can't be choosers."

Trent turned it over in his hands. "I feel like Danny Glover with this thing."

"You look like him, too. You gonna complain all night or what?"

"You're right. Thanks." Trent turned it over in his hands. "Where's the safety?"

"It's a revolver, pal, they don't have safeties."

"Oh." He checked the cylinder again, just to be safe. "So, what am I supposed to *do* with this?"

"Keep it. That's what you're gonna use to kill P.T."

The gun seemed to grow awfully warm at the mention of its intended purpose, like it was anxious to complete the job. "What about you?"

"Don't worry about me, I'm taken care of. There should be some bullets in there, too."

Trent rooted around in Max's glove compartment until he found them. "Hey, Judas Priest. I had this tape. Did you even know this was in here?"

"It's been a while since I cleaned it out. Here's your car."

Max parked behind Trent's Jaguar. It was almost eleven o'clock at that point, the street mostly empty. Trent looked down the sidewalk in both directions before opening the door. "All right, Max, I'll—"

"For Christ's sake, pal, would you *hide* that thing?"

Sheepishly, Trent stuffed the gun inside his jacket and put the box of bullets in his pocket. "Sorry."

"It's nothing. But tomorrow I think you should spend some time at a firing range, make sure you can hit your target. We want to kill him, not scare the shit out of him. I know of a good one, I'll call you tomorrow and give you directions."

"Yeah, sure, all right. What about you?"

"I'm telling you, I've got it covered. Besides, I figure you're the one who should have to shoot him."

"Why me?"

"Because it was your idea, wise guy. See you Monday."

Trent closed the door and watched Max drive off. Then, already convinced that everyone on the planet knew what he was up to, he hurried to his car and deposited the gun in his own glove compartment. He wanted to put it somewhere else—the cops always looked in the glove compartment first—but there wasn't anywhere else to hide it.

So, they were really going through with it. All that was left was to break into P.T.'s impregnable home, find him amidst his 4,000 rooms, and shoot him before he could unleash his own private arsenal—which he was certain to have—on them. That seemed like a fair week's work. In fact, there was only one question that nagged at him as he drove home.

With a world this insane, who needed Reality TV?

][

The next day was Saturday, and just after ten o'clock Trent pulled into the parking lot of Big Bob's Firing Range. The ad had touted Big Bob's as "the largest firing range outside of the Middle East," which didn't seem like a particularly solid selling point. If he saw anyone with a rocket-propelled grenade, he was leaving.

He had no idea where he was. He'd just followed Max's directions, driving east on the 10 Freeway for almost three hours until he was a little more than halfway to Phoenix. There were firing ranges closer to home—he could have driven through Compton or East Los Angeles for that—but Max had argued, and Trent had agreed, that the last thing they needed was for anyone they knew to recognize Trent. Right now he was parked alongside a dusty strip of road that may as well have been in the Mojave for all the urban hospitality it offered. There was a bar across the street, though—Uncle Jim's, the wooden door framed by a series of hubcaps. Ah, guns and beer, America's two favorite pastimes. Real shame they couldn't combine the two buildings into a single establishment. Add a church and a strip club and you'd have a perfect cross-section of the American dream.

Trent sat in his car for a moment and took a deep breath. Except for a trip to Arkansas he'd made as a child, Trent had never seen so many pickup trucks in one place. And here he was without any overalls.

He closed the door to his Jaguar and set the alarm. There were a couple of people standing by Big Bob's front door, and they looked up at the sound.

"Well," one of them said in a drawl that belonged in Appalachia. He was about sixty with a cannonball gut and a military haircut. "Looks like we got ourselves a city boy."

Trent blinked. Where was he, the backwoods of *Deliverance*? Maybe if one of his car doors had been a different color, they would have been more welcoming. "I've come here to learn how to kill things."

That seemed to satisfy them. "Well, you've come to the right place. I'm Big Bob. Let's get you signed up."

Trent followed Bob inside. Compared to the near-blinding noon sunlight, the interior looked rather dark and unwelcoming. The air was filled with a dim popping sound, like a hundred firecrackers exploding underneath a thick mattress. Bob lumbered his way through a waist-high saloon door and took his place behind the main desk. On the wall above his head was a collage of shell casings, arranged neatly by size and culminating in something that must have come from a tank. How charming.

"So," Bob said with a grunt, "you want to learn how to kill things."

"That's right," Trent said. He tried to puff his chest out. "That's what we men do, isn't it?"

"Got that right. Y'ever shoot before?"

"Not since I was a kid."

"Need lessons?"

"No thanks."

"All right, Mr. . . . ?"

Trent panicked. "Smith. John Smith."

Big Bob gave Trent a long, blank look. "John Smith. Right. Well, whatever you like, Mr. Smith. You brought a weapon?"

Trent pulled his six-shooter out and held it up. "Right he—"

With a lightning-fast lunge that belied his appearance, Big Bob grabbed Trent's wrist and slammed it down on the counter. Before he knew what was happening, Trent was twisted into a ball, pinned in place by Bob's right hand.

"First rule, son. Don't ever point a weapon at anything you don't want to shoot, understand?"

"Yes, sir. Sorry."

Slowly, Bob relaxed his hold. "S'all right. I can tell you're new, but I can't afford to take any chances, y'understand."

"Of course. Sorry." He should have known better; he'd seen *Pulp Fiction*.

"Ain't nothin'." Only then did Big Bob completely release him. "All right, Mr. Smith, I've got you set up in stall thirty-four. You need ears?"

"Ears?"

"You bring your own?"

Trent squinted. "Yeah. They're on my head."

Big Bob shook his head disdainfully. "You need hearing protection." He reached under the counter and withdrew a black pair that looked especially well-worn. There was no telling how many sweaty, backcountry heads they had been on. "Need ammo?"

"Ah, no, I've got some, thanks."

"How much d'you have?"

"One box. Isn't that enough?"

"You're gonna need more. Stall thirty-four, door's to your right. There's a one-hour minimum. The first five targets are free, come back here if you need more. Pay when you're done."

"Thanks," Trent said. He took a couple of steps and reached for the door handle.

"Put your ears on first."

As soon as he opened the door, the mild popping sound became a roar. Men and women of all ages were standing in an unbroken line, separated by what looked like bulletproof partitions as they decimated paper targets with their weapons of choice. There were a few families present, fathers teaching their sons and daughters how to properly gun down a potential intruder. One little girl—she couldn't have been more than seven—giggled as he walked past. But she did remember to keep her pistol pointed at the target.

There was already a target set up for him when he reached number thirty-four. It was about five yards away, and a small red joystick attached to the right wall allowed him to adjust the distance. He left it alone for now, then started shooting.

The gun kicked more than he'd expected, and the blast caused him to close his eyes as he fired. When he opened them a second later, there was a small, ragged hole just left of the target's black torso. His second shot went just to the right. Well, at least he would have scared the man.

Trent spent the next hour in his firing booth, pumping round after round after round into dozens of targets. It was so much easier than he had thought it would be. Once he got used to the gun's action and recoil, there really wasn't anything to it. After fifteen minutes he wasn't missing anymore, and by the end of his hour he felt he was a decent shot. Of course, P.T. probably wouldn't do him the favor of standing in one place while he took aim. It would have been nice if he could have practiced with a moving target.

"Hey," he asked Big Bob after his first hour, "do you have any moving—"

"Door to your left. It costs more."

"No problem. I'm going to need some more bullets, too." He cleared his throat. "I mean, ammo."

The next hour was considerably less successful. Moving targets had an irritating tendency to move out of the way of his bullets. He took some consolation in the knowledge that P.T. probably couldn't run as fast as these targets were moving, but it was still evident that he would need to come back.

When he was finished, Trent went back to the front counter and paid, making sure the barrel of his gun was pointed directly at the ground. He peeled the earmuffs off his head—despite having stood in one spot for the past two hours, he was covered in a light sweat—and thanked his host.

"Ain't nothin'," Big Bob said. "Good luck killing whoever you're aiming to kill."

Trent froze. "Excuse me?"

Big Bob didn't blink. "You ain't using that gun to go huntin', that's for sure. Like I said, good luck gettin' whoever done you wrong." He winked. "Mr. Smith."

Trent thought it best not to talk any more. He nodded slowly a few times, then turned around and walked out.

It took about thirty seconds for his eyes to readjust to the blinding desert sun. He couldn't even see his car, much less start walking toward it. When he was finally able to see, he left Big Bob's front step and started toward his car.

Suddenly there was a terrific squealing of tires. Trent whirled just in time to see a rusting pickup truck jump the curb and barrel onto the sidewalk. His stomach collapsed. The out-of-control truck was heading directly for his Jaguar.

There was nothing he could do. With a sickening crunch of metal and glass, the truck smashed into the driver's side of Trent's car. Windows shattered, and the front tire exploded like a gunshot. The car was thrown across three parking spaces so quickly it almost left the ground; if he'd been in the driver's seat, he would almost certainly have been killed. The truck came to a halt, its front fender horribly dented and steam leaking from the radiator.

Amazingly, Trent's first impulse was not to worry about his car. "Hey!" he shouted, racing for the truck, "Are you okay?"

The driver was a man, grizzled and dazed and obviously uncertain about what had just happened. At first Trent thought he might be in some state of shock, until he saw the empty whisky bottle in the man's lap. How it hadn't been thrown through the windshield was a complete mystery.

"Jesus, do you even know where you *are*? Come on, get out of the truck."

In response, the man swung his head toward Trent, looked at him with yellow, bloodshot eyes, and then—with the theatrical majesty that only the monumentally drunk can muster—threw up on his own passenger seat. Then, without a word, he lurched his truck forward and drove off.

"Hey!"

It was no use. By the time Trent realized what was happening, the pickup truck was back on the road, weaving its battered way toward another accident. Trent watched him leave. He hadn't even thought to get the number of the license plate—as if Cousin Jethro actually had insurance.

With a long sigh, Trent turned to his more pressing problem. It didn't take a mechanic to realize that his Jaguar was completely totaled. He was going to need a tow truck, and someone to drive him back to town.

He pulled out his cell phone. Thank God he was still close enough to civilization to get a signal. The first person he called, in part because he was the first person on his call list, was Adam.

On the fourth ring, the answering machine picked up.

"Hi."

Trent looked at his phone. That was a woman's voice, not Adam's, unless he'd had some operations in the last week.

The message continued. "Adam can't come to the phone right now. He's busy with me. Oh. Oooohh."

Then Trent realized. He knew that voice, had heard it every Monday for the past two years. It was Candy.

And she was moaning.

"Oh, I'm afraid you're going to—ooh—have to. . . . *oooohhhhh* . . . call back later. Bye. Oh!" Beep.

He didn't bother leaving a message. Instead he called Max, who also didn't answer. He left a message this time, pleased that at least Max's message didn't involve anyone having an orgasm.

"Looks like someone did a number on you."

Trent turned around. Big Bob was standing in the doorway to his firing range, looking at the wreck with odd satisfaction, as though Trent's ruined Jaguar were a ten-point buck killed with a single shot.

"Wasn't one of my customers, was it?"

Trent shook his head. "Some drunk guy in a pickup truck. Any idea who it might have been?"

"Drunk guy in a pickup truck? Could-a been anyone, 'round here. Come on inside, I'll call you a tow."

Five minutes later a tow truck was on the way, and Trent was back in the parking lot, sitting on the curb and occasionally staring back at his broken car. He tried Max again, and again Max didn't pick up. Then, after a few minutes of debating whether or not he should, he dialed Rachel's number.

She picked up on the second ring. "I've been waiting for you to call."

That sounded promising. "Really?"

"Yeah. I'm in need."

That sounded even more promising. "I'll be happy to oblige. But I need you to do me a favor first. Can you come pick me up?"

"What happened?"

"Car accident. Don't worry, I'm fine."

"I wasn't worried. Where are you?"

He told her.

"Where the hell is that?"

"About three hours from you. Have I mentioned how nice you look today?"

Two hours and ten minutes later—Jesus, how fast did she drive?—Rachel's bright red Mini Cooper pulled into the parking lot. She left the car running and got out. For the first time since he'd known her—in both a professional and Biblical sense—she wasn't dressed for the office. Instead she was wearing frayed jean shorts and a white T-shirt that she'd actually tied in front. Trent highly approved.

She took her sunglasses off and squinted at him. "You want to explain what you're doing at a firing range in the middle of nowhere? Since when do *you* own a gun?"

Trent walked around to the passenger side and opened the door. There was no use in hiding anything; she'd probably guess anyway. And besides, she'd probably love the idea.

"I'll explain on the drive back," he said. "It'll give us something to talk about."

"You're paying for me to get my car washed."

"Fine."

She looked at the roof of her car. "If I'd known how dusty it was out here, I would have borrowed somebody else's car."

"I'll pay to get it waxed, too, all right? Let's just go. We've got more important things to discuss."

[CHAPTER TWENTY-FOUR]

"You had to go and tell her, didn't you?"

"She's up for it, Max."

"That's not the point. A woman's just going to fuck things up."

"I'll fuck *you* up if you don't watch it."

"Go ahead, darling. I might like it."

It was Sunday night. The three of them were at Max's apartment, and their conspiracy was suffering from some internal discord.

"Get over yourself," Rachel said to Max. "You can't get rid of me now, so you might as well deal with it. Besides, I'm looking forward to it."

That was an understatement. When Trent had first told her, Rachel's eyes had lit up like a child's at Christmas. She'd been giddy, so much so that it had been difficult for her to make the drive back to L.A. When he'd asked her why, she'd said, "I've always wanted to kill somebody." From that moment on, Trent had sworn never to wear a blindfold again while having sex with her.

Max threw his hands up. "All right all right all right, what's done is done. I just wish we had a little pro*fess*ionalism here."

"What we *need* is a plan," Trent said.

"Exactly. And fortunately, I happen to have a perfect one."

"I can't wait to hear it," Rachel said.

"You're on thin ice, darling."

"Would you guys cut it out?" Trent said. "This isn't a reality show, you know. We're on the same side here."

Max grinned. "Sorry. I'm too used to trying to bring everyone else down. Especially Todd. I *hate* that guy."

"Not a problem," Rachel said, "we can kill him next. Relax, Trent, I'm just kidding."

"I'm not so sure."

"*Any*way," Max said, "here's what we're going to do. Sometime next week I'm going to get myself invited over to P.T.'s house for dinner. Don't worry about how, that's my job. Then, Trent, you're going to hide in the trunk of my car. That's how we'll get you inside."

"What if they check the trunk?"

"They're not going to check the trunk."

"But what if they do?"

"Trust me, they're not going to check the trunk."

"But what if they *do*?"

"Then you'll get caught," Rachel said matter-of-factly. "They'll probably shoot you both."

Trent stared at her.

"I'm just saying."

Trent turned toward Max. "I'm not sure I like this plan."

"For Christ's sake, what do you want? You expect him to walk around in circles with a target on his forehead? There's going to be some risk, pal, that's just the way it is. Seriously, you ever watch *The Sopranos*? That's how it *really* works."

Trent doubted that the producers over at HBO used Mafia men as their creative consultants. "I just want to be careful."

"I will be. Trust me, if there's one thing I can do, it's talk my way out of trouble. I've been practicing since I was a kid, you should've *seen* some of the things I got away with."

"As much as we care about your childhood," Rachel said, "you want to tell us the *rest* of your plan?"

Max looked at Trent. "Seriously, pal, why her? Of all the people you could've told."

"Guys," Trent said. Was killing someone *always* this difficult? That might explain why more people weren't killed every day. "Like it or not, we're in this together. Understand? Together."

"Yeah, yeah yeah," Max said. "Whatever. So once I'm inside, you'll crawl out of the trunk. The back seats open up, and I'll make sure the release is off. Then you'll come inside, shoot P.T., and run back into my car. Meanwhile I'll tell the guards that someone, I couldn't see who, ran out through the opposite window. They'll know it wasn't me because I don't have a gun on me. Anyway, while they're distracted with trying to find you, I'll start shouting that P.T.'s still alive. Before anyone can say anything I'll scream something about taking him to the hospital, then put him in the back seat of my car and peel off. And *that's* how we'll get out. I'll drop you off somewhere and take P.T. to the hospital. Not like they'll be able to do anything for him, but just for appearances. And that's that." He leaned back, triumphant. "What do you think?"

"Not bad," Trent said. "What's my alibi?"

"You won't need one. There's no reason to think you're in on it. If anyone asks, tell them you were at home sleeping. You don't own a gun—at least you won't after that night—and you've never bought one, so the police won't have any reason to suspect you."

"What's my job?" Rachel asked.

"You'll be driving the getaway car in case anything goes wrong."

"The getaway car? I don't want to drive the getaway car."

"Someone has to, darling. Killers always have a getaway car."

"Ha!" Rachel said. "So you *do* need me after all."

For the next two hours the three of them hammered out the details. Aside from Max and Rachel throwing the occasional barb at each other, things seemed to be going smoothly. Not like Trent really had anything to compare it to—planning a murder wasn't exactly like deciding what movie to see. Still, by the time he finally left Max's apartment a little after midnight, Trent was starting to think that this might actually work out after all.

][

But the next morning, disaster struck.

For once, Trent was on time to work. It wasn't his fault; it was Rachel's, since she was driving him while his insurance company decided whether or not his car was worth repairing. Even so, everyone else was already waiting in the conference room. They did that quite a lot, he was beginning to notice; apparently they all liked their jobs enough to get there early, which was somewhat disturbing. He opened the door and began to apologize.

That's when he realized that something was very, very wrong.

P.T.'s face was aglow, literally. His cheeks and forehead were flushed and red, and the smile on his face made him look like that guy in the Viagra commercials. In all the time Trent had worked at Nova, he had *never* seen his boss that happy, not even the day after Dyson was killed—and that couldn't be a good thing.

"Sorry we're late," Trent said softly, even though they weren't. "Traffic was—"

P.T. stopped him with a wave of his hand. "Don't worry about that! It's nothing, doesn't matter at all! Get some coffee and sit down, we've got a *lot* to talk about."

The room was eerily quiet while Trent poured a cup of coffee. Todd and Taylor were giving each other confused looks, and Tad was busy drawing little stick men with abnormally large penises on the inside cover of his notepad. Trent poured two cups of coffee, one for himself and one for Rachel, and sat down. Max did not make eye contact.

Trent took a long, tentative sip of coffee. Still nobody said anything. P.T. was grinning like a child, so excited he might actually have wet himself.

Naturally, Max was the first to break the silence. "You okay, boss?"

"Okay?" For only the second time since Trent had worked at Nova, P.T. laughed. "Am I okay? Hell, Max, I've never felt better in my *life*. This is a *great* day for me, a great day for Nova, and a great day for America."

"Well," Tad said, "sounds like *some*one's had some fun this morning."

"You sound like you're running for president," Max said to P.T. "You sure you're all right?"

"I'm better than all right. I'm *better* than all right. You know why?" P.T. looked at each of his employees in turn. When he came to Trent, his gaze lingered for an uncomfortably long time. "We're *back*, people."

"What do you mean, we're back?" Taylor asked.

"I mean we're *back*." P.T. leaned forward, grinning like a fanatic. "All that talk about changing our format and coming up with *nice* shows? Gone. Done. Finished. We're back where we started, people, we're going back to making the kind of shows we *should* be making. All that family-friendly bullshit I told you to come up with 'just in case'? Don't need it. I want you to toss it, I want all of it out of this building by the end of the day. I mean it, people, we are *back*."

There was a somewhat awkward silence that followed, sort of the same kind that comes after a man says "I love you" to a woman who doesn't love him back. People cleared their throats and looked at their hands. Trent tried to catch Max's eye, but Max's attention was riveted on P.T.

"Um." Todd immediately looked as if he wished he hadn't said anything. "I mean, that's great and all, but what about . . . what about Armsburger?"

"The FCC," Taylor added. "They didn't just disappear overnight, did they?"

"No," P.T. said, still smiling. "But I've got an inside line. There are about to be some significant changes over at FCC headquarters, and I can say for *cer*tain that those changes will be in our best interests."

"What happened?" Max asked. "Armsburger get the boot?"

"I can't talk about it," P.T. said. "Not yet at least. But trust me, things are about to happen. Big things. This is what we've been waiting for, people. We're finally going to get the government off our backs. We're finally going to be able to make whatever shows we want."

Suddenly P.T. leapt up, bumping the table and knocking his own coffee cup onto the floor. He glanced at it for a second, before he stepped over the spreading puddle. "All right, people, this is what we're going to do. Taylor, I want you to repackage *Take It Off!* and pitch it again. ABC's got first refusal, but tell them we've got three other networks ready to pounce if they're not ready to run with it. Todd, I want another *Gangland Romance*. But make it bigger this time, more violence, more . . . I don't know, more people getting stabbed with icepicks, got me? Tad, you do the same. Come up with something really . . . gay. You know what I'm talking about."

"Yes sirree," Tad said. "Can we do full frontal?"

"Eew," Taylor said. "Even *I* don't want to see that."

"Exactly," P.T. said. "Run it. Whatever you can think of. The sky's the limit here. Rachel, where are we on *Extreme Animal Lovers*? I want it ready for presentation by this Friday, understand? Trent, I want you to call everybody—Walter, Barry, Jack Morgan over at TNT, call the public access channels while you're at it—and tell them that we're about to unleash a barrage."

"What's *happened*?" Max said. "You're making this look like the Google IPO."

"Bigger," P.T. said. "This is bigger than Google, bigger than Microsoft, bigger than everything. *This* is the moment we've been waiting for, people, and I need you to be ready for it when it happens. We've got an empire to build here. You all know what you need to do? Good. Now get to work."

There was no slow shuffle back to the cubicles after that. They all jumped to their feet, excited and energized by a promise whose details none of them knew. What had happened? What was *going* to happen? No one could say. But at the moment, that didn't matter.

P.T. was still sitting there, beaming, staring at the opposite wall with the sunny-eyed confidence of a conqueror. Trent waited until the others had left, then closed the door.

"You've got to tell me."

The General shook his head. "I can't."

"You have to."

"Not until it happens."

"Until what happens? The FCC leaves us alone? That'll never happen, not while Armsburger's the chairman."

"Exactly. Not while Armsburger's in charge."

"What are you saying?" Trent asked. "He'll never step down, not with only eight months left on his term, and not while we're over here trying to ruin America, as he would say. He'd rather see us dead first."

"Likewise."

"So what *is* it?"

But P.T. wouldn't say. "You're going to have to trust me. Now get moving. Oh, and when you talk to Barry, tell him congratulations on his grandchild."

][

Trent spent that afternoon with his ear glued to the phone. He called everyone—including the Home and Garden Network and ESPN Desportes—and told them about the onslaught they should begin to expect in the next fourteen days. Every one of them wanted to know what had happened, and to every one of them Trent gave the same lame answer.

"No idea."

"Not a clue."

"Wish I could say."

"I was hoping you could tell me."

"I'm in the dark just as much as you."

"Been wondering that myself."

"You know I'd tell you if I knew anything."

Despite not knowing why a show surplus was coming their way, most of the networks were eager to jump on it. Fox had a Tuesday night slot opening up, the Discovery Channel was ready to work its way more deeply into the Reality game, and NBC was looking to add variety to its Friday night lineup. Even the History Channel, in an effort to undo years of atrocious dramatizations, was looking for ideas—which meant that hundreds of bad actors and actresses were soon going to have a more difficult time finding work.

Between calls, Trent couldn't help thinking that the timing for all this was perfect, at least for him. P.T. was setting everyone up to expect shows they'd never seen before. So if he could take care of P.T. and get control of the company, he'd be able to package *The Samaritan* as the vanguard of the new Reality era. The networks might balk at first, but Nova's record of success would convince them to give it a try, and once the shows started to take off . . . well, it was possible everything would turn out the way it was supposed to. The way it should have been all along. Maybe P.T.'s unexpected excitement wasn't such a disaster after all.

On the other hand, it meant that one way or another, *some*thing was going to happen soon. That didn't leave them very much time. If Max couldn't figure out a way to get himself invited over to P.T.'s, they were going to have to come up with something else, and fast.

Noon came and went, and the hours began to drag. Trent took only thirty minutes for lunch, not because he was eager to keep working, but because he didn't want P.T. to start thinking he wasn't committed to his job. The last thing he needed right now was to cast any suspicion on himself. The butts in his ashtray steadily piled up, and by three o'clock the air in the room was slightly hazy with cigarette smoke. Take *that*, California lawmakers.

At three-fifteen, Lynette poked her head in the office. She was dressed as though she was about to go on a walkabout with Paul Hogan. "Trent?"

He put his hand over the receiver. "I'm on the phone, Lynette. What is it?"

"Frank from CBS is on line three."

"Why's he calling the main line?"

"He said he's been dialing your extension all day but can't get through. Oh! Speaking of not being able to get through, you'll never *guess* who I saw today!"

"I'm on the phone, Lynette."

"Oh. Right."

"Tell Frank I'll call him when I'm done."

As soon as Trent finished his call—it had been a long shot, but the marketing director over at PBS had actually sounded curious—he called Frank.

"What is it, Frank?"

"Trent! I've been trying to get through to you for *hours*. Where have you *been*?"

"I've been on the phone for the last six hours. What's the crisis this time?"

"You tell *me*! All day long I'm hearing rumors about something *huge* that you guys are about to unload on us. Everyone I've talked to, that's all they can talk about. 'Have you heard from Nova? What do you think's going on?' What I want to know is, how come nobody's calling *me*?"

"I was going to call you, Frank. I hadn't gotten around to it yet."

"You were *going* to call me? I've been hearing about this since ten o'clock! When were you going to call, tomorrow? Three days from now? Who'd you call first, the goddamn Home and Garden network?"

Trent decided not to tell Frank the truth about that one.

"I thought we had a relationship here, Trent."

"We do."

"Then how come you haven't called me yet?"

"I was *going* to. We're talking now, aren't we?"

"I can take our business elsewhere, you know."

"No, you can't," Trent said. It was going to be even more enjoyable to put people like Frank in their place when he was running the company. "There's nowhere else to go, remember? Dyson's . . . finished."

"Look, the bottom line is, if you're going to cut us out of the loop, we'll just do our creative work in-house. We can do that, you know."

"Fine. Do that. I know the kind of winners your in-house will come up with. If that's what you want, go right ahead. Perhaps I was mistaken when I thought that you actually wanted to be a competitive network."

Frank paused. "I can't afford to be last on your list, Trent. We don't want to be known as the guys who take whatever's left over."

"You're not. If you had any patience at all, you'd know that. Now I don't know what you've heard, but I can guaran*tee* that you haven't heard a word about any specific shows. That's because we're not releasing any yet. I'm just calling people to let them know that we're *about* to open a few dozen up for bidding. This is just a heads-up call."

That seemed to pacify him a little. "What kind of shows?"

"I can't tell you."

"Why not?"

"Because I don't know."

"Stop bullshitting me, Trent. If you want to treat me like this, I—"

"*Frank*, I'm not lying to you. I really don't know. P.T.'s got something big planned in the next couple weeks, but he hasn't told me what it is."

"But you're the vice president."

"And don't think I haven't tried to find out."

"Does this have anything to do with Armsburger's speech next Saturday?"

"I'm telling you, I don't . . ." Trent cut himself off. "What did you say?"

"Armsburger. He's flying to L.A. on Friday to deliver the keynote speech for the AMP convention. I thought maybe P.T. had an inside tip on what he's going to talk about. You didn't know about that?"

The blood began to leave Trent's cheeks. "No, I didn't. Do you know when he set this up?"

"Just a couple days ago. I think he's doing someone a last-minute favor."

Oh God.

"I've, I—I've got to go," Trent managed to say, then hung up. All of a sudden, things had become desperate.

[CHAPTER TWENTY-FIVE]

"All right," Max said, "you wanna tell us what all this is about? You look like you're gonna explode. You want a Valium or something?"

Once again they were at Max's apartment. It was just before six o'clock; Trent had insisted that they meet as soon as they left work.

"No, I don't need a Valium. Look, I found something out this afternoon." Trent took a deep breath, closed his eyes, then opened them again. "He's going to kill Armsburger."

Max and Rachel looked at each other. For a long moment they said nothing. Then Rachel adjusted her glasses.

"So, what, is that a problem?"

That wasn't exactly the response Trent was looking for.

"Yes, it's a *prob*lem! He's going to kill Armsburger! We can't let him *do* that!"

"How do you know that?" Max asked. "He tell you?"

Trent told them about his conversation with Frank. "Look, he didn't have to *tell* me, all right, I just *know*. P.T. comes in this morning saying that everything's going to change soon, and it just so happens that Armsburger's coming to L.A. this weekend? That can't be a coincidence."

"Why not?" Max asked. "Maybe Frank's right, maybe Armsburger's going to announce a policy shift. Or maybe he's going to announce his retirement—*you* don't know."

"He's not retiring," Trent said. "And he's *sure* as hell not going to change FCC policy. You've heard him before, you know that isn't going to happen. There's only one explanation, Max. P.T.'s going to kill Armsburger, I *know* it."

"I'm still trying to figure out why that would be a bad thing," Rachel said.

There was a pause.

"She's got a point, pal."

"Have you both lost your—"

"Whoa, pal," Max said with raised hands, "just hear me out. Armsburger's the chairman of the FCC, right?"

"Right."

"And you wouldn't exactly consider the FCC to be on our side, would you?"

"I'm not a fourth-grader, asshead."

"Hey, patience is a virtue. Isn't that right, Rachel?"

"Fuck off, Max."

"Sorry, I couldn't help it. But seriously, Trent, we're talking about a man who's dedicated his life to keeping us from being able to do our jobs. Now *if* P.T. is planning to kill him—and I still think you're full of it, but just for the sake of argument—*if* that happens, what do we lose? Actually, I think he'd be doing us a favor."

"You've got to be kidding. You can't just *kill* a man because you disagree with him."

Max blinked. "You didn't just say that, did you? Because correct me if I'm wrong, but aren't we planning to kill our boss?"

"That's different," Trent said, and he lit a cigarette. Fuck the movies; they always made this look so easy. Conspirators weren't supposed to sit around and argue semantics.

"It won't bother me if Armsburger gets it," Rachel said. "I don't like him."

"Do me a favor," Trent said. "Stop talking. You're not helping."

"Fine. Enjoy sleeping by yourself."

"Do I need to leave you two girls alone?" Max asked. "I feel like I'm a fucking babysitter here." He turned to Rachel. "You two are . . . ?"

"Until today," Rachel said.

"How many times?"

"None of your business."

"None of my business. So, Trent, how is she?"

"More than you can handle," Rachel said.

"Can we *please* focus on the real issue here?" Trent shouted. Ashes from his cigarette went flying onto the carpet. "We have to stop P.T. from killing Armsburger."

"Listen," Max said, "I appreciate what you're trying to do, being all nice and thoughtful and shit. Save the whales, plant a tree, so on and so on. But seriously. *Seriously*, pal, think about it for a second. Once P.T.'s out of the way, we're going to be in charge, and then we're going to be the ones who have to deal with people like Armsburger. Now I don't know about you, but I wouldn't mind having someone a little more—I don't know, agreeable?—running the FCC. Don't you think so?"

"He's got a point," Rachel said.

"I don't *care*," Trent said. "Armsburger will be out of the picture in eight months anyway, that's when his term expires. What's wrong with waiting?"

"Takes too long," Rachel said.

"I can't figure out why you're so worked up about this," Max said. "You ever *met* the guy?"

"No."

"Well, I have. And trust me, he's a dick. There's a reason P.T. has a picture of Armsburger with a target around his head. The man's trying to stop us from *evol*ving. He's one of those people who actually thought the Teletubbies were immoral. He's bad news, pal."

"The man's just doing his job," Trent said.

"He's not letting us do ours, pal. What are you, defending him? Look, I don't want to kill him. But if that's what P.T. has in mind—and I still think you're being a little paranoid here—but if that's what happens, I'm not going to cry about it."

"We should probably send something to his funeral," Rachel said. "For appearances."

"There's not going to *be* a funeral," Trent said. "When Armsburger flies in Friday, we're going to be at the airport. We're going to follow him to the AMP conference, and if we see anybody trying to do anything, we're going to stop them. Is that clear?"

"So wait," Max said. "Lemme get this straight. You want us to look out for a guy we all hate and tail him all weekend on the off chance that our boss is planning to have him killed?"

"Exactly. I'll pick you up after work on Friday."

"In whose car?" Rachel asked. "You don't have one, remember?"

Trent looked at her.

][

"If anything happens to my car," Rachel said to both of them, but probably more to Trent, "I'm going to kill you."

Friday had finally arrived. All week the office had seemed restless, as if the building itself were waiting for something monumental to happen. By Wednesday the atmosphere had become oppressive, and that afternoon as Trent had walked out the door he'd felt as though he were escaping from an abandoned mine. It was abundantly clear that P.T. was anticipating a significant event, and Trent was now more certain than ever that he'd been right to assume the worst.

"Did you guys hear me? If anything happens to my car—"

"Relax," Trent said. "Nothing's going to happen, I promise."

"How can you be sure?"

"Jesus," Max said, "it's in the goddamn parking lot. What do you want?"

"If it's scratched when we get back, you two are paying to get it fixed."

They were on their way into LAX. Trent was leading the way, of course, though he no longer worried that Max and Rachel would vanish on him. They both seemed resigned to his insistence that they save Armsburger, although Max was still convinced they were wasting their time. As for Rachel, she'd been true to her word. Trent hadn't had sex all week.

As soon as they walked through the sliding glass doors into the airport, Max turned to Trent. "What now, fearless leader?"

For the twentieth time in as many minutes, Trent looked at his watch. "Armsburger's plane should be arriving in half an hour. Terminal six, gate 67. Let's go."

It was amazing what you could learn by making a few phone calls under a fake name. In less than two hours on Tuesday morning, Trent—alias Herbert Poonsplatter, a name so ridiculous no one would think it was false—had found out everything he needed to know about Armsburger's flight information, including his seat number and the fact that he was traveling alone. Good thing people were still gullible enough to be trusting; otherwise nobody'd ever be able to get anything done.

In order to meet Armsburger's plane at the gate, Trent had been forced to purchase three tickets, which neither Max nor Rachel had offered to help pay for. The terminals were packed, of course, and as loud as a circus. There were parents everywhere, talking hectically on cell phones and dragging groaning, obnoxious children by their sticky fudge-covered fists. Businesswomen with rolling suitcases stood next to blue-haired teenagers at the coffee kiosks, and the overhead intercoms were constantly reminding passengers not to entrust their belongings to strange people with explosives.

"*God*," Rachel said, after they saw a five-year old boy hit his sister in the head with a plastic baseball bat. "I'm never having children."

"Don't worry," Max said. "They don't want you for their mother, either."

"Come on," Trent said. "We need to make sure we're on time."

Ten minutes later they arrived at gate 67. All of the seats were taken, most of them by sprawling teenagers playing video games. The sign above the gate counter said that Armsburger's flight was on time and scheduled to land in fifteen minutes.

"Okay," Rachel said. "Now what?"

"Now we wait."

"I still don't think this is a good idea," Max said. "I mean, what if P.T. really *is* planning to kill him?"

"Do you think you could talk any louder?" Trent asked.

"I'm just saying, what if he is? And what if his hit men recognize us and tell P.T.? How are you going to explain *that* to him?"

Hmmm. Trent hadn't considered that possibility. "I'm sure you'll think of something."

They waited.

"This is boring," Rachel said.

"It's what you do," Trent said. "Haven't you ever met someone at the airport?"

"Yes, I have, and it's boring."

"So, Trent," Max said, "when the two of you are together, does she fall asleep if you don't get her off in the first thirty seconds? Cuz it seems like—"

"Fuck off, Max."

"All right, you two." Was it too much to ask for a little solidarity? How were they supposed to prevent somebody from being killed if they spent all their time arguing?

Another five minutes went by.

"This is ridiculous," Rachel said. "I'm going to get a cinnamon roll."

"Good idea," Max said. "Get me one too, will you?"

"No!" Trent grabbed her by the wrist before she could take a step. "We have a job to do. You can't just leave!"

Slowly and quite deliberately, Rachel removed her wrist from Trent's grip. "Look. Right now my car is parked in an airport parking lot next to two *minivans* full of soccer equipment. Do you have any idea how I feel about that? Do you have any idea what I'll do if some parking attendant drives his golf cart into my car? So, *you* can stay here and wait, *I'm* going to get a cinnamon roll, Okay? Okay. Do you want anything?"

Actually, a cappuccino sounded excellent. "No, I don't. Hurry up, all right?"

She walked away, the sound of her thin heels audible for twenty feet. Armsburger's flight would be arriving in approximately seven minutes.

"Nice try," Max said when Rachel was a long way out of earshot. "She's probably an on-top girl, isn't she."

"Max."

"Just asking. No harm in that. So is she?"

"Max."

"All right, all right, I get the hint." He paused for a moment. "So you haven't been getting any lately, huh?"

"I'm going to kill you, Max."

"Whoa, pal. We're here to save a life, remember? Not that I think there's any point in it, but if it makes you happy. Because that what friends do, isn't it, we suffer for each other. And that's what I'm doing right now, I'm suffering."

It would have been *really* nice to have a cigarette about now.

Rachel returned two minutes after Armsburger's plane pulled its ponderous way into the gate. "Here you go," she said, handing Max an enormous ball of sugar. The smell was overpowering, and it made Trent's mouth water.

"Thanks," Max said. "Oh, this is good. This is *great*. Hey pal, you want some of this?"

Yes. "No. Just keep your eyes open, he should be coming out any minute."

"I hope so," Rachel said. "I'm getting bored again."

"Seriously, what *is* sex like with you? Five minutes and—"

Trent cut Max off. "There he is, guys."

Ronald Armsburger had just emerged from the tunnel. He looked every bit as stiff and hawkish as the picture in P.T.'s office suggested, his nose even more pronounced and beaklike in person. He stood painfully erect and walked without looking to either side. His cheeks were beginning to jowl, which only added to his gray severity. There was no trace of a smile on his face or a wrinkle on his three-piece suit, and he was evidently in a hurry.

"Looks like he just got back from burning some witches," Max said.

"Come on," Trent said.

They kept a discreet distance, although Armsburger had no reason to suspect he was being followed. The whole time Trent was trying to look everywhere at once, straining to detect in every strange face the telltale marks of a professional hit man—a hand inside a jacket, dark sunglasses, perhaps an eyepatch or a monocle.

"Relax," Max said. "I doubt they're going to hit him at the airport."

Trent took a breath. "You're probably right. Rachel, pull your car around outside baggage and wait for us. As soon as Armsburger gets his bags, we're going to need to be able to follow him."

"Sure. But if *anything's* wrong with my car, you guys are—"

"We know," Max said. "We know."

Rachel started off. She breezed right past Armsburger, and for a moment Trent was afraid their cover was blown. But the man didn't even look at her.

Trent and Max followed him to the baggage claim. For ten minutes they waited near a concrete pylon, watching Armsburger as he stood motionlessly by the baggage carousel. When it started up, Trent's heart gave a little lurch.

"You know, pal, the more inconspicuous you try to look, the more obvious it is."

"I just hope Rachel's waiting for us."

Armsburger's bag—large, black, and unadorned—was one of the first ones out. He picked it up and headed for the taxi line. Trent and Max were right behind.

"I still think we should let P.T. shoot him."

"We can't do that, Max."

"I don't see why not. Maybe it's God's will. Maybe we're—"

"Since when do you believe in God?"

Max shrugged. "When it suits me. Like most people."

As soon as they got outside, Trent relaxed. Rachel's bright red Mini Cooper was there, lights on and engine running. She was standing by the driver's door with her arms crossed in front of her chest. Trent faked an excited wave for appearances, then hurried to her car.

"He's getting into that cab," Trent said as he climbed into the passenger seat. "Follow him."

"I know what I'm doing. Hold on."

With a fierce lurch, she pulled into traffic. The two cars left the airport, then turned onto the interstate and headed toward the heart of Los Angeles. Despite the amount of traffic and the number of identical taxis clogging the road, they had little trouble keeping up. Once they got into the city, it didn't take long to figure out what Armsburger's destination was.

"He's going to the Beverly Hilton, isn't he?" Rachel asked.

"Looks like it," Max said. "Man, I love seeing our tax dollars at work, don't you?"

"Shit," Trent breathed. "I don't want to pay for a room *there*. Why couldn't he stay at the Days Inn?"

"Probably not moral enough," Max offered.

The Beverly Hilton looked like what the Palace of Versailles could have been if the Sun King's architects had tried a little harder. The only thing missing was a bulletproof glass display of some small country's crown jewels. In any other city in America, the hotel would have stood out like an over-opulent, exorbitantly-priced thumb, but in Beverly Hills it somehow fit right in.

Slowly, Rachel pulled into the large circular driveway. Aside from the taxis, her car was the only vehicle that wasn't black.

"At least it's foreign," Max said as he got out. "Otherwise I don't think they'd let you park here."

She handed her keys to the valet. "Don't let anything happen to this car."

"Yes, ma'am. Do you have any bags?"

Trent's heart skipped a beat. What kind of person, much less *three* people, went to a hotel without bags? "Um. Bags? Hmmm."

"They're arriving separately," Rachel said. She gave him fifty dollars. "See that they're taken care of."

"Thanks," Trent said as they walked inside.

"You could have let him think you were hourly."

"Fuck off, Max."

"Quiet," Trent whispered. "He's right in front of us."

They walked inside and went up to the front desk. It was impossible to hide now with Armsburger directly in front of them, his back still rigid while he waited to receive his key. Trent was barely able to hear his room number, 708, before another clerk offered to help him.

"We'd like a room on the seventh floor, please," Trent said. "Preferably 707? The view is simply perfect from there."

A few minutes later, they were safely installed in their room. The door was had a peephole that would make observation easy, and the bathtub had Jacuzzi jets and was big enough for two. As well it should be, considering how much the room had cost.

"There's only one bed," Rachel said.

"How many do you need?" Max asked.

She looked at him. "More."

"Nah. One's all we'll need. I mean, we *are* partners, right?"

"Not *that* kind."

"So no threesome, huh?"

"I'm not touching you, Max."

"Hey, no harm in asking."

"Would you two cut it out?" Trent said. "Okay. We'll need to take shifts watching Armsburger's room for anything suspicious. Three three-hour shifts ought to get us through the night. I'll take the first watch, then Max can take the second, and—"

"Whoa whoa whoa," Max said. "What are you talking about shifts? *I'm* not going to stare at anybody's door for three hours."

"Me neither," Rachel said.

"We *have* to. What if someone comes in the middle of the night? We'll need to be ready so we can stop them."

"Stop them?" Max asked. "With what, our complimentary bathrobes? Look, pal, *I* don't have a gun on me, and unless you know tai chi or something, I'd say you're not gonna stop anybody from doing anything."

"*And*," Trent went on, "we need to be ready to leave as soon as he wakes up."

"Oh, this is ridiculous." Rachel removed her shoes and picked up the phone. There was a short pause. "Hello, can you tell me what time the AMP convention starts tomorrow? Seven o'clock? Thank you." She hung up. "There you go. Problem solved."

The AMP was an acronym, albeit a backasswards one, for the Association for the Preservation of Morality, which sounded a little like a religious cult. And it was, in a way; its members were the kind of people who boycotted Zest commercials for showing too much skin. Nobody outside of their own group took them seriously, and they wielded almost no social, financial, or political power. Why Armsburger had agreed to speak at their convention was still something of a mystery.

"We can't just assume he's going to stay here all day tomorrow," Trent said. "What if he leaves? What if they decide to hit him in his sleep? They could strangle him and make it look like a heart attack."

"Hey," Max said, "you're welcome to sit up all night if you want. Me, I've got better things to do." He stood up and gave Rachel a once-over. "Sure you're not up for a little guy-girl-guy?"

She glared at him.

"Doesn't hurt to try. All right, if either of you needs me, I'll be down at Trader Vic's. There's bound to be some lonely woman waiting for me there. Call me when something happens."

"You can't just *leave*," Trent said. "I thought we were a team here."

"We *are* a team. One guy does all the work, and everyone else takes the credit. You're that guy." Max patted him on the shoulder. "Relax, pal, you know I wouldn't leave if I didn't think it was all right. Nothing's going to happen tonight. I'm telling you, we're wasting our time. I'll see you guys in the morning." Without another word, Max slipped through the door and closed it behind him.

Rachel let her hair down. "I'm going to take a shower." She disappeared into the bathroom, and soon the steady hiss of running water filled the room.

Trent listened for a while, then sighed and took his shoes off. He filled the coffeemaker with water and set the pot to boil. It was looking to be a very long night, and he was going to need all the help he could get.

][

"You're blocking the door, Trent. Trent. *Trent*, get up, I'm hungry."

Slowly, and somewhat painfully, Trent opened his eyes. Or one of them, at least; the other was plastered to the door. For a moment he forgot where he was. Gingerly he set his hands on the floor and pushed himself to his feet.

"What . . . what time is it?"

"Nine-thirty," Rachel said. She looked perfectly rested, even though she was wearing the same clothes she'd worn yesterday.

"Nine-thirty?" Then, suddenly, Trent remembered why he was there. "Nine-thirty! Armsburger, where's—"

"Don't worry. Max just called, he's down by the pool eating breakfast. Armsburger's at the table next to him. I *told* you we didn't need to stay up in shifts." She gave him an appraising look. "That can't have been very comfortable."

It hadn't been. Every muscle in Trent's back and neck was furious with him, kicking and biting like angry children whenever he made the mistake of moving. Currently it was impossible for him to look left without turning his entire body. He felt like a senior citizen without his medication.

"Take a shower," Rachel said, more an order than suggestion. "We'll be downstairs."

He took a quick shower, which did wonders to loosen up his crumpled muscles, then hurried down to the pool. Rachel and Max were still there, and so was Armsburger, sitting alone at the table behind them. He was reading *The New York Times* and had probably eaten something made from whole grains.

"Rise and shine, lazy," Max said with far too much perkiness. "How'd you sleep?"

"Wonderfully," Trent groaned as he slid into his chair. "Thanks for the help last night."

"What? I'm here, he's there, end of story." Max tore off part of his bagel and continued talking around it. "You should be *thanking* me, pal. . . . Well, I'm waiting."

"Give me some coffee."

"Say thank you first."

Trent closed his eyes, which was a mistake; they didn't want to open again. "Fine. *Thank* you, all right. Now give me some coffee. And where's the menu?"

A waiter appeared. "Good morning and welcome to—"

"Coffee," Trent said. "Black. Two cups." He cradled his head in his hands and looked blearily at Max. "So, what happened to *you* last night?"

"Nothing big, just one girl."

"Sorry to hear that."

Max shrugged. "Eh, you take what you can. She wants to become an actress, her parents are rich, put her up here for a couple weeks, I told her I was in television, so on and *so* on, you know how it goes. She's still sleeping upstairs, so if we could make this quick, I'd appreciate it. I don't feel like dealing with her, you know?"

"Charming," Rachel said. "What room's she in?"

"I don't know. Fifth floor somewhere. I wasn't really looking at the room numbers."

"What's her name?" Trent asked.

Max chewed thoughtfully for a moment. "Sarah, Susan, I don't know—something with an S."

"How old is she?"

"She *looked* eighteen. What are you, my mother? I didn't ask, and I don't want to know. Our 'relationship' is now officially over." He took another bite of his bagel. "You want any of this, it's not bad."

Trent declined—the chance of contracting some rather unpleasant disease was just a little too high—then gestured toward Armsburger. "What's he been up to?"

"*Nothing*," Max said. "Reading *The New York Times*, cover to cover it looks like. He's been at it for half an hour now. Seriously, is there even half an hour's worth of news in that thing?"

The waiter returned with two steaming cups of coffee for Trent. He drank the first in large gulps. He wasn't sure if it was the caffeine or the scalding liquid that did it, but he felt pretty wide awake after that.

Unfortunately, the rest of the day did everything it could to put him back to sleep. After breakfast Armsburger rented a car and spent all day sightseeing. Trent found himself sitting in parking spots all across Los Angeles while he waited miserably for the chairman of the FCC to buy himself a new valise or take a scenic tour of North Hollywood. Max and Rachel spent the day with him, bickering incessantly or leaving the car altogether whenever it suited them. Once Max followed Armsburger into a hair salon—yes, the man actually went into a hair salon—and got himself a manicure while a host of Korean women trimmed Armsburger's graying locks.

"I'm telling you," Max said after the three of them spent forty-five minutes waiting outside a boutique on Rodeo Drive while Armsburger bought himself a tie, "someone had *better* try to kill that man, or I'll be pissed."

By three o'clock they were hell and gone from Wilshire, wallowing somewhere near Los Olivos while Armsburger took his third winery tour of the afternoon. Max and Rachel were thrilled and drank themselves into a relatively happy stupor. Trent, on the other hand, was not excited. This was becoming intolerable.

"Man drinks like a fish," Max said at one point. "Very moral of him. What a guy. What's the deal, pal, you not drinking?"

"No," Trent said. Now was not the time to let his guard down. Besides, there was only so much Chardonnay a man could endure.

"Hey," Rachel said, "you ever notice how your fingers are, like, *really* funny-looking?" She giggled. It was a sound he'd never heard out of her before, and he'd heard her make a lot of noises.

"Sounds like someone's had a good time," Max said. "You think she might be up for a little threeway now?"

"Pssshh," she said. "Go ffffuck yourself, y'asshole."

"Give me your keys," Trent said. "I promise I won't hurt anything."

Finally, at a quarter to four, Armsburger looked at his watch and headed directly for his car. It was clear from the way he walked that he was preparing to head back. Trent ushered the slightly intoxicated Max and more royally drunk Rachel to their car, put them both in the back seat, then followed Armsburger as he headed for the 154.

"Quick!" Rachel said, pointing at Armsburger's car. "There he goes! Let's go get him!"

"Try to restrain her," Trent said.

"Go get 'em, cowboy!"

"Remind me again," Max said, "why are we looking out for this guy?"

"We've already been over this."

"I mean the guy's our mortal enemy. He's spent the last four years trying to shut us down. You know how many shows he's forced us to abandon? Of course you know, you're the vice president."

"Heyyyy, Trent!"

"Not now, Rachel."

"Seriously, pal, this guy's in our *way*. Why don't we just—"

"Because it's not right," Trent said.

"I don't see why not."

"You can back out any time, Max. I can do this myself."

"Heyyyy, *Treeeeeent*!"

"Not now, Rachel."

"I'm not backing out," Max said. "I'm Sicilian, if we start something you can bet we're gonna finish it. I just don't think we're looking out for our best interests here."

"Hey, asshole!"

Trent glared at Rachel. "*What* do you want?"

"I was *going* to tell you," she said with heavily-lidded eyes, "I was going to tell you that I think someone's, I think someone's following us."

"What?"

Trent whirled in his seat, straining to look out the rear windshield. "Which one?"

"The blue Chevy. It keeps changing lanes when you do. I think there's two of 'em."

"Two cars?"

"People."

He could see them too, now. "Keep an eye on them," he said. Then, to Max: "What do you say to that?"

"I say that if they were going to kill Armsburger, they would have done it at the winery."

"Maybe it was too public. Maybe they were afraid they wouldn't be able to make a getaway."

"And maybe they live in Los Angeles and are driving back home like we are."

They continued to drive. Every few minutes, Trent checked his mirror for the blue Chevy, and every time it was still there, four or five cars back, keeping a comfortable distance. The more Trent looked at it, the more convinced he became. These were the men P.T. had hired to kill Armsburger.

Half an hour passed, then an hour, then an hour and a half. Soon they reached the outskirts of L.A. Still the blue Chevy was behind them. Then, suddenly, just before they turned off the 405, the car pulled in front of them and settled into place behind Armsburger.

"You see?" Trent shouted. "You see?"

"All right," Max said, "so maybe you're right. Congratulations, I'll buy you a drink. Now what?"

"Now, we stop them."

"*How*, asshole?"

Trent took a deep breath. "I don't know. I'll think of something."

The truth was, though, he had no idea what to do now. He hadn't brought Max's gun and he didn't have any other weapons.

"Hey, Rachel, do you have a tire iron in the trunk?"

"Oh," Max laughed, "you are *not* going to beat anyone to death with a tire iron. I think you'll have some trouble explaining that one to the jury."

"It's just a thought."

"Well, Trent," Rachel said, who was still not completely sober, "it was a dumb thought. Try harder."

"Too late," Max said. "Here we are."

Indeed, the Hilton was coming into view. There was a line of almost a dozen cars waiting to be handed over to the valets. Armsburger's car pulled in behind the last car. The blue Chevy had pulled in as well and was now positioned two cars behind Armsburger's. Trent parked Rachel's car on the inside curve of the driveway and idled, tense and waiting.

"You can't park here," Rachel said.

"Shut up." He strained to see what the two men in the blue Chevy were doing. "These people can't all be here for the AMP conference. What do you think's going on?"

"NBC's doing a casting call for *Last Woman Standing* tomorrow, remember?" Max said. "Half these people probably flew in from Oklahoma."

Trent barely heard him. He leaned over to the passenger seat and pressed his face to the window to eliminate the glare. The Chevy's two occupants were sitting motionlessly while the line of cars slowly inched forward. Armsburger was now third in line.

Tense moments passed.

"So," Max said, "do you think they're going to kill him before his speech or wait until after?"

"Shut up, Max. Rachel, would you sit back? I'm trying to see what's going on."

"Trent, pal, this is *crazy*. What are we supposed to do here?"

"Be quiet," Trent snapped. "Something's going on in that car. Something's . . . oh my God."

"What?" Rachel asked. She leaned forward onto the console. "What is it?"

It couldn't be. It *couldn't* be. But he'd *seen* it, there was no mistaking what he'd seen. One of the men in the blue Chevy had reached into the back seat and grabbed a small, long, black suitcase. There was only one thing a suitcase like that could be used for.

"They're going to shoot him," Trent whispered.

"Really?"

"About time. When?"

"*Here*!" Trent said, "now, right now. I saw the gun, I *saw* it. We have to *do* something!"

"They're not gonna shoot him right here in front of all these people, pal. You're overreacting."

No, Trent thought, he wasn't overreacting. He knew what he'd seen, and he knew what it meant. Already Armsburger's car was at the front of the line. Any second now he'd open the door and step out, and as soon as he did he was a dead man.

Just then, one of the valets started toward Armsburger's car.

Suddenly, as if anticipating the moment, the blue Chevy turned slightly away from the curb. Its passenger side now had a clear line of sight to the driver's side of Armsburger's car.

"Okay," Max said, "so maybe I was wrong."

Trent's heart was pounding. There was only one thing to do.

Frantically he put Rachel's car into gear. Her Mini Cooper lurched forward, tires squealing against the pavement. The movement was so sudden and unexpected that Rachel and Max were thrown back against their seats.

"What are you *doing*!" she shouted.

There was no time to answer, no time to explain what had to be done. He slammed on the gas and pointed the car straight for the blue Chevy.

"Oh, no you're *not*!" Rachel shouted, suddenly stone sober. "Trent, what the fuck are you—"

But she was powerless to stop him. Like a giant, crimson fist, Rachel's Mini Cooper slammed into the other car with the sound of a tremendous punch. The blue Chevy leapt forward almost ten feet, blocking the driveway and sending a spray of shattered glass in every direction. The airbags burst open, and Trent's head was whipped into his at the impact; for a moment he thought he was going to lose consciousness. But his senses returned quickly, and before anyone could say anything, he unbuckled his seatbelt and jumped out of the car.

"Oh, my God!" he shouted. He ran around the side of the Mini Cooper's dented front end and up to the Chevy's driver's side door. "Oh, my God, I'm so sorry I didn't see you pull out, are you guys okay?"

Both men were bleeding, one from his nose and the other from a nasty cut just above his left eyebrow. The suitcase was there—he hadn't made that up—but it was upsidedown, spilled onto the floorboards along with a few dozen cigarette butts. Trent couldn't see what was inside.

"Are you guys okay?"

"You wrecked my *car*!" Rachel screamed. The sound of her door slamming was somehow louder than the accident. "You wrecked my fucking car!"

Trent tried to ignore her. "Hold tight, I'll call an ambulance."

"No!" the driver barked. He was at least twice Trent's size, completely bald and with a jaw that could have been used as a chisel. "That won't be necessary."

"You bastard, you wrecked my goddamn *car*!"

So he'd been *right*. He glanced up and saw Armsburger disappearing into the hotel; the man hadn't even turned to witness the spectacle.

"No, I insist," Trent said, struggling to maintain his composure. "You guys are hurt. Don't worry, I'll have them here in just a couple minutes. Let me help you out of the car."

The driver didn't answer. Instead he slammed down on the accelerator and peeled off, leaving behind a profusion of shattered glass and the acrid smell of burning rubber. Before anyone could do anything—indeed, before anyone could really understand what was happening—the blue Chevy circled around the driveway and sped away from the hotel.

He'd done it. Holy shit, he'd *done* it! Those were the guys, the men P.T. had hired to kill Armsburger, and he had thwarted them. Nothing else could—

Trent's moment of triumph was interrupted by Rachel, who immediately started doing her best to beat him senseless. "I can't—*believe*—you *did* that!"

"Rachel—"

"You *wrecked*—my *car*—you wrecked—my *car*—you *wrecked*—"

"Rachel!" Trent caught her by the wrists, which was not an easy thing to do. At least she was unhurt. "There wasn't any time, I didn't know what else to do. They were going to *shoot* him."

"I don't care!" she screamed. "We're talking about my *car* here. You wrecked my car, you wrecked my goddamn—"

"I'll pay for it, all right? Don't you realize what we've done? We just saved a man's life!"

"It's not *worth* it. Es*pec*ially not *his*. I can't believe you *did* that!"

"Get over it already. It's just a car. What did you want me to do, sit there and watch him get shot?"

"*Yes*. That's *exactly* what I wish you'd done."

At that point Max joined them. He hadn't been wearing a seatbelt and looked a little worse than they did. "So, that was them, huh?"

Trent nodded. "That was them. I *told* you—"

"Yeah, yeah, yeah, you were right, I was wrong. Happy now? How's Rachel doing?"

"Look what he did!" she shouted in response, pointing wildly at the passenger side of her Mini Cooper, which had crumpled like tin foil. "Just look at it, Max. *Look* at it!"

"It's pretty fucked up," Max agreed. "I'll bet I know *one* person who's not getting laid tonight."

"You're goddamn *right* about that!"

Just then a valet came up. "Is everyone all right?"

They spent the next half hour cleaning up the pieces of glass and metal that littered the driveway. Fortunately Rachel's car was still driveable, and they got it to the side of the road without any trouble.

"You know," Max said at one point, "P.T.'s going to be *mad* on Monday."

[CHAPTER TWENTY-SIX]

As it turned out, *mad* wasn't quite the right word to describe P.T.'s mood Monday morning. Jack Nicholson in *The Shining* was mad. Robert De-Niro in *Taxi Driver*—that was mad. When Richard Widmark tied an old lady to her wheelchair and pushed her down a flight of stairs in *Kiss of Death*, that was also mad. No, P.T. wasn't mad.

He was furious.

The first indication Trent received came from Tad, who burst out of the front door into the parking lot just when Max—who was driving Rachel and Trent since *both* their cars were in the shop—pulled up.

"Oh, my God!" Tad said. He ran over, wrists flipping like there was no tomorrow. "Oh, thank *God* I've caught you in time. Listen, take it from me and *don't* go in there. I have *never* seen him like that."

"What's going on?" Trent asked. Best to play innocent.

"Don't ask me. I've never seen anything like it. I mean, I've seen angry men—you're lucky you didn't know me four years ago when I caught my boyfriend masturbating to pictures of Steve Buscemi, I swear I've never *felt* so betrayed—but this is . . . this is . . ." He swallowed. "This is *bad*, boys and girls. B. a. d. *Bad*."

Max got out of the car and shut his door. "Hey, Tad, do me a favor. Don't ever tell me anything about you or your boyfriends again, all right?"

"All right, all right," Trent said. "Let's just get this over with."

"I'm telling you," Tad called as the three of them walked toward the door, "don't do it. Go get some croissants or something. Let's all just go shopping. I'm telling you, you're asking for trouble! Don't say I didn't warn you!"

They walked slowly up to the second floor. Lynette was sitting at the front desk, silent and white and far from her usual perky self. When she saw them, her eyes grew wide.

"Why, hello! Welcome to hell, hope you have a great day!"

"Cute," Rachel said.

"Where is he?" Trent asked.

"In his office. I wouldn't go in there if I were you, he's a little out of sorts."

Taylor and Todd were there as well, both cowering in their cubicles and struggling to make themselves look busy in case P.T. came looking for someone to put onto a kabob skewer. Todd made a little squeak when Trent peeked his head around the corner.

"Jesus God! You scared the *shit* out of me."

"Morning. So, what's the deal?"

"Hell if I know. I'm not about to go in there. Black guy like me, he'd probably barbecue my ass. *You're* the vice president, *you* figure out what's going on."

Trent sighed. Ah, the perks of the job. "All right. Let me borrow your trashcan lid, though, will you? Just in case he starts throwing things. He has a tendency to do that, you know."

A moment later, Trent opened the door to P.T.'s office and stepped into a wasteland. Papers were everywhere, some still raining to the ground like legal-sized snowflakes. All the too-short chairs had been overturned, and the coffee table was upsidedown. One of the lights in the ceiling had somehow been pulled out of its socket and was dangling by the cords, the bulb flickering. And Armsburger's picture? Unrecognizable. Most of it was lying shredded on the floor, ragged strips of eyes and cheeks torn off and left to rot.

"Morning, sir."

The General was sitting behind his massive steel desk, the only piece of furniture in the office that seemed not to have been damaged. His face and neck were flushed, but otherwise he was completely composed, hands clasped in front of him, breathing regularly. Aside from the destruction he had obviously caused, there was no real indication that anything was wrong.

Trent took another step. "Everything okay?"

P.T. closed his eyes, then opened them. His voice was quiet and level. "You have anything to do with this?"

"I'm not sure I understand what you're—"

"I *said*, did you have anything to do with this?"

"I don't know what you're talking about, sir. What happened?"

"You know damn well what happened, don't you."

Fear was the wrong card to play here. "Look, if you're going to accuse me of something, I'd like to know what it is I've supposedly done wrong."

Somehow, it worked. P.T. cleared his throat and continued more calmly. "There's been a complication in our plans." He made a show of arranging some papers. "We're going to need to push back some of our releases. The . . . climate has not improved like I thought it would. It's going to take some more time."

Trent bent down and started picking papers off the floor, mostly to hide his face from his boss. So, the man hadn't given up on the idea of killing Armsburger. This weekend's failed attempt only meant a slight delay, and next time P.T. was certain to be more careful about it. Trent bit his lower lip. He'd been lucky enough to win this time, but there was no way he'd be able to do it again, much less three or four times.

Which meant he was going to have to act soon.

"Leave it," P.T. said.

Slowly, Trent stood up. "Do you want me to call everyone and tell them—"

"No. Let them wait a little. Besides, I've got something else in the works that may pay off soon." He reached for his humidor. "First rule of business: never leave anything to chance. You didn't think I wouldn't have a backup plan, did you?"

It was a supreme effort to maintain a straight face. "I don't know what you're talking about, sir."

"Of course you don't. Of course you don't." With a gentle *snip*, P.T. cut the end of his cigar. "Get out of here. And send Max in."

As soon as he closed the door behind him, Trent took what felt like his first breath in five minutes. The man *knew*. Or, if he didn't know, he at least suspected. Maybe he suspected everyone, but it didn't feel that way, not this time. Trent lit a cigarette. Forget saving Armsburger; if he didn't do something about his boss soon, he'd be lucky to save himself.

On the way to his office he stopped by Max's cubicle. "P.T. wants to talk to you."

At the moment, Max was on the phone. ". . . no, I'm *telling* you Phil, it's going to be huge. Hey pal, have I *ever* lied to you? Let's try that again, have I ever lied to you? That's right, I haven't. So trust me on this. All right? All right. Talk to you Friday." He hung up and swiveled in his chair. "What's up?"

"P.T. wants to talk to you."

"Me? What for?"

"I don't know." Trent lowered his voice to a whisper. "I think he knows, Max."

"What are you talking about? He doesn't know. How would he know? He's just taking it out on you because you're closest."

"Yeah, well, now he's going to take it out on you." Trent looked over the cubicle walls to make sure that nobody was nearby, then leaned in anyway. "Don't give anything away, all right?"

"What, you think I'm going to walk in there and confess everything? Come on, pal, what kind of guy do you think I am? No, no, you don't have to explain anything, I know you're just under a lot of pressure right now. Boss is mad at you, girlfriend's mad at you—Rachel's still not talking to you, is she?—it's a tough time."

Trent finished his cigarette and crushed the butt in Max's ashtray. "Just don't say anything . . . stupid."

"Hey. I take offense to that. I'm a man, Trent. And as a man, I've spent my entire life learning how to lie. Trust me, he's not going to learn anything from me, all right? All right."

Just then Taylor came around the corner. She was wearing a four-inch mini skirt and a camisole top that looked transparent but somehow wasn't. "So," she said to Trent, "you're not dead. Guess I lose, I bet Todd you'd at least come out wounded."

"Thanks for the vote of confidence."

"So you lost a bet to Todd, huh?" Max asked. "What do you have to do? Anything illegal?"

"Maybe." She flashed them both a wicked smile, then walked off. "See you later."

"Someday," Max said as soon as she was gone, "someday I'm gonna get me a piece of that." He clicked his teeth together. "Don't worry about P.T. I know how to handle myself."

"I hope so. Just be careful."

He watched Max disappear into P.T.'s office, then went to his own. It looked the same as it had on Friday, which was something—at least no one had ransacked his files. Not that there was anything to find; unlike many conspirators, Trent had not taken the time to write down his plans in exhausting detail for others to find and read at their leisure. Why anyone did that was beyond him. If you were planning to kill someone, you probably didn't need to write yourself a memo on the off chance that you might forget.

He sat down and stared at his desk. There were no calls to make, no projects to tweak, and he was hardly in a mood to come up with anything new and fresh. Time began to drag, then creep, then do a drunken pub crawl, until it was finally being pulled by the hair like a prehistoric cavewoman.

What did P.T. want to talk to Max for? Was he going to grill everyone? Or was there something more to it? Did he suspect something? And if he did, how would Max react? And why the hell weren't they finished talking yet?

Trent was spared his morbid contemplations by Lynette, who bustled in with an envelope in her left hand. "Special delivery for Mr. Trent Tucker!"

"What is it?"

"I don't know. It was delivered by courier." She shook the envelope next to her ear. "Sounds like a subpoena. My aunt got a subpoena once, it was so exciting. Did I ever tell you about it?"

"Twice," Trent said, which wasn't true. He took the letter, which was most definitely not a subpoena. No return address, though. "Thanks. Anything else?"

"That's it. Good to see you're in one piece. I didn't think you'd make it out of there alive!"

"He's not so bad if you know how to handle him."

"If you say so. But I'd hate to get on his bad side. Oh, did you see last night's episode of—"

"Just missed it," Trent said. He tapped the envelope on his desk. "Thanks for the letter."

Lynette left, clearly frustrated that she'd been cut off. Oh well, let her sulk. Better that than have to listen to her twenty-minute retelling of a forty-three minute show.

He turned the envelope over—no return address on the back either—then slit it open. Inside was a single sheet of folded paper. When he went to unfold it, though, something else fell out. It was a cashier's check, made out to him for the exact amount of fifteen hundred dollars.

Immediately he knew what it was for.

He didn't need to read the letter, but he did anyway. There wasn't much to it, just a few typewritten lines on a half-sheet of computer paper:

> Trent,
>
> Here's the money you loaned me. I'd have given it to you in person, but things have been so busy lately—I'm sure you understand. I didn't include any interest, so if you were expecting any I'm sorry. Let me know and I'll send some; how's 5% sound?
>
> In case I haven't told you, Dreamworks bought the script. They're just about to start production. I think it's going to be huge, man. Candy's set to star, she says to tell you hi.
>
> We should get together for drinks sometime. Tell me what works for you, and I'll see what I can do.
> Thanks again.
>
> Adam

As soon as he finished reading, Trent balled the paper in his fist. So, Adam had finally made it. He was on his way, and now that things had fallen into place he was too busy for anyone else. *I didn't include any interest, so if you were expecting any . . .* What kind of asshole friend would ask for interest? But that was just it, wasn't it—they weren't really friends anymore. Even his signature had been typed.

Well, that was that. Trent pulled a lighter out of his desk, lit Adam's letter until the edges took, and used it to light another cigarette. When the paper became too hot to hold, he tossed it into the trashcan and watched it crisp and smolder until nothing remained but a pyramid of ashes.

For a moment, for just a split second, he thought about picking up the phone. Maybe it wasn't over. Maybe it was possible to go back to where they'd begun, before Trent had read Adam's script and called it the festering pile of monkey shit that it was. Maybe they could all go out for drinks, Candy too, at a new bar with different beautiful waitresses and a pleasant absence of memories.

But his hand never touched the receiver. Adam wouldn't find the time. More than likely he wouldn't answer; he'd let the machine get it so everyone who called could hear Candy, all breathy and eager and his to display. No, going back was impossible. It wasn't that he and Adam had fought; it wasn't even that Trent had hated the script. If everyone else had hated the script too, then there'd be a chance. But that wasn't the case. Suddenly, and for the first time, Adam was successful, and that had changed everything.

There were only two things that could happen now. The first, and most likely, was that *Deadly Justice* would not live up to expectations. Most movies didn't, especially when someone in the studio made the mistake of over-hyping a film without spending enough on advertising. If that happened, Adam would find himself blacklisted faster than the speed of light. He'd be forced to make independent films or, in a last desperate act to save his once-promising career, hit up the Lifetime channel or TNT for the opportunity to write some of the atrocities more commonly known as made-for-TV movies. He'd be a face without a name, that guy who made that movie that one time, standing by the punch bowl at Hollywood parties and watching more important people talk about more important things. If he was lucky, he'd land himself a disillusioned actress whose transition from amateur porn to mainstream films had not panned out as planned, and together they'd eke it out in a tiny, underfurnished apartment. He'd scrape together a living writing dialogue for pasta commercials, and she'd supplement their meager income with walk-on roles in low-budget epics and the occasional clandestine blowjob.

Or maybe it would all fall into place. Maybe *Deadly Justice* would be a titanic success. In that case, Adam's future would be assured. He'd immediately become a sensation, the most desired writer in Hollywood. It wouldn't matter if he never wrote another successful script again; plenty of screenwriters had made their legacy on the strength of a single idea. If that happened, Adam would quickly find himself in a position where he could do nothing wrong. A few years from now, *People* magazine would name him one of the country's 50 sexiest bachelors, and he'd find himself in the arms of women whose bodies would make Taylor's look natural by comparison. His fame and fortune would grow in direct disproportion to the quality of his work; and, like George Lucas, he would eventually end up a Hollywood hermit, surrounded by sycophantic devotees and barricaded behind the walls of his palatial estate where the paparazzi couldn't hound him.

Trent massaged his forehead with the heels of his hands. There was no going back. Adam would never call him again. Whether it lasted for a minute or a lifetime, Hollywood success was irrevocable. He wanted to blame it on Hollywood, on something inherent in that cesspool of mirrors and cameras that latched onto a decent soul and sucked it dry of everything recognizably human. But he knew better than that. Nobody changed who didn't want to be changed. Hollywood wasn't the problem; the problem was that people wanted there to be a Hollywood.

Just like Reality TV.

Trent was working his way into a monumental depression when there was a knock on the door. "Come in."

Max entered. "Hey, pal, good news. You all right? You look beat up."

"I'm fine. What's going on?"

"It's on." Max closed the door and hurried over to the chair across from Trent's desk.

"What's on?"

"The *plan*." His eyes were bright and anxious. "This weekend. P.T.'s invited me over for dinner this Friday. Nine o'clock sharp."

There was nothing for Trent to say. So, after two weeks of anticipating a moment that he'd never been sure would actually come, this was it.

"You ready to do what we need to do?"

Trent looked at the ashes in his trashcan and sighed. "Let's get it over with. We'll talk more about this later, all right?"

"Sure thing, partner." Max got up. "I think this company is long overdue for some major changes. Talk to you later, pal." He walked to the door, turned around, took a long look at Trent and his office, then left and closed the door behind him.

Trent spent the next fifteen minutes lighting matches and watching them slowly burn down to the nub. Finally, they were actually going to *do* something. Who knew? Maybe they really *would* be able to save the world before it became an absolute shitball. Anything was possible, right?

[CHAPTER TWENTY-SEVEN]

The rest of that week seemed to take forever. Every hour was an ordeal, and at every meeting, Trent kept his eyes locked on the table in front of him in case he might accidentally betray something of his intentions to P.T., who was still livid over the past weekend's "missed opportunity," as he not-so-ambiguously called it. Yes, life at Nova was much like life at any other corporate office: grueling, tiresome, and debilitating. It went without saying that company morale was at something of an ebb.

Monday night after work, Max drove Trent to another firing range to practice for Friday. That's what Max called it—practice. Trent spent half an hour shooting round after round at moving targets, then finished up with another half hour on stationary ones. In both respects he was certain he had improved. Perhaps it was just a matter of getting the hang of it. Or perhaps he was fooling himself. Either way, one thing was clear: as long as he got within fifteen feet, there was little doubt what the outcome would be.

"Feel good?" Max asked when Trent was finished.

"I guess so."

"Excellent. Hey, you up for a drink?"

On Tuesday, Trent finally got his own car. Well, not *his* car—the insurance adjustor still hadn't decided whether or not the poor thing was worth saving—but a temporary replacement. Not that a BMW could actually replace his Jaguar, but it sufficed. It would be nice to get his own car back, though. But if his insurance company decided to scrap it, he'd just have to buy himself another one. Hell, maybe he'd buy himself two, sort of a congratulations-on-the-death-of-your-boss present to himself. Hallmark really should've made a card for that occasion; there was bound to be a huge market for it.

That Wednesday, Trent and Rachel met at Max's apartment to finalize their plans. She drove herself, although hers was also a loaner. She hadn't said anything specific—hadn't said anything at all, really—but it seemed that she was starting to forgive him for wrecking her Mini Cooper.

She got out of her car and slammed the door. "I hate you, Trent."

Or maybe not. "I'm sorry."

"Do you realize how much I hate upholstered seats? And it's a *Subaru*. Can you believe that was all they had? Look at me, do I look like a Subaru driver to you?"

"I said I'm sorry."

"I know you're sorry. I'm sorry. We're all sorry. You know what the mechanic said? He told me it might be another two *weeks* before they're finished."

Together they climbed the stairs to Max's apartment. He hurried them inside, then looked down the hallway in both directions before closing the door.

"Nobody followed us," Trent said.

"Hey, can't be too careful, right? So, let's get down to business. Anyone want a White Russian? I've been in love with them ever since *The Big Lebowski*."

Over a number of White Russians, Max explained how Friday was going to go down.

"Here's the plan. I'm meeting P.T. at his house at nine. Rachel, tomorrow night I'll drive you up there so you can see the layout. Friday, try to get there around eight. Park a couple blocks up from his house, far enough away that the camera can't see your car—I'll show you where. Oh, and put a note on the windshield saying that your car broke down and you've already called a tow truck, just in case anyone gets suspicious. I want you to be there after P.T.'s already gotten home, but before we show up, understand? I don't want to go in there unless I know we've got a backup plan in case something goes wrong."

"You want me to wear all black, too?"

"Couldn't hurt. You look good in black, like a sexy little ninja. Now if everything goes right, we'll drive right back out and you can just follow us home, nothing to it. But if things get hairy, we're gonna need you to get us out of there. So keep your eyes open."

"How's she supposed to know if we're in trouble?" Trent asked.

"Because I figure if things go bad, we'll be on foot dodging gunfire. Just kidding, Trent. Jesus, have a little *fun* with this, will you?"

"Don't worry about me," Rachel said. "I've spent plenty of time in parked cars, I know how to keep myself entertained."

Max stared at her for a moment. "All right, that didn't make any sense. No, don't try to explain it, I don't really want to know. So . . . Trent."

Trent finished the last of his drink and got up to pour himself another. "All right. Shoot."

"Shoot. I like that, very appropriate. Okay, here's what we're gonna do. I'll pick you up at your place around eight. Just to be safe, I think you should ride in the trunk the whole way. Won't be all that comfortable, but you gotta do what you gotta do, right? So, around nine o'clock we'll roll up on the guardhouse, and they'll let us through."

"What if they ask to check the trunk?"

"They won't. That's the thing. When the boss was telling me about his place—thinking I'd never seen it, right?—he started in about the guards and all. So I said, 'Whoa. Does that mean I have to take those illegal immigrants out of my trunk?' Just joking, you know. But he said, 'Don't worry, Max, I trust you.' They're not going to check the trunk, I guarantee it."

"But what if they do?"

"Then we'll back on out of there and buy ourselves one-way tickets to Botswana. I hear it's lovely there this time of year. Look, do you have a better idea?"

Trent did not.

"Then you're gonna have to trust me, all right? So, after we're inside, I'll pull the car up to the house. Now, P.T.'s guards are probably going to be a little edgy the first few minutes I'm there, so I think it'd be best if you wait for about ten or fifteen minutes, give them time to relax. After that, all you need to do is climb out, sneak in the house, find P.T., and shoot him. I'll talk loud so you can hear me."

"That shouldn't be a problem."

"Fuck you very much, Rachel." Max turned back to Trent. "After that it's easy. You shoot out a window and get back in the trunk. I'll scream like hell and get all the guards to come running. They'll start searching the woods behind the house, then I'll start in about how he's not dead. I'll get him into the car, and we'll drive out. Hopefully they'll let me go alone. If they do, I'll drop you off on my way to the hospital. If not, you might have to stay cooped up in there for a few hours, but hey, small price. Rachel, once we leave, you can start up and follow us back." He clapped his hands. "And that's that. Simple enough, don't you think?"

"Sounds like it," Trent said.

"Oh, come *on*, pal, stop worrying! What could go wrong? Monday morning we'll have our own company. Think about *that*. All right, who else wants another drink? I just can't get enough of these things."

][

Thursday came and went. All day long Trent was desperate for a drink, something potent to take the edge off his nerves. But he forced himself to abstain. If he had one, he was bound to have more, and the last thing he needed was to wake up Friday with a hangover.

And then, it was Friday.

Trent got to work early for a change. He'd barely slept that night. Even so, he wasn't at all tired. He poured himself a cup of coffee out of habit, but after the second sip he threw the rest away. For some reason, his stomach wasn't in the mood for it.

The first two hours were all right. He made some calls, cleaned up his desk. Nobody stopped by to see him, and he did what he could not to be seen. It was a long morning, but at least it was soon over.

Then, just before he was about to leave for lunch, the intercom on his desk buzzed to life. "Trent. I need to talk to you."

For the next ten minutes, Trent tried to calm down. If P.T. had suspected anything, he wouldn't have wanted to talk; he'd have broken Trent's door down and beaten his vice president to death with a rusty hammer. There was nothing to worry about. The man didn't know.

He opened the door to P.T.'s office and stepped inside. "Yes, sir?"

Everything was in place again. The only evidence of P.T.'s latest tirade was the picture of Armsburger, whose tattered remnants were still hanging on the wall opposite the massive steel desk.

"Sit down, Trent."

P.T. was sitting as well. His face had an unusually hard look about it, as if the defenseless animal he'd eaten for breakfast had somehow disagreed with him. A cigar was resting in its holder, sending a thin trail of pungent smoke drifting lazily into the air.

"It has just occurred to me," P.T. began, "that the two of us have never really talked."

Trent blinked. "Talked, sir?"

"Talked. You know *my* vision for the future, but I don't know yours. I think now is a good time to find out. So tell me."

"Tell you what, sir?"

"Tell me where you'd like to see this company go. Tell me what you would do if you were in my place."

Trent swallowed. "Are you thinking about retiring, sir?"

"Not at all. I just want to know what my vice president's vision is for this company. That's not so unusual, is it?"

"A little. You've never asked before."

"Well, I'm asking now."

There was no point in stalling. P.T. wanted an answer, and Trent couldn't think of any way to avoid giving him one. "You want the truth?"

"Of course."

Why not? It wouldn't hurt. Besides, P.T. was a dead man anyway. "All right. You remember that medical reality show idea I had? The one Dyson stole?"

"*Lives in the Balance*? That ungodly piece of shit?"

"Yes. That's the kind of thing I'd like to see more of. I feel like we have this great potential to bring people together, and instead we're pushing shows that basically drive people apart. Like *Last Man Standing*. What does that tell people? Every man for himself? Seriously, if you were on a desert island with a bunch of other people, don't you think it would be helpful to work together instead of against each other? I *do* have some experience with that, remember."

"I remember. I also seem to recall *Last Man Standing* being our biggest hit."

"You asked for my opinion, I'm giving it to you. I'm not saying it's a bad show." Even though it was. "I'm just saying that we have all this potential and we're really not using it. We're entertaining people, sure, but we're not improving anything."

"What are you saying, that we should be *educating* people? It's not our job to provide them with moral guidance. That's impossible; entertainment and education don't go together."

Trent attempted a disinterested shrug. "I think they can."

"And so what kind of shows would *you* like us to run?"

P.T. didn't care. He certainly wasn't about to change his mind and start pushing worthwhile shows. But Trent went on anyway, because a few hours from now it wouldn't matter what P.T. thought or did or had in mind.

"Well, here's an example. It's called *The Samaritan*. I've been sitting on it for a few weeks because I didn't think it would interest you. But since you're asking, here's the idea . . ."

For the next five minutes Trent outlined the show, given to him by Dyson just hours before his death. He walked through the entire season: the characters, the obstacles, the rewards, the offshoots, the ancillary advertising, the effect it would have on FCC relations. By the time he was finished he felt alive again, supercharged with an enthusiasm he had not felt for almost a month. It was still there, buried inside him, that drive to make something good and pure before it was too late. *The Samaritan* would be the flagship of Trent's new Reality armada, a herald of a new age. Finally, Paris Hilton and Simon Cowell and Jessica Simpson would end up where they belonged—wallowing in off-screen obscurity.

"So," P.T. said when Trent was finished, "that's your vision. That's what you'd like to see us do."

"You asked, sir. Should I have lied?"

"No. Not at all, I appreciate your candor. I don't agree with you, of course. Personally, I think your vision is . . . what's the best way to put this . . . a complete assbomb. No one would watch it except for you and your treehugging friends, but you're entitled to your opinion."

How very generous of him. "Thank you, sir."

P.T. stood up. "Well, that was all. I'm glad we had this talk. Enjoy your lunch."

As Trent shut the door behind him, he realized that he was also glad they'd talked. For the first time in three weeks, he was no longer nervous. He'd been walking on eggshells ever since Dyson's death, but now he felt unaccountably free. He even found himself smiling as he left the building and got in his car. Tonight, he was going to kill his boss.

And for the first time since coming up with the idea, he couldn't wait to do it.

[CHAPTER TWENTY-EIGHT]

That night, at five minutes past eight, Trent climbed into the trunk of Max's car.

"Here it is, pal, the day of reckoning." Max was dressed in a dark suit and collarless white shirt, perfect for the formal dinner he was supposed to be attending. "You got everything?"

For the fiftieth time in the last hour, Trent put his hand inside his jacket. There, tucked into a fold that seemed designed for just such a use, was the gun Max had given him.

"I've got my half." Trent was dressed entirely in black, including a black ski mask in case any of the guards saw him. He'd had to buy the ski mask, which at first had worried him; there weren't too many things a man in L.A. could use a ski mask for. Fortunately, the cashier had barely glanced at him. "You got the bullets?"

Max tossed him a box. "They're silver tips. The guy told me they'll go through anything."

"He's not a werewolf, Max."

"Just in case he tries to hide behind something. There's a flashlight in the trunk in case you need it. Ready? All right, let's do this."

The trunk closed, and Trent was thrust suddenly into darkness. There was not enough room for him to stretch his legs, and for a moment he worried that he'd get so cramped after an hour that he would hardly be able to walk. But he shoved that fear aside. When the time came, he'd be ready.

They started off. Trent attempted to keep track of where they were, but soon he was hopelessly disoriented. After a few minutes, though, the car gained speed, and Trent recognized the familiar hum of highway travel. There was no turning back now. In fifty minutes they'd be parked in P.T.'s driveway. Again Trent felt for the gun in his pocket.

"Hey, pal!" Max said at one point. His voice was muffled but easy to understand. "Can you hear me?"

"Yeah."

"All right. Just checking. We've got about thirty-five minutes to go. You doing all right back there?"

"Fine." Again he gripped the gun.

Occasionally the darkness became oppressive, and when it did, Trent fumbled for the flashlight and turned it on. There wasn't much to see. Except for the flashlight, Max's trunk was completely empty. A shrill breeze was coming in from somewhere, and Trent tried to find the source, but he couldn't. At least the wind kept the air from getting stale.

Eventually the car slowed down, and Trent realized they were turning off the highway. The sound of the road grew louder, harsher somehow, as though they were going over gravel.

Which meant they were close.

"Ten minutes," Max said.

Trent gripped the barrel of his gun. Ten minutes. What would happen if someone saw him? It was hard enough to get past P.T.'s guards going in; it would be impossible to evade them on the way out, especially if they were on the alert. What if Rachel hadn't made it? Worse, what if he missed?

At five minutes to go, Trent pulled the ski mask over his head. Soon his breath had dampened the fabric around his mouth and nose. The car made several slow, sharp turns and began to ascend slightly. They were getting close.

A few minutes later, Max spoke up again. "There's Rachel. So far so good."

Trent allowed himself to relax slightly. At least that was taken care of. He thought he could tell the moment they passed her car, Rachel lying quietly in the back seat, waiting for them to make the next move. It was only a matter of seconds now before—

"Here we are, pal. Don't make any noise."

That wouldn't be a problem; Trent was so tense he could hardly breathe. The car rolled to a stop. He waited, and listened.

A moment later, there was the sound of a gate being opened. The car moved slowly forward, then stopped again. Trent could hear Max's window rolling down. Then a voice, rough but muffled, saying something too indistinct to understand. Max said something back. Their conversation seemed to take longer than it should have. Had something gone wrong?

Silently, Trent removed his gun from his jacket.

Then they were moving forward again. The car picked up speed, and the window was rolled up. They were through. They were *through*.

Now for the hard part.

The next thirty seconds seemed to take an eternity. The car descended, then climbed a small rise, then descended again. Surely by now they were at the house, but still they kept driving. After a minute, Trent started to get worried. Where were they going? Had Max sensed danger and turned around? Were they being followed? What was it? *What*?

Suddenly the car began to slow down and turned left. Trent knew they were now behind P.T.'s house, out of sight of the road and the guardhouse at the top of the driveway. The brakes squealed a bit as the car came to a halt, and Max cut the engine off. The resulting silence was deafening.

"Wait a few minutes," Max said. "And be careful."

There was a loud noise, like a gunshot, and Trent's heart leapt into his brain. Then he realized what it was: Max had popped the seat release. Trent pushed the seat on the rear driver's side, and it moved forward a few inches, enough for tiny slivers of light to squeeze through the crevices on either side.

Then Max opened his door. The car shifted as he got out, and when he slammed his door shut, Trent was certain the rear seats would fall down and reveal him to anyone nearby. But that didn't happen. The seats stayed up, and soon Trent heard the crisp sound of Max's shoes on the pavement. Then a door was opened, almost too distant for Trent to hear. Max's footsteps soon vanished, and Trent was left alone.

In absolute silence he removed the box of bullets from his pocket and loaded his gun. As each bullet slid into the cylinder it made a tiny *click*, and each time Trent paused, positive someone had heard. No one came. After two agonizing minutes his gun was fully loaded. He had six shots, more than enough. He pushed the box of bullets to the corner of the trunk—no need to keep them in his pocket where they might rattle and betray his presence—then pressed his face against the rear seat.

It was impossible to see anything. Slowly, silently, he pushed it forward an inch, then another. That did it; now he could see where he was.

Max had indeed parked behind the house. The driver's side was pointed toward the rear door—good thinking. There were floodlights on every visible corner of the house, but for some reason the area by the door was dark. Perfect.

But still Trent didn't move. This was no time to get too excited, no time to rush in and make a fatal mistake. He inched his way out of the trunk and peered above the level of the windows. He looked right, then left, then right again, then left again. No sign of anybody, no roving flashlights or dark figures silhouetted against the side of the house. Carefully, he edged his way to the passenger's side. Nothing. He was absolutely alone.

He waited for another minute, listening, straining to hear the slightest indication of someone coming around the side of the house. He heard nothing. No loud breathing, no heavy footsteps, no slight rustle of moving clothes. There was never going to be a better time to do it; any minute now, one of P.T's guards was bound to come around the corner.

It was now or never.

As quietly as possible, and still gripping the gun in his right hand, Trent eased the door open and slid out. Still no one. Quickly he closed the door behind him and knelt into a crouch, careful to keep the car between himself and the grassy lawn on the opposite side, just in case someone was standing there. The door to P.T.'s house was perhaps fifteen feet away, and it was opened a crack. Max must have left it that way when he went inside.

Still no one came.

With a deep breath, Trent burst into a run. His feet pounded against the pavement; his heart pounded in his chest. Surely someone would hear him, surely they would all come running with their guns drawn. But they didn't. Three seconds later he was at the door, and without a backward glance he pushed it open and slid inside. Blessedly, it made no sound.

He was in.

The door opened onto a marble-tiled hallway that ran the length of the house. Heavy oak doors, each ten feet tall, stood closed on either side of the entrance. They were recessed about eighteen inches from the hallway itself, and as soon as Trent saw them he wedged himself into one of those recesses. Now he was hidden, as much as he could be, and it gave him a chance to look around and decide where to go next.

The hallway was immense and well-lit, extending two stories to a frescoed ceiling that would have dwarfed the Sistine Chapel. Aside from the doorway he currently occupied, there didn't seem to be many places to hide. Halfway down on the right side, the hallway spilled into a sunken room, probably a den or a home theater. Along the far wall at the opposite end, a row of windows, closed but uncurtained, were stacked to the ceiling. The inside lighting made it impossible to see through them. There was no telling whether or not guards were patrolling that side of the house—undoubtedly they were—and while he'd never be able to see them, they'd have a clear view of him.

Trent pushed himself deeper into the recess and tried to think. It would be suicidal to start hunting for P.T. without knowing where to look; the house was too big, with too many places to hide and too many eyes. He tried the door at his back, but it was locked. He took a deep breath and waited. There was nothing else he could do, until he knew where to go. And that was up to Max.

Trent glanced back over his shoulder to make sure no one was coming inside; no one was. There also didn't seem to be anyone in the house. Was that usual? Shouldn't there have been somebody? Or maybe they just stayed outside, confident that they could stop any intruder from getting past them. That was possible.

Still, none of that mattered. What mattered was that there wasn't anybody there to see him, no one to stop him. All that remained was to find P.T., do his job, and get out.

"Well, yeah, I'd *love* some, boss."

Trent froze. There no mistaking Max's voice, and it was close. Trent inched his head out from around the recessed corner, desperate to determine exactly where the sound had come from.

"Man, this is some pad you've got."

That was it. Max and P.T. were in a room halfway down the hallway on the left side—Trent's side. He couldn't see the door, but he was sure it was open. It wouldn't be hard to figure out which one was the right one, and P.T. couldn't have been expecting him. The man would have no time to react, even if Trent hesitated a second before firing. Which he'd have to; he didn't want to shoot Max by mistake.

"What is this, Persian? Very nice."

He couldn't afford to wait. Any minute one of the guards might realize that Max's car door wasn't entirely closed, and then there'd be no chance of escaping. Trent adjusted the ski mask around his eyes, then slid out of his recess and into the hallway.

He moved as quickly as he could, back pressed to the wall, gun ready at his right shoulder. There was another recessed door about ten yards down, and he slipped into its welcome shadows. So far so good.

"So, when's dinner? I'm starving."

Again Trent made his way into the hallway. The voices were closer now, easier to pinpoint. One more set of recessed doors, then the next should be them. He crouched behind a pedestal and peered around the vase it supported. Still no sign of anyone.

"You a pool player?"

Trent got up and made it to the next recess. One more to go, another twenty or thirty feet, and he'd be on them. He paused a moment, listening for P.T.'s voice, but heard nothing. Nor did he hear anything else. The two of them must have been alone.

"Mind if I rack 'em up?"

Into the hallway once more. The gun's checkered grip had begun to dig into Trent's palm, and he loosened his grip slightly. Twenty feet. Fifteen. His heart was a drum. Ten. Eight. His body was now covered in sweat. Five. Three. The open door was visible now, and a portion of the room beyond. Two. One. He couldn't see anybody; was he in the right place?

"I tell you, boss, this is some pad."

It was the right room.

"Thank you, Max."

And that was the voice he'd been waiting to hear. P.T. was *there*, waiting, just around the corner. It had to happen now.

Now.

With a wordless roar Trent burst into the open doorway. Two frantic steps and he was inside. He lowered his gun and aimed, searching wildly for his target.

But what he saw was not at all what he had expected to see.

[CHAPTER TWENTY-NINE]

"Surpriiiiiiiise!"

Trent gaped, utterly unable to believe his eyes. They were all there, all of them—Rachel and Max, Taylor and Todd, Tad and P.T.—all of them grinning and smiling and laughing and applauding in a display of exuberance and affection Trent simply could not fathom. Behind them were a battery of cameras, hovering overhead in a wide semicircle and all focused directly at the spot where he stood.

In the face of such a shock, Trent's hands went limp, and his gun fell to the floor. "What the fu . . . what's th . . ."

"Don't try to talk, pal." Max stepped forward, beaming like an idiot. "I'm sure this is all a little overwhelming. Just relax. Let it soak in for a while."

"We've got a paramedic in the wings," Tad said, "just in case you have a heart attack."

"Wouldn't surprise me," Todd added. "Thing like this, it could definitely do a guy in."

"Especially one as out of shape as he is," Rachel said.

Trent swallowed. "What's . . . what's going on here? I thought we had come here to . . . What's the deal?"

"What's the *deal*?" P.T. asked. His face was the epitome of pleasure, shining eyes and a smile that would not die. "*You're* the deal, Trent. You're the biggest thing that's ever happened to television, that's what you are."

At those words, Trent's entire body was seized by a violent convulsion. "*What?*"

"You're a star!" Max said. "You have been for the last two years. And let me tell you, I can't *wait* to see this one when it airs. It's gonna bury *everything*."

"You thought I was in the Mafia, didn't you?" P.T. stepped forward, eyes sparkling. "Come on, admit it. You did, didn't you? That's what I was going for, but everyone said I'd never pull it off. But I think I sold it. So tell me, come on, what'd you think? Did you think I was in the Mafia?"

"Wait," Trent said. All of a sudden he had become the hunted one, cowering in the corner while the jackals surrounded him. "You're not saying . . . you can't be . . ."

"Yes-sirree!" Tad said. "Surprise!"

"Surprise indeed!" P.T. said. There was no malice in him now, none of the megalomaniacal hatred that until this moment had been such an inseparable part of him. "Welcome to your own reality show."

No. It couldn't be.

Trent stared at each of them, at the cameras behind him. For the love of God, there was a *caterer* in the far corner, ready with steaming dishes for the after-show party. It wasn't possible. It just wasn't possible. "Are you trying to tell me that all this—"

"That's what we're saying, pal." Max shook his head. "Man, you have no idea how much fun this has been. We've been at this for two years, pal. Two *years*. And to see it all come down to this, to see the look on your face. I wish you could see yourself, pal, it's priceless. Fucking priceless, I'm telling you."

"Max!" Tad said. "What did we tell you about cursing? We don't want to have to edit any of this."

"No." Trent shook his head and soon found that he couldn't stop. "It can't be. This can't all . . . that's not possible!"

"Yes, it is," Todd said.

"Not only is it possible," P.T. said, "it's already *done*. All that's left is the scoring and the editing."

"It can't be!"

"Come on," Max said. "Admit it, a little part of you had to see this coming. Seriously, you're the newest member of our team! And did you really think you could get away with being late to work every single day?"

"Didn't you ever wonder why we were always there before you?" Taylor asked.

"We've been coming in at eight-fifteen for the past two years," Tad added. "That gave us time to get everything in order."

"I gotta say," Todd added, "I'm looking forward to sleeping in from now on."

Trent took an unsteady step backwards. "You *can't* have organized this," he cried, "it's too big! We got . . . we got stranded on an *island*! The guy had a heart attack, you can't have planned that!"

"Staged," Max said. "There was a camera crew already entrenched. We left the helicopter, and they switched the pilot with a real dead person. Put a helmet on him and you couldn't even tell the difference."

"Oh," Tad said, "you have *no* idea how disgusting that was. When you two pulled him out, *oh* my God I thought I was just going to *die*."

"We did a lot of work on the fly," P.T. said. "Had to, with a format like this."

"Like me and Todd in the helicopter?" Taylor said. "Never happened. He was just banging against the wall."

"We didn't do it either," Tad said. "As if. But what a suggestion on Todd's part, huh? You should have seen the look on your face!"

"He will," Max said. "Everyone will."

"It's been a helluva thing," P.T. said. "But the payoff! Max is right, this is going to bury everything."

Trent whirled on Rachel. "But what about, what about us? Was that just—"

"Part of the show," she said. "I don't even really like you."

"She got a hell of a bonus for that," P.T. said with a broad grin.

"Better her than me," Taylor said. "I'd've done it, but I didn't shed any tears when you turned me down, I'll tell you that."

"It can't be!" Trent shouted. "What about my promotion?"

"Fake," P.T. said.

"The hit men?"

"Actors. You really think anybody would call a hit out in the open like that?" P.T. turned to the others. "I *told* you he thought I was Mafia. Pay up."

"But what about Dyson?" Trent was raving now, so desperate and bewildered that he almost couldn't stand. "You had him killed, I *know* you did! That couldn't just be part of the show!"

But P.T.'s smile only grew. There was a hush in the room, a growing sense of something cataclysmic about to happen that made Trent feel as though he were on the verge of a stroke. When P.T. stepped forward and put his hand on Trent's arm, it was all Trent could do to keep from melting.

"That's the best part," P.T. said. "Tad, Rachel, move aside, will you? Trent, look over there."

Too weak to disobey, Trent looked at the space Tad and Rachel had just vacated. In its place was a voting booth with the curtain drawn.

"Is everyone ready?" P.T. said. "Camera two, camera four, I want a good close-up for this. All right, let's show him!"

The curtain opened.

And there was Dyson, alive and radiant, striding forward on legs that shouldn't have been able to move, smiling with lips that should have been cold. He walked right up to Trent, who was powerless to do anything but watch.

"Hello again, Trent," Dyson said. "Surprised?"

"It can't be," Trent whispered. He took another tiny step backward, and would have fallen if P.T. had not caught him and motioned for Max to bring a chair.

"It is," P.T. said. "Everything you've thought has been a lie. Congratulations."

Trent stared at Dyson. "But why? You two hate each other, why would you—"

"*Hate* each other?" Dyson laughed. "We're partners, son! Have been ever since Vietnam! We've been working together on this right from the start. There is no Dyson Associates, never has been."

"Didn't you wonder how Petersen *happened* to run into you at Lynette's party?" Taylor asked. "Weren't you just a little suspicious?"

"He's from the Midwest," Rachel said. "They trust people there. He doesn't know any better."

"But that idea." It was too much; Trent's shock was starting to pass into something like acceptance. "*Lives in the Balance*. My idea, the one we thought up together. How could you have known?"

"You told me about it," Max said. "Remember? A little phone call and *voilà*, that's all it took. Didn't you think it was a little coincidental that the two of you *happened* to come up with the same show idea? There were an awful lot of coincidences. I mean come *on*, nobody's *that* gullible."

"Looks like somebody is," Tad said.

"It's all fake," P.T. said. "All of it. We've had cameras on you since you arrived. In your cubicle, your office, outside Lynette's house, Max's trunk, Rachael's apartment, in the dashboard of your own car, *everywhere*. We've had you on film ten hours a day for the past two years. And all those 'TV execs' you've been calling—actors. We fed them their lines, told them what to tell you. Frank from CBS? He's a voice actor, does car commercials. The drunk driver who totaled your Jag? Hollywood stuntman."

"My obituary?" Dyson said. "Fake. From a newspaper we got printed at Kinko's."

"The only thing we didn't get on film was you coming to me with the idea to kill P.T.," Max said. "And I'm telling you, *man*, what we wouldn't give to have a recording of that!"

"Everything's been planned," P.T. said. "On the fly, like I said, depending on your course of action. And a little on Armsburger. Let me tell you, that AMP speech of his was a blessing from Heaven. But all my office rampages? A show. They were a lot of fun, though."

"And on those rare occasions when you *did* come up with a decent idea," Tad said, "we just sent them along to our real people."

"You've actually come up with some marketable concepts," Taylor said. "Shocked the hell out of me. *Child Custody Court TV*? I didn't think you had it in you."

"It's perfect, don't you see?" Max's eyes were glowing. "You've been a player, pal! You've been to the sets, you've gone behind the scenes, you've seen things the people of America have been dying to see for years. All that filming for *Last Man Standing* and *Take it Off!*, half of that was about *you*. And now, when this show airs it'll be like watching two, three reality shows at a time. It's golden, pal."

"It's genius, that's what it is," Todd said. "The world's never seen anything like it. You're going to be a star."

Trent shook his head. He could accept that Dyson wasn't dead, that he and P.T. were partners. But he could not accept the idea that everything he'd thought in the last two years had been an absolute lie.

"It's not possible," he said, finding his true voice for the first time. "You can't have known everything I was going to do. You can't have planned all this."

"We didn't!" Max shouted. "Don't you see? That's what made this so real! Because you're right, we *didn't* know what you were going to do. Sure we manipulated, we pushed and pulled and suggested this or that, but you *never* failed to surprise us. When we started this—we're calling it *Executive Delusion*, what do you think?—anyway, when we started this we really didn't know what to expect. But this . . ." Max shook his head, still in obvious awe. "To go all this way, to *actually* plan to kill your own boss. We couldn't have predicted that in a million years, pal."

"We didn't count on you wrecking my car, either," Rachel said. "I almost killed you myself for that."

Trent looked at her. "So sorry to disappoint you."

"Disap*point* us?" Max said. "You *never* disappointed us, not once. I mean there we were, sitting in Rachel's car, thinking, 'What's he gonna do now? Is he gonna jump out and wrestle the gun away, what?' Because we didn't know. That was the beauty, pal, it was so *real*. You've taken us to a whole new level here, something nobody's seen before. Nothing fake, nothing contrived. It's gonna blow everything we've done so far right out of the water."

Trent looked at him, then at all of them, smug and superior and grinning like succubi after a feast of souls. The cameras were rolling, he thought he could hear the tiny buzzing of the reels. There was nothing he could do, nothing except stand there and endure a humiliation he had not thought possible. It was true. They had played him like a fiddle, built him up and torn him down for the amusement of an invisible audience. They had made him into the very thing he hated more than anything else. And he had played right into their hands.

He looked down, wishing he could hide himself.

And then he had another idea.

Slowly he bent down and picked up the gun he had dropped. It felt right in his hand, as though it belonged there. He managed a wavering smile. Was he insane? Of course he was; that had been their goal all along. But they had gone too far, and now it was time for them to pay.

"Go ahead," P.T. said. "Fire away if it'll make you feel better."

With careful deliberation Trent aimed his gun at P.T. "I should have done this a long time ago," he said, and pulled the trigger. There was a tremendous noise.

But nothing happened.

"Blanks," P.T. said. He walked over to Trent and took the gun from his hand. "If you're going to kill somebody, make sure you're familiar with the equipment."

"So," Trent said. He felt as though all his bones were turning to sand, disintegrating one molecule at a time until soon nothing would remain but a pile of skin and clothes. "This is your final insult." He stared again at each of them, daring them to meet his gaze.

Every one of them did.

"I hope you're happy," Trent said. Then he raised his head and faced one of the cameras. "I hope you've enjoyed yourself out there, watching me, waiting for me to make a fool of myself. I hope I've given you everything you've wanted. And I hope you all rot in hell."

"Oh," Tad said, "now that wasn't a very nice thing to say."

Trent looked at Tad, deliberated for an instant, then punched him square in the nose.

Tad squealed and fell down, blood pouring down his white designer shirt. Taylor and Rachel rushed to his side, and before Trent could advance he found his arms pinned behind his back by Todd.

"I hope you enjoyed that, America!" Trent shouted into the cameras. "Anything to make you happy!"

"You're such a bastard," Rachel said.

"That's enough," P.T. said. "He's not going to do anything else." He gestured to Todd, and Todd's hold on Trent relaxed.

"So it was all a lie," Trent said, smiling at the bloody spectacle he'd created. "Rachel, the island, the hotel hit men, Dyson, all of it. I'll bet you had cameras in the firing range too, didn't you?"

"Both of them," P.T. said, seemingly unfazed by what Trent had done to Tad. "Max set it up."

"Seriously, pal, you made it so *easy*. If you'd have done any of the work yourself it would have been hard to keep up, but you kept coming to me for advice. 'What should we do now, Max, how are we going to get a gun, Max.' It was child's play. And incidentally, that brilliant plan of mine? Wouldn't work in a million years, pal. We'd have both been dead in a heartbeat. I honestly can't believe you went along with it."

"And all those ideas," Trent said, turning to Dyson. "Those were all fake, too, weren't they."

"No," Dyson said. "They were real ideas. Real terrible ones. *The Samaritan*? Even *you* have to admit it would never work."

"Is this really all that you're capable of?" Trent asked. "Is this really the extent of your vision?"

"What are you talking about?" Max said. "This is *huge*. We've done something the world has never seen. When you came up with that idea for *Tropical Abduction*, we thought you'd figured it out. I mean here you were, spouting off about a show where the contestants didn't even know they were contestants, and we all thought, 'That's it, game over.' But you never put two and two together. Which I don't mind a bit, I mean the ratings for this thing are gonna be through the fucking *roof*."

Trent looked at Max. He wanted to hit him, to pound all of them into the ground. But he did nothing. There was nothing he could do, not to people like these. They were beyond his reach, blind captains on a derelict ship, driving headlong into the breakers and singing all the while.

"Why?" he said at last. They would give him that satisfaction at least. "Why'd you do it?"

"You have to know the answer to that," P.T. said. "Look at yourself, Trent. Look at the man you were when you came to my office two years ago. Young, idealistic, out to change the world. And now, what are you? A bitter, cynical, hopeless shell of your former self. You're the most jaded fuck I've ever met, you've been com*plete*ly torn down. And that sells, my friend. That sells."

Trent swallowed something that tasted like bile. "Then why me? You interviewed a dozen people for my job, why pick me?"

"Are you kidding?" P.T. said, that damnable grin still on his face. "You were *perfect*, everything we were looking for. We couldn't have *asked* for a better choice."

"Seriously," Max said, "we thought we were gonna have to drape the whole office in plastic sheeting to collect the gallons of blood perpetually dripping from your profusely bleeding heart."

"It really was over the top sometimes," Todd agreed.

"You're not going to get away with this," Trent said.

"What are you talking about?" Dyson asked. "We've *gotten* away with it. It's done."

"Armsburger will stop you. This show will never make it to television."

"Wow," Max said. "Even now you're still the idealist."

"Armsburger's term will be up in eight months," P.T. said. "After that, it's open season. I may hate the man, but I'm patient enough to wait. It's going to be a whole new world next year, Trent, I can guarantee you that."

P.T. was right. Trent knew it, and the knowledge dropped the bottom out of his stomach. He walked over to the catering table, desperate for a drink, something to wash the memory of this moment out of his brain forever. The cameras stayed on him the entire time.

"Give me some champagne," he demanded. "I mean this is *my* party, isn't it?"

"Don't give him the bottle, Sherry," P.T. said. "I'm not entirely sure what he'd do with it."

In a thick silence Trent drained his first glass and was given another. He drained it as well, swallowing it all in one searing gulp, then placed both hands on the table. It felt solid beneath his fingers—real. The only thing in the room that was.

"Come on," Max said, "don't be like that. This is supposed to be a party!"

"So what's my prize?" Trent whirled, the muscles in his neck as stiff and hard as iron. "What do I win, huh? I've got to win something, right? After all, I am the *star*."

"You don't win anything," Dyson said. He looked surprised at the question. "We thought that would only soften the blow."

"You're fired, of course," P.T. said. "Obviously I can't have someone in the office who might try to kill me. I don't imagine you'll be too upset by that, though."

"Probably not," Taylor agreed.

Well. They'd thought of everything, hadn't they. Trent opened his mouth, but he didn't say anything. There was no point in talking anymore. With a deliberateness that defied the trembling in his heart, he walked silently toward the door. Nobody tried to stop him.

When he reached the door he turned. Tad was on his feet now, his bleeding reduced to a trickle, Rachel and Taylor standing by his side. Todd, Max, P.T., and Dyson were all motionless, waiting for Trent to make the next move. And above them all, like leering, voyeuristic gods, the cameras were still rolling.

"Go fuck yourselves," Trent said. "All of you."

"Trent," Max said. "Trent, pal, buddy. You can't leave like this. We've made you an icon, pal! You have no idea how big this is going to be. Ten months from now, when this show airs, you're going to be the biggest star in the history of entertainment."

"Go to hell, Max." There was so much more he wanted to say, so many things bubbling like lava in his throat. But he bit his tongue. None of it would matter, not to them.

As he was leaving he heard Max sigh. "Well, I guess we shouldn't have expected much more than that. Still, you'd think he might have shown a little gratitude. Most people would kill to be where he is right now."

EPILOGUE:
Thirteen Months Later

"The hand that rules the press, the radio, the screen and the far-spread magazine, rules the country."
—*Memorial service for Justice Brandeis, December 21, 1942*

[EPILOGUE]

"Hello, everyone, and welcome back to *The Ann Vapid Show*! I'm Ann Vapid, and we're only halfway through! It's just *too* much fun, isn't it? I'm telling you, it's just *sin*ful how much fun we're having. Now as you know, George Clooney is going to be here in just a few minutes—keep your bras to yourselves, ladies—but *first*, we've got a very special treat for you. Now we don't usually have two guests at once, but for *these* two we're happy to make an exception. Please join me in welcoming two of the biggest stars in the *his*tory of Reality TV, Trent Tucker and Max Sorenetti!"

"Thank you, Ann. It's great to be here today."

"Likewise."

"Let me tell you both, it is so great to have you here today. Now, before we really turn on the heat, let's make sure everyone knows who you are. Why don't you tell our audience a little bit about yourself, Max."

"My pleasure, Ann. I'm the executive vice president of The Nova Conglomerate, which is the largest television consulting firm in the country. We're the ones networks come to when they want to add a new show to their line-up."

"And can you tell us what some of your shows are? I'm certain our audience will know the names."

"Absolutely. *Last Man Standing*, *Extreme Animal Lovers*, *Gangland Romance*, *Julie's Surprise*, and of course the top two reality shows ever made, *Take it Off!* and *Executive Delusion*."

"Isn't that exciting, people! It sounds like some of the people in our studio audience are *big* fans."

"Yes, we're very proud of what we've accomplished."

"What did I tell you, people? Didn't I say we were going to have a great show today? Does Ann Vapid *ever* lie? Of course not! *So*, Trent, *tell* me. I'm sure everyone here knows who *you* are. And I think we're all dying to know, what's it like to be the biggest star in America?"

"Oh, it's fantastic, Ann. There nothing's more delightful than having people you've never met come up to you in the grocery store and tell you everything they think you did wrong. I can't tell you how much I enjoy those moments."

"Ooh, I'm sensing a little hostility from our guest here! So Trent, how does it feel to be sitting next to your old friend?"

"I hate him, Ann. I'd like to kick him in the nuts, Ann."

"*Ouch!* Well, *that's* not a very nice thing to say. How does that make you feel, Max?"

"Doesn't surprise me. But I do have to say I think he's being a little inconsiderate. I mean I helped make this man *huge*, and this is how he repays me. You should be thanking me, pal. You should be thanking all of us."

"I'll be happy to thank you in the parking lot after the show, if you'd like."

"Now *boys*! We don't want to have to call security, do we? Or *do* we?"

"I don't think that will be necessary, Ann. You'd think after more than a year that Trent would be over all this, but apparently he's the kind of guy who likes to hold a grudge."

"So, *Trent*, tell us what you've been doing for the last year."

"Gladly, Ann. I've opened my own television consulting firm."

"Is that right? My, that sounds *fas*cinating."

"Yes, and I have two reasons for doing it. One, I'd like to give people something decent to watch. And two, I'd like to see Nova driven out of business."

"Fat lot of luck you'll have with that, pal. We're not going anywhere."

"I have to say, Trent, I think you'll have your work cut out for you there. I don't mean to burst your little bubble, but we're all pretty happy with the shows Nova's been giving us lately."

"I don't care, Ann, it's a fight worth fighting. *The Samaritan* is a good show. *Lives in the Balance* is a good show. People will recognize that eventually. I don't care if it takes ten years, it's going to happen. David beat Goliath, you know."

"Yes, well. On to something *happy*, shall we? So *Max*, which show is *your* favorite?"

"My favorite show? Oh, God, there's so many of them."

"I know, I know, they're all so good! Every night it's like there's a war inside my head. I mean on Monday should I watch *Burlesque Mothers* or *My Daddy the Pimp*? And then Wednesdays! *Last Woman Standing*, *Take it Off!*, and *Julie's Surprise*, all at the same time! It's not fair, there are *so* many good shows. I'm telling you, thank God for Tivo! But if you had to pick just one, which would it be?"

"Man. That's a tough question, Ann. I don't think I can narrow it down to one. The show I'm most impressed by is definitely *Take it Off!* That one's really exceeded all expectations. It's been a very good thing for our company, and I think for the country as well. Then there's another one that hasn't come out yet. It should be out in about five weeks, you might have seen commercials for it. It's called *The Decision*."

"Ooh. I have, and it sounds de*li*cious! Tell us about it."

"Well it's actually an idea we've had on the shelf for over a year, but we're just now able to market it. Here's the deal. Take some housewife from the middle of nowhere and make her over like they used to do with *The Swan*. But then, ship her to Vegas and give her six weeks to enjoy life as a hot, single woman. We'll film everything—the nightclubs, the men, the *women* if there are any, who knows?—then after twelve weeks, take her back to her house and her family and make her decide which life she wants: hot and single, or hot and married? I just really like the concept, you know?"

"Sounds *fas*cinating. Is it your idea?"

"No. I'd love to take credit for it, but give credit where credit's due, right? It's all Taylor's idea, she's on our creative team. I have to admit, when I first heard about it, I wasn't blown away. But Taylor can be *very* persuasive when she wants to be, and she brought me around."

"Persuasive, huh, Max? What exactly do you mean by that?"

"I'll let you figure that out for yourself, Ann."

"Oh, you're *naughty*. Speaking of naughty, what do you have to say to people who think Reality TV has, I don't know, gone too far?"

"I'll be happy to answer that for you."

"She wasn't asking you, pal. I hear that question a lot, Ann, and my answer is always the same. We don't have any control over which shows are on television. It may seem like we do, but really it's the people. If a show isn't good, you guys let us know that. You in the audience, you guys have the real power. We're just trying to provide people with whatever they want to see."

"What do you say to *that*, Trent?"

"I'd say he's so full of shit—can I say shit? I'd say he's so full of shit I'm surprised it's not coming out his eyes. People will watch what they're given to watch. I think it's our responsibility to give them shows that are worth watching. And, since no one at Nova is interested in doing that, it's going to fall to people like me to do what needs to be done."

"You're dreaming, pal. We're the number one creative firm in the *country*. You know why? Because people want what we give them. That's the way it is, and you're not going to change that."

"We'll see about that, *pal*. It's not over yet. It hasn't even started. And someday, when I've put you out of business and you're sitting on the sidewalk wondering what the hell happened to your life, I want you to remember this moment."

"Boys, *boys*, cut it out. Honestly, I swear I don't know what to *do* with you two. *So*, Max, tell us, what's the future of Reality TV look like?"

"Very promising, Ann. Very promising. We have a new FCC chairman, and he looks to be far more accommodating than the old one. I think we're finally getting a chance to make the kinds of shows we've been wanting to make all along."

"Well, *tell* us about them."

"Be happy to, Ann. But first I'd like to bring up something you mentioned earlier. There are a lot of people out there who think that maybe Reality TV has 'gone too far' in some respects. But you know, my feeling is exactly the opposite. I don't think we've gone far enough. I don't think we've really opened her up to see what she's capable of yet. And that's what I want to do. We've got the potential to make a genuine difference in the lives of millions of people, and that's something I'm working very hard to explore."

"Whoa, Max. That went *right* over my head! Could you maybe bring it down to the level of us ordinary people? Give us some examples!"

"Sure thing. You see, for us, *Executive Delusion*, starring my dear, dear friend Trent over here, was a watershed moment in the history of television. Because let's face it, up until then, Reality TV was never completely real. To a certain extent it's always been staged and scripted just like any other television show. And the reason for that is because, until now, all the contestants on our shows had to try out in order to be picked. They wanted to be on the show, and so it made it hard for them to act totally natural because they knew everything they said was going to be on camera. So what we at Nova want to do is make more shows like *Executive Delusion*, shows that are completely candid, where the 'contestants' don't necessarily know they're on TV."

"Ooh. You mean even *more* shows like *Executive*?"

"Even better, Ann. Here's an example. You remember that show *Cheaters*?"

"Of course! Who doesn't?"

"You're right, it was a great idea. But it didn't go far enough. What we want to do is take it to the next level. So we came up with *Stalkers*. It's just like *Cheaters*, except we're going to pick someone completely at random and follow them around. And I mean everywhere. Unfortunately we can't put cameras in their homes because of the legal issues, but we can do everything else that an ordinary stalker would do: follow them to work, go through their garbage, spy through their windows when they have company over. And the thing that's going to make this so much different from what's already been done is that the person who's being filmed doesn't *know* it. That's the only way to get a real reaction out of somebody, as Trent has so vividly shown us. When most of us are put in front of a camera, we act different. But if we don't *know* there's a camera around—that's when you get a chance to see the real person, not just the person they want you to see."

"Ooh, now you've got me all ex*cit*ed. What else do you have in mind?"

"Well, we're also trying to develop shows that can take audience participation to the next level. So far we've got two in the works: *Did I Kill My Husband?* and *Did I Kill My Wife?*, depending on who died, of course."

"Died? My, now I'm *really* excited!"

"So are we, Ann. You take an ordinary murder trial, but instead of using a conventional jury, you put the trial on TV and use the viewing public as the jury. Think about that. Instead of twelve underpaid people deciding someone's fate—because let's face it, you can't be truly objective when you're only getting paid five dollars a day for your time—you have a jury of millions. *And*—and this is the really big thing, Ann—all the people watching? They're watching because they *want* to, not because the government's making them. This could revolutionize the entire trial process. I mean the reason we had twelve-person juries in the first place is because it wasn't practical for them to be bigger. But now, with television's ability to reach everyone in America, now we can have a truly representative jury. Of course, you won't be able to show *all* the facts and evidence like they do in standard trials—there's just not enough TV time for that—but we're confident that the viewing public will still be able to make an intelligent, informed, fair decision. We're very excited about this, I can't wait to see it take off. Instead of watching *Law and Order* or *Judge Judy* or any of those other courtroom dramas, suddenly you'll be able to actually participate in the legal process. It's democracy at work, Ann, pure and simple."

"Oh, my God, isn't this exciting, people? I'm getting *goose*bumps, I swear! Seriously, Max, feel my arm. Can you feel that?"

"Sure can. I don't suppose you have goosebumps anywhere else, do you?"

"Oh, *stop*! Look out, ladies, this one's a tiger! So, any other teasers for us, Mr. Reality Show?"

"How much time do you have? We've got dozens of ideas waiting to come down the pipe, but there's one more I'd like to talk about, because it really demonstrates where we think Reality TV is heading. It's called *Trials of Job*. I'm sure Trent will love this one, at least it should sound familiar to him. You take this guy—or girl, we're equal opportunity here—and completely ruin their life. You don't tell them what's going on, of course, but you get their bosses in on it, their wife or husband or girlfriend or *family* if you can. Just take everything away from them, until they're left with nothing."

"Oh, that sounds *heart*less."

"Not at all, Ann. Because when we're done we'll tell them it was all a gag and give them some money and a vacation to Tahiti or something.

They'll deserve it, believe me. But the beauty is, for the first time the people at home will actually get to see what it looks like for someone to lose everything that matters to them. There won't be any scripts or interviews or anything like that. It'll be completely real. That's where Reality TV is headed. That's the future for you. And it's a good one, Ann. I'm really excited about it. I know I've said that a few times already, I sound like a broken record, but it's because I truly believe in what we're doing."

"What do you have to say to *that*, Trent?"

"I'd say he's driving all of you directly into hell. They're turning the world into a wasteland. And that's why I'm here, right on the fringes, sitting in the back of the class with my hand up, ready to let everyone know that it doesn't have to be this way. And I want everyone out in the audience, and everyone watching at home, to hear me very clearly. It doesn't have to be this way."

"Mmm hmm. Well I've had *such* a good time today, it's been a real pleasure to talk with both of you. And I think we've all learned something valuable today, haven't we? Who says Ann Vapid isn't educational sometimes? Watch out PBS, here comes *The Ann Vapid Show*! So, everyone, are you ready to meet George Clooney?"

"I think that's our cue to get out of here. What do you say, Trent, wanna head to the parking lot and settle accounts?"

"Oh, don't go away mad, boys! Come on, folks, let's hear it for Max Sorenetti one more time, huh? And what about Trent Tucker? Come on, you can do better than that!"

"It's been a treat, Ann."

"Oh, *trust* me, Max, the pleasure is *all* mine. Before you both go, though, I've just got one more question. Are you as excited as I am to see *Deadly Justice*? Which comes out this weekend, I might add?"

"I can't wait, Ann."

"Neither can *I*. That Candy Tyler is something else, isn't she?"

"You can say that again. I think it's safe to say that *Deadly Justice* is going to be the biggest movie of the year."

"I *totally* agree. What about you, Trent, any last thoughts? . . . Trent?"

CPSIA information can be obtained
at www.ICGtesting.com
Printed in the USA
FFOW03n0912070414
4699FF